1350

Ellen Galford was born in New Jersey, USA, but emigrated to Scotland in 1971, and defines herself as an adopted Scot. In 1978 she joined a feminist writers' group working in Edinburgh and Fife, and – with their encouragement – wrote her first novel, *Moll Cutpurse: Her True History*. Since then, as well as *The Fires of Bride*, she has written two other novels, *Queendom Come*, and *The Dyke and the Dybbuk*. She has also contributed to various feminist, and lesbian and gay anthologies, including the short story collection *Girls Next Door* (The Women's Press, 1985). She lives in Edinburgh.

ELLEN GALFORD
The Fires of Bride

First published by The Women's Press Ltd, 1986
A member of the Namara Group
34 Great Sutton Street, London EC1V 0DX

Reprinted 1994

British Library Cataloguing-in-Publication Data
Galford, Ellen
  The fires of Bride.
  I. Title
  823'.914[F]   PR6057.A38/

ISBN 0 7043 4020 8

Typeset by AKM Associates (UK) Ltd
Printed and bound in Great Britain by
BPCC Paperbacks Ltd, Aylesbury, Bucks

For Ellen Smyth

'Scotland will be reborn the day the last minister is strangled with the last copy of the *Sunday Post*'

(Tom Nairn, 'Three Dreams of Scottish Nationalism' in *Memoirs of a Modern Scotland*, ed. Karl Miller, 1970)

PROLOGUE
Lizzie

'Next item on the agenda: Forward Planning. I'm afraid the time has come for us to do another story on the Outer Hebrides.'

'Oh, no, no, anything but that!'

'Oh, help, not another island!'

'Oh, please, have pity!'

'Jesus, Mary and Joseph – not again!'

'Why?'

The chorus of groans makes the teak-panelled conference room sound like Hell's reception desk on the morning after Judgment Day. But it is merely the setting for the weekly brainstorming session of the Caledonian Television Features and Light Entertainment Department. We are kicking some ideas around the newspaper-strewn table. Its expensive veneer is scarred with ring-marks from the coffee-mugs of a thousand weekly meetings past.

'I'm afraid we have no choice,' says our boss, Shuggie Murray. 'May I remind you lads . . .'

'AHEM!!'

'Sorry, Lizzie dear. May I remind you *people* that franchise renewal time is almost upon us. We have a statutory obligation to provide a certain number of programme hours of cultural and social material covering peripheral Scottish viewing areas . . .'

'Pretty bloody peripheral, I'd say. Some of those islands can't even pick up our signal most of the time . . .' Good old Ewan. A jaded veteran of three nervous breakdowns and a coronary. Historian of the good old days when television was run by gentlemen and scholars.

'Shut up, Ewan. As I was saying, London will be looking very carefully at our programming over the next few months. And if they don't like what they see, you lot will all be out on your arses, or

3

writing up obituary notices for the *Auchtermuchty Weekly Advertiser*. So let's get cracking.'

'Islands, mmm, let me see. What about re-opening the Unsolved Benbecula Axe Murder story?' Jimmy is our gore specialist.

'Come on, Jimmy, not that old chestnut again. I want something fresh – but traditional. Now, as I see it, classic island documentaries fall into three basic types. One, Nature: seals in peril and the effects of oil pollution on the lesser red-beaked silver whatnot. Two, Economics: long-term unemployment and all that. Three, Disappearing Gaelic Heritage: by which I mean folksongs and couthy-drouthy characters. Hoaching with atmosphere and local colour. Now that's the direction I want us to go in. Nothing too political, nothing controversial.'

'Dead boring visuals up there,' sighs Clive, the director. 'A slow pan along Glen Stereotype, then cut to the shores of Loch Cliché. You've seen one sheep, you've seen them all. And it's always bloody raining.'

'Fuck this for a lark,' snarls Squinter McBraid, dragging hard on his roll-up. (He used to work down in Fleet Street; never lets us forget it.) 'Let's do something with some guts in it. How about an exposé on extortionist vice-rings on the oil-rigs? I mean, really, Shuggie, who wants to interview a bunch of old Hebridean hags about their eighteenth-century knitting patterns?'

'I do.'

They look at me as if I'd crawled out of a drain.

'Oh well, she would, wouldn't she?'

'Dear god, we're no gonnae get another speech on Rediscovering Wimmin's Traditional Culture, are we?'

Shuggie, to my amazement, comes to my defence. 'I wouldn't be so cocky if I were you, McBraid. I seem to remember that your last little documentary project required us to write thirty-six apology letters and fork out on a god-awful expensive conciliatory lunch for the Secretary of State for Scotland.' He glares around the table. 'Now listen, children. We have a programming gap to fill. We also have a whisky-distiller who wants to run his commercials up against something with a Highland flavour. Lots of lolly, they tell me upstairs. So we are about to redress our shameful imbalance with a nice, socially insightful, visually exciting and culturally enriching but totally inoffensive documentary fillum. I want a real cracker, that we can flog to the whole network.'

'The last time we tried to sell one of our big ambitious

4

documentaries to the network, they wanted us to put on English subtitles.'

'As I remember, McBraid, it might have helped if you hadn't interviewed those Dundee burglars with their backs to the camera. All trying to disguise their voices so the Old Bill wouldn't recognise them.'

'Well, don't think you're getting me up to some bloody Hebridean island to freeze my arse off.'

'I wasn't thinking of you. I'm giving this one to Lizzie.'

'Her?'

'Me?'

Amazement. I am a mere researcher. The checker of facts, the drawer of wood and the hewer of water. The go-fer who runs up to the film library, sets up worthy but tedious interviews with the Scottish Office Minister, and types out all the questions so he can have a look at them in advance. I'm the nice lassie who dries the tears of the accident victim's mother (but only after the camera stops running), warms up the guests with a few light questions before the big-gun macho reporter comes in for the kill. I am, indeed, surprised. And so are the boys from the Features Department. They don't like it one bit.

'Och, it's your big breakthrough, hen.'

'Which island were you thinking of?' I ask Shuggie, ignoring the baleful looks and the hairy fists crushing up agenda sheets.

'I checked the files this morning. And looks like we haven't done much – or anything – about Cailleach. Not for ages.'

'Cailleach? That miserable hole,' sneers Jimmy, 'the outermost island of the Utter Utter Hebrides. Good luck to you, Lizzie love, they're all maniacs up there. Most of them are their own great-grandad's half-sisters, if you know what I mean. It's all incest and home-brewed booze and fanatical ministers ranting on about the wages of sin.' Jimmy is about to launch forth with a few choice anecdotes about congenital disease and alcohol-based brain damage in inbred rural communities when Shuggie cuts him short.

'Ignore the boy, Lizzie. He's just jealous. Ever since we cancelled his film on plane crashes. Now, I want you to take yourself up to Cailleach next week. Read up on the place. Wander around, chat to folk. Take as much time as you need. Then post me down an outline, and if I like it, we'll send up a full feature unit for a three-week shoot. None of your cheap hit-and-run jobs. I want this to look good. You prove your mettle up in Cailleach, and I'll see

5

what I can do about a promotion for you. Go to it. We're counting on you. Right, you lazy bastards, we've got this week's programmes to put out, so let's stop blethering. Meeting adjourned.'

At lunchtime, in the pub over the road, McBraid confronts Shuggie.

'What the fuck was that about?' he demands, banging down his own third pint of Guinness plus a double whisky for his boss. 'Sending that inexperienced little cow up there. I thought I was up for the next big one.'

'Shut up, Squinter and keep your shirt on.' Shuggie glances around the crowded lounge bar to check who's in earshot. 'It's time she had a chance to prove herself. Besides, it may have escaped your notice that the finals for the Miss Galaxy competition are coming up at the Exhibition Hall in ten days' time. We are going to give it the biggest splash since the Kirkintilloch Sweetie-shop Massacre. In-depth profiles of the most attractive contenders from all over the world. Live transmission of the swimsuit heats with lots of close-up shots. Now do you really believe you could give that assignment your full professional concentration with Lizzie boring us rigid about the exploitation of women's bodies for commercial gain? Gie's a break, McBraid. She's well out of the way.'

The first trick is: get to Cailleach. Like Brigadoon, it emerges from the mists only every hundred years or so, but that's not magic, it's the ferry timetable. So, helped by the efficient dynamo Terrible Tessie of the CallyTelly Travel Department, I plot a course to the far north. Up through the West Highland glens by railway, over the sea to Skye, across Skye by bus, across the Minch to Stornoway by overnight ferry ('Whatever you do, don't get marooned in Stornoway,' say the gnarled veterans in the CallyTelly staff canteen. 'The hotels are all either filthy or tee-total, and they're full of trawling Russian trawlermen.') and then another ferry – the *St Rollox* – out to the outermost isles of all.

'Why don't you just fly up to Stornoway and catch the Cailleach boat?' asks Shuggie.

'This is my film, right? And it's my budget, right? Well, I'm spending it on filming, not on frills like first-class travel. Anyway, I want to get the feel of the place, the remoteness of it, the island beyond the islands beyond the hills . . .'

'Dear god, Lizzie, you'll get that all right. And the feel of a sore bum from all those hours on trains and buses, and the feel of an awful queasy stomach when a force tenner blows up on the Minch. Still, as you say, it's your show. And it better be fucking brilliant, or you're back to finding guests for the Housewives' Happy Hour.'

'Don't worry, Shuggie, I'll give you the documentary of the decade. Just give me enough film . . .'

'And enough rope, sweetheart. Mind how you go.'

I have arrived. Dear goddess, what now?

I am used to loneliness in my line of work. A wintry week in Peterhead, surveying fishing-industry fatalities and fending off oil-related sales reps in the hotel bar. A fortnight in the suburbs of Aberdeen, doing an undercover shock-horror probe on battered middle-class housewives (they never screened it). Long nights on the farms of Ayrshire, waiting for the cows to calve after the big Cattle-feed Mutation scare.

But there is nothing quite so lonely as to sit in the bar of the Cailleach-Inn, listening to a jumble of conversation between people who have known each other all their lives. And joining in none of it (as if I could – it's half in the Gaelic). Outside the battering rain, carried on a dirty wind from the mainland, makes escape impossible. But soon, if I'm patient and sit here often enough, a fly on the wall, and for goodness sake get the behavioural codes right, I may somehow find a way into it.

Meanwhile I memorise the maps and study the (skimpy and badly printed) local guidebook, trying to get a fix on the place in space and time.

If, after a perilous and stormy voyage, Saint Columba pulled his coracle ashore on a Sunday, the elders of the Second Schismatic Independent Kirk of the Outer Isles would make him turn round and put to sea again. The hand of the Highland Sabbath lays heavy on Cailleach, and only aliens and incorrigible deviants are excused from Sunday service. The shop doesn't open, the dogs don't bark, and the two bed-and-breakfast ladies close their doors to guests. Even Columba, stranded here on a Saturday night, would have to sleep on the bench down at the harbourmaster's office.

The Cailleach Inn, by the harbour, has incurred the wrath of the kirk by having itself taken over by a new landlord, a godless Glaswegian, who sees no reason why he should not lawfully sell strong drink to *bona fide* travellers and irreligious islanders alike.

But, of course, what else can you expect from an incomer?

'You know, we're all incomers here,' pronounces the English sociologist on a hiking holiday for the benefit of his young lady companion and anyone else in earshot. 'Mankind didn't start on Cailleach, you know.'

'Humankind, you prat,' mutters the barmaid behind her beer pumps. She's an incomer herself, and the landlord's glad to have her; the islanders would sooner let their daughters sell sex than spiritous liquor. (And, far to the south, in the seedy streets around mainline stations, some of them do: 'Well, anything to get away from that hairy oxter of the Outer Isles,' they say.)

What does the outside world think of Cailleach?

'Where is that?'

'Alcoholism and unemployment.'

'Rain.'

'Didn't think anyone lived there any more. Thought they all got themselves evacuated to the mainland in 1929.'

'Isn't that somewhere in Alaska?'

'Very mystical. On a really heavy ley-line. Higher energy than Glastonbury, Iona and Stonehenge put together.'

'Fine if you like storms and seagulls.'

'Isn't that where it's against the law to have sex on Sunday?'

'Wasn't that the place where they drove their ships on to the rocks for plunder, and when the shipwrecked sailors swam ashore the islanders clubbed them to death and ate them?'

'Never heard of it.'

What does Cailleach think of the outside world?

The ignorance is not mutual. The one mistake I do not make is to underestimate the regulars in the bar at the Inn. They've downed martinis in the dark saloons of Manhattan, sipped rum punches in Trinidad, gulped mao-tai on the shores of the China Sea. They will speak knowledgeably about where to find the biggest steak in Sydney, the greenest salads in San Francisco, and they know the difference between a curry cooked in Capetown and one made in Singapore.

If you are young and enterprising, and come from this island, you will have to go off and seek your fortune. The principal export of Cailleach is people. And once they have made their little packet, or given up trying, they think about coming back. Homesickness is in their blood. The first lullabies a Cailleach baby hears are the laments of islanders gone off to fight the clan chief's wars for him, or forced away by the landlord's factors, dying lonely in a country of strangers.

They say the seagulls bring back the spirits of the dead.

I do my homework. I think about scenes from the history of Cailleach. But which scenes? Which history?

History, Political. Barefoot parliaments, government by consensus between the crones and the fishermen, thugs taking over an island flipped back and forth like a tossed coin between the jagged, blood-rimmed fingernails of Picts and Norsemen, Highland chieftains, absentee English milords who came into the title arse-backwards. Questions asked in the House. Literacy rates? Sanitary arrangements? Unemployed heads of household? The Island Problem. Proposals for reform, good ideas admired and forgotten like the rotting hulk of the old Dutch herring buss gone aground in South Bay. A policy decision (made in Edinburgh or London) to smack the Gaelic out of the schoolchildren for their own good. In election years, candidates come because they're told to, faces going bilgy green from seasickness above the bright-coloured party rosettes. A suggestion that the sole Scottish connection may have been no more than a spelling error by a medieval scribe, and really the whole place belongs to the Norwegians by rights.

History, Romantic. Lonely castles guarding rocky coasts, the song of the seabirds, captive princesses, keening pipes. A bard who sings it all from the morning of time, handed down from father's father (or more likely mother's mother who never gets the credit), the whole narration in perfect and neatly translatable pentameters. Probably a fraud by a whimsical eighteenth-century antiquary: don't believe a word of it. Ghost stories by the bucketful, unexplained lights around the ruins of the old chapel, hereditary curses. Possibly a Norse earl stabbed to death with gem-encrusted brooches and buried with his longboat in sight of the seas he conquered. Inscrutably shawled and barefoot maidens crooning. Mists and whimsy, and thank goodness not a whisper of the Little People – it's cloying enough as it is.

History, Spiritual. When the earth was soft and unformed and warm as kneaded dough, the Mother tore off a lump of it and pressed and punched and pulled and pounded. Finally forming the island, she lends it the name of one of her spare incarnations: Cailleach, The Crone, The Old Woman. A grey mare, or white

9

sow, soaring across the sky. The old hag scoops up giant stones in the folds of her apron, tosses or possibly blows them into the sacred circles, cromlechs, dolmens, duns and cairns of the west. Beasts grazing nearby, cows and sheep, always gravitate towards them. What's the pull?

But the ungrateful lot who live there light their fires for someone else entirely: Bride, Brigantia, Bridget. The triple goddess who brings them poetry, smithcraft and the skills of midwifery. Thanks a lot. Put the three together and you can forge a baby, all of bronze, and make it tell rude, rhyming stories. After Bride come the Christian monks, the Moluags, Mungos and Columbas, racing like schoolboys to see who makes it first ashore. Whatever their virtues (and they have many) they do find the three-headed lady a hard act to follow.

History, Sexual. Women living closely in groups bleed in unison; in the hot days of summer the island's breezes are faintly spiced with the scent of it. Twenty-five hundred years or more of combinations and couplings – passionate, dutiful, loving, cold, conventional, incomprehensible and dangerous attraction. Rape as a political statement by raiders, fun for the laird's guests and a perk for faithful servants. Some furtive attempts with sheep – yes the jokes are true. Much fantasising – seeds and juices spilled nightly on to sheets from Nestaval to the cliffs of Crunig. The priests come and go, the Protestants take over; awkward questions in the confessional are replaced by bucketfuls of guilt. From now on, the frissons of secrecy, memories of the night before, flicker behind smooth, bland faces in the Sabbath kirk, whiling away the hours of the sermon.

Late at night, in my room overlooking the beer barrels and empty crates in the yard of the inn, I make notes, draft possible story ideas and outlines, read them over and tear them up. Dear knows what an interested chambermaid would make of the crumpled sheets that fill the little blue bin in the corner. Probably that I'm a spy. Which I suppose I am. To the unschooled observer it might seem that I am mooching around the hotel bar, idling over the obsolete notices in the post office and taking far too much time to choose a bag of sweets at the Co-op. But I am listening to the gossip, sniffing around. And soon I begin to set up some interviews.

Talking Head Possibles: Catriona MacEochan. Local GP as well as Cailleach's version of the lady of the manor. Lives, alone I think, in the square, squat Castle Cailleach, ancestral seat of the Cailleach MacEochans. Seventeenth-century family-founder was an old boyfriend of James VI, received the title to Cailleach in gratitude for unspecified services rendered. And, by dint of a tendency to thrombosis in the male line, two world wars, and the peculiar predilections of one problematical uncle, dead in extremely embarrassing circumstances in Marrakesh, Catriona is the last of the direct descendants. Never mind the Anglo-Scottish cousins, who'd cravenly crawled south after the Act of Union, and are waiting in the wings to scoop up the estate when the old dear, as they whisper cheerfully, pops off.

Had a preliminary, sniffing-each-other-out conversation – not quite an interview – in the Cailleach Inn; I am now angling for a formal invitation to the castle. Over an impressive number of double whiskies, she tells me how she trained at Edinburgh, headed south like so many bright young Scottish doctors, and made good in London, rising rapidly to a consultancy in gynae and obstetrics (much to the displeasure of her male colleagues, who think that a woman in the masculine preserve of female complaints will, with good reason, steal all their customers). Then, and she never said why, she packed it all in and came home to be the Cailleach GP.

She has, as one might expect, an encyclopedic knowledge of local history and folklore. But, what one does not expect, she is also a crackpot. Deeply into the occult. On first name terms with all the island ghosts. Made some cryptic references to the island's celebrated archaeological sites – the ruined convent of St Bride and the Cailleach Ring (see separate notes). One of your grand old eccentrics. (Well, not that old. Fifty-ish maybe, and looking good on it. Must be all that cold, fresh, island air, because judging from the amount of drink she put away, it's unlikely to be clean living.)

She directs me to someone else she thinks I ought to speak to.

Talking Head Possibles: Ina Isbister. One of Cailleach's two bed-and-breakfast ladies. Ina's the friendly but untidy one, who serves the best food; her competitor's the houseproud one, with a smile like a cold bath on a February morning, who – so I'm told – serves margarine with the toast instead of butter.

If Ina's place weren't so out of the way, up at the north end of the island, down a narrow track past the stones, I'd move there tomorrow and forget the clammy comforts of the Cailleach Inn.

Her sitting room's a gallery of framed family photographs (seven children ranging from one still at school to one geologist now making a fortune in Bahrain), nieces and nephews grinning out of wedding pictures, graduation portraits and holiday snaps with Australian settings.

She's a fantastic storyteller, purveyor of juicy gossip spanning centuries: she spins it out with equal gusto whether it happened last week or in 1817. My background reading (see especially Mackie and Mathesen: *Highland Folkways*, St Andrews, 1926) says that island communities usually had semi-official bards, who kept the communal history alive from the days before the written word. Now whether Ina's that, or merely a Gaelic version of your classic Brooklyn yenta, I have no idea, but she's tremendous value.

If I were in charge of Features and Light Entertainment at CallyTelly, instead of You-know-who, I would give Ina a uranium five-year contract at once, and say goodbye for ever to that old fraud Fraser Hardie and his Wee Hielan' Tales.

She tells me about the Cailleach Ring, which looms out of the mist, perfectly framed by the bright floral curtains in her kitchen window. I've got it on tape.

'All that rubbish they talk about those stones. Well, I can tell you the truth of it, dear. I get them all staying with me, you know, the professors and authors and photographers and all. They come up here all laden down with measuring tapes, and telescopes and geiger-counters and whatnot, and leave them cluttering up their rooms – I never touch a thing if I can help it, but you can't just let the stoor lie and leave the beds unmade now, can you?

'Another cup of tea? How about a bacon roll – it's all from our own pigs. Next time, you come for breakfast and I'll fry you up some of my home-made black pudding and a bit of lamb's liver.

'Yes, they're for ever going on about their discoveries and theories. There's one used to go out in the middle of the night at all hours, and sit in the middle of the circle counting the stars or something. They always say they'll send me a copy of their book or their article, but they never do. Honestly, I don't know how their wives put up with all their nonsense.

'But, as I was saying, the real truth of the stones is this . . . in the days before we had Christianity, people used to pray in that circle. That's an old kind of kirk, that's all it is. Not a proper kirk, of course, they were heathens then and didn't know better. It was long before John Knox. They even did human sacrifice. Oh yes. Do you mind that big rock standing apart from the circle? You'll know it when you see it – a big lump half the size of the house. Well, that's where the mothers used to stand and watch them sacrifice the bairns with a big stone knife. Anyhow, that's what my grannie always said, and hers before her, but it's just a load of old superstition and nobody really knows. I cannae mind who'd be interested, it all happened so long ago. I've some currant scones just out of the oven – you'll have to try one with a bit of my cloudberry jam.'

Six More Theories About the Cailleach Ring:

1. *Celtic Twilight*. On moonless nights, the fairies dance there, luring passing travellers into their reels and lavoltas, vanishing at cockcrow, their captives never to be heard of again outside folksongs.

2. *X-rated*. Pulsing fertility rites, celebrated in the shadow of the stones, guarantee a good harvest. At the central altar, of which no trace remains, a masked priest cheerfully drives a bronze knife into the bare white belly of a sacrificial virgin.

3. *We are Not Alone*. Directional signals for spacecraft. Welcome to prehistoric Britain. Please keep to the left.

4. *Herstory*. A tribe of women, who lived in the now-buried earth-houses down by the shore, set up the stones as a lunar calendar, so they might know their fertile days and arrange their periodic, strictly-business copulations with the tribe of men from the opposite end of the island.

5. *Matriarchal Geology*. The Goddess sucked up the stones from a far country, and blew them here on her gael-force breath, to mark the site where she wanted her sacred fire, to be tended and guarded by the descendants of the tribe in Theory 4.

6. *Paranoid*. The real stones were taken away during World War II and used as part of the anti-submarine barrier in Scapa Flow. The present, cunningly designed replicas (washable synthetics with the feel of real Lewisian gneiss) are the highly sensitive receivers through which NATO intelligence forces monitor the conversations, movements and metabolic rates of all deviants and dissenters between Shetland and the Scilly Isles.

Talking Head Possibles: Maria Milleny. An incomer (it takes about three generations to lose that tag), known as the Daft Artist on the Far West Side. But the islanders seem rather proud of her, as if she's some kind of rare migratory seabird, blown miles off her natural flightpath, who's chosen to make a nest here. Thirty-five or so? Hard to tell. She's one of your weatherbeaten types wearing hundreds of jerseys under an old blue boiler-suit. Red-headed

13

stringbean. Doesn't look like someone who cares much about home comforts.

My first contact is an introduction, courtesy of Catriona, when we all three coincide in the post office queue. I write her a note (no phone, of course) and ask if I can visit her at her studio.

The studio turns out to be a corrugated-iron shed behind the souvenir factory. Dotted about are some half-finished projects ('I'm always working on half a dozen things at once'). Amazing stuff. She's not much of a talker, to begin with, but if she were properly coached I'm sure she'd make an interesting subject for an interview. Her sculpture is definitely worth a look. As long as we have a cameraman with a little imagination to shoot it. Dermot or Sandy, maybe, but for lord's sake not Mitch or Douggie. They'd only try to chat her up ('Well it's fair game, eh, she's female and she's under eighty') and if they tried she'd probably smash their Arriflexes over their heads.

I'd have to work hard softening her up before she'd cooperate. She's wary of the media, she says, after a particularly idiotic newspaper piece someone did a while back. I ask if I can see the cutting – background research – but she says she was so pissed off about it she literally tore it up for arse-paper. Anyway, she's had some impressive reviews in the posh arts magazines. (That's according to Catriona MacEochan, anyway. Maria Milleny herself never mentioned them. She is, as they say, rather backwards in coming forwards.)

So I try to start an interview. Fortunately I have a bottle of wine in my bag – thought it was the only polite thing to do, since I've invited myself here. She takes off her welder's mask and says, pointedly, that it's thirsty work. She is constructing a five-foot-long Viking ship, small and sinister and shining. She looks at my bottle.

'Well, that will do for a start. Later I might have something else for you to try.'

I do my bit. The old interviewing technique. Get them talking, let them relax, ask a few leading questions once their guard is down (or, alternatively, encourage them to babble on, untrammelled, about themselves, the universal favourite subject, and they will hardly notice when you switch on the tape). Here goes.

'You came up here from London originally, didn't you?'

'Yes.'

'How long ago?'

14

'Long.'

'I think I remember reading a piece about you in one of the art magazines.'

'Probably.'

Terrific. Brilliant. An interviewer's dream. Just what I need – a real live zombie. An interview with her could be like pulling out finger-nails. Goodbye my embryonic notion for doing the whole damned film around Maria Milleny. And I had it all drafted out on the drive over here, too. 'An Artist's Island World.' Moody shots of her sculptures set among misty grey island landscapes (there are, in fact, dozens of them dotted about the island. Nobody seems to take much notice, as if they'd been there for centuries). A voice-over of Maria talking about her way of life, her sources of inspiration, her techniques, her reasons for leaving the London art scene, et cetera, and so on. It would have been wonderful, if she weren't so bloody laconic.

'You're not an islander by birth, then?'

'No.'

'What brought you here?'

'The *St Rollox*. Same as you.' She grins and raises her glass – a grubby plastic cup, to be more accurate – in the sketch of a toast.

'But why? In three words, or less of course.' I grin back at her. Two can play this game.

'I'm sorry. I'm winding you up.'

She rises. (We have been sitting cross-legged on a battered mattress, the plastic cups and the wine bottle between us.) Goes to a green metal cabinet marked FLAMMABLE hanging at a drunken angle on the wall, and takes out a murky bottle of what looks like disinfectant.

'If you want to understand Cailleach, try this. But you may never be quite the same again.' She pours, a generous dram into her own cup, a cautious dribble into mine. 'Go slowly, it's a painfully acquired taste.'

The amber liquid slides silkily on to my tongue, where it swiftly explodes into a hissing-hot radioactive white snake, its hundred heads spiked with laser-beam fangs, and hard bright diamond eyes that search out and set on fire all my brain's folds and furrows. As my eyes melt into waterfalls and spill down my glowing cheeks, I search for breath and scrabble furiously for a bolt-hole into homey old reality, applying the usual tests: my name, my birthdate, my current salary, the list of my five favourite English poets, American films and French cheeses, and – to bring me back with a thump – the seven demands of the women's liberation movement.

Finally there seems to be only one Maria Milleny, instead of a photomontage of six of her.

'Now, what was your question?'

'Typical boring journalistic drivel. Forget it.'

We laugh, then I begin to feel mildly irritated. This raw-boned eccentric in a boiler-suit has outfoxed me.

'No, I take that back. Not so boring. I really want to know. What brought you to Cailleach, and what keeps you here?'

'Now that is an interesting question, after all. But a tricky one. Sometimes I'm not so sure that I know, myself.'

In the long, peaceful silence, Maria Milleny looks backwards.

Time rewinds, ten years or so.

16

ONE
Catriona and Maria

Fenced in by small violet flames, Dr Catriona MacEochan sits with perfect composure in the centre of a pentangle. When the sun finally rises and the fire dies out, she steps across the chalk marks on the stone-flagged floor and puts her clothes on.

'All right, then, demons, do your stuff,' she says, lacing up her shoes.

Hundreds of miles to the south, behind the bay-window of a London bedsit, Maria Milleny wakes up to the worst day of her life. It begins with the definitive ending to a terminally ill love affair, and proceeds by way of a stolen bicycle to a polite letter from the polytechnic, lamenting budget cuts and dispensing with her services as a part-time lecturer in the Department of Art and Design.

You'd think she was made of iron filings, so strongly does the magnetic North attract her. Whenever she has escaped from anything, she does so by working her way to the top of the map. But so far, except for an unsuccessful walking tour in the Yorkshire Dales and an illicit weekend in the Lake District, she has never gone beyond the reach of the London *A to Z*.

Now, though, she's heading north in a big way. She has bought an Ordnance Survey map, a pair of hiking boots, and an elderly second-hand *Guide to the Outer Isles*. With the warmest woollens she can find stuffed into her rucksack, she is turning her back on her personal version of inner-city blight and going on the lam.

When she comes off the Victoria Line at Euston Station, she starts to run. As always she has left herself far too little time. And she knows that if she misses the 13.30 train to Glasgow, the forces of darkness are going to catch her. She frets and fidgets on a long, slow ticket queue. Everyone ahead of her has intricate and time-consuming demands. A pair of German tourists with problematical English are trying to organise themselves a return trip to Llandudno stopping at Chester on the way out and Chepstow on the way back. They pay with a set of discount vouchers that the ticket clerk studies suspiciously; he compels them to fill out half a dozen ambiguously worded forms, and when they finally receive their tickets they turn back again to ask a few more detailed questions about alternative routes. Next, a meticulous old gentleman pays for a first-class ticket to the Home Counties in five-pence pieces. He is followed by a go-ahead young businessman who wants to do it all by credit cards and needs to know the fastest, smoothest, smartest route from here to there by way of somewhere else, and does that train stop at Birmingham and if not why not; he'd be better off driving but the bleeding motor's off the road today, and so much for all those British Rail commercials, waste of taxpayer's money, innit?

Maria finally reaches the window, pays with a fistful of notes (she's cashed her last forseeable pay-cheque) and runs to the farthest platform, with half a minute to spare, sidestepping a conga-line of baggage carts, a clash of rival football supporters, a crocodile of name-tagged transatlantic tourists following their guide's uplifted red umbrella as if it were the Pillar of Fire, leading them out of this desert and into the Promised Land of their air-conditioned hotel.

But at last Maria's on – after a gazelle-like leap, completely out of character, that leaves her breathless. She stands in the aisle gasping for air, and strains her ears to catch the crackling loudspeaker announcement explaining that the Glasgow train will experience an hour's delay due to staff shortage, points failure at High Wycombe, fallen leaves on the line, and technical difficulties. The no-smoking carriages are crammed with prudent travellers who arrived in plenty of time, complacently eating cheese rolls. Finally she stops and stares down a man whose slimline attaché case sits beside him, atop his *Daily Telegraph*, on the train's only empty seat. He lifts them, grudgingly, then sprawls and spreads the way pin-striped men do who are used to deference. So she wages a small territorial war by dint of elbows and some judicious footwork with her Doc Martin boots. Finally, she wins the day by pulling out her packet of wondrously garlicky salami sandwiches. Her enemy decamps to the buffet car and is never seen again.

Maria sprawls luxuriously. The two nuns opposite, bolt upright and compact, leave her plenty of leg-room. She can feel the speculation in their gaze: her Irish-red hair hangs down her back in a long, thick plait. She wonders if they will suddenly order her to recite the Catechism.

This brings back awkward memories: Mother's note to Sister Mary Claire of Primary One, explaining that Religion was the Opiate of the People, and could little Maria please be excused from any lessons on the subject, and given extra tuition in drawing and spelling instead? The resulting row made local history. Twenty-odd years on, Maria still feels a nervous thrill. Nuns are dangerous. They hit people. And these two, with their shy smiles, wouldn't like her if they knew her. Especially in the unlikely event of their hearing about her one-woman show, two years before: the temporarily scandalous, mildly successful but now forgotten exhibition of paintings, *Lives of the Saints*.

You are invited to a private view
of an exhibition of paintings by Maria Milleny
LIVES OF THE SAINTS
at the marginalia gallery, clerkenwell
10 April 19XX
RSVP

A gallery typist with larger ambitions and a sly sense of humour sends a batch of invitations to Westminster Cathedral, and an equal number to the rival firm at Lambeth Palace. Plus half a dozen to the Jesuits at Farm Street, a scattering to rich old recusants in the art and antiques trades, plus a sufficient number for the whole of Sister Mary Joseph's fifth-form art class at Our Lady of the Precious Blood, Palmer's Green, who – fortunately, perhaps – do not turn up. Most of the others do. Including reviewers. This particular gallery is a current favourite of the Pretty People, whose fingers perpetually rest on Culture's pulse, and the wine is known to be free-flowing, if slightly acid on the tongue.

'Milleny's colours are luminous – the glowing rubies of Chartres windows, the soft-washed blues of old Limoges enamel, the rainbow glitterings of a gem-encrusted psalter. Her subject matter, alas, is a blasphemous travesty. A tragic waste of a fine talent,' – *The Catholic Review*.

'Naughty, but an artist worth watching,' – *Financial Times*.

'Go along to the Marginalia and see the fun,' – *Islington Newsrag*.

'More nonsense from London's over-subsidised art colleges. This rate-payer, for one, was not amused,' – *Evening Standard*.

Preoccupied as she is at her first-ever Private View, Maria, with nervous cramps and her eye on the door, finds time to notice the stranger circling the gallery. She is certainly not a reviewer, being far too interested in the canvases on the walls, and certainly not a gate-crasher, having politely declined the cheap Muscadet in favour of Perrier water. Then the gallery owner, who fancies herself to be north London's answer to Gertrude Stein, drapes her black-velvet arm across the newcomer's sturdy shoulders, and leads her to Maria.

'This, darling, is an old, old chum of mine. We were Scottish schoolgirls together.' A long, slow wink. 'And she's very taken with your work. She's going to buy at least six. Aren't you, Catriona?'

'You always did exaggerate, Louise. One painting will be quite enough. And, with your mark-up, all I could possibly afford. I'm sorry, Miss Milleny, you must think I'm as impolite as Louise, who has forgotten to finish the introductions. I'm Catriona MacEochan. How do you do?'

This is not a phrase of common currency in Maria's world, but the cool, dry handshake is a welcome relief after the sweaty palms of important reviewers and their hangers-on.

'I'm most intrigued, although I must admit I'm not an expert on the contemporary scene. Raeburn portraits are more in my line, and Highland landscapes; Louise despairs of me. But perhaps I could persuade you to give me a bit of background on the ones I like the best. I simply can't make up my mind.'

Catriona MacEochan is tall, but the gallery owner is taller. Just visible behind the Scotswoman's iron-grey curls is the sleek head of Louise, nodding vigorously.

'I'll handle the mob of admirers, Maria. Off you go.'

Fanning herself meditatively with her chequebook – the crowded room is stuffy – Catriona paces like a deerstalker from one painting to another. She stops several times in front of those she likes the most, asks intelligent and respectful questions about colours, planes and brushwork, and finally chooses.

Not 'Saint Veronica', although she praises Maria's rendering of the peasant girl scrubbing frantically at the strange, face-shaped stain on what is clearly her only veil.

22

Not 'Saint Anne', although she nods approvingly and says, 'How like life,' while contemplating the horrified expression on the saint's face, discovering her unwed daughter's swollen belly.

Not 'Mary Magdalene', in spite of the graceful curve of the bare flank being fondled by a langorously post-coital Jesus.

'Now, that's the one,' she announces. ' "Saint Bridget." Quite, quite wonderful.' On a moonlit shore, in a cold northern landscape, the saint strokes the arched neck of a blue-grey swan who has come to light on the edge of a turbulent sea.

'You've been to Cailleach, I see.'

'Where? Oh, Cailleach. Isn't that in the Hebrides? I'm afraid my geography is patchy. I spent most of my schooldays drawing caricatures of the teachers.'

'But you've captured it exactly. The landscape itself, the light. Are you absolutely sure you've never been there?'

'I'm afraid I've never been north of Hadrian's Wall. Perhaps it was a photograph that stuck in my mind. Or I might have dreamed it. I do sometimes dream my pictures before I paint them.'

'Well, it must be in your blood. You'll be Scottish.'

'On my mother's side – and she was away from Scotland long before I was born. The other half's Irish, and that's the half I know best.'

'The Celtic memory is a powerful inheritance. And I suppose your mother's the source of that splendid red-gold hair. So pure a colour is rarely seen among the Sassenachs. That's the Viking strain, of course, but those grey-green eyes are thoroughly Gael.'

Which is of little interest to Maria, pressing on what she hopes is the first of many red SOLD stickers. She is tired of doing publishers' paste-ups all week, and painting only on Sundays.

'The exhibition comes down in three weeks. You can collect the picture from the gallery any time after that.'

'Oh, but I shall be away home in Cailleach by then.'

'That's no problem,' says Louise, at Catriona's elbow. 'I can easily organise a . . .' but she stops as something suspiciously like a shoe presses firmly down on her buttersoft leather boot.

'Perhaps I could persuade you,' says Catriona to Maria, 'to deliver my purchase yourself?'

'Myself? To the north of Scotland? I'm terribly sorry, but I couldn't possibly afford the . . .'

'Don't be silly, girl. I'll pay your fare, of course. What do you take me for? And it won't cost me any more than it would to insure and ship the damned thing in the usual way. Don't tell me you wouldn't appreciate a little holiday, all expenses paid? I know how hard you young artists work, putting your first exhibitions together. Louise has told me all about it . . .'

'It's very kind of you, but I don't see how I could impose . . .'

'You wouldn't be imposing. I live in a ghastly, draughty old castle, but there's plenty of room. Although don't be disappointed – it is really quite tiny, as castles go. And if you're afraid of being stuck on an island with an old hag like me with whom you've nothing in common, well, don't be. I'm far too busy for idle chit-chat with house-guests. You'd be left to your own devices, right enough. And I'd expect you to bring your painting things. The light's perfect for an artist. Other-worldly. You'll find it irresistible, I promise you.'

Maria looks warily at Louise, who is nodding and blowing kisses to some new arrival at the other end of the room. She seems oblivious.

'Now you don't have to commit yourself straight away. I know you have plenty of things to think about, tonight of all nights, and you've been far too generous with your time already. Here's my address. Just drop me a note when the show is over, and we'll settle it all then. Now off you go and talk to all these connoisseurs and people. I understand they're a bit like dry toast – they need to be buttered. See you soon.'

After the show comes down, Maria Milleny does not go to Cailleach. She writes a short, polite letter telling Catriona about the part-time teaching post she's been offered, at a truculently progressive polytechnic, on the strength of the small flurry of public outrage caused by the paintings, 'Mary Magdalene' in particular. 'Saint Bridget' will have to be shipped after all. Would Catriona kindly send instructions to Louise at the gallery, who will see to everything. She is, hers sincerely, with warmest good wishes. So the Saint and her swan travel north in the care of an ancient firm of carriers, long trusted by the aristocracy to ferry its plunder up and down the realm. And life goes on.

Two years later, Maria sends Catriona MacEochan a second note, saying that she might be passing through that part of the world after all, and hopes the invitation is still open.

'Passing through?' muses Catriona over her breakfast kipper. 'Passing through? Where on earth could she be going – Greenland?'

24

No one, if you look at the map and check the ferry schedules, ever just passes through Cailleach.

Now Maria is half-way up England, watching the landscapes slide past the train. Some workmen are standing by the track, leaning on their pick-handles and waiting for the train to pass. For safety's sake, their dark blue anoraks are tabbed with patches of highly visible orange dayglo, but underneath they are wearing moleskin breeches. Behind them, on the embankment, are the huts and tents they live in: they cultivate their walrus moustaches, send their wages home to Ireland where the potato crop has failed again, and serve as unwitting guinea-pigs for a newly patented explosive: the inventor grows rich and important, and they die in a blaze of grit and glory.

But now they are out of sight and Maria presses her nose to the window to see the motorway running parallel to the track. A long parade of angry lorries stands nose to tail, because of some unknown snarl-up ahead. As the train advances Maria sees the source of the trouble: along the road, where tarmacadam has given way to pounded mud, strings of over-burdened ox-carts pass a waggon upset in a ditch and a pair of highwaymen methodically robbing the passengers in the Manchester coach. Next, above the train wheels she hears the smacking swords and bucklers of a battle between rival barons: on higher ground, their crumbled keeps have risen up sound and whole again.

Guarding the ramparts of a tall square fort, a lugubrious Roman soldier watches phlegmatically as the train goes by. He is bored and cold and homesick. This is a bad posting, punishment duty. Forests, impossibly thick, cut out most of the sunlight and for a few miles, wolves run alongside the train.

Maria avoids their ruby eyes, and closes her own.

A flat, metallic light washes over the housing estates beyond Crewe, promising thunderstorms. Maria, looking into gardens and kitchen windows, imagines herself hanging washing that stirs in the wind of the passing express, or peeling potatoes at a sink, and watching the train, homesick for all the places she's never been.

The table that separates her from the nuns is sticky with spilled coffee, and littered with discarded newspapers. She wonders where the holy sisters are going. Heads bent over their leather-bound breviaries, eyes down and mouths slackly open, they might be

25

dozing, or dead and gone to their Heavenly Bridegroom, or spinning in a Saint Theresiac trance. She opens up her Ordnance Survey map, purchased the day before to acquaint herself with Cailleach, and finds that the island occupies barely a quarter of the sheet – the rest is sea.

Staring at the map, Maria falls asleep herself. When she wakes, the train is passing the red walls of Carlisle, built to keep out raiders from the north. The nuns have vanished.

As the train crosses the border, climbing high, hills furrowed with old glacier trails or ancient plough-marks gloom over the track. In the narrow passes she can feel them breathing. For the first time, she feels sufficiently far away, sufficiently safe from pursuit and capture. Silly Maria, the train wheels say, nobody's after you, nobody knows, nobody cares.

Her legs are cramped and numbing, so to ease them she walks the length of the train, stiff-legged as a Wild West desperado, listening for her pardner's gunshots where she's robbing the US Mail van up ahead. Back in her seat again, she riffles through her guidebook. The island of her intentions only merits a paragraph. It's no better value for money, she thinks, than the map that's mostly sea.

So distant is Cailleach, says the book, so difficult of access, that few tourists will take the trouble to visit its clutch of antiquities: a small castle (*circa* 1200) still inhabited and not open to the public, a large stone circle, some ecclesiastical ruins, and a few unidentified mounds of probable Bronze Age origin. The population of 500 souls (approx.) depends on a struggling economy based on crofting, fishing, tweed-weaving, government subsidies and social security. The name Cailleach – Gaelic for Old Woman – is thought to derive either from one of the names of an early Celtic goddess, or from the oddly-shaped crags at the island's southernmost point, resembling a crone with a sharp nose and a jutting chin. The island has its own rapidly disappearing dialect – an amalgam of Gaelic and Old Norse – plus the harshest climate in the west of Scotland and a form of Christianity that matches it, icy blast for icy blast.

As the daylight fades, the train comes down out of the hills and crosses a wide plain bleak with the hulks of abandoned steelworks. This is not the postcard Scotland of Maria's fantasies, but people around her are pulling down their cases, so she must be near the end of the journey. Soon, crossing a bridge, Maria looks down and sees the Clyde below her, and the Glasgow riverfront, backed by sloping streets and a huddle of gables and rooftops under a violet sky.

Maria walks along the embankment next to the River Clyde. She's done her homework and come up with a solution to the problem of where to spend an evening on her own in a strange city. She is looking for a pub called the Thane of Cawdor. A Scottish acquaintance in London has recommended it – 'mostly boys, but everyone's friendly.'

Never over-fond of pubs, Maria at home avoids most gay bars and dykes' discos. But an evening seated on the edge of a lumpy divan in the Balmoral Guest House is unappealing. She finds the pub easily, but walks past it in the pearly twilight, wanting to see more of the city. It's not what she imagined Glasgow to be like at all, this dreamtown, its streets empty except for a gliding ghost or two. She's piqued, disturbed, wants to know where the cobbled alleys lead. An incautious walk for a woman alone in an unknown town, but she feels safe and invisible, a tourist from another dimension.

Soft rain strokes her face, and the late summer evening begins to feel more like early winter, so she retraces her steps and enters the pub. She walks into a brown room full of tiny old men in flat caps and raincoats, each with a pint of beer in one hand and a glass of whisky in the other. She wonders if her informant has been away from Scotland too long, or if she's written down the wrong name altogether. But the barmaid catches her eye, winks, and points her to a stained-glass door (a Victorian mosaic of purple grapes and green garlands) in the corner beyond the cigarette machine.

She climbs a stone staircase and enters a paradise of purple dralon, flocked wallpaper, suburban curry-house meets New Orleans whorehouse in a fantasia of fringed lampshades and chandeliers. Even the bobbles on the heavy fuchsia draperies are rocking and rolling to the thumping disco beat, and the little square of dance floor shines like satin. But there is nobody on it, and the music plays to an empty room.

'Yurra tottie bit early, hen . . .'

'Pardon?'

The lassies, explains the grandmotherly barmaid, never turn up much before nine. But Maria is not here, she tells herself, for any of That Sort of Thing, and if they speak the same dialect as the woman behind the bar she'd need subtitles anyway. This is merely, she says to herself again, a place of diversion and safety for the evening.

She orders a whisky. The measure is generous, twice the size of an English dram, and cheaper, so she indulges in a packet of crisps as well. Then retreats to a banquette with a ringside view, just in time to watch the first customers of the evening filtering in. They are a rich mix – down in London they'd thin themselves out among twenty different specialist venues. But here they have only each other, so leather men rub shining black shoulders with elderly cravatted theatricals, neat-bottomed Botticelli angels, teachers and solicitors still in their sedate daytime dress and letting their hair down. A new face in town, she's glanced at, identified as the wrong gender, dismissed and forgotten.

Relieved, Maria settles down and opens up her map of Cailleach.

Suddenly a shadow falls on Nestaval (700m), covers Cailleach Castle, obscures the Cliffs of Crunig, Gosta Ness, and the Three Lochans. Then a long, pale hand, tapering to scarlet nails of exotic length and elegant curvature, floats across the sea and comes to rest upon the Cape of the Winds.

'Cailleach! You can't be serious! You're going to Cailleach of your own free will? Och, I can't stand it! Nobody in their right mind would do it. You are in your right mind, darling, aren't you? You take it from me, sweetheart, you'd have more fun spending your holidays in Barlinnie Prison.'

Maria looks up. The owner of the lilting accent (Maria has heard that singsong, or its close cousin, before) sits down next to her, gently smoothing the shark-blue satin sleeves of his skin-tight fifties cocktail gown.

'Howdy, stranger. I reckon you're new in town. Just blowed in off the Big Smoke Express and waiting to catch the Highlands and Islands Stage . . . Well, save yourself a passel of trouble and heartbreak. Go anywhere else in the world you fancy, but Cailleach is no place for a nice kid like you.'

Maria says nothing, still taking in the vision before her. The upswept, platinum-blond coiffure looks oddly at home above the droopy black Zapata moustache, which itself matches perfectly with the dangling jet earrings.

'I suppose your mammy told you never to speak to strangers. Well, let me introduce myself and we'll solve that little problem. I'm Davie. But all my pals call me Dinah.'

'Hello.' Maria is too tired to resist, and too curious. 'I'm Maria.'

28

'Now I don't mean to intrude . . . perhaps you vant to be alone, but dear knows you'd hardly be wasting your time in this dump if that were the case. And, of course, if you only want to talk to the sisters I won't be offended at all: some of my best friends are lesbian separatists – at least there's no competition, it's so-o-o relaxing. Anyway, I simply can't sit there in silence watching a poor innocent who is obviously about to commit themselves to the terrible folly of a trip to Cailleach.'

'What do you have against Cailleach?'

'A lifetime of scars, my dear. It's the armpit of the universe. And it's where I come from, so I should know.'

This is not what Maria expects to find up there on the northern rim of the known world. 'Are there any more like you at home?'

'If there are they're so deep in the closet they've turned into coat-hangers. Anyone with any smeddum, whatever their persuasions or perversions, buggers off – pardon my French – as soon as they're old enough to raise the money for a ferry ticket. Oh, it's lovely and peaceful and all that, and very scenic, if you like sheep. But no jobs, no privacy, no freedom, no fun. Unless you're a pillar of the kirk who gets off on denouncing folk. Otherwise it's a fusty wee place. Take my advice and go to Paris instead.'

'I'm trying to get away from it all. I want some place far away and peaceful.'

'Well it's far away, right enough, and I suppose it's peaceful if you're a stranger. Nobody is going to leap out from behind every rock telling *you* to get a haircut or a job or a wife or anything. But I think you'll be sorry.'

'If I buy you a drink, will you tell me about it?'

'I thought you'd never ask, dear.'

She buys him a gin and tonic, while he writes a phone number and address on the margin of her map.

'That's where you should stay. It's the best Bed-and-Breakfast on Cailleach – well, there's only one other – and I don't suppose you want to squander your pennies at that pesthole of an inn.'

'What's wrong with the inn?'

'Well you're all right as long as you don't try to eat the food or sleep in the beds. Unless you're an entomologist. In which case you'll adore it. You could write your whole PhD dissertation on the fauna that live under the kitchen worktops. I was a washer-up there once, for a holiday job. Believe me, I know. Anyway, you take my advice and stay at Ina Isbister's. She's a real old

29

sweetheart, but for lord's sake don't tell her you met me. She's my auntie, and you'll never have a minute's peace once she finds out that you've seen me. Anyway, unless you like heather and old ruins, she's about the one good thing in Cailleach.'

'Well, I do want to see the Cailleach Ring. It's supposed to be amazing. Better than Stonehenge. No tourists.'

'A few hours freezing your arse off, dearie, and you'll soon know why.'

'You really have a down on the place, don't you?'

'Well, look at me, petal. Do I strike you as the classic homesick highlander?'

'Do you know most of the people up there?'

'Only too well. Except I've been away for three years now, so I'm a bit out of touch with all the gossip.'

'A friend of a friend of mine gave me a name. Said I should pay a visit. You know, chance of a free meal, or something.'

'Nothing's really for free in Cailleach. Who's the name?'

'MacEochan.'

'MacEochan. There's plenty of those. There's Betty MacEochan who has five screaming weans – well, its probably eight by now, she's pretty prolific . . . and Jean MacEochan but she's about one hundred and only speaks Gaelic anyway . . . and Mrs MacEochan who does the payroll at the fish-processing factory . . . and of course there's the Dreaded Catriona . . . oh god, don't tell me it's the Queen of Castle Cailleach . . . I have a horrible suspicion that it is.'

'Well, as it happens . . .'

He shrieks, a high falsetto that cracks, just briefly, into baritone, recovering himself only to find that his pearl necklace has burst. The beads roll gently across the sea and over Cailleach, where Maria swiftly gathers them up as they slip across South Bay.

'Thanks, darling. I think we've got them all. They were a present from an old admirer. I'd hate to lose them. Anyroads, as I was saying, you'd better watch yourself if it's Catriona MacEochan. If I were you I'd stay well clear. She's gey sinister. With a face like Glencoe on a winter's morning. And she's always up to something funny. If you're determined to get yourself a free dinner at the castle, you'd best keep your back to the wall. That's all I can say . . .'

Maria thinks that with the help of another drink she can probably induce him to say plenty more. But his eye is suddenly

30

caught by someone standing in the crush that has now built up around the bar. He lights up, blows a winsome kiss, and rises, adjusting the tatty but sweetly scented fox fur around his neck.

'Must fly now, darling. It's Cruise Time. But thanks for the drink and it's been lovely talking to you. Just take my advice, and if you've got any sense, steer well clear from La MacEochan. Don't say that I didn't warn you.'

On the narrow bed in her guest house, somewhere in the southern suburbs, Maria tosses, turns and speculates on the scenario to come.

In the gothic thriller, Maria is lured to the island by Catriona on behalf of a select circle of upper-class Scottish satanists. Forked lightning illuminates their gathering, in the square, sombre tower of Castle Cailleach. Charmed by Maria's talents and beauty, the coven first attempts to recruit her into their fiendish communion and, then, when she has rebuffed them, threatens to sacrifice her on an expensively draped altar, in honour of some imported, goat-faced Mediterranean godlet.

In the late Victorian romance, Maria and Catriona spend some weeks exchanging pleasantries and guarded good manners. Tempted, just once, to a delicate exchange of sisterly kisses, they fly apart and head off in separate directions, to follow noble destinies: Maria to marry a handsome but dissolute aristocrat, Catriona to work among the poor in the slums of Dundee. Fifty years later, they meet again – Maria a wealthy widow, bruised in soul and body, Catriona dying of some infection contracted in the course of her selfless works of charity and piety. Maria brings Catriona to end her days in a sunny villa in the south of France, where their only communion – Catriona being past all speaking – is a gentle pressure of their cool, pale hands. When Catriona dies she leaves an unsuspected fortune to Maria, who buries her friend in the English cemetery at Nice, and comes every day to leave a bunch of violets by her grave.

In the wicked caper movie, Maria charms and flatters her eccentric, elderly hostess, and swiftly establishes herself in Catriona's confidence as well as in her bed. In an episode of cleverly feigned passion, she ascertains the secret location of the legendary MacEochan emeralds, bequeathed to the family by a grateful Bonnie Prince Charlie after a narrow escape. With the jewels concealed in her black leather boots, in a cleverly hollowed-out heel, Maria descends from the tower by an improvised rope of satin bedsheets. She is assisted in her escape by the pert house-parlourmaid, who joins her on the ferry to Stornoway, and in a sybaritic ever-after in some unspecified Caribbean paradise where the sun always shines.

An alternative ending, should the houseparlourmaid be uncooperative or non-existent, is a daring aerial escape from the castle via a hijacked RAF helicopter, ably piloted by a strong, silent lieutenant – female, of course – who whirls her to the mainland where the two dispose of the loot and take up their new identities, breeding spaniels on the Dorset coast.

'Lots of famous people have come to Cailleach, you know. We've had the Queen Mother, and Andy Stewart, and that Aileen Whatshername who reads the news on the wireless. You'd be surprised who's sat in that seat you're sitting in.'

Maria is in the Cailleach taxi, summoned on her behalf by Ina Isbister when she rang Ina from the harbour call-box, just off the ferry, to book herself a room. She has not mentioned who sent her, nor has Ina asked.

'Aye, the weekend will be fine, and perhaps a night or two beyond that. There's no need to make up your mind this minute. I'll send Hector for you – I'm miles out of the way. Although I think you'll find it perfect for the Cailleach stones and other places of interest. Very handy, but lots of peace and quiet.'

'That's what I'm after,' replies Maria as the money runs out.

She is sharing the taxi, she discovers, with two small lambs and a large sheepdog, who rests his cold nose on the back of her neck. Hector, unable to make a living between the visits of the aforementioned celebrities at ten-year intervals, is also a crofter, the island plumber and assistant postmaster.

As they drive along the dark roads, illuminated only by the glow showing through chinks in the curtained windows of a few scattered houses, he entertains her with tales of his previous passengers.

'And then there was this wee fat American with a wee fat cigar, who said he was from Hollywood. He wanted to put Your Quaint Little Island Here – that's how he talked, mind, but I can't do the accent right – into a Major Motion Picture. He said we'd be gey famous. But we saw him off all right. I've kept this as a souvenir.' He pulls off the road – they have arrived at Ina's – but insists on foraging in his pockets for a creased and furrowed scrap of paper. It is the duplicate of a telegram form, and Maria can barely read what's written there. He switches on the light inside the car, and deciphers the message for her:

HARRY YOU AND YOUR COCKAMAMIE IDEAS STOP THIS PLACE TOTALLY WRONG FOR BRIGADOON STOP PEOPLE UGLY WEATHER LOUSY FOOD INEDIBLE STOP LET'S SHOOT THE PICTURE ON THE BACKLOT WHERE IT BELONGS AND STOP SENDING ME ON WILD GOOSE CHASES REGARDS SAM

Somehow Maria feels that Hector doesn't quite get the accent right. But no matter. She has arrived.

Looking out of her bedroom window at Ina Isbister's, Maria can just make out the shapes of the stones on the far side of the field: hooded figures, leaning towards each other, engaged in deep deliberations, a council of cowled elders. Inside the ring the night seems darker, black wine in an obsidian cup.

'The auld wifies used to say,' explains Ina, plumping up pillows, 'that on summer nights the stones would come alive and whirl round in a dance. But I think that those who've seen it are those who've had a drop too much of the cratur first. Fancy a load of old rocks jumping up and doing a jig. I take no notice of it. Now here's a hot-water bottle for your bed, so you should be nice and comfy. But you'd best keep your window open just a crack, and the curtains shut tight. There's an awful dirty wind coming off the sea. You can have your breakfast any time you like, as long as its after seven – when I feed my family – and before half-past eight.

But Maria is up at sunrise, for her first look at the stones, and comes in ravenous to mountains of home-made bread and a lake of creamy porridge.

After breakfast Maria takes her map and goes for a walk along the beach. The warm sun surprises her; she has come north expecting to be wet and cold. She decides to grant herself three days of peace before she contacts Catriona – she has, after all, only said she'd be coming sometime this month, never naming a day. And for all she knows, Catriona has never received her postcard. Perhaps she'll be distantly polite, vague about the invitation, and relieved when Maria goes off on the next available boat. But for the moment Maria will do nothing but walk and read and rest and eat

Ina's wonderful food, and perhaps the demons of paranoia, sloth and self-doubt will lie quiet within her. Just to make sure they don't, she has deliberately forgotten to pack her sketch-blocks. But none of this means anything under a hard, hot sun, so she sprawls on a flat-topped rock and the lapping water lulls her to sleep.

A cold wind wakes her. Something stands between herself and the warm sun. She feels its presence before she shakes off her dream and opens her eyes. A polite cough places the intruder directly behind her. Catriona MacEochan stands on the rock, looking down from a great height; she has leapt up quite soundlessly for a Valkyrie in gum-boots.

'Made it, have we? Very good.'

Maria flusters, feeling caught out. 'Just last night. Very late. Ferry was hours overdue. Couldn't possibly ring you at that hour . . . just up for a little sightseeing, famous Cailleach stones and all . . . thought I might be imposing on you and I'm sure you're dreadfully busy, and just because you bought one of my paintings is no reason to think I can make free of your hospitality, so I thought I'd wait until later today, and telephone you from my bed-and-breakfast place, and . . .'

'Shut up, would you. I'm delighted to see you. There's no need to fuss about it.'

'Do you live close by?'

'No.'

'What a coincidence. I mean . . .'

'There are no coincidences in Cailleach. I've come up to fetch you.'

'How did you know?'

'Scryed you in my crystal, of course. The usual way.'

Maria looks doubtful.

'Ah well, have it your way. You young people are so prosaic. Would you be happier if I said that your Mrs Isbister told me when she dropped off the eggs and milk this morning?'

'Does she report to you on all her guests?'

'Only the ones that interest me. Anyway, I knew you were there.'

'How?'

'Hector told me last night that he'd driven a tall, skinny red-headed lass up to Isbisters'.'

'And how did he come to tell you that?'

'Had him in fixing a burst pipe around midnight, and asked him who came off the *St Rollox*.'

'Just passing the time of night . . .?'

'I had a hunch you'd be on it. And I'm rarely wrong. You'd better realise that this isn't London you're in now. You can't go mooching around unnoticed for twenty years without your neighbours knowing your name and your business. Cailleach's a wise old wily island; her hills have eyes and her breezes carry gossip, and there isn't a bird flying overhead but is in my pay. Now are you coming to me for dinner tonight, or aren't you?'

Maria can't quite think of a reason not to. The voice of Davie-Dinah against the disco-beat of the Thane of Cawdor grows ever fainter; she crumples up his words of warning and flings them out to sea. After all, this is why she came to Cailleach isn't it? To take up Catriona's invitation. She says she will, if it's no trouble at such short notice.

'Well, I'm glad about that, because the main course is already marinating in herbs and garlic, and the wine's been brought up from the cellar. You wouldn't dare say no.'

'How do I get there?'

'I'll drive up and collect you. Say quarter to eight? That should give you time for a good long day's walking.'

'I'd better tell Mrs Isbister I'll be out for dinner.'

'She already knows. See you later.' The wind whirls in and blows away Catriona's footprints.

'So you're dining at the castle tonight. Isn't that lovely?' Ina Isbister pours Maria a cup of tea, and presses her to take a second scone, the size of a saucer.

'I don't think I'll be back very late.'

'Oh you'll be late, right enough. Don't worry, though, the door's never locked.'

Maria hears a snort of suppressed laughter behind her, and turns to see that someone else has entered the kitchen, soundless in dirty plimsolls. A small, dark woman, skinny as a ten-year-old boy, leans against the doorjamb, arms folded across the front of a sweatshirt that proclaims 'Rosa Luxemburg Died for Your Sins.'

'Well, I had better make the necessary introduction, although you two ladies will have nearly missed each other. This is Dr Stonebridge, our archaeologist from Edinburgh, and this is Miss Milleny, up from London for a wee holiday. Dr Stonebridge has been here all summer, working on the excavations, but she's leaving us tomorrow, aren't you dear?'

'Where are you digging? Over at the stones?'

'Wouldn't touch them with a barge pole. Airy-fairy speculations about neolithic astronomy, and all that counter-cultural claptrap. A total waste of time and energy. And anyway, it's not my period. No, we're up at the old nunnery. Been doing it for two years now, over Easter breaks and summer vacations. Digging up the garden, to see what the old girls grew and how they grew it.'

'I'm amazed you can find anything to go on.'

'We have our ways. And seeds are tenacious little bastards. Besides, the sisters were far too thrifty to throw anything away. And I mean anything. Now I know Ina finds it all very distasteful, so I won't bore you with the technical details . . .'

'No, really, I wish you would. I'm very interested . . .'

'Well I'm not. Anyway, I'm off to the inn now. Have to meet my insufferable co-director and the rest of the team for the end-of-dig party. I tell you, Ina, if I don't get that man off my hands next year, I'm not coming up at all. Nice meeting you, pal. Enjoy your evening with the ruling class. But Ina's right. Don't expect to be back early. You haven't a chance. Cheers, Ina.' She disappears.

'Now don't take any notice of her dear. Dr MacEochan is a fine woman, whatever anybody says, and I'm sure you'll have a lovely evening. And I'll be pleased to put my feet up with nobody to cook for, and have a good read of my library book. It's a biography of Marie Curie, and I've just got to the bit where she knows she's on to something when her fingers start glowing in the dark. Now away and run your bath – there's plenty of hot water – so you'll be ready on time. Oh, and one little reminder. She's a great one for her rare old wines, Catriona, just like her father was before her. So if you think she's maybe a touch over-tired at the end of the evening, you be sure you stay put and let her make you up a bed in her spare room. Not that she isn't steady as a rock, mind you, but there's a nasty curve on the road just above Tarvig, and she's had a little mishap there once or twice before on a dark night. But for goodness' sake, don't tell her I said anything. These roads are terrible on a wet evening, and there's more than one has had their problems, especially after a night at the Cailleach Inn. There are some of my neighbours, I regret to say, who do not know how to hold their drink, which is not a skill to be proud of really now, is it? Although I've nothing against the stuff myself, being partial to a wee refreshment on Hogmanay and on my birthday, although if you ever meet our minister, Reverend MacNeish, never tell him that I told you. But he's got a point, you know, to be fair, there is far too much drunkenness in the world these days, and if our island is in a state of decline then we have only ourselves to blame, which is what he said to us in kirk last Sunday. Now away you go, don't stand here listening to me rabbiting on, or you'll be late for your dinner engagement. If you'd like to use some very special perfumed bubble bath, help yourself, it's in that big cut-glass jar on the shelf, with the purple tassels on. 'Harem Rose', it's called. My nephew Davie sent it up for my birthday; he's down at the Uni in Glasgow just now, and doing very well.'

'Aaaahhhh . . .' says Catriona, swirling her glass and inhaling the vapours. 'A year of sunshine and splendour. The world breathing a sigh of relief. The first decent vintage after the war. You can almost see that far away summer when you taste it. Go on . . . no, don't guzzle it, girl! Sip . . . just a little bit . . . draw it through your teeth, swirl it around, think about it, listen to what it tells you, then swallow it. That's right. Pure nectar . . .'

Maria has successfully negotiated the lobster soup, but the main course is proving more of a challenge.

'Now tell me about yourself,' commands Catriona, staring hawklike at Maria as she deftly carves the slices of roast island lamb, pink and rosemary-scented.

'Mmm, lovely lamb,' replies Maria, stalling for time and unsure of what to choose and where to start. She cuts into it enthusiastically, and with a hideous screech of knife on porcelain sends it skittering off the plate and into her lap.

'Easy, my dear. You'll find it's very tender. Cuts like butter.'

'Sorry.'

'My fault. I should have warned you.'

Maria wonders whether to lift it off her lap with her fingers, or whether a fork would be more appropriate. She watches helplessly as it slides down the crisp linen napkin and on to the stone-flagged floor.

'Sorry.' She dives after it.

'Just leave it. I'll pick it up later. For the cats. Have a bit more.'

Two more tender slices are slipped on to Maria's now dishevelled plate.

'What painters have been your most important influences?'

The lamb, going down, hits a sudden nervous knot, as Maria feels she's resitting her last art college finals. She chokes, splutters, almost recovers the morsel as it slips resolutely down the wrong way.

Catriona rises, strides round the table, seizes her from behind and thrusts her ribcage upward with a vigorous authority. The morsel shoots out of Maria's mouth and arcs delicately into a dish of sautéed wild mushrooms.

'Heimlich manoeuvre. Sorts it out every time.'

Maria, catching her breath, tries to lift the murderous mouthful out of the serving dish, so she can conceal it from view in her napkin, and manages to retrieve it while spilling her glass of wine all over the table.

'Oh god. I am so sorry.'

'Never mind, my dear, never mind,' beams Catriona warmly. 'It gives me the chance to show you a very neat trick.' She rises, disappears through a low, lintelled doorway on the far side of the baronial fireplace, Maria hears her footsteps clattering lightly down a spiral staircase, and soon Catriona reappears with a bottle of white wine. 'This will stand you in good stead for ever,' she remarks, uncorking it and pouring it with a theatrical gesture over the red-stained cloth.

Maria gasps.

'Don't worry, it's a completely insignificant little Muscadet that I keep for times like this. Now, you'll see that the white wine will completely neutralise the red, and the cloth will come up just fine. Once you know this, you need never feel embarrassed after a spill. And believe me, they can happen at the most awkward occasions, at the grandest dinner parties. It will save a fortune on cleaning bills. I think there's something fiendish about the way red wine always chooses to spill itself on to white fabric.'

'This is a lovely castle,' says Maria lamely, once things have settled down again. She is playing it safe and toying with a slice of delicately gratinéed potato.

'No it's not,' snaps Catriona. 'It is quite, quite hideous. But it's home. I can live here rent free. Which is why I can afford this not-bad claret. Have some more.' Ignoring Maria's gesture of protest, she pours the wine into the crystal glass.

'Has it been in your family a long time?'

'Since the heyday of that blond boy in the heavy gilt frame on the first landing.' Catriona tosses her head towards the stone staircase, lined with a gallery of ancestors who all appear to be glaring disdainfully at the dinner guest.

'And who is he?'

'That's Alasdair the Ambidextrous. Divided his favours more or less equally between his lady wife and King Jamie Stuart, taking them in turn on alternate week-nights. In grateful thanks he was awarded the castle, and the island along with it. There's a rude song about it in Gaelic that the local women used to sing while weaving the island tweed. But nobody can remember the second verse any more, which is a great pity, because it apparently said some things about the king's assumption of the English crown that would make your hair curl. Anyway, that's on father's side. On my mother's side the island stock goes back much, much further. Which did not endear Mama to her friends and neighbours, who always thought she was letting the side down by marrying the laird. Now, perhaps I could interest you in a little taste of cheese? There's another bottle I've decanted, from the same vintage but a different château. I thought you'd find the comparison interesting.'

'I don't really know much about wine,' says Maria apologetically, 'I think it would be wasted on me.'

Catriona sits upright, taps Maria smartly across the knuckles with her butterknife. 'Don't sell yourself short, woman. You're young enough to learn!'

She sweeps the serving platters and dinner plates away to an ancient oak sideboard, as long and heavy as a Victorian railway carriage, then returns with a board of cheeses and a fresh loaf of bread.

Maria nibbles morsels of unknown cheeses in nervous silence, waiting for the next phase of the inquisition, but Catriona, sniffing meditatively into her wineglass appears to have forgotten her existence.

Suddenly Catriona sits bolt upright, nailing Maria to her chair with a pointed, penetrating gaze. 'What you need,' she announces, seizing Maria's right hand and pulling it towards her, 'is your palm read.' Her grasp is strong, her fingers cool and silky. Maria stares, hypnotised, at the square-tipped fingers gently tracing curves and spirals over her palm.

'It's very clear to me that you have reached some kind of crossroads.'

'I'm sorry, but do you really believe in all this? I mean, you being a doctor, and all, I would have thought . . .'

'You know nothing about it,' snaps Catriona, 'but if you are going to be sceptical then I think there is no point in searching further. At least not for the moment.' She hands Maria her palm back. 'Coffee? We'll have it by the fire.'

'Oh, that would be lovely,' says Maria, rising with a sigh of relief and swiftly sending her empty wineglass flying as she does so. The crystal tinkles musically as it shatters on the stone. 'Oh, Christ. Oh Jesus, Mary and Joseph. Oh, Catriona, I am so sorry, I just don't know how I . . . you must think I am a complete idiot . . . I . . .'

'On the contrary, my dear, it's been a most amusing dinner. You must not be so apologetic. It doesn't suit you. Anyway, I've always loathed this crystal. A birthday present from a very annoying second cousin. Perhaps if I invite you back next week, you'll do me an enormous favour and help me destroy the rest of the set.' Placing her hand firmly on Maria's nervously hunched-up shoulder, she steers her towards an overstuffed armchair by the fire. 'Now sit there, and I shall bring in the coffee. No, don't bother to help me. I'm really rather fond of this particular pair of cups and saucers. So do us both a favour, and just keep still.'

Sipping the coffee, freshly-ground and strong and fragrant, Maria begins to feel slightly dizzy. She thinks it's the wine, reaching her addled brain at last.

'Now, as I was saying,' says Catriona, settling into another deep chair on the other side of the fire, 'I am not going to let you leave here until you tell me more about yourself. Go on, sing for your supper.'

So Maria does. About light and colour and the problem of how to capture and create it when all the world about you is turning grey and flat and fogbound. About her early efforts at sculpture, and the scathing remarks of an instructor that sent her back to the comparative safety of paint and canvas. About her life in London and its recent, total disintegration. About her loss of her job, her self-confidence, and, worst of all, her creativity, for the fund of ideas and images has dried and shrivelled like a sloughed-off snakeskin in the sand, leaving her feeling empty, but riddled with guilt and frustration. She rouses herself from looking inwards, and wonders if Catriona is growing bored.

'Not at all,' says Catriona, smiling gently, her gaze continuing to flick lizardlike across Maria's face, and up and down her spare and anxious frame. 'But I think that it is high time you came to Cailleach. You almost left it too late.'

There seem to be four or five Catrionas sliding across her vision in a gentle dance. She wonders if her hostess has slipped something into the coffee, from an elegantly chased silver phial concealed in her black silk sleeve. She wonders if she will pass out, yet another mortification, and wake up to find herself en route to the brothels of Old Havana. ('Never take food from a stranger.' Her mother's long-ago warning rings like a bell across time.) Or, perhaps, in more classical vein, she will find herself transformed into a squealing pig, penned up in a sty with other bewildered ex-dinner guests. More likely, she decides, looking at the two bright pinpoints of firelight reflected in Catriona's steel-grey eyes, she will soon be lying on a baking tray on the scrubbed wooden table in the castle kitchen. Catriona will be pressing currants and bits of angelica into her body, just before she slips her into the ancient oven and bakes her into gingerbread.

'But first I'll have to fatten you up,' Catriona says softly.

'What?' says Maria, startled, sitting bolt upright.

'I said, I think it's time I drove you back to Ina's. It's getting late.'

Maria doesn't know whether to be relieved or disappointed, as her hostess helps her into her anorak.

In Catriona's land-rover, on the drive back to Ina's, Maria sits quietly, faintly mortified that the evening has ended without even the slightest attempt at a seduction scene. She feels that she has, somehow, blown it, and that Catriona is probably very sorry she ever asked her to visit the island.

Outside, beyond the glow of the headlamps, she can just make out the humped shapes of the low hills, sheep drifting across like puffs of low-lying cloud, a few unlit houses dark against the deeper darkness, and a pool of purple shadow where the road ahead curves sharply, where the rocks go down to the sea. Catriona takes the curve with a gust of speed.

'Is this Tarvig?'

Catriona glances at her, Maria sees the glint of a grin. 'And what do you know about Tarvig . . .'

'Oh, just the name. I've been trying to get my bearings on the map. I think maybe I read it in the guidebook . . . I don't know . . . a Viking battle maybe, or a standing stone.'

'Nothing,' says Catriona flatly, 'nothing at all. Of general historical interest. What else did Ina Isbister tell you?'

'What?'

'Come now.'

'Well, she said that if you seemed tired, I should get you to make me up a spare bed. She said you overwork yourself dreadfully . . .'

41

'Rubbish. That's not what she said at all. Anyway, never mind. I am not, as Ina so delicately puts it, tired. And I think you are better off for tonight anyway, staying at Ina's. Tomorrow, however, I shall collect you at half-past ten in the morning, and take you on a little tour of the island. I'll bring a picnic. There's plenty of leftover roast lamb . . .' She grins wickedly.

'But, if you're sure that it's no imposition, I mean, if Sunday's your one free day, and . . .'

'Just stop it. At once. These niminy-piminy petit-bourgeois good manners do not sit well with your image. You're a child of the sixties. A starving, at least in the metaphorical sense, artist. And you dress like an anarchist. So don't behave like an Edinburgh lady from Morningside in a flowery bonnet. Just take what you're offered. And I am offering you a Sunday drive unlike any you will ever get anywhere on the mainland. With an excellent picnic. So just shut up and accept it with a bit of good grace.' She jerks the land-rover to a stop. 'That's it. Get out. We're at Ina's. Goodnight.'

Wide awake in bed, Maria thinks about Catriona. Tries to analyse why she finds her so disturbing. Hopes that will exorcise it. Makes a list, counting on fingers that still smell faintly of rosemary.

1. She must be nearly fifty. What do I want with an older woman? Quite a lot really, I'm sick of overgrown adolescents.

2. She is a member of the ruling class. Well, sort of. Near enough anyway. That would irritate good old Marxist mother nicely, if she knew. (In her mind's eye, she sees Catriona, smiling, extending an open palm, producing a tiny silver knife and cutting straight across the line of Venus. Drops of blood, bright blue, harden into a sapphire bracelet. Then the image laughs and says, 'So I'm descended from an old, old family. What's so special about that? So's everyone. Or where do you think your lot started – a potato sprout?')

3. She may call herself poor, and strapped for money and all, but that's only inverse snobbery, or suppressed guilt. The old dear has a castle full of antiques, and probably owns the whole island . . . ('A liability if there ever was one,' snaps the image. 'What do you think the whole shebang would fetch on the open market? The place is an economic desert. The Secretary of State for Scotland doesn't even know how to spell it properly. They'd give us independence in a flash, you know, we're really just an encumbrance. But

I suppose they're saving us for a uranium dump.')

4. She's weird. Who ever heard of a palm-reading GP? (Catriona smiles enigmatically, a ruddy-cheeked Mona Lisa. A gypsy hoop dangles from one ear, and when she smiles a front tooth is revealed to have a gold star set into it.)

5. If she accepts hospitality from Catriona, she is putting herself in a compromising position. But the woman has virtually offered to keep her for an indefinite period. A Renaissance patron of the arts in a pair of corduroy breeches. Or perhaps Maria's blown it. Catriona was interested two years ago, but a lot can change in that time. ('Don't be ridiculous,' says Catriona. 'Things don't change that fast on Cailleach. Unless I let them. Now go to sleep.')

Just before she falls over the edge, Maria hears brakes and a banging door and unsteady footsteps. Unwillingly, she listens to Dr Stephanie Stonebridge being copiously sick in the sink on the other side of the wall. 'Oooh, never again. Serves me bloody right.'

The next thing Maria hears, as she wakes to a blaze of sunlight, is Dr Stonebridge shouting, 'Bless you, Ina love, and see you next year. If they don't blow us all to kingdom come before then . . .!'

'Well, that's our excavation over for the season,' announces Ina, as she pours out Maria's breakfast cup of stiff black coffee.

'I didn't think there was a Sunday ferry.'

'Oh, there's not. That would be unthinkable. No, someone is coming to collect her and her old bits and relics in a helicopter. The students are all away tomorrow on the *St Rollox*, but she and that wee professor chappie are taking the latest discoveries away in style. Courtesy of a Royal Navy helicopter. Something to do with getting the bones to a lab as fast as possible, or something. And don't think that our minister isn't furious about it. A helicopter landing on the Lord's Day. Of course, he really doesn't hold with all this archaeology at all, you know. He says it's against the Bible's own commandment to leave well enough alone and don't poke your nose in where you're not wanted. I can't quite mind the chapter and verse.'

Catriona, in the land-rover, summons Maria with a few staccato blasts of her horn.

'Fasten your seatbelt. I drive like a demon.'

To prove it, she presses down hard on the accelerator with a well-worn hiking boot and they lurch down the bumpy track that links the Isbisters' croft with the road.

'Of course, you know this road already,' says Catriona as they head down the coast towards the castle.

'It looks different, though. Because of the light.'

The sky is brassy, with thundery weather blowing in from the west. Spurs of rock run down to the jagged shoreline, where grey-green lumps of island, bitten off by the sea, float in the black water, seeming to keep pace with the car as they drive along the coast. On the landward side, the ground rises sharply. Blackface sheep, their tails higher than their heads, browse on the bracken of the hillside.

'A special breed. Their front and back legs are different sizes. Evolved for hill-walking.'

'You're joking.'

'Yes. Half of what I say is rubbish, the rest is true. Up to you to sort out what's what.'

They roar down the road for a while in silence. Maria tries to think up something to say. Catriona is someone else this morning, no longer the lady of the manor but the general of an invading army, making a dangerous reconnaissance of the enemy's ground. Her khaki army surplus trousers, tight against sturdy thighs, reinforce the image, and her eyes, behind dark glasses, search for snipers. Maria feels a frisson of attraction, slaps it down, and studies the scenery.

A few crouching cottages huddle together on a stony promontory, looking as if they're grown out of the ground.

'Blackhouses,' says Catriona, following Maria's curious gaze. 'Built without windows, to keep things cosy. A few of the older people still live in them. Everybody on the island did, once upon a time.'

'Except for those of you who lived in castles?'

'A medieval aberration. Newfangled nonsense. And pretty useless in a Hebridean winter, as you'll find out in good time.' She juts her chin towards the tower. 'There's the old heap now.'

'I don't think I'll be staying that long. I'm only here for a week or two.'

'We'll see.' Catriona puts her foot down hard, and they roar past the castle, sitting on its island, linked by a causeway to the shore. The sky clears suddenly, and the old stone glows warm and golden in the sun. 'Weather changes fast here.'

Catriona toots her horn and waves at a weatherbeaten woman helping a small boy stacking up blocks of peat against a cottage wall. 'That's Morag. I suppose she and young Ruari have been out since sunrise cutting peat for the winter. She'd never get her man to do it. If he did he'd probably drown himself in the bog. Which might be a good thing for Morag, in the long run.'

'Do you know everyone on the island?'

'Silly question. Down to their underwear and their intimate secrets, I'm afraid. I've done most of their horoscopes too, but that's our little secret. Here's the village.'

They speed past firmly shuttered shops, all three of them, and see no one but a yellow dog lifting his leg outside the post office and grocery.

'Where's the population?'

'Where do you think, lass, on the Lord's Day? They're in their beds. Or in kirk, if they're among the Elect. Even a damned and hopeless sinner like yourself should remember the Sabbath. And if I were a decent woman instead of Satan's own consul on Cailleach (at least according to our dear minister), I'd have you in there right this minute, listening to a good improving sermon for an hour or three. Instead of careering about the countryside leading you down the paths of corruption.'

They are beyond the village now, passing a small, steeple-less, stone-faced church. It sits on a little rise of ground, flanked by tombstones, scowling out to sea.

'Not very welcoming,' shudders Maria. 'Bring on the corruption.'

'All in good time,' says Catriona, tapping her lightly on the knee.

For several wordless miles Maria feels the ghost of Catriona's finger-tips, reverberating gently under the faded denim.

They have turned off on to a narrow track that climbs sharply through a glen, hills on both sides raked deeply with ancient ploughmarks. Maria wishes she could think of something intelligent to say, wonders if Catriona will find her boring after a whole day together.

'What are those ridges?' she asks, made edgy by her own self-consciousness.

'Do you really want to know?' says Catriona with a sharp sideways glance. And launches into a lengthy disquisition on ancient island agriculture, run-rigs, worship of the earth goddess and the Hebridean eco-system past and present, with divagations into the radical changes caused by the introduction of new sheep breeds by nineteenth-century improvers and the devastating

45

alterations in the climate since neolithic times. Maria, lulled, stops listening as the road climbs higher, looking down the steep sides of the glen, changing colour as the cloud-shadows pass over them.

At the highest point, Catriona slams on the brakes. 'Look!' A golden eagle soars above them. 'Out!' She leans over Maria, opens her door for her. 'And look behind you.'

Maria obeys, wondering for a brief irrational instant if she is going to be abandoned here in retribution for a moment's inattention to the lecture. But when she turns around she sees the bay, and its flotilla of islands, with the honey-coloured castle turning suddenly black as a thundercloud looms over it. The water is green and glassy, then glitters as the wind pushes the cloud away. A gust of icy rain, coming up from behind, surprises her, and she stands on the top of the island in a downpour, watching the sunshine down below.

'Get in,' calls Catriona. 'I don't want you soaked before we start walking.'

Through the glen, under high steep hills, then the track rises only to reveal even higher tops before Catriona turns suddenly on to a better road and heads northwards.

'Look – a double rainbow. Over there.'

'You'll find we have lots of rainbows. Probably because we have lots of rain.' She points to a high, rounded hump. 'That's Nestaval over there. Highest point on the island.'

'What's up there?'

'Iron-age broch. Probably built on the site of a prehistoric look-out point. And under the hill lies the crystal castle of the Shining Ones.'

'Who?'

'Damn!' Catriona bangs on the brakes to avoid a suicidal sheep. 'Not a good place for a breakdown.'

'Which always happens in the dark of a winter night, when you're five sheets to the wind or bone-weary from sitting in at a death or a birth, and it's a mere five miles rough walking to Graeme Isbister's excuse for a garage on the far west side. Who, if he isn't too drunk to hear the banging on his door, will obligingly bring his truck up here at any hour. Ask any of us. We've all been through it.'

'Who are the Shining Ones?' Maria isn't interested in engine troubles.

'A local legend. The Old Gods, not dead yet, biding their time.

They stay out of the way, mostly, but keep an eye on things.'

'Very picturesque. Do you really believe that Celtic-twilight stuff?'

'Only when my moon's in Venus. How about you?'

'Religión's not my strong suit.'

'Judging from your exhibition of paintings, I'd say you were rather obsessed by it.'

'Only for purposes of demolition.'

'Wheesht, or they'll hear you.'

'I didn't think you were so fey.' Maria, seeing Catriona's lips tighten, thinks she's overstepped the mark. Clams up.

'Fey has nothing to do with it.' And for the next ten miles Catriona curdles Maria's blood with tales of supernatural vengeance, thefts of corpses, changeling babies grinning up ferally at crofter parents from their cradles, shape-shiftings and curses whose grisly effects long outlasted the memory of the quarrels that inspired them. Massacres, witch-hunts, blood feuds and other traditional pleasures.

'This is not always an amiable island,' grins Catriona, as they pass the burnt-out hulk of a blackhouse that was the scene of a famous turn-of-the-century murder. With professional accuracy, Catriona spares none of the details.

They are down from the hills, on the road that rings the island again, close to the sea.

'We'll walk now. I'll carry the hamper. That's our lunch. Hungry?'

'I was before you told me what she did with those sheep-shears.'

They walk along a path on the edge of the cliff, wordlessly because of the wind and the screaming gulls. A barbed-wire fence, tagged with little tufts of wool, bars the way, but Catriona pulls off her jacket, tosses it over the wire, climbs up and over herself and helps Maria do the same.

'Aren't we trespassing?'

'Nonsense. This isn't England, you know. Our laws are different. As long as you close the gates and don't trouble the sheep you're welcome. Anyway, the land belongs to me, more or less. The tenant has it on a thousand-year lease, for the current equivalent of two baskets of peat and a newborn lamb. And I suppose if I want to fight a war against another island, or pull a raid on the missile base at Benbecula, I can ask him to bear arms on my behalf. Don't look down, by the way, if you're nervous of heights.'

Thus tempted, Maria does, to find gulls wheeling gracefully two hundred feet below them, and the sea crashing into a fissure in the striated rocks.

'The Cliffs of Crunig. Lovers' leap.'

Maria's head spins. She freezes on the narrow path, brushed by a sudden panic. Catriona reaches out a hand, and Maria flinches, as if it's to push and not to steady her.

'Come away from the edge if you're frightened. And just relax. Take a deep breath. That's better. Now there's nothing to worry about, the path's nice and wide here. And we haven't bothered with human sacrifices from these cliffs for simply ages.' She puts a protective arm around Maria's waist. 'Besides, this is good Christian ground. Look over there.'

Across the field lies a large, rambling ruin.

'What's that?'

'A rare example of Hebridean-Romanesque. *Circa* tenth century. The Convent of Saint Bride.'

'Isn't that where the archaeologists have been digging?'

'Ah, yes. You'll have met the good lady at Ina Isbister's. I forgot she was leaving this weekend. Well, thank goodness they're all gone for the season now. Infestation of intellectual fleas upon the body of our Cailleach.'

'You're not very impressed by them, are you?'

'Hardly. Bunch of bloodhounds with blocked sinuses, if you ask me. Barking up the wrong tree entirely. But at least they haven't made too much of a mess on the site. That's it all nicely battened down for the winter.'

She points to a neatly fenced-in rectangle of ground, covered with heavy tarpaulins and thick plastic sheeting. 'The old convent garden. Let's hope they've left the nunnery itself alone.'

At this distance, the pile of stones seems to be covered in patches of yellow hair, but as they come closer Maria sees that the crumbling walls are overgrown with grass, and smeared with mosses and lichen.

'You can see why I was so keen to buy your Saint Bridget, as you call her. Bride belongs to Cailleach. And Cailleach to her.'

'It's an old-feeling place.'

'Even older than you'd imagine. Before they put the convent up, there was a temple here.'

'Were they here for a long time?'

'Who?'

48

'The sisters.'

'I suppose that to the islanders it seemed like for ever. They were as solid as the stones. Kept the place alive in evil times.'

'What happened to them?'

'Something sudden. There were a lot of hasty burials. The archaeologists found them a while back. Done inexpertly, they said, by clumsy hands.'

'It's peaceful here, but there's something else, isn't there? Something bad.'

Catriona studies her intently. 'And how do you know that?'

Maria is reticent, doesn't want to explain about the humming in her head, the little snail of terror cold at the pit of her stomach.

'Just a feeling. I don't know.'

'No, I don't suppose you do. Does it upset you? Would you like to go now?'

'No. I'm just being silly. Too fey for my own good, mother always said. I like it here. I'd like to look around.'

'I'll leave you to it. I won't be very far away.' Catriona disappears.

The first visitor of the New Year knocks on the gate, and the extern sister opens up, with a blessing on her lips, in time to see the glint of red-gold beards before a club thumps down and cleaves her skull in two.

Some are killed and then violated, some violated and then killed, some – the oldest ones – simply slaughtered. One or two were blessed with the small compensation, first, of seeing scratched-out eyes streaming blood underneath the bronze helmets. A souvenir to remember us by. But the Fire itself finally goes out, when a crouching bundle of rags rises up from a dark corner, and pushes the last invader into it.

Maria finds Catriona staring fixedly down at the earth in the centre of the cloister, as if she can see through it.

They skirt a wall that stands by itself, supporting nothing, a little apart from the rest of the ruins. It is a broad wedge of piled-up stones, twice as high as Maria. Near the top, the curving capitals of two Ionic columns are set into the rough-hewn surface, as if an ancient Greek doorway had suddenly materialised in the wrong century, only to be sealed up, slapdash and quickly, in an effort to keep time from leaking through.

Picking their way through heaps of tumbled stones, they wander

49

in and out of the roofless rooms, around the oblong cloister with its broken arches.

'Damn!' Maria, distracted by a far away blue hill, framed by a gap in the chapel wall, trips over a bush growing out of the broken stone floor, and falls headlong.

'Are you all right?' Catriona appears at the top of a steep staircase set close to the wall, and leading to nowhere.

'I don't know.'

'Is it your ankle?'

Maria rises, steps gingerly. 'No, it's fine.'

'Shall I have a look at it?'

'Really, it's perfectly all right.' But you'd love it, wouldn't you, she thinks, to roll up the leg of my jeans, ever so carefully, and stroke and press with an ostensibly professional detachment, then pick me up and carry me home, and place me ever so gently in your wide, warm bed, and feel all over for broken bones or bruises that you could tenderly rub away and . . .

'Maria!' Catriona is standing looking fixedly at her, peering into her eyes over the lowered spectacles.

'I'm fine. Fine. Fine.' She backs away, caught out in her daydream. Beware your blasted redhead's blush, Milleny, she tells herself, then sprints away down the length of the cloister at speed. 'Look, that proves it. Nothing broken. I'm perfectly fit!'

'Just as well. I supposed I'd have had to carry you home, or do first aid or some damned dreary thing. Too much like work on my day off. Thanks to the goddess Bride!'

'I thought she was a saint.'

'That, my dear, was much later. And merely an aberration.'

They wander through the skeletons of cells and halls and cloisters a little longer. Sometimes, out of the corner of her eye, Maria thinks she sees something moving . . . the flutter of a long dark skirt, the white flash of a wimple, the glitter of a silver crucifix. She hears, just faintly, alto voices soft and far away, rising in a *Kyrie eleison*. Entranced, she walks towards the source of the chant and finds, on an overturned slab that might be altar or gravestone, a feast spread out for her: wine in goblets, cheeses, fruits, crusty rolls in a cloth-lined basket. The music dies away.

Catriona presides over the picnic, beaming up at Maria from her seat upon a block of stone. 'Didn't know I could whistle, did you? Come and have lunch.'

The light at the convent is soft and pearly grey. On the far north of the island, near the lighthouse, it is a hard, hot blue. The weather has changed again. They stare out to sea, lulled by the sounds of waves and the birds.

'Perfect peace,' says Maria.

'Not quite,' says Catriona. 'Not always. This is where the Norsemen landed. And around that point there it's all rocks and reefs. Shipwreck country. Perhaps you've heard the unpleasant bit of Hebridean gossip about us. They say the Cailleach people used to hide among the rocks when a ship was in distress. Any survivors that struggled to shore were clubbed to death and salted down for winter meat.'

'Is it true?'

'Nonsense. A vile canard, put about by our jealous neighbours of Lewis and Harris, because we stood up to the Norsemen better than they did.'

'I've heard of such things happening.'

'Who knows? We island folk have a taste for strange delicacies . . .'

They drive down the coast road again, turning inland, and walk along the shore of a long, narrow loch. At its far end stands a tower, cracked like a broken chesspiece.

'What's that place?' Catriona doesn't hear her. Quickens her pace. Maria asks again.

'No one ever talks about it,' snaps Catriona. 'A very nasty history. Stay well away.'

And, however hard Maria tries, Catriona will not be drawn.

'Look up there – did you ever see so many geese in a single formation?'

Maria isn't sure she's ever seen any wild geese, anywhere at all.

'They're deserting us early. Prepare for a hard winter.'

'It couldn't be harder than the last one.'

'I didn't think the weather was so bad, down south.'

'It's not the weather I was thinking of.'

'Why not stay here for a while then?'

'It's tempting. At this minute, I'd be happy if I never saw London again.'

'Watch what you say. If you make a wish when the winds change, it may come true.'

Right on cue, a breeze blows over the loch and drenches them with spray.

'But I'd like it very much if you came and stayed for a while.'

'I don't know . . .'

'Keep thinking. In the meantime, let's finish up with one more local landmark.'

Rain pours down on them on the path to the Cailleach Stones.

'I've been here before,' says Maria.

'Yes, I know,' responds Catriona. 'But when? In which of your many lives?'

'I meant yesterday morning, actually.' You are one weird lady, Catriona, says Maria to herself.

'Of course. How silly of me. Well, then you'll realise that you're nearly home again.'

Suddenly, as if alerted by their voices, the twenty-seven stones of Cailleach spring out of the ground on the far side of the field. The tallest stones slope inwards, towards the centre of the ring, as if in whispered consultation, or contemplation of something helpless that lies at their centre.

As they approach, Maria begins to ask what she thinks might be an intelligent archaeological question, but Catriona sharply silences her. 'Don't say anything. Just go and see for yourself. Listen to them. Forget about me.'

Some government department has built a small protective fence around it, with a creaking gate. Maria thinks the barrier is incongruous, like gingham curtains on a cathedral's stained-glass windows.

'Not very effective,' she says to Catriona, stepping over the band of barbed wire. 'Who are they trying to keep out?'

'Or keep in.' Catriona is behind her; she doesn't look back, wondering if the good doctor will have metamorphosised into a painted stone-age priestess, brandishing a ritual knife. Maria feels the gaze piercing her shoulder-blades, a sharp, clean needle-thrust, in and out again, not quite painless.

'Just walk the ring, Maria. Widdershins would be best.'

The stones are not uniform, the ring is more an ellipse than a circle. Some are tall jagged spikes, piercing the air like angry jabbing fingers, proving a point. Others are short and stumpy, broken teeth, wider than their own height, with their edges rubbed and scalloped by four thousand years of harsh winds. Disappointed that no mystical relevations are exploding before her eyes, that the place feels so ordinary, she picks up speed and orbits the ring more rapidly, feeling tired, chilly, and all too aware of a blister rising on her ankle. Catriona is nowhere to be seen, so Maria feels free to hurry past three and four and five of the stones at a time, without according them the lengthy contemplation that Catriona clearly expects as their due. She is suddenly overcome by a flood of homesickness; what on earth is she doing here? Why did she come? She relives the last humiliating quarrel with her lover, craves the stinging heat of the vindaloo from the curry-house at the end of her London street, hears the rippling clarinet solo from a gifted busker in the underground. She smells the paints and oily rags from her studio at the art college, and hears the faint praise, the judicious compliments, the jovial demolition job from her various lecturers. The reds of her first serious painting, the one she felt truly proud of, remind her of the unexpected menstrual blood welling on to the white summer-holiday shorts: Mother would have told her, but it happened far too soon. She wonders whatever became of her closest friend at primary school, whose tongue flicked in and out of her mouth like a small, nervous lizard's, and she flinches at the stinging slap when some alien adult catches them together, up to no good, in the airing cupboard. Then redness again, and a roaring, and a movement from light, too much light, into darkness, and she is deep inside a mountain, wandering down a track to an underground city, her way barred by heavy, intricately carved metal doors; she thinks, even in the faint light of flickering torches, that she can recognise several sculpted madonnas, a flayed and tortured saint whose name she can't quite remember, and an Indian goddess, a whirl of many arms, and hot little ruby eyes on the sixty skulls that make her necklace. The goddess laughs at her, cruel and cackling, and she bridles at the incoherent injustice of it all, until she realises that the cackling is the cry of gulls, and the great bronze door is a squat stone in the Cailleach Ring, pockmarked with circular depressions, cups in the stone, and a trailing spiral that might have been scratched by a whirling finger-nail, idly tracing the line for a thousand years or so, a little absent-minded vandalism to while away the long Hebridean nights.

'Eighteen times round the ring is really quite enough for the first go, my dear,' observes Catriona, leaning against the broken-off stump of a stone that must once have been three times her height; its tumbled pinnacles lie on the ground behind it.

'Well, I . . .'

'Don't say anything. Whatever you want to say about them has

53

probably been said already. I'll take you back to Ina's now. I hope she's baked some of her celebrated madeira cake. I would kill for a cup of tea.'

There is, Maria notices, nothing feudal about Ina. When the lady of the manor comes to call she must, if there are no clean teacups, wash them herself. Ina meanwhile produces the hoped-for madeira cake and piles three different sorts of scone on platters. They sit at the kitchen table, waiting for the tea to stew to Ina's desired state of blackness.

'If it doesn't set your teeth on edge, it isn't ready,' she explains, lifting the lid of the pot and nodding approvingly at the murky brew within.

Catriona, thickly spreading Ina's cloudberry jam on a snowy scone studded with currants, clears her throat. 'Maria is quite taken with Cailleach.'

'I thought she would be,' smiles Ina. 'I can always tell with my visitors if they're deserving of us or not. You wouldn't believe this, my dear,' she says confidingly to Maria, 'but there are some folk as come up here and hate the rain and the black stretches of peat bog and complain that the hills are awfully bare. They usually only stay for a day or two, then scuttle back to Skye or some such soft place on the conventional Highland Tour. And good riddance to them.'

'She'll be staying for a while.'

Maria, her third slab of cake suspended in mid-air, is mildly miffed to find the decision made for her.

'I'll sort out her bill myself if you care to make it up – no rush, Ina, after you've had your second cup.'

Maria puts the cake down. 'Now really, Catriona, I . . .'

'You are my guest. Have you forgotten? That was the arrangement we made two years ago, and I'm not aware anything has changed.'

'I'm not sure I like having my bills paid for me . . .'

'You needn't worry, I'll make sure you sing for your supper.'

'But I've booked in with Ina until Wednesday, I can't just . . .'

'Oh dear,' sighs Ina, 'did I not tell you before you went out this morning? I really must be slipping in my old age. I have to go away to Stornoway on the *St Rollox* tomorrow. A hospital appointment – no nothing serious, just a check-up for an old complaint. I wasn't meant to go 'til November, but my GP here,' she winks at Catriona, 'tells me they've had a cancellation, and I'd best go now and get it over with before the weather closes in. I'm an awful one for seasickness, believe it or not. Hardly what you'd expect for someone living on an island. But maybe that's why I hate to leave it. I'm really quite a homebody, you know, and what with the B and B and the croft to run – the weans are a help, but my man can't do it all any more – and I wouldn't want that tight-hearted old besom McKay down at the harbour to capture all the passing trade, such as there is of it . . .'

'So you see, my dear,' says Catriona, peering over her spectacles, 'you are really doing Ina a favour by coming to stay with me.'

'I suppose I'd better pack up my rucksack,' says Maria, rising and wondering where she put the leaflet with the ferry schedules. 'But I don't think I'll be troubling you for very long, Catriona . . .'

'Oh, it's no trouble . . .'

'Because I haven't really brought enough clothes and things for a longer stay.'

'Oh, I wouldn't worry about that,' laughs Ina, 'I'm sure Cailleach can supply whatever you need.'

'Besides,' adds Catriona, 'you're forgetting your Greek mythology. Don't you know that once Proserpine ate the food of the underworld, she had to stay for ever.'

'I don't know much about Greeks,' says Ina, 'although I do believe there's one has opened a dry-cleaning shop over in Stornoway. But you know they say the same thing about the Good People . . .' here she spits, tidily, into her teacup . . . 'once you eat their fairy food you're locked inside the hill for ever?'

'So I guess you're for it, Maria.'

'I guess I am.' She feels pleasantly smothered.

The land-rover shoots up the castle causeway. Maria thinks she hears the sound of a portcullis banging down behind her.

'I suppose you'd better have a tour of the castle. I don't want you breaking your neck looking for the bathroom in the dark.'

At the top of the tower, Catriona shares her bedroom with all the birds of the north. Skuas glare contemptuously at solan geese, whose fish-stinking flesh is much prized as a delicacy by the older islanders. Terns, herring gulls, gannets line the bookshelves, and an owl under glass on the shelf over the bed looks thoughtfully upon the black-and-white patterns of the island tweed that covers the counterpane. Little Arctic butterflies, pinned down in pretty patterns by a sadistically artistic great-grandmother, stand framed in rows in between the tall windows, where gulls – flapping too close to the panes – catch sight of the feathery necropolis and wheel away again in horror.

Where there are no birds or butterflies, there are dried flowers and dusty catkins jammed into milk bottles and priceless Chinese vases and old medicine jars. A shawl, knitted fine enough to pass through the eye of a needle, hangs neglected over the arm of an Orkney chair, with its high basketwoven back good for keeping Arctic draughts and Viking axes off the thick necks of its occupants. The gigantic cat asleep on the bed is not stuffed, despite its upholstered appearance and perfect immobility. A rocking chair by the window nods gently back and forth, although there is nothing in it. The shifting foundation of the castle, explains Catriona.

Maria flushes rose-red to see her own painting, 'Saint Bridget', mounted on the wall four-square above the double bed, behind the baleful owl.

'I hope you approve of the position. I've put her opposite the windows. If you come up here tomorrow, when it's light, you'll see that the scene you painted is the mirror-image of the view from this tower. Quite eerie that, don't you think?'

'Perhaps I saw a photograph, or a postcard once, and forgot about it.'

'There isn't one. But never mind. Come over here, there's something I think you'll like.'

Beyond a high black oak press, in the farthest corner of the octagonal room, stands a low door. Its threshold is guarded by another cat, smaller, wide awake and fierce-faced, sitting sphinx-like on a velvet cushion black as itself. She is most displeased when Catriona steps over her.

'Come in,' beckons Catriona, 'but mind your head.'

Maria finds herself in a narrow cell.

'This is my little cabinet of curiosities. It's set into the tower wall. Just odds and ends that have come down in the family, and a few personal favourites of my own. All stolen goods, of course, one way or another.'

Maria is surprised by the sparseness of the treasure-trove. An oaken chest, crudely carved with suns and smiling faces. Some glassed-in bookshelves, blanketed in dust. A tray of shells and small fossils, an ancient fly embedded in a lump of amber. On a spindly-legged Chinese table, clay vases containing a bundle of peacock feathers stand next to a small velvet frame enclosing a brooch of intricately-twisted metalwork. On a low chest, tossed there almost carelessly, lies a Viking helmet on its side, with the Viking's skull still in it.

'What's in the chest?'

'Maps and deeds and family papers. Manuscripts that crumble when you touch them. Some rainy day, I tell myself, I'll sort them all out. But there's a lot of rain falls here, and I've never done it yet.'

Maria sneezes, and Catriona hustles her back into the bedroom. 'Sorry about the dust. I keep a clean kitchen, but I never catch up with the rest of the housework. But you can see that I've made myself nice and comfortable up here, although the rest of the house is rather bleak.'

Some comfort, Maria thinks, avoiding the gaze of the stuffed skua. Like dossing down for the night in the Natural History Museum.

'I'm afraid your room, down below, is rather spartan. But whenever the cold gets to you, just come up and make yourself comfortable. The fire's rarely out.'

That first night, they sit on the rug in front of the peat fire, with a map of the island spread out before them. Catriona shows Maria the best footpaths, beaches, caves and sea views, plotting out the walks that Maria ought to take, ornithological, archaeological, topographical and historic.

'I might just take some time to lie around and do nothing.'

'Oh, we can't allow that on Cailleach. This is a Protestant island now, you know. Here, fornication is a mere peccadillo, compared to idleness, on the league table of Deadly Sins. Did you bring your painting things? I didn't see anything that looked like them when we brought your bits and pieces in.'

'Well, actually, the last few months I haven't done much . . .'

'And you thought that if you escaped up here without a brush or a canvas you'd have the perfect excuse to do even less . . .'

Maria stares gloomily into the fire.

'Crisis of confidence? If it's any help, I thought your work was very exciting. I know I'm not an art expert, but . . .'

'Thanks, but it's not much help, really. I've dried up.'

'Cailleach may get your juices flowing again.'

'Don't get your hopes up.'

'Wait and see.'

'No, I won't wait and see. It's like looking for Nirvana. Or trying for an orgasm. If you think about it, it never comes.'

'Well all right then, suppose you never painted a stroke again. What about it? Wouldn't the world be the poorer for it?'

'The world wouldn't even notice. And it wouldn't make a bit of difference. What's the point?'

'Your trouble, young woman, is that you aren't arrogant enough. Now go to bed. I trust you can find your way to your room in this old rabbit warren. If not, I suppose we'll find your bones in some dark passageway, fifty years from now. Good night.'

'A few rules of the house,' announces Catriona at breakfast, expertly pouring hot milk and freshly brewed coffee simultaneously into a shallow bowl. 'One, I go off to my surgery at about nine every morning, and I am in no mood to face anyone before that. So keep out of my way, if you don't mind. You can have your breakfast later. Two, you may, if you choose, do a bit of cooking or washing up or whatever, but it isn't compulsory while you are my guest. Should your stay extend to the point when you are a lodger instead of a visitor, we'll think again – but that won't be for a long time. Three, you are welcome, as I said last night, to spend time during the day in my room, but please respect my privacy as regards cupboards, drawers and boxes. I'm sorry if that offends you, but I have to say this after one or two unfortunately unhappy experiences with house guests past.'

'What happened to them?'

'Just don't look in the cupboards, drawers and boxes.'

'But I don't mind helping around the place . . . I don't want to be a parasite . . .'

'Well then, I'll leave you a list every morning – polish the brasses, scrub the stone staircases, black-lead the old kitchen range, buff up the not-so-old Aga, sweep the chimneys, dust the books in the library – although not those in the cupboard behind the mummy-case which are under no conditions to be touched at all. Walk down to the village to do the shopping, clear the dust of centuries out of the cellars and mind out for the skeletons, re-organise the wine-cellar with its bins going back to my great-grandfather's time, clean the stone sink, re-point the windows, repair the roof, boil up a fresh cauldron of lead to keep intruders away, cook us a five-course meal of Edwardian proportions to be ready on the dot of eight-thirty, and wash up after it, taking special care with the antique china and the crystal. Breakages will be charged in full.

Also, I'd like you to catalogue my rare collection of seventeenth-century French pornography, serve as governess to my twelve imaginary children and do a spot of psychotherapy for the madwoman – my last Duchess – locked up in the attic. Now as for the afternoons . . .'

'All right, I give in.'

On the Monday Catriona disappears for twenty-four hours, and returns to report that she has delivered twin daughters to the postmistress's wayward niece. They are not identical and the postmistress whispers darkly about the possibility of different fathers. 'It was the night of yon Hector MacEochan's twenty-first, no doubt,' she mutters to Catriona as she sees her to the door. 'They were up to no good, the lot of them, drinking and dancing to the devil's own tunes. But that one will say nothing about the fathers . . . I swear she doesn't know herself. My sister Bella will be turning in her grave . . .' Catriona's scientific doubts are dismissed with a grim laugh.

Maria has spent the time staring out of the tower window, watching the steady fall of rain on the wind-whirled waters of Cailleach Bay, and feeling almost as sorry for herself as she does for the disconsolate-looking sheep she can just make out on the tiny island opposite.

On Wednesday night Catriona, much refreshed after a long sleep and an uneventful afternoon at the surgery, beckons Maria to a little velvet-draped table she has placed in front of the fire. She pours out two generous drams of the island malt and produces a long, flat rosewood box. It opens out into a board printed with the letters of the alphabet.

'You seem a bit troubled. I thought we'd get some advice for you.'

'From a ouija board?'

'I suppose you think it's just a quaint Victorian parlour game.'

'Well, yes. I suppose I do.'

'Those who come to sneer often stay to honour. Give me your hand.'

Maria dares to dabble her fingers in the cool, dry hollow of Catriona's palm, and finds them placed firmly on to the triangular planchette. 'Don't be frivolous!' But Catriona is gazing, searchingly, into her eyes. 'Now what's the trouble?'

'This is silly.'

'There is nothing silly about it. You feel silly. That is quite a different thing. Be precise.' She addresses the board. 'Is anybody there?'

Maria stifles a giggle. The planchette begins to move.

'There, I told you.'

'Come on, you're moving it somehow.'

'Look carefully at my fingers. You'd notice something, wouldn't you? If I were cheating? Now then – what's your name?'

The planchette moves to the letter G. Then to R. Then to A. Then along to N. Then stops.

'It's somebody's grandmother. Grandmother MacEochan, is it you?'

No response.

'Granny MacNeil . . . my mother's mother,' she whispers to Maria, who is still suspicious. 'A very wise old woman. Island stock going far back before my father's lot.'

Nothing.

'You ask, then. Perhaps it's one of yours.'

'Not bloody likely. My grandmother on one side's still alive and well in Australia, drinking her pint of Guinness a day and taking snuff for her catarrh.'

'What about the other one?'

'I never knew her.'

'That's immaterial.'

The planchette begins to move. H.U.R.R.Y.

'Greetings, honoured spirit,' intones Catriona solemnly. 'We beg your guidance.'

The triangle travels. R.U.B.B.I.S.H.

'Perhaps you'd better have a go,' whispers Catriona. 'I think whoever it is, is probably annoyed by your cynicism. Try to mollify them. Ask a sensible question.'

'Oh. Um . . .' She grimaces at Catriona. 'No, you. I can't think of anything.'

'This child is troubled,' confides Catriona to the tortoiseshell triangle of the planchette. 'She fears that she has lost her inspiration. Can you encourage her? Will she recover it?'

No movement.

'You try. She must want you to ask the question yourself. After all, she's your grandmother.'

'That's ridiculous. How do you know? Maybe it's just a spirit named Gran. Short for Grantchester. Or Granite-face. Or Grant from the Arts Council, No Chance of.' She nudges Catriona's foot with her own. Catriona glowers. 'Or you cheating.'

The planchette stirs. G.O.O.D.B.Y.E.

'No, wait, please don't go. All right, you win,' she sighs at Catriona. 'What's my future as an artist? Should I give up trying?' R.U.B.B.I.S.H.

'Wait a minute. My future is rubbish . . . or do you mean that it's silly to give up trying? Explain yourself. You spirits are so . . . so . . . nebulous.'

D.O. N.O.T. G.E.T. C.H.E.E.K.Y. W.I.T.H. M.E. L.A.S.S. O.R. I.L.L. S.K.E.L.P. Y.O.U.

'I'm sorry. I didn't mean to offend your sensibilities.' She appeals to Catriona. 'I've insulted it. What do I do now?'

'I'll try.' She strokes the planchette gently, stroking Maria's fingers as well. 'What subject should Maria address herself to next?'

The planchette does not respond.

'See, Granny's as devoid of inspiration as I am. Runs in the family, doesn't it, Gran?'

R.U.B.B.I.S.H. L.E.A.V.E. A.N. O.L.D. W.O.M.A.N. I.N. P.E.A.C.E.

'One more thing, oh kindly spirit . . .' breathes Catriona.

S.T.O.P. M.E.D.D.L.I.N.G. The planchette jerks violently, slides off the table, and flies straight into the glowing peat-fire.

'Oh my goodness! I don't think she liked being patronised.'

'Nothing like that has ever happened before. It must be your cynical attitude. You're emanating the most sceptical vibrations, even now. And I'll have to send all the way to London for a new planchette. That last one was an antique. Belonged to my great-great-uncle. A student of spiritualism. Studied for years with the Siberian shamans. What a pity.'

'I am sorry, Catriona, really. I never thought . . .'

'Don't be. It's my fault as much as yours. And it just confirms what I should have known already. Secrets should not be shared with cynics and unbelievers. However, that is your loss, more than mine.'

'Admit it, you're cross because she, or it, or whatever, wanted to speak to me, and not to you.'

'Perhaps. Even the seventh daughter of a seventh daughter is not completely devoid of human feeling.'

'Is that what you are?'

'Sometimes. A little more malt?'

On Friday night, Maria asks Catriona to tell her more about her ancestors. She would like Catriona to tell her more about herself as well, feeling that all the confidences and information have flowed in the one direction. But she doesn't know how to ask. Instead, as Catriona rattles off a catalogue of family skeletons, made safe by the distance of centuries, Maria tries to find out what she can, by studying the lines around her eyes, the play of expressions, the way she licks her lips, and thrusts out her chin. Finally, Maria slips off and finds some paper, then sketches Catriona as she sits like a pirate queen in her high-backed chair. But when Catriona asks to see the drawing, Maria crumples it up and tosses it into the fire.

On Saturday morning, the rain that has battered the island all week has given way to renewed summery sunlight, and Maria finds Catriona more cheerful than anyone has a right to be who has consumed so much whisky the night before.

'If you know what to drink, and how to drink, you never suffer,' explains Catriona, pouring pitch-black coffee into a mug as deep as a well. 'But I wouldn't advise you to try and match me. Our constitutions are very different.'

'I see that,' says Maria, wincing at the explosive crash of a teaspoon being placed on a saucer.

'If you're up for it, I'd like to take you on a little outing this morning. That is, if you don't have other plans.'

Maria, preoccupied with surviving her orange juice, does not rise to the bait.

They drive down to the southernmost point of Cailleach. On the low hills, the gorse, still wet from the storms of the week, glitters as they pass, and a sudden eruption of wings and rainbow colours forces Catriona to bang on the land-rover's brakes. 'Pheasant.'

'Beautiful. I've never seen one.'

'Delicious. Have you ever eaten one?'

'Seems a pity, really.'

'You city-folk with your misplaced sentiments. The hawk will get it if I don't.'

'Is there a difference?'

'Does alcohol bring out the moralist in you? I'd better limit you to tea tonight, then. We've the whole weekend to get through.'

She stops at a whitewashed, slate-roofed cottage. Maria hears a whirring, clacking sound, and someone singing in an unknown language that must be Gaelic.

Inside, a woman is sitting at a large loom, weaving a length of tweed in the greys, greens and browns of the hill outside her window.

'Is that herself, then? You're a long time coming, Catriona.'

'The less you see of me the better.'

'Not when you're here in your private capacity. Which I trust you are today. I haven't called you.'

'This is a friend of mine, Isa, who's come to stay at the castle for a bit. Her name's Maria, and her hair is the colour that yours used to be, or so you tell me.'

Isa nods and smiles at Maria, who sees that the old woman's eyes are sightless, but glow like topazes. 'I suppose you'll be thinking that weaving is no work for a blind woman, and too polite to say so. Well, let us get things straight from the beginning of our acquaintance, and start as we'll mean to go on. I can feel the colours in my finger-tips, and when the tweed is woven I hold it up to my ear, and listen to know if it is good. And, suffering very little modesty, I can tell you that it usually is well near perfect. Every time. Sit down, the pair of you, and tell me what exciting present you've brought me this morning.'

Catriona produces a bottle, and rummages in a drawer until she finds a corkscrew. She goes to a shelf, takes a single glass, and pours a few drops, barely a spoonful, into it.

'Mind the tweed, lass, mind the tweed! That's my rates and electricity paid for, but not if you muck it up with purple splashes.'

'Sorry, Isa. Well, what do you think?'

'A year of many angry noises, but no war within two thousand miles or so. The sun, as you'll know yourself, was dreadfully hot, you can feel it bouncing back up into your face. Nevertheless, the hands that grew and picked them were those of a cold customer, if there ever was one, who had probably strangled his wife that morning of the harvest, if not the night before, and hidden her body behind the vats before they filled them. In the place where the grapes grew there had been a period of drought, but perhaps fifty years before this vintage, and some metal coins, Roman gold I'd guess, were beginning to float upwards in the shifting, sandy soil. There were quite a lot of them, not very far away from these self-same vines, a large hoard, with somebody's face on them. One of those fat pagan emperors. Nasty man. The winds were warm and coming from the east on the day of the picking, though by the time they reached this particular valley they'd been softened down to the whisper of a breeze. I can tell you, my old bones would be pleased to have some of that hot sun right now, but they say it's a terrible thing for our northern complexions, so I'll just bide where I am.

'But, where was I? Oh yes, the cellaring was good and careful, although the family quarrels between the sons who were due to split the property on the old man's death were obviously something awful . . . there's just the faintest hint of their vitriol in one of these droplets. And the journey over was uneventful, although it is apparent that he who purchased it first had no knowledge of what he was buying, or intention of drinking it. It was purely to impress his rich in-laws with his fine tastes, but they disinherited their daughter anyway, and she was as happy with cheap German hock as anything, so this was all stored down below stairs and forgotten. Did you bid for it at auction? Yes, I thought so. But all by telephone, of course, with an angry gentleman from somewhere in the American West – Texas I think – trying to force you out.'

'Surely you can't tell that, Isa! Not from the wine itself . . . that really is stretching credibility too far.'

'Well as it happens, that about the auction I know from Dugald who drives the lorry and collects the tweed. He said you told him all about it when he came to get his bad shoulder seen to. Bursitis he says you told him. But I say different.'

'What do you say?'

'I say it's sex with his wife in unnatural positions. Now I think I'm ready for another glass of that wine. I'd offer you some as well, but I'm sure you've plenty more bottles at home. Don't bother to stick the cork back in, I'd like it to breathe a wee bit. Particularly since Ina Isbister's due any time now. She's bringing me some of that good Dunlop cheese for my lunch. And you'd better leave me in peace to think up something interesting to say about the cow that gave the milk for it.'

'I wonder if I might come down and watch you work some day?' ventures Maria.

'Oh, I don't know if I could allow that, dear. Mustn't profane the mysteries of the craft, you know. But I'll tell you what – you let me pluck out two or three strands of your silky hair, and I'll weave it into this tweed of mine. Then you and the wearer of it will always have good luck on the same day.'

'That's an interesting idea, Isa,' remarks Catriona. 'I've never heard that one before. Must be a purely south-of-the-island superstition.'

'Indeed it is. Very local. And freshly minted by me, right here in this house this morning.'

That night, after some peaceful but wordless hours watching an allegory of Hell played out among the glowing peats, Catriona rises from her armchair.

'Well, I'm for an early night tonight. I'll leave you to it.'

Maria wonders if Catriona is bored. She wishes she were a more amusing house-guest. Perhaps she should think about packing her rucksack. Catriona, half-way up the stairs, comes down again, stands behind Maria's chair.

'Maria . . .'

'Mmm?' She is absorbed in poking at the peats, wondering if they need art teachers in Papua New Guinea, or waitresses in Wolverhampton. She hunches morosely over the hearth.

'It's been a good week. Thanks for being here.'

Maria drops the poker, straightens up, braces herself for the dismissal.

'I hope I haven't been in the way. And I'm sorry about your great-great-uncle's planchette. And that glass I broke, and . . .'

'Shall I submit a list of breakages with the final bill?' She puts a hand on Maria's shoulder.

'Does that mean this is check-out time?'

'Do you want it to be?' The hand tenses slightly.

'Not really.'

'I'm sorry my life's so dull. I've tried to think of things to amuse you.'

'You shouldn't. And it isn't. What I mean is . . . I don't know. You're so . . .'

Catriona's hand moves from Maria's shoulder to the nape of her neck, massaging gently.

'Don't get flustered. It's all right.'

'No it's not. I feel like a parasite. I'm just so useless. I . . .' The grip on her neck tightens.

'I will drive those demons out of you whether you like it or not.' The finger-tips send little tingling bolts of gentle lightning down her spine. 'For your own good.'

Maria feels her colour rising, everywhere. Makes a stab at flippancy, to keep from falling over a cliff. 'You sound like my mother.'

'That was the wrong thing to say.' The hand is withdrawn. 'Good night.'

The next morning, Sunday, Maria waits for a long time at the breakfast table she has set so thoughtfully, while rejecting all the possible lines she wrote for herself during a restless night. Catriona doesn't appear. Maria goes for a long walk on the rocky beach, looking over her shoulder at the castle tower; its windows, blocked by thick curtains, give nothing away. When the rain comes on heavily, she turns back to the castle, which is still cool and quiet, as if it's still early morning instead of late afternoon. She starts leafing through the pile of books Catriona has set out for her – natural histories of the islands, old travellers' tales, Victorian sketchbooks, learned tomes on Hebridean folklore. Nothing distracts her. Finally, with the care of an acolyte performing a solemn rite, she brews a pot of China tea, selects a pair of small, fine porcelain cups, arranges everything on a lacquered tray, and climbs carefully with her offering to the tower.

'Catriona, are you awake?' she whispers through the keyhole.

'I should hope so, at five o'clock. Come in.'

She finds Catriona, sitting cross-legged on her bed, wrapped in a satin kimono the colour of a peacock's tail, bent over an enormous volume bound in brass and dull crimson leather, its pages crumbling with age. The text is bold and gothic and unreadable. Next to Catriona, the large black cat, coiled like a cobra, rears up his head and peers at the intruder, a sacred snake guarding the goddess.

'I hope I'm not interrupting,' says Maria.

'On the contrary. You're what it's all about.'

The tea tray is placed, carefully, on the bedside table. The cat, disgruntled, is dropped with a resounding thump to the floor.

When, finally, she leaves Catriona's bed late on Monday morning ('Christ! Surgery opened an hour ago' cries the doctor, racing for her land-rover with her shoes in her hand), Maria goes for a long walk. She heads inland, following the rising ground, climbing an old sheeptrack, but never leaving the sight or sound of the sea. She carries a battered map, folded in all the wrong places, and wears an ancient, indestructible jersey borrowed from Catriona. It smells of her, faintly spiced, a trace of sandalwood or patchouli.

Maria has slept very little, but she is bursting with energy, throbbing and humming quietly, pleasurably tormenting herself by replaying the events of the night as she climbs. The track passes windowless blackhouses and the rusting hulks of abandoned cars and tractors. She looks behind her, sees the narrow road that skirts the coast and watches a cloud of soft mist enfold the castle in the bay. She turns, jumps at the sight of a tall, thin monk in a cowl and pointed hood glaring down at her from higher up the hill, then looks again to discover he is nothing but a tapered standing-stone, a cold, grey finger pointing up out of the summit. When she reaches the stone, and assures herself that it will not shift back to a menacing monk, she turns and gazes down at the castle again. The mists have parted, a rainbow curves over the crow-stepped gable, and the passing flotilla of fishing boats cuts through water that is green and gold.

She sees, when she finally comes to the top, and the sheeptrack divides into five narrow paths, that she is not on the summit of an isolated peak, but on the highest hump of a long tall ridge. A little distance away, though distances here are deceptive, she can see another hump, nearly as high, but with a flattened, sliced-off crown. She checks her map, sees from the gothic type in which the Gaelic name is set that it is an 'ancient monument'. The Broch of the White Sow, Catriona has promised, is worth a visit.

Sitting on a flat stone, she eats the oatcakes, the apple and the soft white island cheese that she has brought with her and looks down at the bay, and the hills of the other Hebrides blue on the eastern horizon. Then she sets off for the broch. The walking is difficult, for the sheeptracks have vanished. What has seemed, from not so far away, to be smooth, hard, dun-coloured ground proves instead to consist of a sea of tangled grasses, hiding piled-up stones and worn-down furrows. She dips and rises and dips and rises, skirting one patch of bog only to find herself trapped by another.

Tracing her progress on the map she finds herself crossing names without places attached to them, impossible to pronounce, but hinting of stories. Catriona will know them all, if she remembers to ask.

Reaching the broch, Maria finds herself facing a lopped-off tower of rough stones, piled one upon the other. Instead of the imagined flat surface, the centre is a deep hollow, filled with tumbled rocks and rubble. She climbs carefully, finding footholds. Capping the pile is the vestige of a rampart, the gap between two squared-off boulders. The vantage must have been a good one, commanding all the points of the compass, anticipating incursions. If this is a good place, someone will be sure to come and take it away; be watchful. She imagines herself posted, straining her sight and hoping to see nothing: quiet coracles with priests ready to tear the world apart, Viking ships gliding in smooth and sinister, a sea-monster, a dying whale.

She climbs down again, back the way she has come, just a little distance, to see the form of the old broch more clearly against the sky. A tremor, very slight, ripples the dull grey air. She stares fixedly as the stones almost, but not quite, slide out of focus, and realises that a silence has wrapped itself around her. No wind, no gulls, no wave-sounds. It has been there for a while.

This is what it feels like, she reflects, in the moment before something comes up out of the crest of the hill and pulls you down into it. This is what Tam Lin felt, and Binnorie, and all the others unremembered, before the thin silvery pipes wheedled them away.

Don't be daft, Milleny. Don't be conned by the Celtic twilight. You're an urban anarchist, a smasher of sacred cows, a city-kid, streetwise. Out of your depth? Stand your ground.

As if she could do otherwise. She freezes, watches the silvery shimmer of what might be heat-waves if the air were not so cold. Fighting hard against the impulse to bolt, she is struck by a thought. The gentle, benevolent queen of the fairies is a soft, silly Victorian invention. Up here, she leads a fierce, unsentimental army; her face is angry and her eyes glint ice. It is death to meet her. She wears snakes in her hair. And she's coming closer. 'Now!'

Maria turns on her heel and runs faster than she knows she can, tripping over tussocks, pounding headlong down the hill, almost somersaulting, doesn't look behind her. She finds herself safe on the road again. In no time. But she thinks that in her flight she's lost something. Searches about herself, can't think what. Her small pack, with the old map, is still on her back, the Swiss army knife's safe in her pocket. Nothing's missing in the inventory. Maybe it will come to her. She goes back to the castle, walking quickly as if in the midst of a rush-hour crowd, and wishes there were a drawbridge she could pull shut behind her as she comes over the causeway. Barely stopping to wipe the mud from her boots, she climbs to the tower room, still warm, although the fire was carefully banked. Then she slides into Catriona's bed, shuts her eyes against the glowering gazes of the bird-collection, and sleeps for a long, long time. Maybe for ever.

'Feeling good?'

'Mmmm.' Maria, languid after a mostly sleepless but thoroughly satisfying night in Catriona's tower room, opens her eyes to meet the stony stare of the stuffed skua. Behind him, out the window, the sky is grey-green and the air is heavy. Catriona, presenting a mug of coffee, appears to be fully dressed under her embroidered kimono.

'What's the point in getting up on a day like this? Why don't you just come back and join me in bed for an hour or six?'

'Can't.'

'No work today. It's Saturday.'

'Yes, but . . .'

'Getting bored of me? It's five weeks today.'

'On the contrary. If I had my way in the world I'd lock us in here 'til Christmas, and arrange for the Air-Sea Rescue helicopter to drop in regular deliveries of champagne and caviare. Best Beluga, of course. But the real world is calling.'

'Not me it isn't.'

'Yes, but you're just a counter-cultural little scruff aren't you? No responsibilities, no ties . . .'

'That's a sore point . . . Come back to bed and make it up to me. Please?'

'Impossible. I'm afraid I have some rather horrific news for you, my dear.'

Maria sits upright, pulls the covers to her chin, reluctant to receive her congé or hear the announcement of some rival lover, when her shoulders are exposed to the chilly autumn air. Her stomach clenches into a fist. 'Well . . .?'

'It's that today is the Anniversary.'

'The what?'

'The three hundred and seventy-somethingth anniversary of the granting of the charter for Isle Cailleach, Castle Cailleach, Cailleach Bheag and the Chapel Isle; the fishing rights for the Straits of Stourie and the Dragon Loch, plus other assorted privileges within the gift of his Glorious Majesty King James the Sixth of Scotland. Conferred by the royal gracious favour on to the previously humble but politically astute head of my remote but direct ancestor Sir Alasdair MacEochan, member of the Privy

Council, Keeper of the Wine-cellar Keys at Holyrood House, and honorary Gentleman of the Bedchamber in more ways than one.'

'Congratulations on the anniversary. I'm impressed. But so what? What's the horrific part?'

'Wheesht, my love. Listen . . .'

Underneath the gusts of wind and spatterings of rain against the windows, Maria hears another sound, the rumbling hum of marine engines.

'Is that the ferry? It's awfully early for it . . .'

'No. Special charter, I'm afraid. Go and look out the bathroom window, on the landward side.'

'Must I? I'd rather stay in bed.'

'I'm afraid you'd better.'

Maria wraps Catriona's thick tartan dressing-gown around herself (never the brilliantly hued kimono, which is not for borrowing even by the best-beloved), and does as she's bidden.

'God in heaven! Who are all those people on the beach? There must be hundreds of them!'

'Those are the members of the Clan MacEochan. Come from such distant compass points as Vancouver, Alabama and the Falkland Islands. It's the gathering of the Clan, my dear, and, alas, they're all heading this way for a welcoming breakfast in their ancestral hall. I should go down to greet them in person. By some interpretations of the law of primogeniture, I have a fair claim to be the current Clan Chief. However, since it seems to me like the most tedious honour imaginable, I have gracefully yielded the position to my stuffy Cousin Roddy, the Edinburgh advocate. As a matter of fact, I think that's the gentle tread of his hand-made shoes on the stair just now.'

Maria slams the bathroom door and locks herself in.

'Don't panic, my little dove. I'll hand you in some clothes and pour you some coffee with a slug of whisky in it. Then you'll be fit to face the festivities.'

In the great hall, rugs and furniture have been cleared away, and replaced by long trestle tables, where Ina Isbister, the postmistress, and several other women Maria doesn't know are doling out porridge and mugs of tea. As Maria edges down the staircase, past a group of chattering transatlantics admiring the family portraits, the crowd in the hall bursts into cheers, whistles and an isolated rebel yell. The MacEochan of MacEochan, Cousin Roddy of the Edinburgh law courts, has just finished his welcoming speech. He is resplendent in a kilt of blue-green tartan, and a sealskin sporran. Next to him, a robust, ruddy-faced *grande dame*, in a long skirt of the same plaid, a black velvet waistcoat and antique lace jabot proves, on closer inspection, to be Catriona herself, who has nipped down the back stair while Maria was gathering her courage.

Maria slithers into the queue of visitors inching along the receiving line, and waits patiently to shake her lover's hand. Who mutters through her social smile, 'One snide remark and I'll throttle you, Milleny.' She nods graciously, turns to her cousin, takes Maria by the hand and says, 'Roddy, this is Maria Milleny. My house-guest.'

The sharp-featured chief of the Clan MacEochan shakes Maria's hand with a bland lack of cordiality, and eyes her fishily. 'Charmed, I'm sure.' Then, to his cousin, 'A bit young for you, this one, isn't she, Cat?'

'Excuse me, Miss,' drawls a voice behind Maria, 'But do you happen to know the skedjool for the day's events?'

Maria turns, adjusts her gaze upwards along a broad, six-foot-plus expanse of tartan crimplene to the jaunty peak of a scarlet baseball cap.

'Tulsa Oilers,' he explains. 'Never miss a home-game when I'm in the good ole US of A. How-de-do. Scotty McCrumb's the name, from Indian Graves, Oklahoma. My maw's a MacEochan. She's from Glasgow. Except now she's from Palm Beach, Florida, since I set her up in a nice little condo. I suppose I'm from Glasgow too, but that's a long, long time ago. Come on over here and meet the wife.'

A smiling Flora MacDonald, her gown and bodice protected under a transparent plastic rain-cape, extends a white-gloved hand.

'Hi there. I'm Jerry-Sue, but my friends all call me Pinky. Nothing to do with politics, you understand. I'm a Pinkerton by birth. Of the famous detective Pinkertons. Scotch of course. You a MacEochan, too?'

'No, just an interloper.'

Scotty encloses Maria's hand in his beefy fist. 'I don't think I know that clan, honey, but welcome just the same. Now what did you say your name was?'

'Maria. And I'm afraid I can't help you. I don't have a clue about the programme.'

'Now wait a minute, Scotty-hon, I might just have that old brochure scrunched up in my purse. Hang on.' Pinky rummages in

71

a purple shoulder-bag capacious enough to hide a Christmas goose. 'Can you hold this stuff for me, sugar? It's here somewhere.' She hands Maria a camera, a Thermos flask, a copy of *Time* magazine, a road map, a packet of chocolate biscuits, a roll of toilet paper, and a plastic pouch full of medicine bottles, tubes of cream and gaily wrapped sticks of sugar-free chewing-gum.

'Always be prepared, I say,' she says, passing her husband an electric torch, a plastic rain-hat, and a fistful of foil-wrapped butter pats marked with the imprints of several international hotel chains. 'What did I tell you? Here it is, tucked right down there behind the water-purification kit.'

'Well, let's have a gander.' Scotty unfolds the paper, holds it at arm's length, squints and scowls. 'Oh my gosh, we'd better hustle our butts Pink, or we'll miss the parade.'

Sallying forth from the castle go the Dallas, Texas, Pipettes, flicking tiny tartan skirts as they punctuate their march with high can-can kicks, to the accompaniment of massed bagpipes, flutes and sousaphones. Behind them, nipping doucely at their heels, the Auckland, New Zealand, Combined Churches Choral Society strolls across the causeway, humming gently, as six sopranos sing 'My Heart's in the Highlands'. As their song wafts them towards Cailleach Village Hall, they are succeeded, at a distance carefully calculated to express tactful disapproval, by the Kearney, New Jersey, Pipe Band. The pipers, kilted in authentic MacEochan Dress Tartan, wail out a series of previously unrecorded pibrochs, the subject of a prize-winning dissertation in ethnomusicology at Yale, awarded to Ms Kiki MacEochan, formerly of Kearney High School.

Maria, gazing down on the scene from a vantage point originally designed for pouring boiling oil, cranes her neck to read the banners as the massed clan members take a sharp left turn off the causeway and step smartly on to the narrow road. Some of the place names tell of homesick exiles – Jock's Misery, Montana; New Caledonian Falls; Glasgow Prairie; Argyll Acres; Invernessville; Cromarty Park. Some recall other tribes, as scattered as any in Gaeldom: Sioux City, Chippewa Falls, Winnipeg, Coonawara.

'Aye, it's a grand sight,' says a voice at Maria's shoulder. Ina Isbister, wiping her hands on a tea-towel apron, joins Maria at the narrow window. 'But it makes you wonder why they're all so keen on coming back to honour the old place. Half their people mooched off on the first boat as would take them, the other half

72

were flung forcibly into the sea by the clan chief of the day. Old Hector Blood-and-Thunder. Spitting image of our Catriona, round about the cheeks and chin, so they say. Still, it looks as if they've all done not so badly for themselves out there in the great world. They wouldn't have those fine drip-dry, no-iron clothes and fancy hairdos if they'd all stayed in Cailleach. And, we'd probably be fighting each other for turnip tops and rotten fish-heads, like they did in the old days. Still, it's harmless fun today, in spite of what the Reverend MacNeish said about it in kirk last week, about the inn extending its hours, and crates of whisky in amounts you've never dreamed of coming off the *St Rollox*. And dear knows what strange ideas our young people will pick up from those distant cousins and clansmen they meet at the dancing tonight. Well, look, that's the last of them. Do you mind those thumping great Australian laddies in tartan bunnets, you'd think they'd blush to see themselves. Anyway, I'm away to get a hurl from my old man up to the Games. Are you not coming yourself, dear? It's lashings of local colour. Sword dances and the tossing of the caber and all. Except there's not one contender lives within three thousand miles of here.'

The Reverend Murdo MacNeish, of the Second Schismatic Independent Kirk of the Outer Isles starts his preparations for the Lord's Day on Saturday evening, with a long soak in a steaming hot bath. Morag feeds the boiler to keep the water hot for him, and bathes the children in the kitchen sink with the tepid leavings; Murdo believes that goose-pimples, like regular beatings, build their characters. Floating in warmth, he goes over the main points of tomorrow's morning and evening sermons, for he speaks without notes and prides himself on a long and vengeful memory.

Murdo is a man of scrupulous cleanliness. He scrubs vigorously at his private parts until he is satisfied, admiring the Lord's good workmanship. As he rubs himself dry he reflects on the unseasonable mildness of the evening, and decides on a moonlight walk along the beach, to flush out adolescent sinners. All names will be mentioned at kirk in the morning.

With a swift zip that rasps across Maria's brain, Catriona – smart and chirpy – closes up her black bag and says she must be off now. Babies are no respecters of Sundays.

Maria, fogged in by a heavy hangover like none she has ever known, squints at her, too queasy to speak.

'Now you'll have to learn to take your drink better than that, my girl, if you want to qualify as an honorary islander.'

'Don't remember a bloody thing. Went out for some fresh air after dinner, didn't we? Nice night. Warm. What next?'

'You sang me some old art college songs, about sex and drugs and rock and roll and revolutions. Then we started dancing. You took your shirt off.'

'Wasn't I freezing?'

'It was warm for the time of year. Almost balmy. Just as well. You took mine off, too.'

'We were on the beach.'

'No, the castle causeway. The beach came later. You were looking for sea-monsters.'

'Did we find any?'

'Yes, but when we did you were afraid to look. So I sent it away again.'

'Liar.'

'What a pity it's rained this morning. Otherwise you could have seen the spoor.'

Maria only moans, folds her arms on the scrubbed kitchen table, puts her head down.

'Don't do that. You won't be able to lift it up again for ages.'

'Don't care.'

'Now, there's a pot of good strong tea – not ordinary tea, a very special blend – and I want you to drink every drop of it. And in three or four hours, whether you are hungry or not, you will find some soup simmering on the Aga. Not sooner – it's only started cooking. You must have at least three large bowls of it. Not only is it extremely delicious, but it is the most effective hangover remedy I know. It's an old Turkish recipe. You start with . . .'

'No. Please. Don't tell me.'

'Never mind, then. Just be sure you finish it. And no cheating. Otherwise you've only yourself to blame if you feel like death all day.'

Maria goes back to bed, and dreams of being buried alive.

The kirk elders meet.

'With all due respect, if she wasn't who she is, I'd have that woman up before the Kirk Session.'

'No use. She'd never come.'

'It was always a gey queer family.'

'Hamish says that the castle rubbish is three-quarters wine bottles. Even when there aren't visitors.'

'She'd not be the first among us cursed by the drink.'

'It's her duty to set a moral example, Donald. Not to cause scandals.'

'Perhaps she needs reminding.'

'As I said in my Sunday sermon . . .'

'There's the rub, Minister. She never comes to kirk. Never has, nor her father before her.'

'My grandfather always said there was a smell of incense about the place . . .'

'She could be a secret RC.'

'She'd have a long way to go to find a mass to hear in these parts.'

'Who knows? Has our Hamish seen any empty biscuit-packets when he goes round with the dust-cart? Add that to yon wine bottles and you could have the evidence to accuse her of DIY Holy Communion. And we could not be doing with that on Cailleach.'

'That's enough of your sarcasm, Donald.'

'Please, gentlemen, we are straying from our agenda. And the issue remains undecided. She has been observed behaving with extreme indiscretion on the castle causeway. With a companion. A foreigner, unknown to us, thank the Lord. Not one of our own. Now the causeway is her own property, her front garden as it were, and technically we have no right to interfere. But she might have been seen by one of our young people. Fortunately it was well after midnight when the Minister caught sight of her. But nevertheless . . . Now are we agreed that she must be spoken to? And, if so, who will take responsibility?'

'I saw her myself,' declares Murdo, 'so I will have it out with her myself.'

The spiritual leaders of Cailleach have not always gone hand-in-glove with the keepers of the castle. Catriona is treated with a certain, mild deference – more because she is a doctor of medicine than because she is a MacEochan of the Castle Cailleach Mac-Eochans. She is also looked upon with some suspicion. She went away, which was bad enough, in her youth, then, what was worse, came back again. Her father was a nonentity, who confined his indiscretions to the fleshpots of the south, and was treated with courteous contempt by his tenants. But her grandfather has never been forgiven, by those who remember him, for inviting Keir Hardie to stay at the castle, and walking about with him on the beach.

A MacEochan of Queen Victoria's time passionately collected insects, which would have been nothing in itself had he not practised his habits conspicuously on Sundays.

An earlier MacEochan was an enthusiastic improver of his estates. When he decided to evict three hundred tenants from his lands and replace them with more profitable sheep, it was the island minister himself who broke the laird's jaw with an angry blow, and was jailed for ten years at Inverness.

And so it went, back through the generations. There was the laird who invited a new minister to supper, and served him up rats and toads baked in a pie. Before him, the previous ecclesiastical incumbent developed a certainty that he could fly, and, encouraged by his lordship, experimented by stepping out of the tower's top window, calling curses on the MacEochan name all the way down.

Earlier still, in Papist times, before Jamie Stuart gave the island to his fancy boy, who had ancestored Catriona, things were even worse. One savage earl liked to exercise his *droit de seigneur* upon all the island maidens. When the priest came to admonish him, he locked up the good father in a wine cellar under the castle, and forgot all about him until the following summer.

Another lord, more pious, set off on the Great Crusade to free Jerusalem, leaving his new bride in the care of the castle chaplain. Five years later he came home safely, full of vows to build a church as round as the Holy Sepulchre itself. And what should he find but his lady's belly, temporarily swollen to the same rotundity.

'Oh, I was guilty of spiritual pride,' she explained, 'and boasted far too much of your holy mission. Father Confessor imposed some most peculiar penances.' Clearly, she'd been a most recalcitrant sinner, for the crusader discovered two curly-headed brats, with the priest's own face, hiding behind her billowing skirts. That very day, bastards and wife and belly and Father Confessor were all put to sea in a leaky boat. But the projected Round Church of Cailleach was never built.

Reverend MacNeish has no control over the incomers, so he pretends they don't exist, or that they inhabit some separate, secondary island attached to Cailleach only by the fragile pontoon of the post office and the Co-op. He has, alas, no control over Dr MacEochan, either, but she is much more difficult to ignore. Especially when she chooses to make a public show of her own depravity.

Murdo is sorry he ever mentioned the matter to the elders (but how to keep such delicious scandal to oneself?). Now he can hardly go back on his promise to confront Catriona; the eyes of the kirk are upon him. Mulling over the problem, he decides that Monday morning will be an auspicious time to call at the castle. An early hour, when the mists still lie on the waters of the bay like a guilty conscience. Invigorated by the spiritual scourings of the Sabbath, he will be at his best; he can feel the fires of righteousness glowing in his belly. But she, the whited sepulchre, the scarlet lady of Rome and Babylon, will be at her most vulnerable, wan and weary after the unspeakable revels of the weekend.

He finds her, not as he'd hoped, paying out the wages of sin with aspirin and an ice-pack in a darkened room, but starting up the engine of a little motorboat at the jetty near the castle causeway, and roaring across the water, with her unspeakable house-guest on board. Catriona waves cheerfully and shouts something at the Minister but the wind lifts her words away.

In the underground chamber, Catriona suddenly switches off the torch. Her eyes glint yellow in the darkness.

'Where do you think you are?'

'The mummy's tomb?' Maria wonders if this is the moment when Catriona will reveal her true colours, and delicately puncture her victim's neck with two neatly-filed fangs.

'The source of it all.' She floods the cavern with light again, and plays the beam of the torch on the rough shelves that line the walls. Jars, jugs, kegs and carboys stand in neat rows, some of them full of an amber juice.

'This is the kennel of the dog that bit you. The source and fountain of the local poteen. I thought you might like to see where it comes from.'

'I never want to see the stuff again, or taste it, or hear of it, thank you very much. It nearly killed me.'

'Nonsense.'

'Isn't this all a bit . . . illegal?'

'What do you think? Would I bring you out, by a circuitous route, to a small island hidden behind two other small islands (this one, by the way, is called Pabbay – the Priest's Isle; the others have Gaelic names that translate, roughly, as the Earl's Arse and the Hog's Snout), scrabble in the bracken for a hidden trapdoor, lead you down a steep and rickety ladder and make you crawl through a passage slightly wider than the average birth canal if you could pick up a litre of this stuff at the Cailleach Co-op?'

'I'm shocked.'

'Why ever so? You smoke your marijuana or whatever, don't you? Why such a double standard?'

'It doesn't fit – the cases of amazing claret and Burgundy from your pukka wine merchants, the fifteen-year-old single malts after dinner . . . and this.'

'The *grand crus* and malts reflect my father's side of the family. The taste for this comes straight from my mother. She was from an old island family . . . or have I told you that already? Never mind.'

'How long has it been here?'

'The place itself is, officially, an unexcavated ancient monument, too dangerous to be open to the public, and, in any case, inaccessible. It is, in fact, an earth-house, probably Pictish, but the Papish priests used it too, as a hidey-hole when Cailleach first turned Protestant. Since that time, it has also been the centre of our small local poteen manufactory – if one can put so mundane a name to the midnight alchemy that goes on here. The pipes for the still itself are down that passage. Ina Isbister's husband is in charge of the place, and they say that young Jamie's shaping up in a promising way to follow after him.'

'If it's illegal, aren't they afraid of getting caught?'

'Oh everyone knows about it. So there's no one to tell.'

'What about the island policeman?'

'He is usually off the island when there's a batch ready.'

Catriona turns her torch on a stoneware jar with a spigot set into it. 'That's just ready for sampling. Fancy a bit?'

'I'd rather drink horse-piss.'

'Don't be so silly. Try it again. The first time is always the worst.' She produces two murky-looking tumblers, spits into them and polishes them on the sleeve of her jersey, and hands Maria a brimming glass.

'That's enough to kill an army.'

'Nonsense; it's still at a very weak stage. Try it.'

This time it tastes like molten honey to Maria, but honey all the same.

'Just as long as it doesn't have the effect it did last night.'

'It won't. I promise. This is another batch altogether.'

The cellar is suffused by a rich, golden light, and Maria is dazzled.

78

'Catriona, could you move your torch a bit; it's shining in my eyes.'

'Nonsense, my dear. It isn't even on.' She grins wickedly. 'Anyway, it seems you're beginning to appreciate it. Which is just as well. It's an essential part of your introduction to Cailleach. And there's an old island saying that those who have drunk of the Old Woman's fiery milk will never stray far from the teat it flows from.'

'Meaning?'

'Whatever you like.'

They climb the ladder again, and emerge, blinking, into the grey but glaring light outside. The weather has turned, and a cold, wet wind is coming in from the east.

'Smells of winter,' says Catriona.

'You might find this amusing,' says Catriona at breakfast, handing Maria a thick book bound in elaborately tooled leather. 'Island lore. Edited and privately printed by my great-great-grandfather. He was an antiquarian, whose profound interest in the history and folkways of Cailleach was matched only by his profound interest in the castle kitchenmaids. The girls were always sent packing, alas. Anyway, it will keep you entertained for a day or two. I'm off to Stornoway this morning. Won't be back until the weekend.'

'Oh.'

'Don't look so stricken. It happens sometimes. Regional Health Authority meetings. Very dreary. Execrable food and a hotel full of garish tartan carpets. Endless agendas of stupefying inconsequentiality, and all the important issues lightly brushed aside and buried. Lots of power-games and politicking.'

'Sounds terrible.'

'This time there's a bright side. My planets are in an excellent alignment for sticking my knife into certain people's backs. Machiavelli rising. Could I bring you anything? A sketchpad, some pens?'

'No thanks.'

'You'll have to get down to work some time, you know.'

Maria becomes obsessively interested in the faded floral pattern on the butter-dish.

'A no-go area? We'll leave it. For the moment. Enjoy the book. And,' she traces a pattern lightly on Maria's back with her finger-tips, 'I'll miss you, of course. In spite of the considerable charisma of the Chief Nursing Officer.'

'Who's that?'

'An old flame. But quite extinguished. See you Saturday.'

Supervised by Catriona's cats and the stuffed seabirds, Maria spends the rest of the day in the tower, reading. The antiquarian ancestor has been tireless in his pursuit of island lore.

Isle Cailleach. Nature notes, continued: Serpents.

Mull, as Hebridean naturalists will know, crawls with vipers, as does Arran. (Surely there are still readers old enough to remember the Brodick Schoolyard Horror?) The furthest isles of the Outer Hebrides are not supposed to have any that will be venomous or troublesome. Cailleach may, if folklore has a grain of truth, be an exception. Or it may not. Cottagers are wont to speak of 'the long scaly beastie as lives in a hole up at Nestaval'. References are never made to a colony of the creatures, only to The Snake. Always singular. The informant himself admits he (or, in rare cases, she) has never seen the beast, but relates some encounter of years past, described by a relative, now dead, or some more recent meeting with the creature attributed to the friend of a friend, now away with the fishing boats. No other physical features are known, save its length and its bright scaliness, but much is made of its significance by the superstitious islanders. They argue among themselves whether it be an omen of death, a token of great good fortune for he who meets it, or the malevolent guardian of some antique and probably accursed hidden treasure. The Snake is always referred to as 'She'; informants invariably preface their remarks by glancing swiftly over their left shoulders, and conclude them by spitting, discreetly, into the wind.

'The Comeuppance of Harald Bloodaxe in the Isle of Stones.' An Extract from The Second Saga of Snorri, as Translated by the Author.

The last of Snorri's near-fatal acts of rashness, as foretold by the Witches of Grey River, was his theft of Freya Stigsdottir, promised bride to Harald Bloodaxe. A few days before the appointed wedding date, five longboats, with red dragon prows, slid silently into Stig's bay between midnight and dawn. Rudely awakened by roars, howls, the sound of stamping feet and the smell of pitch from flaming torches, Stig's wife and slaves barricaded the door with an oaken chest. They thought they were under attack by demons, and – with Stig and his men off collecting tribute round the southern islands – knew they would have to face them alone. Commanded by Stig's wife, a strong-minded woman, they gathered up knives and cudgels and the mallets they used in the kitchen to soften the meat, preparing for battle. But, as suddenly as it erupted, the cacophony of menacing hell-howls died away, and the flares of the demons' firebrands diminished into pinpoints of light along the shore, vanishing altogether as the invaders put to sea.

The women of Stig's house thanked their gods that the danger was over, yet none could sleep again that night. So they sat in a huddle by the fire and drank hot ale to comfort themselves, and passed the dark hours recounting old stories. Only when the morning came, and the dawn turned the black heavens into a pale, cold blue, did they realise that one of their number had vanished. Where, they asked each other, had Freya gone? She of the golden braids like sun on the fields of rye, she who spun threads finer than cobwebs, she who wove cloth soft as swansdown, had disappeared. Missing was fair Freya, pride of Stig's house, betrothed of her father's best-beloved old battle-mate, the mighty Harald Bloodaxe. A great murmuring arose, of fear and wonder. Each woman swore, upon the lives of her own children, that no raider had crossed the threshold, and no one in the house had left it during the night. And they concluded that it must have been sorcery. How else could a maiden be snatched away from their company, by unseen hands, and carried out through solid walls as if they were no stronger than melting snow?

Then they remembered that young Freya had not been among them since suppertime the night before. Fretful, in the manner of young maidens about to be married, she had complained that she could find no rest with all her sisters and slave-women snoring round about, and begged her mother to let her sleep alone, up in the apple-loft. Stig's wife, a kind and indulgent mother, had granted the child's request, for she knew full well that her Freya would enjoy little enough repose once she found herself in the bed of lusty Harald Bloodaxe.

Sure enough, when Stig's wife climbed to the apple-loft she saw that the girl had vanished, nor had her pallet been slept on. But there were no signs of struggle. She resolved that no one

81

must ever know that the girl had been an accomplice in her own abduction, which would have been an unbearable disgrace for all Stig's people. She climbed down the ladder again, and spoke of signs of sorcery – a smell of sulphur, a trace of blood in no human colour (signs of a struggle?) and the marks of claws scraped upon the rafters. Freya had been taken, by witch-work, and everyone in the north-lands knew that Snorri was a friend of the witches. Stig's wife tore her hair and lamented.

The next day, when her husband, Stig, returned, bearing barrels of salted fish, coffers of gold, sacks of spices and hogsheads of mead for the wedding feast, she broke the terrible news. Prudently, she then removed herself and her women from the house while Stig raged, smashing stools and jugs and platters and benches in his fury. Yet the anger of the bride's father was as nothing to the anger of the disappointed bridegroom. How dreadful, to arrive with his followers as an expectant bridegroom, and to bide in the house of his prospective father-in-law as the outraged victim of a cunning theft. For three days and three nights he raged and cursed and plotted, assuaging his own grief, and the grief of his men, by consuming all the provisions intended for the wedding-feast. He abandoned any thought of recovering his stolen bride, for she would be damaged goods by now, and an unfit wife. Instead, he meditated on vengeance. Snorri had to be punished, Snorri his old enemy, who had bested him many times before.

But to punish Snorri, Harald had first to find him. He would have to lure him out of his hiding-place, for in some northern inlet or some unknown island harbour, the Dragon-Boats would be moored, and Snorri would be drinking with his henchmen, jeering at Harald. Now it was well known that Snorri claimed the jarldom of all the outermost isles, even those he had never yet set foot upon to extract tribute. And if he ever heard of any other chieftain sailing towards them, Snorri swooped like a bird of prey, and challenged the interloper to a duel. Armed with his magic sword (a gift, like so much else, from the Witches of Grey River), Snorri was invincible, so everyone stayed away from those places, which became known for a time as Snorri's Islands. Sorely vexed were the sea-lords, for in these isles their own fathers and grandfathers had long preyed happily.

Harald's ships, accordingly, made for those distant islands. 'Let him come after me,' vowed Bloodaxe, 'and I will show him that the thirst for vengeance is a more powerful charm than a sword blessed by old women's magic.'

At every landing-place, slave-interpreters put the terrified natives to the question: Have you seen the Dragon-Boats of Snorri? Which way did they go? And at every landing place, came contradictory answers, for the people would say anything that came into their heads to the angry, red-bearded invaders, in hopes that they would leave them in peace.

But the search was fruitless. Snorri, his stolen bride, and his fleet had vanished into the mists, as surely as if they had sailed into the underworld. As Harald travelled from place to place, his anger grew hotter, for he could not bear another humiliation inflicted by Snorri. Finally, his ships reached the outermost isle of all, that which is called by some old people the Island of Stones, for it has great grey slabs upon it that were planted there in time outside memory by some mighty wizard.

When Harald's fleet sailed into the bay at the Isle of Stones it was midnight. As they came ashore, a strange thing happened. On the hills round about them several bonfires blazed up, as one; they could see the lights, and smell the smoke, but heard no sounds. And, as the fires flared, so did the wrath of Harald Bloodaxe. What could these beacons be but signals, to warn wicked Snorri of his enemy's approach? So he gave the order that every living creature on the island must be put to the sword – man, woman, child, beast, killed without quarter. In vain did the slave-interpreters explain that these were ritual fires, marking the moment when the old year died; in vain did they protest that the fires had nothing at all to do with Snorri. These were merely the signs of a holy feast.

But Harald cared nothing for holidays, nor even knew what season of the year it was, so blinded was he by rage at Snorri, Bride-Stealer. So he led his men up and down the island with swords and axes, intending to feast on blood. Yet suddenly, when the slaughter had barely begun, it ended. The raiders turned on their heels as one, and ran for their ships, then rowed as fast as their oarsmen could carry them out of the bay. For, in the middle of the massacre, their leader, Harald Bloodaxe, had been murdered. Not by Snorri rising up out of some secret hiding-place. Not by some unknown rival warrior, nor by some angry native fighting to defend his home. No, it was sorcery that slew Harald. He died in an house full of unarmed crones.

83

Only later was the tale of his end pieced together by the terrified survivors. It seemed that he, and his closest companions, had cut his way through a houseful of dark-robed virgins, those that the natives call Holy Sisters. After dispatching the women, in the usual fashion, he looked about him to see what treasure could be carried away, for sometimes these places have golden candlesticks and jewelled caskets concealed within their bleak stone walls. Suddenly, out of a heap of corpses on the floor, a ghost rose up like smoke, and seized him by the leg. With a strength beyond anything human, the spectre spun him round like a child's spinning-top, and flung him headlong into a pit of fire. He burned to bones and ashes before his fear-frozen companions could stir themselves from a spell that had been laid on them. Those who could shake themselves free ran for safety, those who could not were turned to stone on the spot. Blasting on their horns, to warn their fellows, Harald's men hastened to their crafts and steered homewards, by a circuitous route that carried them as far as possible from this cursed isle. For it was now clear to all men that this Snorri was no ordinary chieftain. Not only could he snatch brides through thick walls and disappear into thin air with all his dragon-ships, but he could command ghosts and evil spirits to do his bidding. By his murder, through magic, of Harald Bloodaxe, he became known for all time as Snorri Ghost-Master, and nevermore did any other sea-lord question his sovereignty over the wild isles of the west.

When Snorri heard this tale, he laughed and laughed. For during the time that Harald Bloodaxe was scouring the western seas in hot pursuit, Snorri was enjoying a honeymoon with his new bride in the court of the King of Norway (many long days' sail away, in the opposite direction). He had never yet set foot upon the Isle of Stones.

Catriona, on her rounds, stops the land-rover on the road that bisects the island, and leaps out for a closer look at a golden eagle, swooping and soaring over the glen. When it disappears, she stares for a long while at the blue-grey sky, hoping the bird will come back again, and sniffing the wind. In this lonely place, a tap on the shoulder makes her jump. The Minister has come upon her unsuspected. On one of his long tramps across the island, she surmises. Stalking sin.

'Perhaps you can spare me a minute, Dr MacEochan? I've been wanting a word with you.'

As if Murdo has brought it with him, the rain blows in and falls straight down on them.

'Are you on foot, Minister? If so, I suggest we have our little chat in the car, while I drive you home, or wherever it is you're heading. This isn't a good week to contract pneumonia. My stock of antibiotics is running low, and until the new consignment comes, it's mothers and children who'll have priority.'

'I sometimes wonder what the Regional Health Authority thinks of your methods, Dr MacEochan.'

'Oh, I follow their directives to the letter. Most punctiliously. And, as they've often said, they'd be hard pressed to replace me. The bright young medics aren't interested in general practice on the Outer Isles these days. They're all away to Glasgow and Dundee for the lasers and computers and micro-surgery. Not to mention all the private patients. But I suppose I'll have to retire some time.'

She starts the land-rover with a sudden jolt, and Murdo tips towards the windscreen. She pushes him firmly back in his place. 'Sorry, Minister. No seatbelt? You'd better fasten it. Unless you prefer to entrust your safety to the Lord.'

Murdo glares out at the rain.

'Which way are you going?'

'Back to the manse.'

'Now, what's troubling you?'

Steepling his fingers into a little portable kirk, Murdo clears his throat in a manner well known to his congregation, a signal that they are to take down their spiritual trousers and await chastisement.

'There is no doubt, Dr MacEochan, that your professional conduct is unexceptionable, although perhaps a trifle unorthodox. Not a man, woman or child on this island can be anything but grateful for your care and concern in all matters affecting their physical and material health and well-being. Indeed, there are those among us who affirm that you have single-handedly redeemed the good name of your family, so often besmirched by those of your forefathers who – with their ungodly ways and avarice – blighted the lives of our poor ancestors in troubled times gone by.'

'I'm very glad to hear it,' replies Catriona, fingers drumming impatiently on the steering-wheel. 'But get to the point, please.'

'Your personal conduct, however, has given cause for concern in some quarters.'

'What quarters?'

'That's neither here nor there. But some folk are as interested in the spiritual and moral health of our community as you are in its bodily welfare.'

'You and your elders then. I thought so. What's the problem?'

She swerves sharply to avoid a pair of incredulous sheep.

'What you do inside the four walls of your own home . . .'

'Ten actually, if you count the tower and the . . .'

'Be that as it may. Your private life, however we might question it in a moral sense, is your own affair.'

'Excellent. I'm pleased to hear it. I never thought it was anyone else's.'

'But . . .'

'But what? What exactly worries you about my private life, Murdo? I wouldn't have thought it could possibly interest you. We don't actually move in the same social circles, do we?'

'You know as well as I do that Cailleach is a very small place. A close-knit community. And I am the guardian of its moral health.'

'By whose order?'

'God's order, woman! Now hear me out!'

'Which god would that be, Murdo? This island has known quite a collection, in its time.'

'I'll have none of your meddling in theology, Doctor. You're evading the issue.'

'What issue? I've been waiting these five miles for word of it. If you don't hurry up and speak your piece we'll be back in the village, and all your hopes of a private chat will be ruined.'

'To be brief, then. You and your – house-guest – have been observed conducting yourself in a most unseemly manner.'

'And when would this have been?'

'Three Saturdays past. On the castle causeway. You were . . . improperly dressed. Among other things.'

'Ah yes, our moonlight swim. Changed our minds, though. The water was far too cold for her. I'd warned her it would be. Much too late in the year, never mind the warm weather. Well. So there we were, on what is – virtually – the private path to my own front door. And where, may I ask, was the unseen observer who was so shocked and offended by our behaviour? Swimming in the bay, perhaps? Or looking up a periscope from a tiny submarine lurking in the waters? I didn't realise the Church Militant had acquired its own navy. Or could they have been crouching behind the rocks on the foreshore?'

'Does it matter?'

'Strictly speaking, no. Although that beach is part of the castle grounds. My front garden, as it were. I'd be most distressed to think that some sneak-thief or would-be rapist was tiptoeing round my home in the dead of night. Or perhaps it was merely some guilty adulterer, sliding home from an unlawful tryst. And I presume your unnamed observer had some such good reason to be slinking about at such an ungodly hour.'

'Let us digress no further. Sexual perversion is bad enough, with all due respect. But public displays of such perverted affections are unspeakable! Think of the damage that could be done to our young people . . .'

'Might give them ideas, you mean?'

'You know very well what I mean, Dr MacEochan. And I am sure that the management of the Regional Health Authority would agree with me. I intend to write to them about your disgraceful behaviour.'

'I'm sure they will be fascinated. But are you certain they will be as outraged as you are, Murdo? For all you know, they might be perverts themselves. So go right ahead.'

'Are you calling my bluff?'

'I wouldn't dream of it, Murdo. As a professional, I can do no more than encourage any dissatisfied patients to seek satisfaction with a higher authority. But I warn you – the mighty Dr Jamieson himself is gay as pink paint. His amours with the ferry captain are the talk of Stornoway.'

'Then I shall write to the Secretary of State for Scotland about the pair of you. His moral probity is unexceptionable.'

'I'm quite sure it is. And you do that, Minister.' She stops the car. They have arrived at the manse. 'But it occurs to me that I've been quite remiss in my professional duties. Do you remember that little scare you had in July, after your trip to Edinburgh, for the Schismatic Kirk Assembly? Well, as I told you at the time, the blood test proved there was nothing to worry about. However, pressure of work (you remember the chickenpox epidemic?) prevented me from fulfilling my obligations as District Medical Officer. What I should have done was to ask Mrs MacNeish to come and see me. Only a formality, of course, since it proved to be a false alarm. But better safe than sorry. And it's not too late even now. There's a little printed form for just this purpose. I could easily fill it in this afternoon, and pop it through the letterbox.'

He glances over his shoulder, towards the manse. His eyebrows knit into a pair of copulating caterpillars.

'Point taken this time, Dr MacEochan. I knew I should have consulted someone on the mainland, but one doesn't know if a delay could be fatal . . . However, let us call it quits. I will not write the letter. And you, I presume, will let the other matter rest. But I beg of you to act with more discretion. As befits your station and – ahem – your age.'

She glares at him.

'It is hard enough, Doctor, in these lax times, to carry out the Lord's work. I cannot stand idly by and see my little flock corrupted.'

'The don't look, Minister. There's your Morag at the window now, Murdo. No doubt she's put your lunch on the table. Nice and hot. Cheery-bye.'

Snug in Catriona's tower room, while the winds of late November scream around her, Maria riffles through old family albums, packets of letters in faded ribbons, scrapbooks of calling cards and invitations, tea-chests full of sepia photographs in heavy frames: Victorians picnic by a waterfall; a shooting-party displays its bag; mustachioed ghillies steady the reins of small girls' ponies; young officers sit stiffly in armchairs, while their lily-skinned brides, of equally military bearing, stand ramrod-straight behind them.

'Feel free to browse,' says Catriona. 'Anything not under lock and key is there to be looked at. I hardly talk to any of my present-day relatives – you've met my starchy cousin Roddy at the Gathering, so you'll understand why. I'm quite fond of this lot, though. We have excellent relations – or did before you ruined my planchette. Still, I can't think why you're so intrigued by them.'

'I suppose it's a way of knowing you better. After all, you never tell me anything about yourself.'

'Perhaps because you never ask.'

Maria blinks, but says nothing.

'Don't count on finding out anything about me from this lot. I'm the family changeling, you know. Dropped into the aristocratic cradle by a pack of malevolent pixies, in exchange for the rightful infant heiress. Who sits even now in a mud-brown palace underground, making kidnapped mortals dance their feet off.'

'Every time I walk down the stairs,' replies Maria, 'four hundred years of piercing MacEochan eyes follow after me, looking down their fine patrician noses. If we dressed you up in a high lace collar, or a slashed damask jerkin shot with canary silk, you'd complete the set quite perfectly.'

'Oh, but I'm so much nicer than the rest.'

'Is that a fact?'

'When anyone annoyed them, they usually stuffed them down an oubliette. Or chucked them off the top of the tower into the bay.'

'And what will you do with me, if I annoy you?'

'Something far too terrible to mention. So watch your step.'

Refusing to rise to the bait, Maria turns back to her papers, and continues her gentle probe into her lover's ancestry.

Catriona, knowing Maria to be safely under surveillance by the stuffed seabirds and the castle cats, leaves her to it and disappears.

Dearest Cissie,

I trust you have now received my letter recounting the horrors of our journey to the isle of Cailleach. I shouldn't wonder if you smiled to yourself, and thought that I had received my come-uppance. Perhaps I did lord it over you just a little, about my invitation to Algy MacEochan's house-party. But you must confess that a visit to a Scotch castle is a far more thrilling prospect than a month with you and your chaperone at Frinton.

I hasten to assure you that my seasickness is now quite forgotten. Algy's mama, Lady Jean, has made us all quite comfortable. The weather has been fine for an hour or two every day, enabling us to make brief excursions along the shore and into the hills. I am captivated by the wild beauties of this windswept isle, although I must confess that I am mystified by Lady Jean's apparent willingness to remain here all the year round, foregoing the pleasures of the London season.

The castle has belonged to Algy's family for three centuries or more. Portraits of venerable MacEochan ancestors, male and female, hang in the hall and line the great stone staircase, but they are sadly blackened by peat-smoke. Still, I have spent a pleasant hour or two studying them, to see if I can discern any family resemblances.

Even now, in the height of summer, peat fires blaze in every hearth. The castle is bitterly cold. Algy says it is the chill of centuries. Lady Jean has tried to make the hall and the drawing room as comfortable as possible, with thick velvet draperies and carpets in the same tartan that Her Majesty has used to such good effect, so they tell me, at Balmoral.

The other young lady guests are Edinburgh girls. You would laugh to see their idea of fashion. The gentlemen in our party are all officers from Algy's regiment. Their rooms are in the tower, where the sea views are said to be splendid. But I do not envy them their eyrie, for the tower is said to be haunted. We learned this when we accompanied Lady Jean on a visit to Algy's old nurse, who lives in a filthy hovel in the village. We brought her a jar of calf's-foot jelly, and a basket of Lady Jean's cast-off clothing. I found her a horrid old woman, and not at all grateful. But good manners compelled us to sit with her for three-quarters of an hour, during which time she entertained us with gruesome tales of the island in olden times. She said that every year, on the seventh day of the seventh month, a pale lady, in a nun's habit, walks through the uppermost chambers of the castle. The apparition passes through stone walls as if they were no more than air. Lady Jean denied all knowledge of the ghost, but the old woman claimed to have seen the creature twice with her own eyes.

Before we could make our excuses and repair to the more wholesome atmosphere out-of-doors, she spoke of torture chambers, unsolved murders, prisoners walled up alive. By the end of the visit, I felt quite faint.

I am sure that you, darling Cissie, with your rational turn of mind and your readings of German philosophers, will dismiss my fears as the worst sort of feminine weakness. But I defy you to pass a stormy night in my present chamber, without the comforting knowledge that a party of gallant young officers is lodged on the storey above!!!

The thought of ghosts and similar horrors makes me shiver, even now as I write this, in spite of the morning sunshine, and the company of Lady Jean and my fellow guests reading letters or doing needlework.

I shall turn to happier matters. Last night we experienced a most thrilling spectacle. We saw the Aurora Borealis!! The gentlemen went out to smoke their after-dinner cigars upon the castle causeway. Suddenly they hurried back indoors and summoned us to join them. We hastily threw plaids and cloaks over our evening dresses, willy-nilly, and obeyed, to find a most wonderful spectacle spread out for our contemplation. The sky was luminous, with phosphorescent billows of green and purple cloud seeping across the heavens, like vast velvet curtains sweeping across the stage of a celestial opera house. The Northern Lights!! We stood and marvelled. I have no idea how long we remained there, but Lady Jean finally ordered us back into the castle with dire warnings about fatal summer chills.

What a sublime, unforgettable sight!! Neither my poor pen, nor my limited powers as a water-colourist, can do it justice. And that was only one of the remarkable events that took place last evening. The other, and equally unforgettable, was the little squeeze that Algy gave my hand and we stood together gazing up at the heavenly spectacle. Now, Cissie dearest, you must cross your heart and hope to die if you ever breathe a word of this!!

I know what you are thinking, Cissie. You are thinking that if anything should come to pass between Algy and myself, I should be most unsuited to a life in a cold northern castle, staring out at the perpetual rain, with only an old witch and some cottagers babbling in a foreign tongue for company. You may rest assured, my clever friend, that I am not as feather-headed as you suppose. I have already sounded out Algy on the subject of residence, most discreetly.

Yesterday we went on an excursion to see some old mouldering monument, a type of minor Stonehenge, that is one of the picturesque features of the neighbourhood. We spread out our picnic on a tartan rug, and Algy sat down beside me. While helping Algy to a dish of lobster salad, I remarked upon the wild remoteness of the island, and asked if he felt truly at home here.

He confessed that he had never formed a great attachment. He was taken from the arms of his native nurse at a tender age, and sent south to school. Summers, for the most part, were passed with his governess in the Swiss Alps or at Mentone. His own preference, he avers, is for hot sunny climes. He is delighted by his regiment's next posting, for they are off to India after Christmas.

You do realise, my pet, that this gives me very little time to plot my own campaign. I shall have to make the best possible use of the remaining days of this house-party. Perhaps when we meet again in

London I shall have some interesting news for you. If things go according to plan, I shall need your assistance on a tour of all the best milliners and dressmakers in Mayfair. What, I wonder, do memsahibs wear to regimental balls in Delhi?

I remain, as ever, your most affectionate friend,
Charlotte.

'And where have today's researches led you?' asks Catriona, ladling out a steaming bowl of barley broth. 'Eat plenty of this. It's better than central heating.'

'A letter to someone named Cissie from someone named Charlotte. Who was up here on some kind of Victorian house-party. Setting her cap for the first-born son.'

'Ah, yes, one of my favourites. At least you can read it – the handwriting's nice and clear, not criss-crossed every which way like some.'

'But I don't understand why Charlotte's letter is still here. She wrote it to Cissie, who was either in London or Frinton at the time. Was it never sent?'

'Oh, it was sent, all right.'

'I'm confused. Was Charlotte your great-grandmother?'

'No. Her friend Cissie was.'

'Cissie!'

'As soon as Cissie received dear Charlotte's missive, she decided that Algy and his romantic island would be wasted on her frivolous friend. So, with a little deft manoeuvring in the drawing rooms of Berkeley Square and Edinburgh's New Town, she gently nudged her *chère amie* out of the picture, and took the castle.'

'Didn't Algy go to India?'

'Of course, and Cissie went with him. Apparently she went all native, and discovered reincarnation. Caused something of a scandal among Algy's regiment. They came back here when he resigned his commission, and she took up the reins at the castle. Ruled the island with an iron hand.'

'I wonder what happened to Charlotte?'

'Looked for another dashing young officer of good family to take her out to India, I suppose. But I haven't found any evidence that she and Cissie corresponded after that.'

'You're a ruthless lot.'

'That's why we have a castle. Bread and butter?'

Of November and December Maria remembers very little, except amorous dalliance. In between times, Catriona sees people in and out of the world, binds up wounds, drives away viruses and demons ('Much of a muchness,' she explains), listens to complaints and fears and heartbeats. Maria, meanwhile, does little more than wait for Catriona's land-rover to come rattling across the causeway. Thinks about painting, but decides she doesn't have an idea in her head. Concludes that *Lives of the Saints* was simply a fluke, that art-college successes were accidents of luck or results of young lecturers grading with their libidos. Or someone's clerical errors, failures mistakenly transcribed as pass-marks. She's here on false pretences. Artist on an island has a romantic ring; house-guest who helps with the dishes is slightly less glamorous.

She gives up looking in mirrors. Just as well. She isn't there any more.

At Christmas (after a long, soul-searching discussion about the morality of celebrating it at all when it is – according to Maria – a reactionary relic of the patriarchal stone age, or – according to Catriona – a silly modern substitute for the star-shattering magnificences of the Winter Solstice) they exchange presents.

Maria gives Catriona a soft woollen scarf, violet and grey like heather on the hills, woven at her special request by Isa at the south of the island and sent up, secretly, via Dugald in the tweed-mill lorry. A hiding-place is easy: Maria tucks it under the pillow of the spare-room bed she hasn't slept in since September.

Catriona's present to Maria needs legerdemain and logistics. It's far too bulky to be spirited into the castle – especially since Maria is hardly ever out. So the mysterious parcel is stored in a shed behind the post office and spirited across the causeway at the crack of dawn on Christmas morning.

Maria unwraps the bundle – 'not gift-wrapped, I'm afraid,' apologises Catriona – to find a generous quantity of good canvas, an ample supply of wooden stretchers, and a box packed with a rainbow of paints.

'I hope they're the proper sort,' says Catriona.

'Of course they are, but . . .' Maria flusters, protests, blushes red as her hair.

'Catriona, it's all far too much. I couldn't possibly . . .'

'Don't say you couldn't possibly accept it. What on earth would I do with all that rubbish?'

93

'It's far too generous.'

'So am I, dear. But, then, I've an ulterior motive. I thought it was time you got down to some serious work again.'

'You've pulled my best excuse straight out from under me.'

'And you're not sure if you're pleased or not. Never mind, you can start tomorrow. Today is dedicated to eating far too much and drinking accordingly. More champagne?'

In between the pheasant and the apple crêpes, while Catriona removes the glasses that held the *premier cru* claret and replaces them with others to hold the forty-year-old Sauternes, Maria slips away from the table, and returns with a small package, wrapped in a piece of white silk.

'What's this?'

'A little something extra that I nearly forgot.'

Catriona opens it, laughs, and shakes her head. 'You're far too good for me, you know.' She strokes the planchette, a thin wedge of lacquered wood, silky to the touch.

'I hope it's the right kind. I had to make about two hundred telephone calls – not from here, of course – until I found someone in a shop in London who knew what I was on about. It's supposed to be about one hundred years old, and it's inlaid with amber.'

'I can tell, it's very powerful. It must have belonged to someone who understood how to use it.'

'The silk came with it. You're suppose to keep it wrapped that way, the woman said.'

'I'm scandalised when I think what this must have cost you.'

'Less than the paints and things. And you can't fool me about them.'

'You did very well, especially buying it sight unseen. There are far too many cheats in this trade.'

'I liked the sound of her voice. So I sent the cheque and hoped for the best.'

'Oh, did you?'

'She reminded me of you.'

'Oh, dear. Perhaps we'd better put it to the test, then. We don't know what we're getting into.'

After dinner, they set up the board in front of the fire. Before they can ask any questions, the planchette sets off on a majestic progress through the alphabet. It makes no sense to Maria, but as Catriona notes down the letters she laughs and laughs.

'It's all gibberish.'

'Nonsense, it's all in the Gaelic.'

'What's it saying?'

'Oh, I can't possibly tell you. She said I mustn't breathe a word of it to anyone.'

'Who's she?'

'No one you know. Besides, I thought you despised all this jiggery-pokery.'

'I didn't say I was going to believe it. I just wanted to know what the words meant.'

'This particular transmission isn't for the eyes of cynics. But it's absolutely riveting. May I congratulate you on your superb – if purely accidental – choice of instrument?'

'Bloody ingrate. Not if you won't tell me what it's on about.'

'Why don't you just go up to bed?'

'Why don't you just put that away for the night and join me?'

Catriona lifts her eyes from the board, and looks over her spectacles at Maria.

'Taking the initiative at last, are we? This *could* be an interesting winter.'

The board is hastily covered with its velvet cloth, but the planchette in its silk wrappings continues to move from letter to letter, gently but insistently, all night long.

January isn't white in Cailleach, but bleached and grey. Maria mopes in the castle, engulfed by an ever-rising silt of crumpled sketches. She no longer looks out the window, seasick even at the thought of the pale, choppy waves below the tower. Catriona looks in on her, from time to time.

'Well?'

Stop looking over my shoulder, she thinks, stop breathing down my neck. 'Nothing's happening. Sorry.'

'Don't say sorry. Just keep at it.'

Catriona, dustcloth in hand, patrols the castle. She rubs the round-bellied cherubs adorning the massive fireplace. An eighteenth-century MacEochan, lucky at cards and marriage, had imported masons from Italy along with the marble. She walks slowly up the stairs, dusting and adjusting the heavily gilded frames of the ancestral portraits. One is missing from the sequence, having been tossed into the sea after the painter, upon completion, eloped with the youthful sitter. Another shows a young lace-collared lordling posed before a tapestry – now lost – recording the exploits of an early military MacEochan; the needlewomen who produced it were imported from Flanders to create the work on the spot. When the job was finished, they were not sent home again, but married off to local fishermen, who found them very handy at mending the nets. On the upper landing, where the paintings end, Catriona looks speculatively at the well-hewn stones of the thick castle wall, marking the spot where her seventeenth-century ancestor added a new wing to a much older fortress. A pair of skeletons, found during recent repairs, suggest that the master-builder had taken out his own form of insurance on the work, by walling up two live apprentices to appease the gods that were older than God, and to keep the structure standing. Whether or not her predecessor had known of this act is a moot point, but Catriona thinks it likely: the MacEochans had always been patrons of the arts.

'Maria, would you like to paint my portrait?'
   'I'd be terrified.'
   'Why's that?'
   'I could never get it right.'
   'Don't sell yourself short.'
   'It's nothing to do with that. I just don't think you'd be a very easy model.'
   'Try me.'
   'Only on one condition.'
   'What's that?'
   'That I don't have to show you the results unless I'm satisfied.'
   'But you know you won't be.'
   'That's my price, Catriona. Take it or leave it.'
So the sittings begin. Catriona sits in a high-backed oaken armchair, carved with the moon and the sun and the stars, and wears, at Maria's behest, her peacock kimono. Maria sketches, silently, and spends hours simply staring at Catriona, scrutinising every plane and line, exploring every shadow, first with her eyes, then with her charcoal, circumspectly, then more assertively, with her brush. Catriona keeps perfectly still, and says nothing, but feels the soul softly stroked and teased out of her body, and transferred to the painted canvas. On the night when Maria finally gives up in despair and, with a string of curses, throws crumpled sketches and shredded canvas into the fire, Catriona takes to her bed with a fever, and spends the next fortnight with her face to the wall, consumed by a virulent flu.

When she recovers, the subject of the portrait is dropped altogether.

March comes to Castle Cailleach. Lust still flourishes, but conversation wanes.

Maria thinks about leaving. After six months on the island she has little to show for it, except for a few dozen lacklustre sketches of the landscape, the stones, the castle itself. She broaches the subject, nervously, to Catriona.

'Bored, are we?'

Maria denies it, a little too fervently.

'I should be sorry if you went now.'

For the life of her, Maria can't see why. 'I'm doing nothing. I feel as if I'm half-way between a kept woman and a parasite.'

'That's ridiculous. And insulting.'

'Sorry.'

'You give me a lot, you know. You're here, you keep me from feeling lonely, you're someone to talk to in the evenings, but you don't get in my way. And you feed the cats when I'm off the island. And now that you've finally learned to cook a bit, you're practically indispensable.'

Maria sees, or thinks she sees, a glint in Catriona's eye.

'And is that all I'm good for?'

'What more do you want?' snaps Catriona.

Maria wishes she'd never asked.

By April, even lust is cooling.

'Well, well, well. It's the Artist Lady. Still here, after all. And what have you been doing with yourself all winter?'

Maria, back from a long walk across the island, is dismayed to find an unexpected guest. The archaeologist she met in September, staying at Ina Isbister's, sprawls on the hearthrug, helping herself to a well-punished bottle of island malt.

Before Maria can answer, Catriona emerges from the kitchen, bearing a tray of home-made bread and her legendary layered game pâté. Playing the gracious hostess. Maria knows that this particular delicacy takes at least three days to prepare. If Catriona has known about Stephanie Stonebridge's arrival, she has not thought to pass on the news.

'Maria, this is Stoney. One of the people running the excavations at the convent. Comes up for a quick recce every Easter, and then descends on us again in June, accompanied by her eunuchs and handmaidens, to pitch camp for the season.'

'We've met,' say Maria and Stoney, curtly but in perfect unison.

'Ah yes. At Ina's. Well, dinner will be in half an hour or so, and I'll leave you two to amuse yourselves with the pâté. I'd better look to my pots, and baste the duck.'

'You didn't answer my question,' murmurs Stoney.

'If you don't mind, I'm going to go up and have a wash, and change my clothes. I'm covered in mud.'

'Excuses, excuses,' jeers Stoney, reaching for the tray.

When Maria comes back twenty minutes later, Catriona and Stoney are sitting side by side on the floor in front of the fire, roaring with laughter. The whisky bottle is empty and the pâté is finished.

Throughout the meal, Maria attempts to assert her membership in the household by helping with the serving. She breaks a wine glass, drops a ladleful of noodles into Stoney's lap, and splatters vinaigrette all over the tablecloth while tossing the salad.

Catriona makes light of it. The perfect hostess, still.

'I must say, Maria, if I didn't know better, I'd think it was you and not ourselves who'd had a drop too much.'

Stoney explodes with laughter, chokes on a breadcrumb, has to be thumped soundly on the back by Catriona, who then lets her hand rest lightly on Stoney's shoulder.

'You know, this silly girl has always refused my invitations to come and stay at the castle when the dig's on.' She rumples Stoney's cropped black hair. 'So much more comfortable than Ina Isbister's, don't you think, Maria?'

'Ah, yes, Catriona,' smiles Stoney, looking up at her winking, 'but then you know I wouldn't get a stroke of work done.'

'Touché,' mutters Maria.

'What?'

'Nothing.'

After dinner, Catriona and Stoney settle down in the armchairs on either side of the fire. Maria sits on a cushion on the hearthrug, gazing with feigned tranquillity into the flames, listening to the thrusts and parries, feeling contemptuous.

'Catriona, that's a load of bourgeois romantic bullshit, and you know it!'

'Stoney, my love, you simply have no imagination.'

'You can stuff your imagination! In my field, too much imagination is a downright disaster. Otherwise what do you get – Heinrich Schliemann faking his evidence, rearranging things a little, this way or that way, so everything tallies nicely with Homer? Or some daydreaming amateur sticking his spade into a chambered cairn in search of King Arthur, and ruining at a stroke four thousand years of solid data? Or some idiot waving a branch of mistletoe, leaping out from behind a menhir, and threatening to put a curse on us if we violate the Mother's flesh with tools of iron? Come on, Catriona, give it a rest.'

Maria, ignored, marks an invisible scorecard. Stoney 1, Catriona nil.

'I still think you're wasting your time. Excavating a medieval vegetable garden is all very well, I'm sure, if you want to publish some dreary little essay in a learned journal to improve your chances of tenure at the university, but I think you would find there are things of considerably more interest, and considerably older, underneath the nunnery itself. But perhaps you'd be out of your depth.'

Catriona comes up from behind; the score is even. Stoney, it seems, is still working on one-year contracts.

'What's your evidence?'

'I just think you will, that's all.' Weak move, Catriona. Stoney edges ahead.

'That's exactly what I mean, Catriona. Sloppy thinking. Now come on, after all, you've had a scientific training yourself, Doctor. You'd never dream of applying a half-baked approach like that to your diagnoses.'

'Wrong. That's exactly what I have to do. Use guesswork and intuition. Sometimes there're no data to go on. And sometimes there are, but the data lie. Or the patient does. When you get a little older, my dear, you'll cling less tenaciously to the things they taught you in your undergraduate seminars.' Game to Catriona.

The argument continues, in spirals, curves, circles. Maria, fighting sleep, is determined to see the night through to its end. But finally Catriona rises and announces, 'Well, some of us have work in the morning, don't we, Stoney?' She turns to Maria. 'You don't mind that Stoney is sleeping in the spare room tonight, do you, my love? Of course you don't. Sweet dreams.'

Maria goes up to the tower room and waits for Catriona to join her. Waits and waits.

Maria Milleny decides that the time has come to leave Cailleach. She wonders where to go, rakes through a few wild ideas. She might volunteer to teach sewing at a missionary school in Botswana, except she can barely tell a pin from a needle. She might try to get another post at an art college or polytechnic, but thinks she is probably on some kind of blacklist, after being arrested for smoking marijuana in company with three of her students. She toys with the idea of going back to London, to see if her old basement studio is still for rent, but she is sure that the status of the neighbourhood will – in the way of so many London districts – have sky-rocketed in her absence; where once she stacked her canvases and spilled her turps, some rising young barrister will now be living comfortably amid the best examples of Italian furniture design. She wonders about phoning this ex-lover, or that one, but her flesh creeps and she cannot conceive how she ever . . . She muses about offering herself to an upper-class nunnery in the Cotswolds, but doesn't think she would like their rules and regulations, not to mention their version of God. And even if she could reconcile herself to these, she doubts they'd have her: if her name is remembered at all, after *Lives of the Saints*, it is bound to be mud throughout the established churches. Perhaps a dose of self-sacrifice would be good for her soul, if not for her painting, and she should move to Dundee and dole out soup in a dossers' hostel. But the thought of crossing the Minch to the mainland and heading south again sickens her; she has just begun to learn to breathe the crystalline air of the north. Perhaps she should go even closer to the top of the world, drawn ever northwards, to Orkney or Shetland, and take her chances. But then she remembers that she has no money, having emptied her bank account to buy Catriona's Christmas planchette.

Maria Milleny's attempts to leave Cailleach:

1. She packs her rucksack, writes a note to Catriona, saying: 'Thanks for everything, but I think it's time to go.' She hitches a lift to the pier and finds that the ferry has been cancelled because of a seamen's strike.

2. She packs her rucksack, writes a note to Catriona, hitches a lift to the pier. Just as she boards the ferry she remembers that her wallet, with all the money she has left in the world, is still on the kitchen dresser back at the castle.

3. She packs her rucksack, writes a note to Catriona, makes sure she has her wallet, and sets out to hitch a lift to the ferry. But, unusually for that hour of the day, no cars pass her, and when someone finally stops she can hear the foghorn as the *St Rollox* steams out into the bay.

4. She packs her rucksack, writes a note to Catriona, checks her money, and leaves herself enough time to walk the entire way, if necessary, and still have an hour to idle round the Co-op or the Cailleach Inn. Or so she thinks. But her watch, and the castle clocks, have somehow stopped, and by the time she realises this it is far too late to bother.

5. She packs her rucksack, writes a note to Catriona, checks her money, and arranges for the island taxi to collect her from the castle with plenty of time to spare before the ferry sails. She makes it, with a comfortable margin, to the port, and whiles away two hours in the bar at the Cailleach Inn, politely ignored by the same regulars who have been politely ignoring her ever since she moved into the castle. When the time comes, she boards the *St Rollox*, and finds a seat as far as possible from the stale, greasy smells of the ship's so-called cafeteria. She stares out at the grey water and the rain-battered village, until they are out of sight as the ferry rounds the point. She looks straight past the castle towards the dun-coloured hills behind it. The sky is a dull, brassy colour; the sea roughens and the *St Rollox* – a small boat, servicing unimportant islands – lurches sharply in the violent swell.

Crew and passengers appear nonchalant; they've all weathered worse than this on winter and springtime crossings. But they are taken by surprise by a great wall of wind and wave that comes banging up without warning out of the sea, rises into a Himalayan height, and knocks the ship off its cautious course through a tricky chain of islets. With a terrible grating noise, like a taloned finger dragged sadistically across a giant blackboard, the *St Rollox* smashes into the bird-covered rocks of Cailleach Bheag.

Something hits Maria on the head as the ferry slews; she is dizzy, deafened by shouts, sirens, whooping klaxons, and barely conscious of the oilskinned arms that push her along the sloping deck and hoist her into a lifeboat. The sky turns white, and shatters into a thousand pairs of flapping wings; the seabird colonies are disturbed and angry, afraid for their eggs. Maria finds herself eye to eye with an irate skua, identical twin to the stuffed bird in

Catriona's tower, who glares at her balefully as she blacks out altogether.

Maria opens her eyes. The skua is still glaring at her, but this time it is the stuffed bird in Catriona's bedroom.

'You'll be happy to know that you were the only one injured. And it's only a mild concussion. You were all very lucky. A similar freak wave, about sixty years ago, sank the ferry and killed twenty people. The *St Rollox* will be out of commission for a while, but I suppose the company will scare up some old tub to replace her until she's out of dry dock. So we won't be totally cut off. Not that it will matter to you. You aren't going anywhere.'

Maria shuts her eyes again; Catriona's voice is flicked off like a switch.

When she opens them again, Catriona herself has replaced the skua, and gazes intently, with the aid of a little torch, into Maria's eyes; but the concentration is purely professional, and she meets Maria's glance without interest.

'I suppose you'd like to be out of here quite soon. You should be fit to go in a week or so.'

'Did you see my note?'

'Darling, I saw all five of them. You really should tear things up when you put them in the dustbin. So if you're asking if I was surprised, insulted, hurt, relieved, dismayed or delighted, the answer is yes.' She hands Maria a mug filled with a foul-smelling tisane. 'And no. Anyway, drink that. It will bring you back to life.'

'When does the replacement ferry start up?'

'Oh, it's already started. But you won't be on it. You've been out cold most of the time for the past two days. You have exactly fifteen pounds to your name. And I will not have you wandering around the landscape like a displaced ghost. No, I'm afraid you're staying here for a while. You haven't any option.'

'I don't want to live with you, Catriona.'

'That's fine, my dear, I don't want to live with you either. But that doesn't mean I am going to let you go.'

A few days later Catriona hustles Maria out of her bed (she herself has retired to the spare room down below, with its problematical associations, for the duration) and bundles her up far more warmly that the soft spring weather demands. She says nothing as she leads Maria to the land-rover, restricts her remarks to the state of the road and the arrival of the wildflowers as they drive across the island, and finally pulls up in front of a white-washed cottage that stands on the long, sandy beach of the far west side.

'In here,' she says, hoisting Maria's rucksack on her shoulder.

She pushes open the door. The room is warm and slightly smokey; someone has kindled a peat fire on the hearth. 'Blocked chimney, blast it,' says Catriona, fiddling with the damper. 'I'll sort it. Have a look around.'

The furnishings are simple – a narrow box-bed in a recess, covered with a comforter woven of the black-and-white island tweed; a rocking chair; a scrubbed pine table; an old settee and a battered armchair; a pair of wooden kitchen chairs and a three-legged stool; an old chest of drawers.

'Kitchen's that way,' says Catriona. 'Just a hotplate, a sink and a tiny fridge. Didn't think you'd need anything more elaborate, and that's what there was. Loo's over there.'

The canvases, sketchblocks, wooden stretchers, paints and other gear that Catriona gave Maria for Christmas are stacked haphazardly in a corner. 'You forgot those,' remarks Catriona. 'Or was it that they didn't fit into your rucksack, made a quick escape impossible? Never mind. I've no use for them myself, and I don't want them cluttering up the castle.'

'What makes you think I have any use for them either?'

'You will do. I thought you might do a little painting during your convalescence.'

'Catriona, what I do is no concern of yours.'

'All right then, jump in the land-rover, bring your rucksack, and I'll take you to the harbour. Hurry up, stop gaping, there's a ferry at three-thirty and if we're quick you'll just catch it.'

Maria looks straight past her, at the blue-grey light, the cloud-shadows stroking the sea. Rocky outcroppings divide the beach into sections; tiny wildflowers – anemones, foxgloves, wild orchids, beads of colour whose names are unknown to her, bloom in the crevices between slabs and fingers of stone.

'Whose place is this?'

'Yours, for the time being. It belongs to me, I suppose, but it's been lying empty. The locals don't fancy it – too far off the beaten track, too small for a family, whatever – so don't worry, I have not driven out ragged tenants into the snow on your behalf.'

'What's the rent?' Nothing's for free with you, she mutters to herself, that's sure.

'We'll settle that later. Perhaps a couple of paintings would suffice for the present quarter. If you were staying . . .'

'I can't do them to order, you know.'

'I'm not worried.' Catriona heads for the door, 'Well, that's neither here nor there if you're going to make your ferry. But we'll have to hurry. I hope you'll drop me a postcard one of these years. Tell me how you're getting on. I understand it is still possible to get cheap bedsitting-rooms in some of the outer London suburbs. I suppose you'll land on your feet.'

Outside the cottage door, the gulls are swooping and skimming low over the sea.

'You're a wicked woman, Catriona. A sly old witch. Go on, be smug about it. I'll stay. For a bit. But don't make any assumptions . . .'

'About what? Our relationship? My dear, you are naive. That's well and truly over.'

Maria feels herself glowing red-hot with anger, vexation, a sense she's been conned, all spiked with a sharp sense of loss.

'Damn you!' She scoops up a few tubes of paint – rose madder, black, white, cerulean blue – and flings them into Catriona's face. 'What are you doing to me? What are you playing at? Why? It's over, you've said it yourself. I'd think you'd be rushing off to London or Paris or somewhere by now, to find yourself another keen young painter to patronise. Or maybe a wild-eyed poetess for a change? Or perhaps a musician, throbbing with frustrated talent and bottled-up passions? I don't know what you want from me. I just don't, don't, don't, don't KNOW!' She grabs Catriona by the shoulders, shakes her, harder and harder, until the eyeglasses slide off her face, hang for a moment from one ear, then fall to the floor.

Catriona brushes away Maria's hands, as if sweeping specks of dust from the sleeves of her thick jersey. She kicks her own eyeglasses lightly across the floor, out of harm's way, and walks towards Maria, staring fixedly, as if she is about to stride straight through her. Backing off from a gaze as pitiless as a peregrine falcon's, Maria loses her balance and falls backwards on to the bed. Catriona looms over her; her lips part in a delighted grin.

'Very pretty. You'd look like an overturned tortoise, except you're too tall. And at this moment your face is the colour of beaujolais nouveau.'

Maria snarls at her. 'Get away from me!'

Catriona recovers her glasses, restores them, peers at Maria over the frame in her customary fashion.

'You think I've put some kind of spell on you, yes? What arrogance. What makes you think I'd bother?'

'Well, haven't you, you . . . witch!'

'Don't be silly. You don't really think so, do you?' Honeyed tones.

'I think, Catriona, that up in your tower, at the bottom of that black oak press, tucked away behind the butter-soft boots and the Liberty scarves, you have the West Wind captured and tied up in a bag.'

Catriona, once more in sole possession of her tower, testifies before the silent jury of seabirds.

'You've seen the intimate details for yourselves; you know how good it was – when it was good – and how it foundered. But if you believe I cast a spell on her, to keep her here on Cailleach, you're all as silly as she is. We may have our sea-mists and superstitions, but this is not Brigadoon, and I'm not the Wicked Witch of the North.'

They do not quibble, nor lift a feather in dissent. But, in the back of the old oak press at midnight, something howls softly in a leather sack. Maria Milleny swears to it.

Below Catriona's tower, the waters of the bay slap softly against the castle's rocky foundations. But here, on the far west side, the Atlantic smashes itself against the shore. Until the rhythms of her dreams, and the flow of her blood, sychronise with the ocean tides, Maria sleeps very badly.

It is light by four or five in the morning. Maria, looking out at the sea, imagines she sees a woman walking along the beach, putting seaweed into a basket. But there is little to go on, beyond a swift, peripheral movement, seen through the salt-stained window, and Maria wonders if anyone was there at all.

In the pale blue mist that passes for midsummer midnight, Maria walks along the shore in a trance, anticipating slippery stones and avoiding rockpools. She is drawn out every night from her cottage, to look at the light. The seabirds are silent, and the only sound is the hiss of the tide.

If there are any sea-serpents out there, I'll see them now. And if I'm truly a silkie, trapped by a spell in human form, now is the

105

moment when I will turn back into a seal again, and slip into the waves and slide out to sea to find my own kind.

Maria's is the only house on the beach; no one lives within a mile of her. Sometimes, in spite of her pleasure in solitude, she feels oppressed by the isolation. In the brief hour or two of darkness in the nights of early summer, she sits by the window, trying to ascertain where the ocean meets the sky. The wave-sounds are comforting, and the stars never fail to surprise her. One night she strains her eyes at something coming over the horizon. She thinks it is the seaweed-gatherer, emerging from the darkness. This time the woman is not traversing the beach, but riding the waves into shore, like a surfer or like Venus on her cockleshell; the hem of her long, dark skirt skims the whitecaps. By the second glance, she has, of course, vanished, leaving only a faint tingling along Maria's spine as proof of her passage.

Maria quickly draws the curtains tight, switches all the lamps on. She pours a tumbler-full of whisky and crouches in her box-bed, with the crackling radio for reassurance, listening to the fishing-boats calling out to each other, warning of gales in the Pentland Firth or a dangerous hulk afloat in the Minch.

Up at the nunnery, the season has turned and the diggers are back on site again. They pierce the earth with their picks and spades, and carefully turn over layers of time. The past flies out, untrammelled, a genie escaping from an uncorked bottle.

TWO
Mhairi

The Faith changes and doesn't change. The goddesses shrewdly transform themselves (or are transformed by others) into saints. This is how the Fathers of the Church make inroads, faced with wild and deeply suspicious tribes. Tell them their goddesses and ghosts have come over, do a few instructive magic tricks and miracles, and you'll soon have them banging down your door for baptisms, wagging their rituals behind them. Just follow the approved formula: grease the palm or the vanity of the local chieftain, flog the folk across the river in job lots, priest upstream doing the business, and you've extended the frontiers of the Faith even further.

Sound policy, carried along in the coracles: head for the well-established holy places, set up shop where the customers are already waiting. Amazing how you can engineer a takeover, slip in all sorts of new stock in similar packages, and the clientele will never even notice that the old firm's stopped trading.

Thriftily using the assets they encountered, the early missionaries turned the temples into chapels, kept the sacred fires burning, didn't shift the massive stones implanted in the earth – not that they could have, even if they'd tried. The rock on which you build your church was placed there for good reason, by someone else. Even now, put an ear to certain pitted and well-rubbed stones in the Cailleach Ring and you can hear a faint but persistent humming, from deep down in the earth.

Some of the goddesses surrendered without a fight, disappearing into place names and superstitions. Others subsided, disgruntled, into the sinister underground of the fairies and the little people, reduced to souring milk and wiping changelings' bottoms, where once they'd split the skies and caused whole continents to crumble.

But Bride, all-wise healer and midwife, bringer of babies, teacher of smithcraft, teller of stories, put the wafer on one of her golden tongues, drank the blood-black wine and signed on as a saint. And did her loving people notice? Never mind, they went on keeping her fire going, and all the priests and politicos were satisfied.

Only later, when the money's changed hands, or the keys to the kingdom, are questions raised. It becomes imperative to explain how this or that Old One fits into the new arrangements. But underneath the surface of the Authorised Version lie tales older than the language they are told in. Grandmothers continue to warn and to gossip, people still puzzle over dreams. Things are done without a reason, like the pinch of salt tossed over the shoulder. Random relics, perhaps, or a conspiracy?

The Fathers wonder and worry. But the Sisters, patiently and skilfully, transcribe what they can before it all disappears.

North and north and north they go. No place is ever quite remote enough, nowhere far enough away from the world and its agents. Once flooded out, twice burned out, three times starved out and four times hounded out, they carry their bundles and their dubious theology down to the boats and put to sea again.

The Sisters of Saint Bride are expert stonemasons, fine draughtswomen, seraphic choristers and dedicated gardeners. But their true genius is for packing up fast, and covering their tracks.

Scandalously, the convent does not divide itself into lay-sisters and enclosed nuns. No rough-handed, slightly-less-holy ones are assigned to the labours of scullery and dairy and byre while the better-born ladies get on with the mysticism. Everyone scrubs pots and meditates on the Mysteries and tells their beads and sweeps the floors and helps tend the Fire. Even Reverend Mother takes her turn cleaning the privies.

This is a worry and a sore point to the mild, blue-eyed confessors who come twice-yearly from Iona. How, they ask, can you reconcile holinesss and haggling with fishwives? How keep the soul pure while leading the cow to the bull? How differentiate between the cloistered princess and the swineherd's daughter?

'We don't,' says Reverend Mother flatly, pouring him another cup of the Water of Life. She takes some herself; priests hate to drink alone.

Elsewhere on the island live Mhairi's parents. They are soft-hearted people, underneath their ferocious pomp and considerable local power. So when it comes time to negotiate their daughter's future, they offer Mhairi a free choice: marry the old earl and cement a strategically important alliance, or cut off all your hair and live locked up in a nunnery for ever.

The earl has a perpetually greasy face, as if he were for ever gnawing on mutton bones, and smells like the family farm on the day of the great pigsticking. Of the three wives he's outlived so far, one died bearing the seed that had turned into a giant in her belly, one drowned, one fell from a cliff. Mhairi says she'd rather tell rosaries 'til the Resurrection than marry him.

If God wants any of your children, the gentle priest tells the parents often enough, you must give them freely. Refusing your consent is a mortal sin, and you will be boiled in the Devil's cauldron for all eternity.

Nevertheless, they try their small persuasions. A fine comb, carved out of a unicorn's horn, comes as a gift from a loving aunt. What good is that if you're going to be bald as a polished rock? asks Mother, and takes it away.

A mistake in the kitchen one day, and while the rest of the household sup on the golden broth of a cockerel, out comes a bowl of thin, snottery gruel for Mhairi. An unfortunate mistake, says Father, but let the child eat what is put before her. Might as well get her used to convent fare if that's her pleasure.

The ceremonial drowning, one by one, of her pet bitch's puppies. An earl's lady may have all the dogs she desires, they tell her, but nuns can have no pets but their own body-lice.

Still, when the time comes, they pack her off to the nuns with a generous dowry, and wait eagerly for Mhairi's young sister to start her first bleeding; she will not be allowed the same latitude, especially now they've given one child to God. The old earl, too, is patient.

Mhairi worships Sister Bloduedd, who has kept her warm in bed those first homesick nights, rubbing her ice-cold feet and tickling her ear with stories. So no wonder she blushes scarlet from her coif to her sandals when Bloduedd says, 'I've told Reverend Mother about your clever fingers. We think you show a special talent. So now I'm going to teach you something wonderful and new – the mystery of making books with words and pictures in them. It may take you twenty years, if we are spared and if the Fire stays alight, to learn this art, but once you do you will be able to make things

111

that will last longer than any of us.'

They begin with something simple and difficult: the shaping of letters. For a year or more, Bloduedd guides her hand, and Mhairi never traces so much as the cross-piece of an Alpha without those strong, sure fingers bearing down on hers. For five years she writes the stories that Bloduedd tells her, letter by letter, then word by word, then phrase by phrase. Sometimes, by way of a change, she is allowed to copy lines from another book, written down by a long-dead sister, many years before.

'Her name is forgotten,' says Bloduedd, 'but her words still speak to us. Work hard and yours will do the same.'

The two books – the old one for copying, and the new one that is trickling slowly from Bloduedd's lips – tell the same story, but with subtle variations. Sometimes, when Bloduedd pauses for breath, or to struggle with a turn of phrase, Mhairi asks why or how or when. She is intrigued, disturbed, by the tale that she is writing down, but Bloduedd will brook no interruptions. She becomes cross, reaches out and pinches Mhairi in a sensitive place, and says it is far too soon for her to be asking questions.

Before they can make the pictures for the book, they must make the colours. In May and June, Bloduedd and Mhairi walk along the beach and then climb the hills behind it. Wildflowers are everywhere underfoot, the bleak beach has transformed itself, briefly, into a Turkey carpet; every crack and crevice in the rocks is sprinkled with colours. Bluebells, daisies, fairy foxgloves, anemones, small purple stars with no name, go into their baskets along with seaweeds, shells, particular small pebbles, slick and gleaming from the tide. For the summer of that year, and all the summers that follow, Mhairi's life is ruled by the mortar and the pestle. Under Bloduedd's meticulous supervision, she presses out juices, grinds and mixes powders. There are seventeen different shades of blue: for virgins' robes; for sky in time of cold, famine, happiness, summer, danger; for the eyes of the Saint; for the sea at different seasons and hours; for precious stones in crowns and necklaces; for scales of the twining serpent – this last shade must be blended with luminous greens and rich purples whose confection is even more complex. Red comes from berries, found in the inland scrub, dangerous little beads bursting with a poison that must be tamed before the dye can be used. Mhairi learns the particular skills involved in their handling at some cost; she will carry for ever a cobweb-shaped scar where the bright acid has splashed her palm.

112

A certain shade of russet-brown is highly prized for the warm glow it imparts to the small, furry beasts that scuttle through the margins of the text; this colour comes from the Sisters' own menstrual blood, carefully collected and dried out in earthenware basins near the Fire. Gold and silver come, sparingly, from locked boxes; Bloduedd sleeps with the keys under her pillow. If the situation doesn't improve Out There, she tells an uncomprehending Mhairi, we may never get any silvering and gilding again. But so skilled is Bloduedd at spreading the gleaming metals tissuethin, that it will be long past her lifetime before the present stock is depleted.

'In another year, or two,' promises Bloduedd, 'I may trust you to put a little colour on the page all by yourself. That's if we're spared, if Bride protects us, and if the Fire stays lit, of course.'

The Brothers and Fathers on a distant island, who rightly or wrongly believe themselves to be the shepherds of the Sisters' souls, are not altogether happy with the situation on Cailleach. Something not quite right is going on there. But they can't put their pious fingers on it.

Bemused sisters offer honey-cakes and the semblance of attention when a tonsured guest comes – ostensibly – to preach a sermon. They can't think why they are being spied upon. While the Good Father holds forth, from noon to midnight, they sit in the chapel, getting on with their mending, clicketing their rosaries, digging the soil of the garden out of their finger-nails. Scriptorium Sister sneaks a few chalk sketches on the stone wall at her side – a priest in full spate, very pleased with the sound of his own voice.

Look to your flock, Reverend Mother. Inattention is a subspecies of the Deadly Sin of Sloth.

On the contrary, Father Ferret, it's the rule of our Order that hands must never lie idle, especially during a visitor's sermon. A little distraction concentrates the mind, don't you think?

(I wonder what misinformation he'll take back to his bishop?)

The visiting Father delivers his final homily.

'And on this Tree of Sin, my beloved Sisters, there groweth another most dreadful branch, and the fruit of it is yet more deadly than the fruit that groweth on these first six branches of which I have already spoken. This fruit is most perilous for it is bright and fair of colour, ripe and round, and pleasing to all the senses. Yet be

113

ye ware, for this is the trap of Satan, for once bitten the juice is most foul and bitter to taste. It burneth the throat and bringeth canker to the lips and tormenteth the belly like a river of fire.

'And what is the name of this branch of Sin that beareth this terrible fruit, you ask, and how shall we know her? Know her you needs must so that you may shun her, but keep yourselves from her company. Be watchful. Alas, would that you sweet virgins needed not to know of this branch, but how may you guard against her deadly fruits if you know them not?

'This branch is called Lust, my dear Sisters, and upon this branch of the Tree of Sin there liveth a foul serpent, terrible to behold, that twisteth its long neck around the branch like a thick rope, hanging down in great rings to ensnare all those that pass by.

'And even as the other branches on this Tree, the branch that is called Lust hath seven fruits. The first fruit is the lust of a man for a woman that is not his wife under God's law, the second is the lust of a man and his wife that join in lechery for their own desires and not for the lawful engendering of children, the third is the lust of a man for another man's wife, the fourth is the lust of a man for his wife's own sister, and the fifth is the lust of a man for his wife when she bleeds from her womb, for this is uncleanness and no children shall come of this joining.

'But the sixth and seventh fruits, oh my sweet and blameless Sisters, of those fruits I shall not speak at all. For I would shield your innocent ears from their names, lest your ears become the Devil's paths to let in corruption. So I pray you, as you love God and fear the Devil, think not upon these last two fruits, for women living together in holy retirement are their dearest prey. The serpent liketh most to bury her teeth into bodies that are white and pure. So beware those fruits of which I do not speak, beware the branch on which the foul serpent lingereth, beware this deadly Tree of Sins.'

'Mmmm, sounds interesting,' whispers Bloduedd to Mhairi. 'Especially the last bit.'

'Spit in his soup,' says Sister Serena. 'I'm sick of him telling us what to do.'

'It's not the telling I mind, it's the asking. Hanging around, poking his nose into everything, wanting to hear everyone's confessions.'

'Reverend Mother told him that none of us have anything of

114

interest to confess. He told Reverend Mother that she was guilty of pride and blasphemy and disobedience. So she decided to shut him up, and sent Sister Mhairi to make a general confession on behalf of everybody.'

'And what did Mhairi tell him?'

'Oh, you know Mhairi. She said that angels in white gowns slid down on moonbeams and shared our beds at night. And that we're all pregnant with little Holy Ghosts. And that all the snakes that Padraig charmed out of Ireland came swimming over here, and we use them as bellropes in the chapel. And that when the Pope farts in Rome, the monks can smell it on Iona.'

'And what did he say to all that?'

'He told Reverend Mother that Mhairi was a madwoman, and ought to be whipped, thrown into a stone cell, and fed on bread and water.'

'And what did Reverend Mother say to that?'

'Reverend Mother told him that Mhairi was a little saint. And very gifted. All the more reason to wall her up, he said. Every convent needs an anchoress. So he's sent some masons to build a cell, and he's coming over again to supervise the walling-up himself.'

'Reverend Mother wouldn't stand for that.'

'She didn't. She told him he had 'til the next high tide to get off this island, and not to come back ever, nor his holy Brothers neither. She said we'd make our own arrangements with God in future.'

'And what did he say to that?'

'He said that this chapter wasn't ended yet, and when it was, he'd be the one to put the tailpiece on it.'

'So where is he now?'

'In the guest-house, demanding supper before he leaves.'

'Well, then, spit in his soup, I said.'

'But I've already sneezed in his porridge.'

On that night in the year when the light never quite disappears, the Sisters read to each other from the *Book of Bride*. They fill their cups with mead, fermented from their own bees' honey, and listen closely. The story never seems very long, but when it is done, they are inevitably surprised by the warm glow of morning.

The Book offers partial explanations for certain things: their Holy Fire, their special responsibilities, the practices that make the priests of Iona so uneasy. But every year, the words change slightly. Even if the same readers, in the same sequence, take the same passages, year after year, it happens. In the lifetime of an elderly nun, from her novice year to her final solstice, it is likely that certain episodes will alter just enough to skew their meaning; others will disappear from the text altogether.

This is why Bloduedd works so frantically in her scriptorium, and trains up Mhairi to equal or surpass her, to fix the story for all time. But even the written and decorated copies of the Book develop their quirks and differences. Sometimes the words are at war with the pictures, sometimes new marginalia appear, and others vanish. There are, however, certain immutables: the fruit-bearing tree, the linked spirals, the gaily-striped snake nibbling its own tail always make their appearance, and the sow with seven piglets is rarely far away.

And this is, roughly, how it goes:

Good news, as in all Gospels, travels fast. But even better news may not travel at all. Especially if, at the time, no one considers it to be particularly interesting. And in those days, among the Jews and their neighbours, very little fuss was made about girl babies. Selling one, to raise the cash for a boy-child's blankets, was a regrettable necessity, but no sin. And giving one away, although unusual, would excite no reaction save mild surprise that anybody should want one.

So when a nervous Herod, acting on Rome's off-the-record instructions, slaughtered the Jewish innocents, she was well out of the way. And by the time her twin brother was nailed on the cross, as a lesson to all the other local dissidents, she was long forgotten.

Except among those who had taken her in. Or, more precisely, those who worshipped the one who had done so.

Whether the child herself made the long, long journey is unknown, but it is certain that her story did. Over bright, blank deserts and plundered coasts, spinning high above the billowing sails on the sea (a streak of light to the boy on deck, a thin shiver down the spine of the oarsmen), invisible to the jostling tribes on the great, flat plains, leaving few traces anywhere between Bethlehem and Benbecula. One thing is very sure: she did not come back with the crusaders, packed in among their silks and drugs and spices. For she was in the land before they'd ever left it; indeed, she held sway in cold, northern places that were, to most of them, as remote as Jerusalem and more mysterious.

116

While Mhairi and Bloduedd bend over their texts, placing foxes and weasels between the paragraphs, or staking out the margins with interlaced snakes and dragons, other Sisters tend the garden. In separate beds, neat and sensible: camomile, yarrow, comfrey, garlic medicinal as well as for the pot, peas and beans to dry for winter soups, carrots, colewort, cresses, kale, leeks, lettuces, turnips small and great – most nourishing but likely to bring flatulence, although the fennel growing in a nearby bed will drive the wind away. Also parsley, beetroot, borage, bushes of tough northern berries, thyme and juniper.

('Oh, dear,' says Mhairi, back in the scriptorium, 'an accident is about to happen.')

Digging deep, a nun lifts out a hefty shovelful of soil, and feels the earth give way. She pitches forward and disappears.

Peering into the crater, the nuns find Sister Idris bruised and bad-tempered, but otherwise unharmed. A ladder is swiftly lowered, she is helped to the surface and hustled off to her cell. Reverend Mother and a chosen few go down into the pit to investigate, and find themselves in a tunnel, leading to a small chamber shaped like a teardrop. On the hard earth floor, two perfect skeletons lie sleeping. Sister Padraig, expert bonesetter, studies them for a while and says that they were women. In the middle of the chamber, a shallow pit surrounded by smooth stone marks a fire's place.

Padraig, always rash in the search for knowledge, crouches down to touch the ribs of one of the sleepers, which falls away to dust and splinters under her hand. Nearby, her searching candle finds rough pictures scratched upon the wall: a sticklike tree bearing dangling globes of fruit, a striped snake swallowing itself, some spirals interlinked, a sketch of a snouted beast suckling seven smaller ones.

'We're not the first to have our house here,' says Reverend Mother. 'It says in the Annals of our Order that this place was chosen for a reason. Most annoyingly, the chronicler never thought to mention what it was.'

Remembering their manners, the Sisters cross themselves and whisper a prayer for the dead.

'It was definitely a flying dragon,' insists Mhairi. 'Screaming as it crossed the sky. It was breathing smoke. It had winking red eyes. Are you absolutely sure you didn't see it too?'

'Mhairi, I have been sitting here beside you for half the morning. It was warm in the sun, thanks be to Bride in her benevolence, and you fell fast asleep. You were dreaming.'

'I've been mending my torn underskirt. Look. I only started when we sat down here, and now I'm nearly finished. I couldn't have done that in my sleep, could I? Why don't you believe me? Just for once . . .'

'Because I know you too well, Sister. Last time it was a band of soldiers, marching out of the mouth of a sea-serpent risen from the waves. The time before that it was a picture, big as an altarpiece, that could move and sing and talk. Before that it was a ship as big as three churches set end to end.'

'I suppose you think I'm moonstruck mad.'

'Nonsense. I think you work far too hard in the scriptorium. And when you go to sleep, you continue making pictures in your dreams. Especially when you've been lying in the warm summer sun, looking at shapes in the clouds.'

'I was wide awake. And as to all those other things, I saw them with my eyes wide open. Sitting bolt upright, in the refectory, or in chapel, or in the scriptorium, and I still saw what I saw. Dispute that.'

Bloduedd shakes her head. 'There's no persuading you. Perhaps the Saint has chosen you to receive visions. Personally, I don't think you're anything like holy enough for that. Not yet, anyway. Far too greedy at supper, for one thing. But, I'll tell you what. The next time you are granted one of these visitations, why don't you copy down what you see, as carefully as you can. If it's a pretty picture, we'll put it into the marginalia. Chapter VII is looking rather blank, and I've run out of divine inspiration altogether. Will that satisfy you?'

'I suppose so. But I only see them fleetingly. And maybe now that we've talked about it, the magic is off, and I'll never see anything again. Still, if I do see anything strange, I'll try to make a faithful copy. And perhaps then you'll believe me.'

'There go the bells. We'd better hurry back. And if anyone asks where we've been all this time, you must say we were out looking for a special berry to make the crimson hindquarters of the Devil.'

In that oversize organisation, prayer and redemption may be the principal products, but gossip and politics are the *modus operandi*. Though information, goodness knows, is hard to come by, even for those whose business it is to gather it.

118

With dangerous seas, eight months a year of stormy weather, and a thousand tiny islands with unpronounceable names, surveillance is a little difficult. Even an accurate headcount of monks, lay-brothers, friars, anchorites, sisters active and sisters contemplative, is beyond the capacity of any clerk. Just as soon as someone completes a detailed census of the religious houses, word comes – in a roundabout way – that the Brothers of the Blessed Bloodstain have split over a dispute on the acceptability of laughter during Lent, and half the monks have paddled off in coracles taking all the Holy Books and the communion wine. Or a ragged nun will appear, exhausted, at some distant Motherhouse, and relate a tale of debauchery at some outpost of the Order, concerning the abbess's unholy liaison with a local warlord, the weaving of sinister plots, and the unexplained disappearance of dissidents.

If statistics suffer in such a climate, scandal flourishes. Even the simplest thread of a mildly interesting rumour can be twisted and knotted by time and distance into an intricate tapestry of heresy and riot. An anchorite who fasts for a month on Mingulay will, by the time the tale reaches Iona, have lived for fifty years on nothing but cobwebs. An Orkney nunnery, successful once in calming a storm by dint of prayer, will be reported, in Benbecula, to be a miracle-factory, devoted to the salvation of Christians in peril at sea. And some months later, in Lindisfarne, the same northern ladies will be translated into a band of succubi, disguised as holy sisters, who conjure up evil winds and lure Christian travellers to their doom in the far north, at the point where the five tides meet.

The first plate. The Virgin, belly like a great golden pear, squats on the birth-stool. Interested cherubim peer over the top of the rounded arches, while Joseph stands apart and averts his eyes. An old woman in a purple cloak kneels before Mary, reaching out to catch a child whose head has just emerged.

The second plate. The virgin holds her swaddled baby, the edge of its tiny halo resting on her shoulder. Magi, all gorgeously turbanned, their faces midnight-black, present coffers of spices. A cluster of common people looks on at the scene, pointing upwards and exclaiming, from the very bottom of the frame. In the left-hand corner, the purple-cloaked woman from the first plate is seen passing through a low doorway, carrying a second well-wrapped infant in her arms.

The third plate. Still carrying the bundled child, the old woman rides through a cloudy sky on the back of a giant seagull.

The fourth plate. A small girl picks wildflowers inside a circle of tall, jagged stones. She is barefoot, raggedly dressed, but crowned by an ornate silver and gold halo, jewel-encrusted. The old woman, still wrapped in purple, looks on, standing on a flat-topped stone table that might be a primitive shelter, or an altar.

The fifth plate. Bare-legged soldiers, brandishing swords, clamber up a cliff. A ship, crammed full of more soldiers, whose heads are larger than the ship itself, bobs in the sea below.

The sixth plate. Two soldiers menace the old woman with swords and cudgels. Behind her, the small haloed child cowers. The woman stands with her arms spread wide, blocking the attackers.

The seventh plate. A diptych. On the left, the old woman casts her purple cloak over the child with one hand, and with the other brandishes a flaming torch that keeps the soldiers at bay. On the right, the purple cloak lies flat on the ground. The soldiers have dropped their weapons and are fleeing back to their ship. Their comrades, panic-stricken, leap out of the ship and dive headlong into the waves. Meanwhile the old woman points skywards, towards a soaring white bird, still crowned with the jewelled halo.

'Very pretty,' says the Bishop. 'Excellent use of colour. But a total heresy, of course. You'd better burn it. And the makers as well.'

'The Abbess won't name names. Says that it is merely a copy of a copy of an original long lost.'

'I'm a little tired of that house, you know. They're a greater thorn in my flesh than the Norsemen.'

'Shut them down?'

'I can't. They represent the westernmost reach of Holy Church. The last rampart. Beyond them it's only sea-monsters. If we close Saint Bride's, the entire Christian world contracts. We can't afford that.'

'Find a replacement for the Abbess. Someone more . . . tractable?'

'No volunteers.'

'Whatever happened to the spirit of Saints Patrick, Moluag and Columba? Where's our muscle? Where's our zeal to keep the Church pure and unblemished? Where's the fire in our belly? What about removing the Sisters and putting in some Brothers instead? Not nearly so rebellious.'

'Again, no volunteers. They won't go that far, even the fanatics.'

'Well, you're going to have to do something.'

'I'm sending out an order. They'll have to put their Fire out.'

'Well, that's one way to solve your problem. They'll all freeze to death.'

'Not their hearth-fire, Brother. Their Fire of Saint Bride.'

'Oh yes, of course. I'd forgotten. Their quaint little sacred flame. Old pagan relic. Can't understand why they were allowed to keep it to begin with. Still, ours not to question the early Fathers. I suppose they had their reasons. But surely none of the Sisters takes the thing seriously any more. It's all just sentiment and a bit of folklore to them. Isn't it?'

'I wouldn't venture to presume anything about those she-devils. However, the order will make them sit up and take notice. Show them who's boss. Bring the wenches to heel. They'll have to decide, are they Christian nuns or are they pagan priestesses. Whores of Babylon . . .'

'That's it. You tell them.'

'Well, actually, no. You're going to tell them. I'm sending you as my Special Envoy. With a big jar of holy water to quench the damned thing. That should be a nice touch.'

'Are you sure I'm the right man for the job, Your Grace? I'm only a humble scholar, a drudge, a . . .'

'Where's your muscle? Where's your zeal? Where's the fire in your belly?'

'As you will. But pray for me.'

'Did I hear you correctly? Put out the Fire? Bride's Fire? I hope you are gibbering mad, Brother, for if you're speaking in earnest I will have no choice but to slaughter you like a lamb and throw you into it to placate Bride. Cutting your tool off first, of course. We can't have the flame polluted.'

He was speaking in earnest. She did what she said she'd do. The laws of the Saint were strict on the subject. The tool, well-wrapped and preserved in drugs and spices, was sent back to the Bishop in the care of a friendly fishing-boat.

'Perpetua,' says the Bishop, rubbing his bare thigh against hers, 'how would you like to be an abbess?'

121

Her interview with the incumbent Reverend Mother goes badly.

'That's ridiculous. What do they mean by "transferred"? Transferring me where, I'd like to know. To scrub floors in the Bishop's palace? I've been in this Order since the beginning. I have been in this house, on this island, since I first took my vows. I helped place the stones on the new west wall myself. I heal the sick, feed the poor in time of famine, give shelter to fugitive virgins, keep the sacred Fire going. I have work still to do. I bring pagans into the fold, I can dispute theology with priests, and win the argument. When it comes time to choose a successor, I shall choose her myself – for if I do not, she will gain no respect or obedience from the Sisters of this house. I will brook no interference from Iona or anywhere else in the Church. No self-promoted clerk hiding behind fortifications and licking the backside of any kinglet who throws a few coins his way, will have the gall to tell me when to leave here.'

Perpetua, despite her holy vows to higher powers, is a woman of fierce loyalties to her earthly friends. She doesn't like to hear her lovers insulted, and she is angry about the slaughter of the Bishop's last emissary – he happened to be her favourite cousin, who first brought her to the notice of His Grace. Family feeling runs high in these islands. So she blinks back a few tears, grabs Reverend Mother by her awe-inspiring headdress, pulls her head back and pours a phial of poison down her throat. The death is neat and quick – Perpetua is a woman of delicate sensibilities; she loves nothing so much as puppies, snowflakes, and the prospect of having her own little religious community to re-organise and rule.

A howling and keening fills the sky, freezing her blood, until she realises it is the sound of a flock of seabirds swooping low over the convent, disputing some point of avian theology as they fly south. She recomposes her features into an expression compounded of sorrow, shock and pious resignation, suitable for one who is compelled to bring bad news to strangers. She rehearses the phrases of condolence she will soon murmur to the sisterhood, who are now sleeping peacefully.

Mhairi wakes up screaming. Bloduedd is shaking her gently.

'Hush, you'll have the whole house up. What is it?'

Another bad dream. She can't describe it. More a feeling than a clear picture or a story. She feels ashamed, as if she's seen something she shouldn't have. Now she's awake, but feels that the dream hasn't quite ended.

She stands up, shivering, and goes over to the narrow slit of window. 'Before that moon sets, something terrible is going to happen.'

'You've had the Night Mare pressing down on your chest, that's all. Drink some water. There – another sip. Now say a little something to the Saint and go back to sleep. We have to be up soon enough anyway.'

Mhairi's right, though. They have just settled down again, curled warmly together, when there are lights, running feet, shouts in the cloister.

'Get up, get up. Everyone. Now. Reverend Mother is dead.'

'I told you,' whispers Mhairi, slipping on her sandals and tapping away at the ice in the basin so she can wash her burning eyes.

Suspicion runs high, especially in the scriptorium, where Mhairi and Bloduedd whisper speculations as they prepare their vellum to receive the text. But nothing certain will be known conclusively for nearly a thousand years, until Dr Stephanie Stonebridge of the Edinburgh University Archaeology Department finds something unusual among the remains exhumed from the Cailleach excavation.

Meanwhile, there are going to be a few changes around here.

'What? What? WHAT?'

On a rapid-fire inspection tour, the new Abbess – hastily installed on the day of the funeral by the Bishop's personal chaplain – doesn't like what she finds. Anywhere, but especially in the scriptorium. Oh, they meet their quotas all right, copying as many as five texts per year. But the output, instead of Matthew, Mark, Luke and John, is overwhelmingly dominated by a Life of their own saint, Bride, a figure of dubious legitimacy according to current ecclesiastical views.

Perpetua can't help but admire the illustrations; they are, indeed, brilliant, and her only comment, under her breath, anticipates someone's remark (some time later) that the Devil has all the best tunes. The text, however, upon which she is best qualified to comment, being a great user of words herself, upsets her considerably.

'What is this claptrap? What are your sources? And why all this "I" and "Me" – that's incorrect style unless you are quoting Our Lord

Himself. And why does so little of it have to do with the story of Jesus? And this, this travesty – is disgusting. All this heretical nonsense about a twin sister! Blasphemy. Makes me sick. And it's going to make the Bishop and the good Fathers even sicker! These books should all be burned – and their perpetrators with them!'

But, in a stunning display of the new management policy, she does nothing about it. Not until letters have passed, across stormy seas, between herself and the Bishop, and directions are issued from On High. Yet it all takes time, and until they are forced to desist, Mhairi and Bloduedd go on with their work.

So many young women, up and down the coast and all around the islands, have opted for God as a spouse, in preference to their parents' selections, that the whole of the West is peppered with nunneries. Orders sprout everywhere, catering to every spiritual quirk and quibble: the Sisters of the Lamb, the Sisters of the Word, the Sisters of the Sea-borne Virgin, the Sisters of the White Dove, the Sisters of Kindness, the Maidens of Saint Moluag's Chair, the Sisters of the Moon, the Ladies of the Gospels, the Sisters of the White Serpent, the Sisters, respectively, of the Stone, the Cup and the Thornless Rose, the Holy Handmaidens, the Anchoresses of the Blue Sky, the Little Shepherdesses of the Strayed Flocks, the Mothers of the Purification, the Daughters of Eternity, and the Brides of Heaven. Each has its elaborate, often terrifying rules, its patron saint or legendary founder. Some orders number one hundred members, others have less than five.

To be fair, the houses are not merely bolt-holes for reluctant brides. They have work to do in the world, and do it well. Their members like hard tasks, grim challenges, and goodness for its own sake, and they enjoy being the guardians of an ever-expanding set of mysteries.

Some convents co-exist within a few sea-miles, peacefully indifferent to each other. A few engage in long and furious rivalries, theological debates, the hot competition for well-dowered recruits. Occasional slanders, of buried babies or stolen chalices, cross the water. A few Orders flourish for generations; some die out when their founder-members do. Sisters usually sign themselves on for life, but it is not unknown for a nun, after personal frictions or a spiritual change-of-heart, to pack up her few belongings and move from one Order to another.

Perpetua, for instance, began in the dark blue robes of the Brides

124

of Heaven, decided to change them for the dun-coloured apron (but cosier quarters) of the Little Shepherdesses, tired of this dreary habit and progressed, as soon as expedient, to the splendid purple vestments of the Sisters of Kindness. From here she was by special order seconded (some say evicted) to serve as housekeeper to the most powerful Abbot in the Isles, then to the Bishop himself. She saw the command of the House of Bride as a sensible and challenging next step.

Mhairi, ladling out bean soup in the refectory, hears this from her older Sisters, whispering together before the mid-day reading starts.

'What can the Bishop be thinking of?'

'I hear her last Order but one collapsed within a year of her arrival.'

'Could be a coincidence. Well, couldn't it?'

'Probably not.'

Wanting more snippets of gossip to report back to Bloduedd (who is missing the meal as a penance for spilling some ink), Mhairi is disappointed when the hall falls silent. Perpetua has appeared at the lectern.

'In a moment Sister Caitlin will read to us from Saint Elliptica's Third Discourse on Obedience. But first I shall make a few announcements.'

The hall rumbles, long and low, like a hungry giant's stomach.

'Change number one. Cell assignments. There are far too many particular friendships. The new sleeping arrangements will be announced after Vespers.'

The rumble stops, abruptly, then resumes and grows louder.

'Silence! Item two. There is a severe shortage of vestments for the priests on the mainland. To meet this need, the scriptorium Sisters will be redeployed to the sewing brigade, where their artistic talents will be more suitably employed. We will henceforth leave the making of illuminated books to our Brothers in the monasteries of North Uist and Iona, who are, after all, far better qualified for such labours.'

'That's not true!' Mhairi is surprised to hear her own outraged cry above the roomful of mutinous murmurings.

'And, finally, an edict from His Grace. All trees, stones, and fires, formerly the objects of pagan worship, are now decreed to be anathema. In the case of this establishment, this means that the so-called Sacred Fire of Bride is now irrelevant and obsolete. I am pleased to announce that the Bishop himself will shortly visit us, bringing a vessel of Holy Water, and will extinguish the flames with his own hands.'

Pandemonium breaks loose. Quite literally. A fierce gale blows in, carried by a squadron of demons from the bowels of Hell in the cold heart of Mount Hekla, and blows the roof off the refectory in a single screaming gust.

Like a cloud crossing the sun, Perpetua glides into the high-windowed scriptorium.

'A message from Holy Father.'

She is annoyed because Mhairi and Bloduedd neither look up, nor rise reverently. She pauses, considers her tactics.

'Well, at least you're following orders and sewing vestments. Nice stitches, those. I thought you two would be good at it. Don't think I don't appreciate your talents, because I do. It's just that needlework is so desperately important to the Church, much more so than books, I think. Don't you agree? After all, books are for the few, but the masses and the chapels and the priests are for everyone. Think of all those thousands of believers who can't read a word, but whose dear, good souls are uplifted by the sight of a Father in his finely-worked chasuble. After all, any old monk can make a gospel, but men are so hamfisted, aren't they, when it comes to sewing. Oh, they can make a sail all right, or stitch a wound coarsely in the midst of battle, but be honest now, ladies, it is a woman's art.'

They are not placated. Mhairi says nothing, bites off a loose end of thread with a savage snap.

Perpetua persists.

'I thought perhaps you'd like to make some new altar cloths for our own little chapel. I'd leave the decoration entirely up to you. A completely free hand – once I've seen your sketches, of course. Wouldn't it be splendid if we had them ready for the Bishop's visit? I know that's asking a lot in a short time, but if we enlist the help of all the Sisters, and work out new rotas covering night and day, I have every confidence that we can . . .'

'Not enough pins,' growls Bloduedd.

'Since when? I've been through the convent inventories. We should have plenty.'

'They've disappeared.' And I'm not going to tell you, she thinks to herself, that half the beds in the place have little wax Perpetua-

126

dolls tucked under the pillows, all spiked with stolen pins in painful places.

'And where have they disappeared to? Whatever your other faults, the House of Bride is not a wasteful community. Pins are precious. You wouldn't just lose track of them.'

'Island people borrow them sometimes. They usually return them.'

'Well, that's going to stop. We're not pedlars here, supplying the local housewives with their sewing goods.'

'Not for sewing. For protection. Metal to ward off evil.'

'That's heathen nonsense!'

'Used to be they thought our house was protection enough. Not now, though.'

Perpetua paces. Decides not to ask. Presumes the reason for the Bishop's impending visit, and the imminent dowsing of the Fire, are public knowledge. Rumours travel in and out with the creels of fish and the sacks of flour, coming, and the healing herbs and nuns to use them, going abroad at all hours of the day and night. Far too cosy a relationship with the locals, she thinks, and wonders how long it would take her to impose a rule of eighteen-hour silence and turn the place into an Enclosed Order.

'Ridiculous. If this Order did its work properly you wouldn't have these superstitions any more. But never mind that now. You've made me forget what I was going to say. Oh yes, the message from His Grace. About your . . . text. The *Book of Bride*. How many copies are there?'

'Why?'

'It's not your place to ask why, Sister. It's your place to answer my question.'

'Fewer than there used to be. A confessor came and took one away for the Bishop to read. He never returned it. He sent us you instead.'

'Bloduedd, you are insolent. And setting a disgraceful example for a younger Sister.'

'Mhairi? She's disgraceful enough in her own right, Reverend Mother.'

Mhairi suppresses a giggle, pricks herself with her needle, sees the bloodspot on the vestment and curses quietly.

'We have been ordered to collect up all existing copies of the Book, and burn them. They are no longer part of the Received Wisdom. Where are they?'

'Surely you're not stupid enough to think I'd tell you, Perpetua.'

'Surely you're not stupid enough to think I won't find out.'

A silence, broken only by Mhairi sucking at her pierced finger.

Bloduedd flicks a sideways glance at a workbench at the far end of the room, piled high with loose sheets, rolls of calfskin, miscellaneous bundles and pots of ink and dye. The bench stands in front of a low door, set into a deep recess in the stone wall.

Perpetua follows Bloduedd's gaze and sets off grimly, long sleeves flapping. She rummages roughly through the clutter, knocking most of it to the floor. An inkpot bounces off her foot and splatters its contents. She wrenches the bench itself away from the doorway, and tugs hard at the cast-iron handle.

'Key!' she spits out.

Bloduedd tosses it. It falls far short. Perpetua swoops on it, spins on her heel, rattles it into the lock and pulls the door wide.

She thrusts her head through the opening. The cupboard is empty. Except for three irate bats, who swiftly fly out and entangle themselves in Perpetua's voluminous veil.

'You look like an unbreached barrel of mead.'

'Fine thing for you to say, after all these years. Just thank your Saint you've never had to suffer it.'

'You sound bitter.'

'It's not fun. Not like singing hymns and tending a garden and making pretty things and all the other delicate little pastimes you Sisters enjoy up there.'

'Oh, it's not all milk and honey, I promise you. Imagine getting shaken awake two hours after you've fallen asleep to file into a cold chapel for another round of prayers. Imagine having to offer up the juiciest bits of the mutton as a Mortification and swallow the lumps of fat and gristle instead. Imagine never but never being allowed to sit by yourself with your hands lying idle in your lap. Imagine the bossing and the backbiting.'

'Still, I'd change places. Would you?'

'Not really.'

'That's why I'm bitter. If you hadn't been so clever and wriggled out of it, Father would have married you to old Shittybreeks, not me.'

'I'm sorry. Is it awful?'

'Could be worse, I suppose. I'm now a woman of wealth and position. And a mother of three.'

'That was quick.'

'I suppose time runs fast when you're enjoying yourself. Why haven't you been to see me before?'

'Our Rule says we can't go more than an hour's walk from the Sacred Fire. Except for the nursing sisters, of course. And you're a sight farther than that, down here.'

'Well, then, what are you doing here now?'

'Breaking all the rules. If anybody finds out I'll be on bread-and-water for weeks.'

'No fear. I won't tell, and the old hog's away somewhere raping and pillaging. But why have you come? Not just a little family reunion, is it?'

'I want you to do me a favour.'

'Why should I? You've hardly done me one.'

'What about those kittens I saved from drowning?'

'That was fifteen years ago.'

'Well, for the sake of our blood-bond, then.'

'I didn't choose you for my sister, not the way you lot all chose each other, up at the Bride-house. But I do think of you, every so often. And not always unkindly.'

'Thanks. I've said a lot of prayers on your behalf to the Saint, you know. She's particularly good at childbirth.'

'Well, maybe that's been a help. The old swine does beget big babies. Still, I've been a lot luckier than his first wife. She . . .'

'I've heard the story.'

'Well, what can I do for you?'

'Keep this for me. Hide it somewhere safe.'

'What is it?'

'A holy book. Don't be afraid, you can touch it. It won't burn your fingers. Have a look at it. Just handle it carefully. Read it whenever you like.'

'Read it?'

'Sorry. I forgot. Well, look at the pictures, then. They're rather good, if I do say so myself.'

'Did you make them?'

'Some of them.'

'Which ones?'

'I don't have time now. I have to go back. It's a long journey. And I have to be back before the dawn breaks.'

'Will you come back for it?'

'I don't know. That's not what's important. Just keep it very,

very secret. And keep it safe. And if I don't come back for it, and time goes on, and that bump in your belly proves to be a daughter, ask her to do the same. And for Bride's sake, don't ever tell anyone. Especially not your husband.'

'No fear of that. We hardly speak.'

'I'll ask the Saint to make your time easy.'

'Will she listen?'

'I think she will. She owes me a favour, now.'

The Bishop is due any day, depending on the seasonal storms, and the tides.

In preparation, Perpetua identifies those Sisters likely to be most pliable, and keeps them in thrall by knowing their weak points, and playing them like fish. The hungry ones are tantalised and rewarded by extra rations, the homesick ones offered snippets of news from their families, the ambitious ones put in positions of apparent trust and power. The others are kept in line by veiled threats.

She has succeeded in gathering up several copies of the Book – those that have previously been sent to other communities will by now have been destroyed, by order. But she is not convinced that she has found all of them. Neither Mhairi or Bloduedd have responded to threats, or to any form of torment (those at her disposal are fairly ineffectual, this particular community never having had any enthusiasm for hair shirts or flagellation). Perpetua is niggled by the memory of a half-finished copy that she remembers seeing in the scriptorium on her very first tour of inspection; however, a thorough search of the library, the cells and the chapel have revealed no sign of it, although several other fairly distressing or disgusting bits of heresy have been discovered in the process.

Mhairi is a particular irritant; Perpetua knows a subversive when she sees one. She feels the younger nun is probably a more dangerous influence than Bloduedd. The old scriptorium Sister has grown perceptibly weaker since Perpetua put her on a bread-and-water regime in hopes of breaking her will.

But the new Abbess is taking no chances. She wants the house in perfect moral and spiritual order when the Bishop arrives. So she confines Mhairi to the earth-cell underneath the kitchen garden, ostensibly as an act of penance for the infringement of some newly-invented convent rule. Without wishing to influence the

130

judgment of her betters, Perpetua hopes that the Bishop will decide to drown Mhairi along with the wretched Sacred Fire, or consign her to the flames, along with her blasted Book.

Down in the dark hole, Mhairi is hungry, but not cold. The loose sheets of the Book, which she had providentially sewn into her skirt during Perpetua's search of the convent, keep her suprisingly warm; their colours glow like invisible coals. For the first few hours – or days, perhaps, for she soon loses all sense of time – she does little more than crouch in a corner, locked in a trance. Then she forces herself to pace about the little chamber. She can barely stand up straight, and the top of her head sometimes grazes the ceiling, which is a great, flat slab of rock, held up by six upright stones. The walls are hard-packed earth. With her fingers, she traces the scratch marks that she can't see in the dark – the linked spirals, the snake swallowing itself, the sow and her piglets. At the far end of the chamber – not very far, when the whole of Mhairi's world can be traversed in ten long strides – there is a little chink of light. The trapdoor fits imperfectly.

Once in a while, someone whispers her name through the crack, and lifts the wooden lid just enough to lower a loaf of bread or a little flask of ale on a rope. But then she hears far-away sounds that disturb and puzzle her – faint screams, roars, splintering wood, clanging metal. After that, no one calls to her again.

It seems to her that the Bishop is a long time coming. To pass the time, she studies the scenes and pictures that appear before her eyes. She dreams that she has created a whole new chapter for Bride's Book.

Perhaps the Bishop has been lost in a storm in the Minch. If so, the Fire will have to stay alight for ever. With this cheerful thought, she falls asleep.

In other places, in the Burning Times, they went for crones who made cows go dry. Or madwomen who bragged about copulation with the Devil. Or the local abortionist, who knew too many little secrets for her own good – and anyone else's. But in Cailleach, the purge had a different purpose: get rid of the Fire-women. Thrawn and threatening, these harpies were said to hold on to a heresy about Saint Bride and the Stepdaughter, garbled in form and difficult to explain. Not everyone on the island was party to the cult; it was passed on, mother to daughter, in a few families only. And displayed no easily recognisable signs and symptoms: no cavorting naked at midnight sabbaths, no flights up chimneys, no shape-shifting into white dogs or black cats. The sect had no known gathering-places, not even the accursed stone circle, which everyone avoided by order of the kirk.

The persecutors had little to go on, except for rumours: something about a bannock baked with menstrual blood, a whispered blasphemy about Christ's nativity, a tenacious affection for that old papistical Saint Bride (still called upon by Cailleach women in the pains of childbirth, no matter what the elders said about it).

No one was quite sure why they were called the Fire-women. Some opined it was because they knew that hellfire awaited them, others maintained it was because they stared and muttered into their own kitchen-fires. As if every housewife didn't, when her troubles overwhelmed her. Still, the men of Cailleach didn't like to think of their hearths being put to uncanny uses. Imagine the pile of glowing peats, over which your porridge bubbles, transformed behind your back into the blazing heart of something old and evil. It would turn the very broth to poison in the pot. A fine way to tame, enslave, or even kill a husband.

Inspired by such nervous speculations, the men of the place grew ever more vigilant, and zealously dispatched any suspected woman to the boot, the rope and the stake at Inverness.

Thus, the menace of the Fire-women was eradicated. By the time Scotland sold herself to England, the name of the cult was but a trick to scare children, in the catalogue of bedtime threats along with beltings, bogles, or a visit from the minister. 'The Fire-women will come and take you!' But, in time, parents grew kinder, and within a few generations the very name was totally forgotten.

THREE
Maria and Catriona

A storm slams in from the place where the old map-makers put their sea-monsters. Of the twenty-six distinct and specific terms in the old Cailleach dialect describing rain, this is the sort that the islanders call – loosely translated – the whips of Saint Columba. It batters the roof, slaps at the windows, scourges the outside walls, helped by a vengeful Arctic wind. And it goes on for a long, long time.

I want my nights back, says Maria to herself. Except for the demons that haunt her – spiky little memories of mistakes and mortifications that go back years and years – she is lonely. The radio, her constant companion, has let her down: the static has eaten the airwaves, the fishing-boats are silent; any vessel caught out in this thing is either blown half-way to the Dogger Bank or broken up and on the bottom.

But if she stays indoors any longer she will explode, so she buries herself in oilskins and big boots, and battles the wind for control of the door. In a lull, she succeeds in forcing it shut, and goes out to exorcise ghosts of old miseries, snarling devils grown from seeds that Catriona planted, mistimed memories of the good things between them that she'd sooner write out of the history altogether to make the end of it easier. The wind levitates her, skims her along the dark shore.

She lets herself be blown back and forth for an hour or so. She can see nothing – even the stars have been erased. Somewhere on the far side of the sand dunes she can hear some sheep bleating complaints to each other as they huddle in some sheltered place. Finally, she decides she has had enough. She is scoured clean as a pebble, washed by the tide, but she is sodden. Suddenly grounded, she is irritated to find that a rapid movement sends a little flood of rainwater cascading down her sleeve and into her armpit. A romantic demise from a chill is unlikely, but she'd rather not have Catriona paying housecalls and looking smug. Heaven knows what old witch-philtre she'd sneak into the antibiotics.

'Right,' she screams to the sky, 'I've done it. I can take anything you care to dish out. Screw your storms and your nightmares, I'm going home.'

Which is now the cottage, brightly lit and comforting, on its little knoll above the beach.

'Home sweet home.' She likes the thought of it. 'Well, sort of.' Pushes the thorny practicalities away as she pushes open the door. For she sees she's not alone.

Someone has kept the fire going in her absence. Someone crouches there now, feeding in peats.

'Catriona?'

Who else? But not quite. The huddled figure, startled, springs to her feet and turns around. It's the seaweed-woman.

One sharp, startled gasp does for the pair of them. Maria, even through her white-hot panic, sees she's not the only frightened one. Maria's visitor is as waterlogged as she is, and her sodden, shapeless clothes steam slightly from the fire's warmth. Both of them are shivering.

There should be no cause for alarm. A woman, chilled and soaked by the storm, seeks shelter in the nearest house. Maria, had she been at home to the tentative knock on the door, would never have questioned it. Such matters of life and death are the basis for Highland hospitality. But even so, she might have banged the door shut at the first glimpse of what was out there. Because the seaweed-woman's face is identical to her own.

Maria hopes that if she pretends everything's ordinary, it soon will be, and begins to talk herself down from her terror.

'Bloody awful out there, isn't it? And this place is supposed to be warmed by the Gulf Stream. I know there's someone down on the southern tip who claims to have a palm tree in their garden, but really . . . I've seen you before, you know. Gathering seaweed. Is it for the processing plant? I'll make us both a cup of tea in a minute, but perhaps you could move over and give me a bit of my own fire?' She is surprised by the rattling staccato of her own voice, gives up, and walks towards the fire. The stranger, wary, backs away, and for a moment the two women slowly spiral round each other, silently staring.

Maria reaches out, touches the woman's arm, surprised that her

136

own hand doesn't pass straight through it. But the flesh is as clammy and goose-bumped as Maria's own. The woman glances at the place Maria's fingers have brushed, as if expecting bruises.

'Well, it is an extraordinary coincidence. Still, maybe not. I do have Celtic blood. Perhaps we're nineteenth cousins, a thousand times removed. But this is silly. If we stand here gaping any longer, we'll both catch pneumonia. Let's have a dram. Then I'll put the kettle on.'

Maria reaches for the whisky bottle on the mantelpiece, opens it, and passes it first to her guest, once again the well-brought up suburban child in plaits and party dress, remembering her manners. 'After you.'

The woman sniffs it, unsure.

'It's very good stuff. The island malt. But, of course, you'll know it well.'

The seaweed-woman still stands, stiffly, clutching the bottle as if she expects it to explode in her hands.

'Or are you tee-total? One of Reverend Murdo's people? Look, I know you don't approve of strong drink, but think of it as medicinal. Keeps the chill off. Surely you won't get sent to Hell for trying to ward off bronchitis . . .'

The woman hands it back to her.

'Look, I'll take some first myself, then you'll see it isn't poisoned. Here, down the hatch!' She swigs it like a sailor on shore leave, then coughs and splutters. The seaweed-woman's mouth twitches at the corners, then she bursts out laughing, and reaches out for the bottle; she takes a delicate, tentative sip.

'That's more like it. Don't follow my example. This is superior stuff, meant to be sipped not swigged according to my former mentor who shall remain for the moment nameless. And, speaking of names, mine's Maria Milleny.'

Her guest smiles politely, says nothing.

'Soaking clothes will do us no good whatsoever. You'd better have a blanket to wrap round you while we let your stuff dry by the fire – and mine too.' Play-acting the bustling, cheery hostess, she rummages in the press and produces two thick folded blankets, woven of the dark-grey island tweed.

'Isa made these. Do you know her?'

The woman brightens at the sight of the herringbone pattern, strokes the grain of it as if greeting an old friend. Then swiftly peels off her clammy clothing – a long dress, a cloak, an underskirt in a

137

rough fabric of a stained and faded once-dark blue. Maria does likewise, but not so frantically that she misses the sight of the seaweed-woman's body, as thin and freckled as her own. The visitor takes her own clothes, and Maria's, and drapes them neatly over the backs of two wooden chairs, drawn close to the fire. Then the two of them sit together between the drying clothes and the fire itself, staring meditatively into the glowing peats.

Time to try again to break the silence. 'Do you live nearby? I've seen you before, you know, on the beach. Gathering seaweed. And once . . .' But stops herself short, decides not to mention the night when she saw the woman floating across the water. Doesn't want even this strangest of strangers to join the local consensus that the Milleny person is a wee bit daft in the head. But the woman is still smiling at her, tentatively, looking as if she'd like to say something.

'I've only been here a few months myself,' Maria continues, 'but I was staying – in the castle. Wore out my welcome, though, but couldn't bring myself to leave the island.' Well, put it that way if you like, Milleny.

Despairing at her own stupidity, the truth dawns. 'You don't understand a word of what I'm saying, do you?'

The woman spreads out her hands, helplessly.

'Well, I knew there was quite a bit of Gaelic still spoken, but I thought everyone knew English, too. I'm surprised the good doctor never mentioned you, or showed you off to me as a tourist attraction. Unless of course you're another one of her guilty little secrets. After all, if I'm her type, so are you.'

The woman replies suddenly, with a stream of incomprehensible words, a soft, lilting gabble.

'Is that the Gaelic? I'm ashamed to say I haven't learned it, although yours doesn't sound like anyone else's I've heard. There's one thing I can say, though,' reaching for the whisky again, '*Slanche va* . . .'

The woman brightens, takes the bottle herself, repeats the same words in a wildly different accent.

'Well, it's just as well I'm not terribly talkative. All this is just nervousness, you know. Anyway, make yourself comfortable.' She points to herself. 'Maria.'

The woman gets the message, taps her own chest, says something that sounds like 'Varri'.

Tired by these efforts, they fall silent again, soaking in the warmth of the whisky and the fire.

138

Maria feels there is something she hasn't done, hears her mother's voice somewhere in the background, and remembers just in time. 'Would you like something to eat?' She mimes, pointing to her mouth, opening wide, taking a huge bite out of an imaginary apple, chewing vigorously, then gulping it down, rubbing her stomach in satisfaction.

The visitor suppresses giggles, then nods enthusiastically. But, before Maria can rise, she scuttles across the floor, on her knees, still wrapped in her blanket. Rummaging among the cast-off clothes, she produces a bulky leather pouch, and digs out a large chunk of coarse grey bread. She breaks it in two, offers half to Maria.

'But I was going to offer *you* something. Not that there's much in the house.'

The woman shakes her head, pulls Maria back to the hearthrug, holds out the bread. Afraid of offending some mysterious code of island hospitality, Maria takes a tentative bite, expecting it to be hard and stale as old bones. Instead, it is sweet and yeasty, tastes as if it were just out of the oven. She chews, watched keenly by her guest, and finds, as she eats, that a faint iodine sharpness, a spicing of seaweed, comes to her tongue. She isn't sure if it comes from the bread, from the leather pouch it was stored in, or from the fingers of the woman herself. It is, at once, tantalising and slightly repellent.

'Would you like some hot tea?' She mimes a drink from a cup.

The woman shakes her head, yawns, looks hopefully across the room towards Maria's bed.

'Well, I suppose you'd better stay the night. The storm's still going strong out there. You were crazy to be out in it, you know. But, then, so was I. I can't think what possessed us.'

She lifts up the blankets, lets her guest slip into bed, then switches out the light and joins her. They lie, for a moment, stiff and separate, until the seaweed woman reaches out and pulls Maria to her. Her lips, fingers, and everything they touch glow in the darkness.

Mirror-images, copper-speckled moonstones, flow together.

In the morning, Maria is not surprised to find herself alone. But she is slightly disappointed to find that neither the bed nor the tweed blankets nor the hearthrug smell of anything but peat-smoke and

139

her own patchouli. She dresses, and goes out to the beach, sparkling after the storm under a blue sky sharp as a knife. The tide is out, and she buries her face in a clump of gleaming blue-black seaweed.

Up on the hill, young Dougie Isbister, looking to his father's sheep, sees Maria down below and wonders what on earth she's doing. 'That woman,' he says to his dog, 'is gey strange. Definitely away with the fairies.'

'Right,' says Maria Milleny. 'It's time to pay the rent.'

She flips out a blade on her Swiss army knife, and cuts through the cords that bind her sketchblocks, canvases, neatly stacked frames and stretchers. Then, once she has turned a corner of her cottage into a working studio, she hikes to the phone box at Graeme Isbister's garage, fishes a hoard of coins out of her pockets, and begins to sort out her messy life. A transfer-charge call to the gallery down in London tells her that they have – at long last – sold two of the *Lives of the Saints*, and now they know where to find her, the cheque is in the post. A brief chat with the woman who drives the Co-op Mobile Shop sorts out her food supplies (in future, she'll pay for her own groceries; they are no longer to be charged to the Doctor's account). And a conversation with Graeme Isbister, while skipping stones into a lochan by the roadside, leads to a new and totally unexpected *modus vivendi*.

She goes home satisfied, then remembers that she has one or two bits of business still to take care of.

'You want some paintings, do you, to hang on the stone staircase at Castle MacEochan? Well, formerly-dearest Catriona, you shall have them.'

Working from memory and a couple of prudently purloined old photographs, she makes some sketches: Catriona smiling, Catriona lustful, Catriona in pensive mood (probably wondering which claret to open), Catriona attempting to commune with the Other Side, playing her planchette like a tiny piano. Once loosened up, Maria gathers her paints and gets down to work. She loses track of time, and can only guess by her rumbling stomach, her cat-naps and her stiff fingers when the fire dies out, how long she is at it. Settings, costumes, colours change, but the subject's face is always the same. Obliging Catriona has stepped up and stuck her face through the appropriate holes in the painted backdrop, the unwitting patsy at a carnival coconut-shy. Maria, candyfloss in one hand, paintbrush in the other, hits the target and wins her prizes. Catriona is transformed first into a muscular Flora MacDonald, booting Bonnie Prince Charlie out of her rowboat; into an old witch dropping snakes and froglets into a bubbling cauldron; into a stone-carved fertility goddess, all mountainous bosom; into an angular, monocled Paris salon dyke eyeing up the talent at a *thé dansant*; into a Roman empress fanned by slave-girls; into Mary Queen of Scots bravely approaching the headsman's block; and – her favourite of all – into a black-caped vampire queen, delicately drinking at the distended throat of a swooning victim, watched by an audience of stuffed birds and faded family portraits.

On a hot, sunny day in late August, Maria is sitting outside her cottage, perched on a flat-topped boulder that, with forethought, rolled down the hill during the last ice age to make her a comfortable seat. She is mildly annoyed, but not particularly surprised, to hear the sound of a land-rover that could only be Catriona's rattling up the track. She has been expecting this visit, knowing how often and when Catriona settles up her grocery bills and other accounts.

'Well, I am surprised,' says Catriona, 'you've put on an ounce or two. I thought you'd be dying of starvation.'

'Why's that?'

'A perceptible reduction on my Co-op bill. Just enough to account for the absence of your usual order of tinned baked beans, processed cheese and other execrable little delicacies.'

'Did you ask the Co-op?'

'Mrs MacFee was very tight-lipped. Besides, she and I are at war over a prescription that I won't renew. The woman doesn't need diet pills, she needs to stop scoffing the sweeties she borrows from her own shop.'

'Well, perhaps she believes in professional discretion. Doesn't go telling people her customers' business. Not like some.'

'Mmmm. Point taken. Never mind, it's not a secret; the entire debate between us was conducted – on her part – at high volume in the post-office queue. But don't deflect me – what are you eating?'

'All the usual execrable delicacies, Catriona. Except I've decided to pay for them myself. Aunt Catriona's Good Samaritan Free Arts Supplies and Grocery Service is about to lose its best customer.'

'What have you done, dear, robbed a bank?'

'I managed before I met you. I'm managing again. In my own sordid, inelegant little way. And your old friend at the gallery's come through; she's sold a couple of my paintings. Seems she dragged a few of them out of storage to fill up some empty wall space in the gallery's summer show. I'm apparently going to hang in an ageing pop star's retreat in Provence . . . at least, two of my *Saints* are.'

'Well, there you are. I always said you had Promise. How much did they go for?'

'I can't see that it's any business of yours.'

'It never ceases to amaze me how people can be so free and easy about sex, and so prudish about money. You won't stoop to tell me how you're managing to keep yourself alive, but you're perfectly uninhibited about what you'll say, and do, when we're in the middle of . . .'

'Catriona . . .'

'Why, don't you remember that night when you wanted to . . .'

'Catriona, would you like to drop the subject, shut your wicked mouth and listen to what I am going to tell you?'

'All right. Just don't pretend it never happened.'

'How could I? My fingerprints are for ever on the tower chandelier.'

'That's what I mean.'

'I'm painting again.'

'Are you? That's fantastic. I knew it was only a matter of time! Where are they? I must see them!' Catriona rushes past Maria, a frenzied wind out of the sea, pushes open the door of the cottage and bursts out laughing.

Maria, reluctantly, trudges up the beach to join her.

Catriona sits on the edge of the box-bed, doubled up, wiping the tears from her cheeks. 'They're perfectly awful,' she gasps, fighting waves of uncontrollable guffaws and hiccups, 'but very funny.'

Maria is disconcerted. 'You mean you're not annoyed?'

'I've always wanted to be the heroine of my own comic strip. Of course I'm not.'

Catriona suddenly straightens up, calms down, catches her breath and looks inquiringly at Maria over the frames of her spectacles. 'Why? Did you want me to be?'

'Well . . . yes, I suppose I did.' Maria looks anywhere that will keep her from meeting Catriona's gaze, busily engages herself in brushing crumbs off the kitchen table.

'What do you call these . . . artefacts?'

'Well, if you must know, the working title is "Up Yours, Catriona".'

'I see.' The gold in her teeth glints as she grins delightedly.

Maria feels mildly piqued. Hands jammed in the pockets of her jeans, she paces glumly.

'Were you hoping to make me angry? Oh, dear, I'm so sorry to disappoint you. I think they're priceless. And speaking of price, how much do you want for them? I'd like the set.'

'They're yours. Rent for the cottage.'

'Don't be silly.'

'You said so yourself, remember? That if I painted anything while I was here, you might accept one as payment.'

'That was if you did any painting.'

'What's this?'

'A comic strip, just as I said. A bit of doggerel. And now that you've poured out all your bile, perhaps we can look forward to some serious work. Now stop glaring at me. You look as if you're about to burst into tears. Pull your socks up, lass. You're well on the way; you've just let yourself get lazy and sloppy.'

'I thought you wanted to be my patron.'

'Well, sometimes the job of a patron is to give you a kick up the backside. And I did offer to pay. I want them for my surgery waiting room. It will make a pleasant change from NHS no-smoking posters and diet charts.' She begins to stack them up, whistling. 'Should give the customers something to take their minds off their aches and pains.'

'Well, accept them with my compliments.' Maria slouches, sulking.

'I said, I'll pay you for them.'

'I'll send the money back, Catriona. I won't be in your debt. And if you won't take it, I'll send the money on to your favourite charity. The Old Necromancers' Home, or the Satanic Liberation Front, or whatever it is you're partial to, these days.'

'Why are you so insistent?'

'I told you, they're my rent. And I shall continue to pay it – but the rest will be in cash. I don't want to be kept by you any more . . . not as your lover-of-the-moment, as was, and not as your penniless but artistic tenant. I'd like to put things on a strictly business footing.'

'How unsentimental.'

'Maybe so. But I want my soul back.'

'Oh, that's quite impossible, dear. I lost it in a dice-game with Beelzebub. So sorry.'

Briskly, Catriona carries her booty to the land-rover. Maria, in a temper, leaves her to it, running full tilt up the hill behind the cottage. When she reaches the top she watches the land-rover lurching along the track far below. She wishes there were a large boulder handy, that could be thrown down, with flawless aim, to stop Catriona dead. But, like her own distant Celtic ancestors, faced with an invading army, she can arm herself with nothing but old sheep-droppings, and once again, the MacEochan clan marches on its way across the island, undeterred.

Maria Milleny roars into the wind which, probably at Catriona's behest, spirals suddenly in his course and knocks her sideways.

The next morning, after a restless night when all the perfect ripostes presented themselves, Maria walks the two miles to Graeme Isbister's garage and starts her new job, pumping petrol.

'Have you seen the lassie who's working down Graeme's garage?'

'Aye. Yon incomer with the red hair. Looks like a big stick insect, she's that tall and skinny.'

'A gey queer one.'

'Aye. I thought at first she'd be one of that hippy lot down in the clarty commune at South Bay. But my boy Willie says she's a pal of Dr MacEochan's. From London.'

'Well, if she's that posh, what's she doing working in a garage?'

'I couldn't say. But if you want my opinion, I'm not over-fond of incomers taking island jobs. Dear knows there aren't many of them.'

'Oh now, Morag, be fair. Do you know a single person in Cailleach who'd willingly work for Greasy Graeme in his midden of a garage? If you ask me, he pays worse than the dole; it's not what you'd call a thriving business, is it?'

'He could make a lot more of it he weren't so bone lazy.'

'My Jimmy says he sniffs up the petrol from his pumps and gets staggering drunk on it. Even on a Sunday.'

'Well, good luck to him and his new assistant then. The pair of them are well matched; I think she's some kind of drug addict herself. Dougie Isbister said he saw her scrabbling around the beach a while back, snuffling up a clump of seaweed.'

144

'I don't know what this island is coming to.'

'Never mind. If gambling weren't a wicked sin, I'd wager you next week's housekeeping that the lass won't last the month.'

At summer's end, the nights begin to eat away at the grey and chilly afternoons. Maria sleeps deeply and long, but dreams of unfamiliar colours, incoherent scenes, urgent messages tapped out in a code she cannot break. She goes without speaking for days on end; the garage, never busy, demands little beyond murmured greetings and nods of assent.

The garage on the far west side is not the most scenic spot on Cailleach. Between the jumble of corrugated-iron sheds, battered petrol pumps, and the sand dunes of the beach beyond, stand three large scrap-metal mountains. Heaped up in pyramids, old car-doors, fenders, dismembered fridges and skeletal bedsprings glint in the sun, or – more commonly – sparkle with hail and raindrops. Each one is marooned in a rusty puddle. Nevertheless, Maria forages among the mounds, picks her way through the innards of the island's abandoned cars and tractors, retrieves mysterious pieces.

'What do you want that old rubbish for?' asks Graeme, when he's sober enough to notice, which is rarely.

'Just playing,' she says, hauling her prizes into the workshop (which looks like a tumbled rubbish-heap itself, except for its door and stovepipe chimneys). She tinkers with the welding equipment. She's used it before, reluctantly, in art college, a compulsory unit in the foundation course. She'd hated the lecturers, hated the assignments, loathed the claustrophobic safety-mask almost more than she'd feared the sparks that could ignite her hair into a flaming pyre. But here, on Cailleach, the mask makes her feel strong, an armoured knight. The oxy-acetylene torch becomes a weapon of power, blessed by a witch. With so much scrap metal handy about the garage – some would say it's the principal crop of the island – Maria feels free to experiment.

In time and after many false starts, tall, tortured, semi-human shapes come unbidden out of her blowtorch. She disclaims all forethought and responsibility, but keeps going.

Walk, work at the garage, eat (something simple, not what Catriona would call eating at all), walk again, along the shore or up into the hills. Look at the tumbled pile of stones behind the cottage,

145

left over from some calamity or simply abandoned, some fifty, five hundred or five thousand years ago. When the hours of daylight have narrowed to a thin slit in the long wall of winter nights, walk faster, work more frantically and spend the rest of the time sleeping.

On the other side of the island, Catriona follows her own routines. She enjoys her evening glass of claret, her after-dinner malt, her suppers solitary but impeccable. During the workdays (and, as often, the worknights) she sees a surprisingly large crop of babies into the world: a statistical curiosity, for by all regional forecasts the island's population should be ageing and dwindling. Must be something in the water. As always, she spends more hours filling in forms than she does healing the sick and the injured. She takes her regular, quarterly deliveries from the Edinburgh wine merchant that served her forefathers, reads the books she selects at intervals from the catalogue of a fine old antiquarian firm in London, knocks on the door of the spirit world, and tries patiently to consort with a better class of demon. She treats herself to one of her periodic holidays off the island (last winter, amorously distracted, she missed the opportunity). She does not go to her despised cousin Roddy in his Georgian house in Edinburgh, nor to her grouse-shooting cousins in Perthshire. Neither does she take up the long-standing invitations of her favourite former lovers – who raise red setters in Donegal; own an impeccable restaurant on the shores of Lake Constance, known only to the cognoscenti of four continents; run a *samizdat* printing-press in Prague; teach gymnastics in Catalonia; or cheerfully rise at five to sing to the cabbages on a holistic-organic commune in the Yorkshire Dales.

In a spirit of benevolence, she sends a postcard to Maria Milleny. Greetings from Glasgow announces the photo-montage of the City Chambers, the Kelvin Hall, two Scottie Dogs and a Floral Arrangement in George Square. 'Having an interesting time,' writes Catriona. 'Have discovered a good cheese shop that will fill orders by post, explored the Victorian tombs of the old Necropolis, and had a most interesting consultation with a speywife who lives on the twenty-first floor of an East End council block. Yours aye, C.'

Harold Robbins, Shakespeare, Agatha Christie, Sir Walter Scott, Annie Swan, James Joyce, Hugh McDiarmid, Catullus, Rimbaud and Barbara Cartland slither up against Karl Marx, P.G. Wodehouse, Alastair Maclean and the Brothers Grimm as the Mobile Library van trundles off the ferry. The librarian, Stuart Macleod, in candy-striped shirt and a decorous tie, knows these are perennially hot items, and makes sure there are plenty to go round. Other choices are more eclectic. Isa the weaver sends a neighbour to the port to collect her Braille copy of *The Autobiography of Alice B. Toklas*, while the Reverend Murdo MacNeish arrives to collect his special order of the *Collected Sermons of John Knox*, Volume eleven, and the latest edition of Francis Gay's *Friendship Book* for his wife. (The Reverend is a great one for special orders, and after he has finished at the library van he will slip across to the post office in expectation of another special order, in unmarked wrappers, of *Naughty Nights* and *Spanking Stories*.)

Behind the Reverend, in the library queue, two earth-mothers, dripping fringes, and a heavily-bearded ex-dentist from the enclave at South Bay, are awaiting their organic-gardening handbooks. Last in line is Maria Milleny, celebrating the occasion of a rare trip to Cailleach port with a baggy but freshly laundered boiler-suit. She borrows a copy of *Teach Yourself Gaelic*, a guide to edible seaweeds of the British Isles, and orders three textbooks on metal-working. These requests provide rich meat for Ina Isbister and the librarian's Auntie Jeannie to speculate over, but they will pose no problem for the Outer Isles Library Service.

Maria waits for the seaweed-woman to come again. Waits and waits.

Meanwhile, she continues her experiments. The innards of scrapped tractors, flattened oilcans, bits of corrugated roofs are all grist for her mill. The garage forecourt blooms into a glinting, metallic garden.

'Stalactite Sequences One and Seven' flank the single petrol pump. The spiky, gothic 'Gates of Hell' loom over the shed where Graeme stores the paraffin. 'Mandorla', a radiantly rusty aureole of spiralled bedsprings, hangs behind the cash-desk. At the roadside, where the cars pull in, the 'Rainbow Kings', a family of thorny-fingered giants with spray-painted crowns, stand in a conversational group to welcome visitors and passing trade. And, to be sure, more cars are pulling in these days. Graeme Isbister's garage has become a talking-point for all the island.

Even those who have seen no reason to stir themselves far from

Cailleach port for years on end now find an excuse to give their ageing motors a wee run; or they come out riding pillion on their neighbour's motorbikes. Nobody would be seen to gape or be curious. It just happens to be a nice afternoon for a trip to the far west side. Or they suddenly remember a jelly-bag they borrowed from Graeme's mother three or four years ago urgently needs returning. And while they're over that way, they might as well stop by the garage and pick up a tin of anti-freeze, or have their tyres checked. Graeme's glad enough of the extra trade, but Maria's annoyed, since the increased business leaves her less time for her own private banging and bashing. Still, she knows the reason, and she admits to being flattered by the interest.

They have a nervous moment, though. The Reverend Murdo himself decides to pay a visit, spurred by a rumour that the far west side is sprouting life-sized crucifixes and other Papish idols. But the items in question turn out to be the supporting cross-pieces for 'Cailleach Clothesline', bedecked with shirts and trousers, all made of well-hammered sheet metal, sticking out stiffly as if lifted by a strong wind off the sea. The idols, true enough, are beginning to proliferate, but they bear no connection with any Roman excrescences that Murdo has ever railed against in a sermon.

Once a week, as precisely to the hour as the ferry will allow, the bank arrives on Cailleach. The blue-and-white van trundles off the ramp of the *St Rollox*, and parks just outside the Cailleach Inn. The driver, a navy-blue tie just visible under his neat blue overall, hops out of the van, goes round to the back, lowers a set of steps giving access to a small wood-panelled door. Then he opens the door to reveal a banker, in all his three-piece-suited splendour, presiding behind the polished teak counter. The islanders queue, politely, and the door is firmly shut behind each customer, whether the business is the cashing of a cheque, a ten-year-old's deposit in the Junior Savings Club, or a stern lecture about a mounting overdraft.

The queue is not cheerful and gossipy, like that at the post office, or raucous like the Friday-night crush at the bar of the inn, but silent, sober, churchly. Privacy is guaranteed by a shared illusion that everyone, before and after, simply isn't there at all.

Except when a breezy, booming English voice breaks the mood. 'Good god, it's Maria Milleny!'

It's Stoney, wearing a sweatshirt that proclaims 'Old Archaeologists Never Die; They Just Go Out of Date.' And standing right behind Maria.

The rest of the queue ripples with a faint murmur of disapproval; Maria glowers.

'Still here, are we, after all this time? What are you, some kind of fugitive from justice?'

Maria says nothing.

'It must be over a year now, no, nearly two; you were just arriving when I was leaving, dig before last. Still, can't say I blame you. This place may be the back of beyond, but the grub at the castle's all right.'

'I'm not with Catriona any more. I thought you knew.'

The queue is finding it harder and harder to pretend it isn't there. Ina Isbister, for instance, is almost reluctant that her turn to climb the steps has finally come, in spite of the healthy sum she's about to tuck into her deposit account, what with the Oban men working on the telephone lines all spring, and Molly MacNee's Australian over-spills from her Golden Wedding celebrations, and the first trickle of mystics communing with the Cailleach stones (they come every year, like migratory geese, as soon as the weather improves).

'My dear, I can't imagine why I should have known. Did you announce it in *The Scotsman*?'

'I thought Catriona might have mentioned it.'

'We're hardly bosom buddies.'

'Oh?'

'Well, I did have supper with her once or twice last summer when I was up for the dig. But I must admit, your name didn't come up.'

'I'm not surprised.'

The bartender from the inn is sorely disappointed when Ina Isbister emerges from the van; she has finished her bit of business far too quickly for his liking. She can find no reason to linger, and drifts off reluctantly; he shrugs, straightens his tie and goes up the stairs as if ascending the scaffold.

'You're well out of it, you know.'

'Isn't that a bit disloyal?'

'I don't know what you think has been going on, mate, but it isn't . . .'

'I'm really not very interested.' She digs her carefully hoarded pound notes out of her pocket; the pay at the garage is paltry, but so are her needs. She has decided to turn herself into a solid citizen and save a bit. 'Sorry, I think my turn's next, and then I've got to find the person who's giving me a lift back to the west side.'

'Is that where you've been hiding? Well, be prepared. I may just come and root you out of your burrow.'

Maria nods at the bartender as he exits, looking woebegone, and snaps the door shut behind her. Stoney, who has no business with the bank at all, discovers that she is next in the queue, and rapidly invents a request for some leaflets about mortgages and insurance. She glances over her shoulder as Maria emerges and marches past her without a word. Four pairs of eyes immediately drop to the ground, and the Co-op manageress, the island taxi-driver, the primary teacher and a crofter from the south of the island immediately fall into a feverish discussion of the weather.

Maria is sleeping late on a Sunday morning, dreaming about the seaweed-woman, when a pounding on the door pulls her into the real world, where it is grey and wet and more like November than June.

Staggering to the door in her jumble-sale dressing-gown, she finds Stoney, holding out a plastic bag full of Ina Isbister's celebrated fruit scones and a jar of instant coffee.

'Don't shoot. I come in peace. Bringing breakfast.'

The rain hitting her face helps Maria focus. 'You'd better come in or you'll get soaked. But the place is a tip today, I warn you.'

'Who cares? I'm not your mother,' says Stoney, stepping over the heaps of clothing on the floor. 'Got you out of your pit, did I? Sorry about that, you struck me as the early-riser type. Why don't you get yourself dressed, and I'll light the fire and put the kettle on.'

Maria, vaguely resentful of the unfinished dream (the seaweed-woman was unrolling some sort of scroll, and the edges of a richly-coloured, gilded illumination were just appearing when Stoney burst in and exploded it with her knocking), pulls on jeans and a flannel shirt. She watches Stoney light the fire, but forgets to warn her about the tricky wiring on the electric kettle. A spark flies, and Stoney leaps backwards.

'Damn! You trying to kill me, Milleny?'

'Sorry, I should have warned you . . .'

'Before I go any further, are there any other booby-traps I should know about?'

'Not unless Catriona's put a curse on the place again. Last time she did that, all uninvited visitors turned into marmalade cats.'

There is a scratching at the kitchen window. Maria opens it, admitting two orange kittens. 'See, they've come to claim you.'

'I thought Catriona was the weird one . . . maybe I was wrong about you.'

'I promise they won't lift a paw against you if you give them some of that milk.'

Once the cats are placated, they settle down to coffee and scones.

'Hope you don't mind the invasion. Brought the scones as a bribe so you'd let me in. Ina says they're your favourites, and she thinks you're looking a bit scrawny.'

'Tell her thanks.'

'I'll go if you want me to.'

'No, I don't mind.' She doesn't think she does, but has no idea what to say.

'I thought we might have one or two things to sort out.'

'Do we?'

'About Catriona.'

'There's really nothing to talk about.'

'Did you think I was . . . in some kind of . . . thing with her?'

'Well, I suppose I did. But don't flatter yourself. It really doesn't matter. That isn't why I left.'

'Why did you, then?'

'You're a nosey bugger, aren't you, Stonebridge?'

'Sorry. Just wondered.'

'Keep wondering.'

'Well, I wasn't, you know.'

'Wasn't what?'

'Her lover.'

'No? You seemed pretty cosy that Easter, at the castle.'

'Just a little dance we do together, sometimes. Ever since I was the number three research assistant on the expedition, with a nasty throat infection, and she was the totally unexpected and ever-so solicitous island GP. There I was, enfeebled by fever, and there she was, throbbing with years of bottled-up lust . . .'

'And?'

'Like you said, keep wondering.'

'Checkmate.'

'How about more coffee?'

'There's a price on it. You'll have to submit to being sketched. I was planning to spend some time today drawing. And just because you're here, I'm not going to alter my plans. It's the first time in

151

ages that I've felt like it. Can't afford to waste the urge, you never know if it will hit again. And since it's pissing wet outside, I might as well sit by my own comfortable fireside and use you as a model.'

'I can't imagine what you'd want to draw me for.'

'Don't be coy. You have interesting bones.'

'Are you sure you wouldn't rather dissect me, then?'

'It amounts to the same thing.'

'Do I have to? I hate being photographed.'

'I'm not a camera. I won't steal your soul, you know. You English. Such a sweet, shy, primitive race. Now, how about that second cup of coffee?'

'You do it.'

'Afraid of the great electricity god? Powerful Celtic fire-magic, that is. Leave it to me.'

'You don't have to sit there so stiffly, Stoney. Just relax.'

'I am relaxed,' grits Stoney, through clenched jaws. 'May I talk?'

'As long as you don't fidget. Like that. Stop it!'

'If I think about not fidgeting, it makes me fidget.'

'So just don't think about it.'

'But that's impossible. Haven't you ever heard the old folktale about the dragon and the gold?'

'Don't think so. Tell me. But keep your hands where they are.'

'Well, once upon a time there was a wonderful treasure, a great chamber full of gold, deep in a cave that was guarded by a very powerful dragon. Anyone who wanted the treasure was welcome to walk straight into the cave and claim it. But there was a catch. They were not allowed to think the word "dragon". If the word even entered their minds while they were inside the cave, the dragon itself would hear them thinking it, and would leap out and gobble them up.'

'And what happened? Did anyone get the treasure?'

'Millions of people tried, but no one ever succeeded. They simply *had* to think the word "dragon" no matter how hard they clenched up their brains. And pow! So the treasure is still there. And so's the dragon. But he's getting very, very, very, fat, and he has terrible indigestion.'

'See! You've been able to sit there for ages now without fidgeting.'

'That was because I was afraid you'd eat me.'

'I might still.'

The first sketch shows Stoney sitting cross-legged on a cushion, holding a mug of coffee. The drink has cooled, unnoticed, while Maria asks Stoney about her work, and about herself. She finds out quite a bit about the first, not much about the second, except for the fact that Stoney comes from Sussex, did her degree at Edinburgh and stayed on to join the department, that she lives near the university in a flat 'with some other people', that she doesn't like 'silly twits who romanticise about ruins. It's all bullshit. A rubbish pit tells me more than a stone circle ever will. A kitchen midden's more significant than a church.'

Maria learns that archaeological expeditions, in spite of the muddy boots and the fancy equipment, are 'workplaces like any other. Nasty little nests of office politics, with rain and wind thrown in. It took me five years of backstabbing to get to be in charge of this one.'

The second sketch shows Stoney in profile, sitting in the rocking chair and staring out the window, a kitten asleep in her lap. Maria has opened a bottle of wine and produced some cheese biscuits. Stoney has drunk too much of the wine far too fast, and is feeling slightly sleepy. She is listening to Maria's stories about her left-wing parents. 'They ran off together. Her family was horrified because he was an Irish Catholic. His family was horrified because she wasn't. So I never knew my grandparents. Nobody spoke to anybody – an unforgiving lot. And my parents moved to Australia, years ago. They're busy organising the Sydney dockers or the Adelaide ambulance-drivers or something. We don't write much. Anyway, they think my artworks, as they call them, are a load of bourgeois tripe. They wish I'd settle down and become a radical poster-printer, or a documentary film-maker exposing imperialism or something. I'm sorry they didn't see *Lives of the Saints*, though. Mother would approve.'

'What's *Lives of the Saints*?'

'Ahh, fame is so short-lived.' And she tells Stoney about her exhibition – Stoney says she likes the sound of it. Which leads, inevitably, to Maria's first meeting with Catriona and her visit to Cailleach.

'Visit? Some visit . . . you've been here nearly two years now.'

'Well, it started as a visit. It isn't any more. I feel I belong here now.'

'Rubbish. The islanders will never accept you. You'll be an incomer 'til you're one hundred and three.'

'Don't care. Anyway. I'm half Cailleach myself as it happens.' Damn. She hadn't meant to say that. The wine must be going to her head. Or Stoney is.

'What?'

'I told you – KEEP STILL. If you were a model in my art-college life class, you'd get the sack in the first five minutes.'

'Don't deflect me. What do you mean, you're half Cailleach?'

'On my mother's side.'

'I thought she was a lefty.'

'She is. So what's the contradiction?'

'This is hardly the Hebridean Socialist Republic, is it?'

'Ooh, you may have lived up here longer than I have, sister, but you really don't know your Scotland, do you?' She rummages among her pencils, then continues her story.

'Anyway. Mother was always a bit of a rebel. Left home at seventeen to work in Glasgow, met Father at some Baby Trotsky-ites summer-camp or something, and came home for a visit several years later with him in tow as her fiancé. Who was revealed to be, lord preserve us, one Michael Milleny of Dublin. He was as much of an atheist as she was, but that cuts no ice up here with the Calvinist mafia. "Papish blood will out," they said ominously. So the two of them were packed off on the next ferry, and never seen here again. I suppose I came back to reclaim the territory.'

'Well, well, well.'

'If you breathe a word of this to anyone, Stonebridge, you'll be found sprawled dead over your research notes with my hammer embedded in your skull. Not even Catriona knows.'

'Why on earth didn't you tell her? I think she'd love the story.'

'She probably knows it. But my father's surname doesn't mean anything to anyone up here. I don't think the introductions got that far. Anyway, I don't know why, I just decided not to say anything . . . it's complicated . . .' And, she thinks, I am not going to tell you, dearie, how Catriona marvelled at my grasp of the light and the scenery in my painting of Saint Bride. Only invited me up here because she thought I had some kind of deep psychic bond with the place. Which I suppose I do, anyway. 'Anyway, I'll kill you if you breathe a word of it.'

'A touching show of trust. I'm flattered. I didn't think you liked me.'

'I'm not sure that I do, yet. More vino?'

The third sketch is softer, less precise than the pair before it. In the late afternoon, the sun has finally come out, and they go for a long, wordless walk on the beach, listening to the sounds of the birds and the rhythms of the waves. Stoney produces an expensive-looking hip flask from her pocket, and, when that is finished, squats down on her haunches and rolls a joint. They lie on their backs, on a sun-warmed sand dune, and look up at the cloud patterns changing in the sky. As the light goes, they feel chilled and head back to the cottage. Unsteady as she is, Maria is determined to do a final drawing, and sits Stoney firmly down on the cushion before the now-extinct fire, sketching frantically before the light goes.

She works in silence, afraid of what other secrets Stoney might worm out of her. But she has nothing to fear. Stoney, sitting stock still, has fallen asleep. When she finishes her picture, she shakes Stoney awake, and shows her all three of them.

'You're not much of a realist, are you? I could never look that good.' Nevertheless, Stoney is a little miffed when Maria refuses to part with them.

'I like to live with my stuff for a while,' explains Maria.

'I'll tell you what, then,' slurs Stoney. 'Give me the drawings and you can come live with me.'

Maria knows they are both drunk, and still slightly stoned, and pours gallons of black coffee down Stoney before she sends her out into the night.

Stoney's room at Ina Isbister's is as neat as a tent, and as cold. She has a narrow bed, a tartan blanket folded over it, a table with a portable typewriter – very battered – and a shelf holding a row of labelled box-files. Her clothes hang on hooks behind the door, or lie folded away in the little chest of drawers beside the bed. She offers Maria the only chair, and sits on the bed, her head bent, rolling a cigarette.

'When I'm here I'm never here, if you see what I mean. So it's a waste to have anything more comfortable. The short-stay guests have nicer quarters. But, of course, you'll remember from your own brief visit.'

She goes out, comes back with a tray. 'Biscuits with the tea tonight. It must be on your account. I'm out of favour after leaving a ring in the bath. Nice to see you. To what do I owe the pleasure?'

'Thought I was mean, last week. Of course you can have one of the drawings. I thought you might like the one I did last.'

'I do. It's the least like me. Awfully dreamy.'

'Maybe I know more about you than you do.'

'Don't be cocky.'

Maria licks the chocolate off a digestive biscuit. She can't think of anything to say.

'We have two options,' announces Stoney. 'Act as if we've been leading up to this since our first brief encounter a year ago last September, or act as if it's a bolt of lightning out of the blue. Which do you like better?'

'Both,' says Maria.

Stoney smiles wryly at the narrowness of her own bed, but seems to take no notice of the icy sheets. Maria, however, shivers as she touches them.

'I thought you were the seasoned islander,' Stoney teases her. 'You're the one who's spent two winters here. I'm just a summertime bird-of-passage.'

'The secret of survival is a roaring fire in the room, and a nice hot-water bottle in the bed.'

'Sorry, but I didn't know you were coming.'

'Unless I get some circulation back, I probably won't be.'

'Shameless hussy!' Stoney wraps herself around Maria. 'You're not such a demure little flower after all. Well, let's see what we can do to warm ourselves up.'

Stoney makes love much the same way she excavates a site, and with the same serious concentration. Slowly, carefully, undistracted, she is meticulous and patient and determined. When she finds something interesting, she pauses and considers it, then searches further.

Maria makes love much the same way she makes a sculpture, feverish, excited, full of ideas, unaware of passing time.

So she is surprised when Stoney suddenly sits up and says, 'Hurry up – it's nearly midnight. Whatever will Mrs Isbister think we're up to?' She tosses Maria her clothes, scrambles into her own. 'I'll run you home. Not much chance of hitching a lift at this hour on a weeknight.'

When they drive uphill, past the castle, Maria sees a faint glow coming from the windows of Catriona's tower. Stoney notices her head turn. 'That woman is a menace,' she mutters, changing gears.

Catriona hears the van climbing the brae. But she is standing inside a pentangle, marked out with candles on her bedroom floor, staring very hard at something in the empty air in front of her. She has other things to think about.

For thirty days and thirty nights Maria eats little and sleeps less. Even when the garage is closed she is to be found there, pounding, hammering, scraping, blasting away. Flying sparks bounce off her welder's mask, her overalls are saturated with the smell of hot metals. Steam furs up the windows as the fiery glow from the workshop collides with the cool night air. This summer is harder than the last one; everyone complains about it.

Women's faces, none of them known to her, swim up out of her dreams. They pique and plague her until she finds some way to reproduce their planes and angles. One figure takes a week to make, others come forth two or three in a single night. As she works, she overhears, above the whining and banging of her tools and machinery, scraps of conversation, incomprehensible jokes and quarrels, tastes strong broth and coarse, over-salted porridge in her mouth, smells warm wool and sweat and menstrual blood (not her own). Long flapping sleeves brush against her arms as she works, thick bands of serge weigh down her forehead, coarse cloth lies heavy on her shoulders and sometimes as she moves around the workshop she is tripped up by an invisible hem round her ankles.

Sometimes she stops for breath or for a gulp of cold, stewed tea. She pauses, puts down her tools, stands back and considers. The result doesn't always satisfy her. Displeased, she takes a heavy hammer, a saw, a torch, and swipes and smashes and burns away her failures until the imperfect shape is battered into something more acceptable.

When the garage is open, she serves the customers politely but with vacant eyes, nodding absently in response to greetings, thanks, and the endless complaints about the weather.

'Are you paying that lassie enough?' people ask Graeme Isbister. 'She's looking awful peely-wally.'

'I ken fine,' he replies, 'but I'll say nothing more about it. The other day I asked her how she was keeping, told her she looked a bit off-colour, said why didn't she have Dr MacEochan look her over. Do you know what she did? Nearly rammed my own Stornoway screwdriver down my thrapple and said the only thing wrong with her was people poking. So as long as she works her hours, and stays handy about the place, I'll not complain. Do you fancy another pint, Donald? I think it's your round this time.'

When, at last, she decides she's finished, Maria asks Graeme if she can borrow the breakdown lorry.

'After closing time. To shift some stuff I've done.'

'Are we not to have it for your collection in the forecourt?'

'No this time, Graeme. Sorry. It's a . . . surprise for a friend.'

'Pity that. Every time you add something new, trade seems to treble.'

'Never mind, boss. I promise, the next one will be specially for you. How do you fancy a twenty-foot high minister of the kirk preaching a sermon over the air-hose?'

In the morning, Stoney, as always, arrives at the site before her team. She likes to be first at the dig every day, just in case something interesting turns up. If it does, she wants to be sure that hers is the name attached to the find. To reach the excavation from the track where she's parked the van, she takes her usual shortcut through the ruined cloister. Out of the corner of her eye, she catches a flash of something black and shiny. She turns, starts, jumps and freezes, then laughs until the tears run. The convent is once again full of nuns, made out of scrap metal and fourteen feet tall.

The Reverend MacNeish is not well pleased by the sudden sprouting of scrap-metal nuns on the convent site. Not that he's bothered by any notion of desecration, for, as he repeatedly reminds his congregation, that pagan, papistical place has well deserved its fate of being tumbled down in ruins. Instead, he feels the statues represent another little slide down the slippery slope towards the worship of graven images. First came the television (its perpetually bad reception, whatever you might say about static and radio interference and climatic conditions, is, according to Murdo, God's expressed opinion on the programmes). Now come these abominations made out of old cars and cisterns and whatever. Some fool on the island's community council has even proposed that they actually buy one of these specimens, to decorate the entrance of the new Cailleach Hall. Thank heavens one or two kirk elders have managed to quash the proposal, on the grounds that statuary was a bit over the top for the entrance of what is no more than a large, prefabricated hut. However, the council was not swayed by its theological scruples, preferring to reject the idea solely on the grounds of cost.

158

Unfortunately, the afternoon that Murdo chooses to drive across the island and remonstrate with Maria in person is also the afternoon when a reporter and photographer from a popular Dundee-based family newspaper have arrived on the island to do a story on Maria's work. For, in a modest way, word has begun to spread beyond Cailleach. A Swedish museum – in the person of its backpacking curator on holiday with her four solemn blonde teenaged children – has purchased a tall, spike-studded cast-iron cylinder entitled 'Thor', at an encouraging (and, to Maria's mind, totally astronomical) price. In the same week, a retired pop-star (visiting his young sister at the counter-cultural commune down at the south end) has carried off a large rectangular slab of smashed bonnets, fused headlamps and chrome for his combination recording studio and detoxification centre on the Isle of Skye. Soon thereafter, an Edinburgh gallery admired from Brooklyn to Bulgaria requests a piece (of Maria's own choosing) for their celebrated summer show. Even the Scottish Arts Council bestirs itself to send a letter of polite enquiry.

So when Murdo pulls into Graeme Isbister's forecourt, hoping to catch his quarry unawares, he finds her, instead, arguing with a fat man in a bright blue anorak, and a tall boy with a bad complexion, draped with light meters and cameras. Striding forth, the Minister dissolves the little knot of onlookers – village children, Mrs McConachie from over the road, and Graeme Isbister himself, who nods and smiles deferentially as he slips a flask discreetly into the waistband of his baggy dungarees. Standing a little apart, waiting to be deferred to, he strains to hear the conversation, which is being conducted on all sides through tightly clenched jaws.

'I told you,' grits Maria, clenched fists jammed into the pockets of her overalls, 'I do not have a skirt. Short, long, or otherwise. And if I did own a skirt, I don't see why I should trek two miles home and back to put it on for you.'

'Now, dearie, you can't want your photograph taken in that mucky old boiler-suit. My colleague here will be delighted to give you a hurl up the road in the motor, so you can change into something prettier. After all, it's not every day you get your picture in the paper, is it?'

'I thought you came to do a story on my sculptures. Not on my wardrobe.'

'Now listen, lovey, let me explain to you about journalism. We wouldn't be over here just to take a picture of your metal bits and pieces there, very fine though they are, I'm sure, if you like that sort of abstract avant-gardie stuff. But our readers, god bless 'em, aren't your common or garden intellectuals, ken. They're interested in people. Now if you were some old bag with a face like a prune we probably wouldn't even be doing a story – unless of course you were a plucky wee pensioner in a wheelchair, in which case we'd take a different angle entirely. But you're a very attractive lass, hen, and that's nothing to be ashamed of.'

'Do you want to take your pictures of my sculptures, or don't you? I really don't have time to hang about like this. We're very busy in the garage today. Aren't we, Graeme?'

'Now don't you worry about that,' says Graeme heartily, profoundly stirred by his first encounter with the media, and at his very own garage too. 'You just take as much time as is needed for these lads to get a good picture and a good story for their paper. And we'll buy an extra copy when it comes out and stick it up by the cash desk.'

The photographer has sidled past the onlookers, hands cupped protectively round his lenses, and is wandering around 'Cailleach Clothesline', making passes with his light meter.

'Over here, I think, Willie, but we'd better get a move on before the rain starts again.'

The man in the anorak shoos the locals – including a greatly offended Murdo – well out of range, and places Maria in front of the sculpture.

'Won't I be blocking the view of it if I stand here?'

'Now, just you leave us to do our job, darling.' He steps back, considers the effect. 'Now Maureen, do you think you could . . .'

'Maria.'

'What?'

'Maria. My name is Maria. Not Maureen.'

'Oh. Right enough. Now, as I was saying, Maria sweetheart, do you think you could maybe pull the belt on your wee jumpsuit a bit tighter, maybe with your hands on your hips, stick your right shoulder out a bit. Don't be ashamed of that nice figure of yours. And give us a smile, please, hen.'

'No.'

'Pardon?'

'I said No.'

'Now look, lass, I'm a great supporter of your women's lib and all, but just give us a break, will you?'

160

'You came along and said you wanted to do a shot of my sculptures. So do one. And I'll be perfectly happy to stand next to them, like a normal person, to give you your so-called human interest. But if you want me to pretend I'm some kind of pin-up, you can stuff it.'

'Och, we're just a couple of hard-working lads trying to do our jobs, missus . . .'

'I think you're a pair of little shits. And I think your paper is a disgusting little rag, not even fit for lining a cat-box. And if Graeme hadn't asked me, as a personal favour, to do it for you, I would never have agreed, and . . .'

'Ah, that's a red-head for you, a right wee spitfire. I bet she's a tiger in bed!'

'PISS OFF! GET OUT OF HERE!' Spluttering with fury, she raises her hands above her head, as if to call down the wrath of the gods upon them.

'Dougie – *now*! That's it.' Snap. Click. Snap. Click. 'You know, you're beautiful when you're angry, darlin'. Ta very much, and cheery-bye.' As Maria moves towards them, murder in her eyes and a hammer in her hand, they leap into their car and speed away.

Murdo, unwilling to be upstaged by hacks and hirelings, decides to postpone his attack until a more propitious time. Asking only to have his petrol topped up and the oil checked, he drives off, disappointed. However, like everyone else on Cailleach, he duly buys a copy of the *Sunday Sentinel* the moment it comes off the Monday ferry. Although he strongly disapproves of the fact that it is published on the Lord's Day, he feels its values are sound, and its editorial heart as close to the right place as it is possible for a work of Mammon to be. And, more than once, its little homilies and anecdotes have helped him out when he is stuck for a theme for a Sabbath sermon.

And, indeed, in the latest issue, there is Maria for all to see, in between the Wee Thought for the Week and the Queen at Balmoral Enjoying a Joke with the Royal Corgis. Photographed with arms akimbo and legs wide apart, she is shouting something at the camera. Those who know no better will think she looks – sort of, more or less, if you squint – like some sort of jump-suited comedienne. But the small group of eye-witnesses will recognise the pose as a cleverly-angled shot of Maria leaping up and down in rage. Barely visible, the sculpture behind her seems to be some sort of strange projection rising up from the top of her head. The headline reads: RED-HEAD MAUREEN TURNS SCRAP INTO ART. The short caption below the picture says, 'Lissom Maureen Molony, from Cailleach in the Outer Hebrides, turns her job as garage-girl to good use by making sculptures out of wrecked cars. "I think my boss Graeme Isbister is a super bloke to let me do this," smiles winsome Maureen, "and folk come from miles around to look at the things I've made. It's great for business at the garage." Woman's-libber Maureen wanted your *Sentinel* photographer to take her picture in her welder's mask, but we think you'd rather see her as she is.'

Maria soon discovers that Stoney's appetites are as precisely cyclical as the moon and the tides. She knows almost to the hour when, on a clear summer night or a drizzly Sunday morning, there will come a cheerful tapping at her window or an imperious knock at the door. She never thinks to go in search of Stoney, but she never feels inclined to send her away, even if she sometimes wishes that the visitor were the seaweed-woman instead. But for a long time now, nothing has skimmed over the sea except birds and moonlight.

They do not meet often. Stoney is far too busy digging holes in the island, sifting soil through her scientific fingers, giving each granule its number and name. Maria, in turn, is far too busy fighting with each new bit of stubborn Cailleach scrap metal, struggling to bend or blast or melt it to her will. She is producing a series of massive hulks, jagged fragments, and tiny objects of great intricacy, which she calls 'Machines from Before the Ice Age': winged engines; gears and fuses all densely decorated with spirals and scrolls and wildly frilled flowers, of no known species but meticulous detail; dials and levers smoothly moulded for use by a hand with six fingers; coils and wires knitted into sinuous coats of armour, retaining flecks and splashes of the colours that must have once covered them completely.

Nevertheless, she has to stop sometimes, and Stoney always finds her in; if she ever comes knocking in vain when Maria's not home, Stoney never lets on.

'She's a vampire, you know,' observes Stoney on one such Sunday. They have been in bed all afternoon; they have risen now to eat oatcakes and lentil soup.

'Who?'

'The Good Doctor. Who bloody else?'

'You really are obsessed with that woman. You're always talking about her. Why don't you just go off and sleep with her; scratch the itch.'

'Ugh!'

'Are you maligning my taste? We had our good times.'

'You've grown out of her, thank goodness.'

'And what does that make you? The next higher stage of evolution? My post-graduate degree?'

'Don't be cheeky. Anyway, she was terrible for you. Lady Dracula.'

'Come now, you're a woman of science,' Maria nods towards Stoney's sweatshirt, which states, 'Hypatia Had It All Figured Out'. 'You don't believe in vampires.'

'I'm speaking in purely psychological terms, of course. She's an energy vampire. Battens on to you and sucks you dry. Lives off the blood of younger women.'

'That's a bit heavy.'

'Well, look at you. You lived with her for months and didn't do a damned thing. Not a stroke of painting, zilch.'

'I sketched some . . .'

'Don't be silly. Nothing serious. You know what I mean. Nothing substantial. And yet look at you now. You move out, get your act together, and look what happens – bang, you're working again. In a whole new medium.'

'Maybe I just needed the germination time. Maybe if I'd never been with her, I'd still be doing damn all. Or struggling with paintings that never get finished, or tearing up my sketches as soon as I finish them. She gave me something I needed.'

'She used your lithe and delightful body, pal. Besides, you're the one that pissed off and busted it up.'

'I think she was waiting for me to go. Anyway, so maybe it wasn't the most wholesome and spiritually pure relationship, but I'm still very fond of the old bat. She may be a little unscrupulous, but she's one of the most open-handed, generous people I've ever met. And she's taught me a lot.'

'Like how to cook, for instance.'

'Well, yes.'

'I thought I recognised the old Catriona touch in this lentil soup. Lemon juice, spices and garlic. Lots and lots and lots of garlic.'

'So there. How could she be a vampire?'

They go back to bed. Just before Stoney leaves she announces,

'I'm going back to Edinburgh this week. Dig's over for the season.'

'Already? Time flies. See you next summer, then.'

'Is that all you can say?'

'What else do you want – a proposal of marriage?'

' "Thank you for a very pleasant summer," maybe? Or, "I'll miss you, Stoney." Go on, you ice maiden, give it a try.'

'Thank you for a very pleasant summer and I will miss you, Stoney, well, sometimes anyway. It's been – pretty good.'

'And the same to you.'

'Do you want me to get out my widow's weeds? Throw myself in the wake of your departing ferry? Come now.'

'I guess I'm used to people being a little more – upset when I go.'

'You don't look too upset yourself.'

'Ah, but I'm the one doing the leaving. You're the one left behind on this godforsaken island.'

'If you don't like it, why do you keep coming back?'

'The period and the place have been a good career move. Another season or two and maybe I'll make it to the big stuff. South-eastern Turkey or a site I've got my eye on in Peru. Anyway, I should be turning up again, probably around the Easter break, to organise the accommodation for the team and all. And if you're down in civilisation, or would like to come and visit, here's my number. Give me a buzz.'

'Not likely. I think I'll stay put for the winter.'

'She has cast a spell on you, hasn't she?'

'Cailleach? Yes.'

'I meant Catriona. Anyway, you keep nice and busy with your banging and blasting, and don't let that old spider lure you back into her web.'

'You sound awfully possessive. Anyway, are you going to miss me? You haven't said.'

'Ah, but I'm off to the sinful city, love. I have lots of fish to fry.'

'*Bon appetit*, then. Go south and be a superstar.' Maria looks past her, out the window towards the sea.

Just before closing time at the Cailleach Inn, when the regulars in the public bar are bracing themselves to go out and face the gusts of rain whipping in from the west, Graeme Isbister announces that he is closing down the garage and emigrating to Australia. His best mate, who has done well there, has summoned him with promises of strong beer and perpetual sunshine. He has sold his premises to a

Mr Scotty McCrumb, a Scot who has gone to America and Made Good, and fancies a little financial interest in the old country. According to Graeme, he plans to use the garage site to build a small factory.

'Heavy industry,' they pronounce, at the inn and in the post office and outside the Co-op and in the kirk, 'will never come to anything on Cailleach.'

'And Graeme Isbister,' they pronounce, at the kirk and outside the Co-op, and in the post office and at the inn, 'will never amount to anything in New South Wales.'

Nevertheless, most of the drinking population of the island crowds into the lounge bar of the inn on the night before he leaves, to give him a proper send-off.

For the first hour or so, Maria simply sits in a corner, pleased that she's been invited in spite of her status as raw incomer. She watches the festivities, listens to the fiddlers, straining her ears to sieve out the English chat mixed in with the Gaelic. When the fiddlers take a break, they are succeeded by the island's own rock band, Snorri's Marauders. Their star singer and lead guitarist, Stuart Macleod, has abandoned the crisply-pressed peppermint-striped shirt and neat floral tie he wears for his rounds with the Mobile Library van, and replaced them with skin-tight black leather trousers and a carefully torn singlet exposing a surprising amount of orange chest-hair. A gold pirate hoop glistens in one ear. As he sings of menacing footsteps, killers' feet, behind you in the city street; of black holes in the soul; of what he and you and those three over there could do together ohso sweetly ohso indiscreetly all night long, Maria observes the small contingent of the island's youth impressing each other on the dance floor.

Wee Maggie, Ina Isbister's second-to-youngest, is lately back from a holiday in Glasgow; Maria wonders if her skin-tight, iridescent fifties evening gown and earrings of dripping rhinestones and peacock-feathers indicate a city shopping spree with her cousin Davie-Dinah. 'For heaven's sake, don't tell your mother, you wee besom, or I'll murder you . . .'

Maggie is well aware that she's a fantastic dancer; she's developed her style with fierce dedication in front of her bedroom mirror, and now she's living dangerously, working hard to fascinate Billy the lobsterman, who is far too old for her, but deeply flattered. The Marauders' drums and guitars are pounding and throbbing, the music and musicians gyrating pelvically, and wee

Maggie zeroing in for the kill when, with a plaintive whine, the amplifiers die and the lights go out. By the time the generator is repaired, and the music going again, Billy is deep in an argument about new EEC regulations with the crew of the *Jeanie Deans*, and Maggie is commandeered by her mother to help with the sandwiches.

Maria is reaching for a sausage roll when an agitated voice whispers in her ear, 'For heaven's sake, woman, save yourself! Don't fill up on that muck! They'll be bringing out the fresh prawns and crab claws in a minute.'

It is Catriona, close behind her, cradling a tumbler full of the island malt.

'Long time no see.'

'I've been busy.'

'So I gather. Where's your friend?'

Maria looks at her blankly, then flushes. 'Away back to Edinburgh.'

'Of course. Migration season. However do you pass the time?'

'I've been working on a very complicated sculpture.'

'Ah well, you'll have plenty of time on your hands now, with the garage closing down.'

'I'll manage.'

'I was thinking of buying the nuns.'

'I don't need charity, thanks.'

'I'm not giving it. But I don't want some idiotic little Edinburgh bureaucrat from the Ancient Monuments lot trying to get them removed from the ruins. I think they add the perfect touch. And they do a lot less damage to the spirit of the place than those licensed vandals and their archaeological excavation. So I thought that if I bought them, officially, I could gift them, equally officially, to the people of the island, with the condition they be kept on site. The Sisters of Saint Bride should be preserved for posterity.'

'I'd like that.'

'Excellent. But let's talk business some other time. In the meanwhile, here are those crab claws. Lovely, aren't they? Silly fools usually export the whole lot to the French – not much local demand, they say. Pity. But now, tell me about you and our archaeological friend . . .'

'Catriona, I'm sorry, but I don't think that's any of your business.'

'Well, not yet it isn't.'

166

'What?'

'Just be careful you don't catch something.'

'Now, really . . .'

'I mean it. She's a bit of a wanderer. Even does it with men.'

'Catriona, you're disgusting. And I don't believe you . . . bloody malicious . . .'

'Just how well do you know the lady? Not very, in spite of your . . . intimacies, I'll wager. But don't say I didn't warn you when you turn up in my surgery with some embarrassing little problem.'

'You're just jealous.'

Catriona laughs so hard she nearly chokes on her malt. 'You do think a lot more of yourself than you used to, Milleny. Anyway, take it as it was meant. A friendly warning. Word to the wise. Besides which, she's a triple Scorpio with far too much Venus in her sixth house. I know. I've done her chart. Had to obtain the information by stealth, of course. Now if *that* doesn't convince you . . .'

Someone taps Maria on the shoulder. Graeme Isbister stands at her side, beaming through his maudlin tears. 'May I have the pleasure of the next dance, Maria? As your former employer, I'll always remember the grand day when you walked into my wee garage and said you were desperate . . .'

Maria looks sidelong at Catriona. 'Shut up, Graeme, never mind. I'm not much of a dancer, but let's go.' And they rock and roll out of Catriona's grasp.

Soon it is time for the farewell speeches, while the crowd is still able to stand.

'I remember when you were just a wee boy of eleven,' says Stella Duncan from the south of the island, 'and you stowed away in your uncle Hamish's herring-boat . . . the *Isa May*.'

'No, that's wrong. He was fourteen . . .'

'And it was his cousin Davey's trawler, *Maid of the Sea*.'

'They were half-way to the Dogger Bank before they found you . . .'

'Never. They cotched him before they were out of the Minch.'

'Asleep in a rope locker, with the brandy bottle from the First Aid box hanging out of your jaiket pocket . . .'

'No, no. He stumbled out of the forward hold, choked with diesel fumes and greetin' for his ma.'

'You're a bad devil, Graeme lad, but we'll never forget you.'

Murmured assents, another twelve rounds, and they're singing

167

'Viva Espana', humming 'Gypsy Rover', crooning 'Danny Boy', and whistling the 'Eriska Love Lilt', all at the same time. Tears flow freely during 'The Northern Lights of Old Aberdeen'. Graeme promises to send everyone present a plane ticket to Australia when he's made his first million.

The night ends, but the party continues. There is a last-minute panicky scrum when the ferry hooter goes, and Graeme in no fit state to board it. Then someone in a corner, under a heap of snoring bodies, calls, 'Never fash, never worry, lads, there's half the crew doon here, and they cannae load up nor leave without us.'

The one fiddler still upright plays a farewell lament.

The next afternoon, her brains still thick as muck from the harbour-bottom, a hungover Maria returns to the vacant garage to gather up her sculptures. She is moving them, as carefully as blown glass, to the ground outside her cottage. Catriona is bringing the land-rover, the lorry from the tweed-mill is helping out, and a couple of crofter-neighbours of Ina Isbister's are bringing their tractors to shift what they can.

Waiting for her helpers, Maria balances in the broken swivel chair behind the till, looking at the heap of greasy rags, out-of-date calendars and empty oilcans on the floor. She wonders what comes next. Her sculpting will go on. Graeme has left her all the necessary metalworking equipment as a parting gift, and although one rich source of scrap metal may be drying up, the island will sprout more; it grows wild as heather. She's lost an ideal workplace, though, and money will be a problem, in spite of the sales she's beginning to make as word spreads round the more progressive galleries.

She and Catriona may be on speaking terms once more, even friendly, but she will never ask her for another penny. Never.

Suddenly she hears the squeal of brakes, and looks out to see the island taxi swerve to avoid a fat sheep that has planted herself in the middle of the road. The car pulls up in the forecourt, lets out a passenger. Maria goes to meet him; she recognises his baseball cap and his drawl.

'Hi there, ma'am. I'm Scotty McCrumb.'

'We've met.'

He squints, judging her like a prize heifer or a potential oilwell. 'Well I'll be damned. So we have. You were the nice young lady at the Clan Gathering a while back. Well, what a coinkydinky. Wait'll I tell the wife.'

Maria shakes hands, matching his bone-cracking squeeze; all that working-out with a blowtorch means she can give as good as she gets. Hopes he doesn't mind that she hasn't finished clearing out her things yet . . . everyone's running a little late today. There was this party, and . . .

'Never you mind, hon. I saw Mr Isbister getting on board this a.m. just as I was getting off. Say no more.'

'Anyway, I'm taking all my sculptures away. It may take us a while, but . . .'

'Oh yes, the famous junk-statues and all. Heard about them. Very nice, but not the sort of thing to have in front of a new factory. Now don't get me wrong. I'm all in favour of creativity and all that stuff. Can't do without it whatever they say. No profits without prophets, if you get my meaning. In fact, art is the name of my game. Which is why I'm delighted to meet you. I never realised, back at that Clan Gathering, that I was talking to such a talented little lady . . .'

'Well . . .'

Mr Isbister told my agents all about you, when they asked what those peculiar bits were, sticking up all around the garage. It occurs to me I might be able to offer you a deal . . .'

'Do you want to buy one?'

'No, just hang on in there and hold your horses. Hear me out. This factory of mine is partly funded by a Highlands and Islands Development Grant. I suppose the local busybodies have been telling everybody it's gonna be a steel-mill or a uranium smelter or lordy knows what. Well that couldn't be further from the truth. First of all, this island would be dead useless for anything like that, and second of all, I've got myself an extra top-up grant for the purpose of encouraging traditional handicraft skills.'

'Are you opening another tweed-mill?'

'Nope. Guess again.'

'A new distillery?'

'I'll leave that to the boys who know how to do it best.'

'I'm sorry. I really can't imagine.'

'Souvenirs, darling.'

'Souvenirs?'

'You know. Little dolls in kilts. Scenic ashtrays. Teddy bears with sporrans. Shellcraft tie-pins. Elkhorn cigarette-lighters. Typical stuff.'

'Not very typical of Cailleach, I'm afraid.'

'So what? It's not for sale in Cailleach. Not enough tourists here to turn a penny out of a pay-toilet. We're talking export, sweetie-pie. To Canada and New Zealand and the Yew Ess of Ay and Hong Kong. Balance of trade. Just what this country needs. And socially useful, too. Not a drop of smoke or smuts or fumes, no pollution to muck up your little old island paradise, here. Some nice wee part-time and outworking jobs for some local ladies who'd like a little spare cash. Plus vacancies full-time for a van driver and a foreman and that sort of thing. And, say, ten hours a week for a designer. That's where you come in, sugar.'

'Me? I don't know the first thing about designing any of that . . .'

'Come on, hon, it's easy as falling off a greased raccoon. You just choose the colours for the dolls' kilts, and lay out some nice postcardy views for the ashtrays, and keep the ladies up to the mark when they're sewing up the teddy bears (this is a quality operation, remember), and sketch out a few new designs for costume jewellery and egg-spoons and card-cases and such like. Nothing you can't do, what with your undoubted abilities in the drawing and painting line.'

'I really don't think I'm qualified.'

'If I say you're qualified, you're qualified.'

'Don't you think the job ought to go to an islander?'

'Well, what are you?'

'I live here, but . . .'

'Now look, I'm a member of Clan MacEochan on my mama's side, remember. And I know fine about the unemployment on this island and whatnot. But you tell me if you know of any unemployed artists, designers, or illustrators hanging about here. Apart that is, from your good self. If anyone from this island has any training in art, they've hightailed it down south long ago. And anyway, you didn't bother about all that when you took a job with that thirsty old squirrel Isbister at this garage.'

'Nobody else wanted it.'

'Well, this time it's me don't want no one else. Besides, once we start turning over the profits, you might just be able to take on a wee trainee. So here's the deal. I pay you twice what Isbister did, and for half the hours. Let you get on with your artwork in your spare time. I'll even give you a little shed or something out the back, big enough to do your statuary in.'

'I'm not sure . . .'

170

'You sure are one reluctant little lady.'

'It will be some time before the factory is built, I suppose.'

'Are you kidding? End of this month we'll be ready to roll.'

She looks around the derelict garage, and the piles of scrap-metal.

'Aint't a mess? But there's nothing can't be done fast if you got the money to buy the time. And besides, the factory itself is nothing but a lightweight prefab shell. Goes up in no time. Easy to build, and easy to take down. These little old grants don't last for ever, you know.'

'I suppose you wouldn't have it any other way.'

'Well now, that's what I call perspicacity. Do we have a deal? You're hired.'

'Now here in the needlecraft department, ladies, we'll be working on a variety of products. Soft toys, stuffed animals, et cetera. We'll turn out Loch Ness Monsters in turquoise, orange and a tasteful green-and-yellow polka-dotted pattern. Also seals, teddies, and wee Scotch terriers in tartan coats. All very simple patterns, nothing you girls can't do with both hands tied behind your backs. We'll have a little production line for teatowel printing: I'd like to feature some good old Scotch recipes, so go home and write down all your grannies' ways of doing porridge and shortbread and your Auntie's mutton broth and the like, and we'll offer a cash prize for the best ones used. We'll also work on bathroom sets – tartan bath-mats, toilet-roll holders, and little rugs for the seat and the tank of the . . . convenience itself. That's a very popular item in my factory in Puerto Rico, and I'm sure the Scotch motif will make it a bestseller for this plant too. We'll also be getting in our first consignment of dollies from Taiwan next week, so we'll get cracking first thing tomorrow on making the costumes – Scotch lassies and brides for a start. Maria Milleny here will be sketching out the patterns for you to follow. You folks all know Maria, don't you?'

'Next we come to our assembly line for elkhorn products: cutlery, cigarette-lighters, keyrings and so forth. Now these are manufactured elsewhere (in the Philippines, to be exact), and your part in the process is simply to stamp them in gold letters: 'A present from the Outer Hebrides' or 'A Souvenir from Bonnie Scotland' or 'Found on the Road to the Isles' or whatever. Then we parcel them up in these attractive gift boxes, decorated with dancing Highlanders and wrapped in what I'm assured is an authentic MacEochan tartan, transferred on to best quality plastic film.

'Step this way please, and mind your heads – this is our ceramic and china-painting workshop. Ashtrays, spoonrests, old-fashioned chamber pots to put flowers in, your attractive little ornaments and gifts for the home. We'll be decorating them with little bluebells, thistles and other appropriate flower-type items. Also mugs, of course. We'll have them with photographs of the Royal Family printed on, and some with little poems and old Scotch sayings. Won't that be nice?

'Well, that just about wraps it up. I hope you've all enjoyed your little tour. Now if you'll just follow me back to the front reception desk, I think we're ready for the official opening ceremony. I'm sure you'll be glad to know that your own lady-of-the-manor and our honoured clanswoman Dr MacEochan is going to cut the ribbon across the new factory loading-bay. After which the Reverend Murdo MacNeish who I'm sure you all know and admire as much as I do will say a few words of blessing, over this new business enterprise. When I asked him, he had a few qualms at first, on account of all these graven images, but I said they were purely for export, and the only things we worshipped around here were low overheads and high turnover, so he kindly consented to come along and christen us, so to speak. And just to end things on a friendly note, we'll then adjourn to my private office, where the Mesdames Duncan and MacKay have laid out a lovely spread of sandwiches and scones.'

'No, you don't have to sit still. Honestly. Just keep knitting. Forget that I'm here. Just go on with your story.'

At the factory, Maria has been left in temporary charge; Scotty's gone back to look after his American companies, and the foreman's off sick with bronchitis. So she borrows a bit of company time to make sketches for her next sculpture, 'The Three Knitters of Cailleach West'. From all possible angles and perspectives, she draws Jean MacTaggart finishing her sock, Betty Mackay half-way through a fisherman's jersey and Flora Duncan starting on a scarf. To keep them from stiffening into self-conscious poses, she gets her models gossiping and reminiscing.

'Ah well, as I was saying, the Auld Man was not so happy about his daughter going in for the doctoring. He'd much rather see her married to someone from another old Highland family. Talked a lot about honourable alliances and the old traditions. He was a great one for the old traditions, when it suited him, not like his own feyther who was a tearaway if there ever was one. Came around the crofthouses preaching socialism, of all things, suggesting the royal family be pensioned off and the House of Lords abolished. Anyway, his son, Sir Angus, Catriona's daddy, decided that if she was set on the medical school she'd have to make her own way. He would pay not a penny for her training. Now in those days, all these grants and things weren't so easy come by, and anyways, seeing she had a family with its own wee castle, they'd hardly let her qualify. Never mind that those MacEochans have cried poor-mouth since the days of the Forty-five.

'So what does young Catriona do but start up a quarrel with him, right in front of the whole island, at the opening ceremonies of the Cailleach Games. Now I cannae mind what year that was, but it must have been the first games after the sweeties came off the rations, wasn't it, Flora?'

'That was it. My wee Gordy was so full of black strippit balls and soor plooms that he was sick all over the starting line for the caber toss, and they had to mark out a new place on the other side of the field.'

'Anyway, so as I was saying, there's the old man, in his finest kilt and all, with his wee mean eyes keeking through his glinting spectacles, and that wisp of a moustache that was all he could ever manage . . .'

'Not like his brother, with those great walrus whiskers . . .'

'But with a temper twice as hot. Dear knows what the lass said to provoke him – her just out of hair ribbons herself – but he exploded, in front of the minister and all, and roared, "Damn your cheek, girl, you will *not*!" '

'And you could have heard a pin drop, all over the ground. Not a whisper. Even the gannets circling over the tea-tent held their wheesht. There she was, all smartly turned out for the games, with her hair in one of those long horses' tails the lassies used to wear, and she tossed her head and said something so coarse and crude to her own father that the minister's wife, who was standing nearby, came all over queer and had to be revived with smelling salts . . .'

'What was it . . .?'

'Och . . . it was . . . I can't say it. I just can't.'

'You're a daft jessie, Flora. It was something beginning with a B.'

'Will you listen to the pair of them, Maria, you'd think those two old biddies were the original Foolish Virgins. What she said was "Bugger off you bloody old fool, I'll pay my own way and you can put your plans for my future where the monkey put his nuts."

'And just like that, she turns on her heel, picks up the nearest bicycle (it was Hamish Isbister, Graeme's uncle's old push-bike, but he didn't mind, he was too dead guttered by that time of the day) and pedals herself home to the castle. Packs a big satchel and goes away on the next boat.'

'And what happened next?' Maria rummages for a fresh sketchblock.

'Well, none of us saw hide nor hair of her for ages, after that. And it would be more than your life was worth to ask the Auld Man about his daughter, should you meet him at kirk or in the port. There were plenty of rumours flying about, of course, that she'd gone south and got the money from her other relations – but that was highly unlikely seeing that the various branches of the MacEochan family were rarely on speaking terms. And then there was a story that she'd got wed to some Greek millionaire, but nobody really believed that one either, although you never know.'

'Then, when my brother Davie got the scholarship, and went to study engineering at Edinburgh University, who should he meet in the refectory but herself. She was carrying a big stack of medical textbooks, dropped them all down the stairs at the sight of him. She was pleased to see a face from home, she said, and told him she was half-way through her course. Well, its a big place, Edinburgh, and he only saw her two or three times after that, jumping on to a bus, or rushing for a lecture or whatever.'

'When we heard she was there, we all wondered how she'd raised the money, but as she never came home for her holidays, there was no way to find out. That housekeeper up at the castle was a close-mouthed old biddy. Nobody spoke to her. She was English.'

'Then the summer after that, I had to go away down to Glasgow for a few weeks, to help out my sister Bella. She'd just had her twins, and needed a hand with the three other weans. One night, just to give her a wee break, my brother-in-law and I took the three big ones to see the fair on Glasgow Green. They went on all the rides, and Bella's husband won a beautiful big candelabra in the shooting gallery, and then they all said that it was time for me to have a treat. So I decided to have my fortune told. There must have been five or six different palm-readers there, but you know what I'm like. I didn't fancy the look of this one's tent, and there was too long a queue in front of that one's and so on, but it was getting past the bairns' bedtime, so I made up my mind I'd go to the last one, just before the exit. And so I did. "Madame Brigantia" it said in fancy letters over the door of the tent. And it looked quite respectable, with a nice clean curtain and all. So what should I see when I went inside but a gypsy with a bright green heidsquare and big dangly hoop earrings, and she said, "Next please," and looked up, and jumped just as high as I did. Because it was Catriona MacEochan herself, all done up in a fringey striped shawl, with black paint round her eyes and purple lipstick. I nearly fainted dead away. You'd scarcely credit it. And, of course, she knew that I'd recognised her. So she just said this was how she was paying her way through the Uni, and she'd done not too badly, all things considered. And would I like my palm done, or my cards read, or both together? Whatever I wanted, she'd do for half-price, being from Cailleach and all. I swear I was more embarrassed than she was; she seemed cool as anything.'

'So what happened next?'

'Now you should know that it's bad luck to tell the world what the speywife tells you. But I'll just say this, that I went through with it, and she told me a few things that later came out just as she'd said they would. Then we settled down for a good old crack about Cailleach people, until my brother-in-law shouted through the curtain that the bairns were asleep on their feet. So I had to go.'

'Did she swear you to secrecy?'

'Did she whit . . . No, she gave me her calling card, all funny foreign lettering, and told me to send my friends along whenever they were on the mainland and wanted their palms read. I never told the Laird that I'd seen her, though. I was feared it would bring on his second heart attack, and they'd all say I'd murdered the auld boy on purpose.'

For months, Granny's Hielan' Hame Industries hums with activity and lucrative overtime: the Hogmanay rush (beer mats, Auld Lang Syne teatowels and a new line of printed aprons that don't quite reveal what a knobbly-kneed Scotsman wears under his kilt) is rapidly followed by a panic, all-hands-on-deck attack on the backlog of plush Haggises needed in time for Burns Nights across the world. Things simmer down briefly in the darkest months of winter; lighting the factory on days of little daylight is not cost-effective. Maria uses her free time to work on a massive piece she calls 'The Sacred Fire', a circle of luminous sheet-metal flames traversed by a line of leaping dancers with snakes and lizards entwined in their spiky wrought-iron fingers. She also breaks into her now modestly thriving bank account and buys herself a second-hand motorbike from an Isbister cousin who's gone off to join the merchant marine.

On a day that is cold but unseasonably sunny, she heads down to the south of the island to pay a call on Isa in her weaving shed. The atmosphere around the loom is thick and steamy: a peat-fire is roaring, two paraffin heaters are belting out their moist and fumy heat, and Isa herself is taking a break from her work to imbibe a hot toddy that emits a heady fog of lemon juice, heated honey and warm poteen.

'Well it's long past time you've been to see me, dearie. Help yourself to some grog. How's the motorbike suiting you?'

'I'm learning,' says Maria. 'If there were more traffic on Cailleach I'd be dead three times over. But I thought today I'd try a good long run, and I have something for you anyway, so here I am.'

'Ahh, let me guess. It's never a bottle of fine wine – you'd shake it up far too much on that bike of yours and you're well enough trained by Catriona not to do that. And it's never some item from that dreadful factory of yours – for I'll grant it's given us a few more jobs, but you must admit it's a gey dreadful thing they're doing in the name of traditional crafts. The bossman, that American person, asked if I'd join them, you know – but that's only because he gets some sort of extra government grant if he hires the so-called disabled. I told him where to put his tartan teatowels, I did. I'll stay with my tweed.'

She unwraps the parcel that Maria hands her, and strokes the object that emerges, caressing it with her palms, brushing it with her finger-tip, tracing its outlines.

'It's all of stones and clay. I thought you worked in metal.'

'This is an experiment. Metal didn't seem right for it . . . or for you.'

'It could be the body of a sleeping woman, or it could be a line of hills and valleys.'

'It's the hills of the island; that's Nestaval in the centre. The view from your cottage window, looking north. I thought you'd like to

176

have it for yourself.'

'That's true, that's very true.' She strokes the curves of Nestaval, dabbles her fingers in the valley of the lochan, where the ruins with the curse on them stand on their tiny islet. 'Ah, that's the little tower . . . you have been faithful to the fine details, haven't you?'

'Lots of sketching, long nights with the Ordnance Survey map, walking the ground when the weather let me.'

'It's a good gift. I can touch the hills now and know what's happening on them – feel the cloud-shadows moving across the tops, learn how the sheep are faring, spot the hawks and the golden eagles, see who is walking near the broch, where they have no business to be . . .' she waggles her finger in warning at Maria.

'I only went up there once . . . when I first came to the island.'

'And you didn't stay long, did you?'

'It didn't feel . . . right. I didn't like it.'

'That's just as well, for if you had, you'd still be up there. And you wouldn't be the first, either . . .'

'Tell me about it.'

'Not today. We're expecting another surprise visitor, in about three minutes time.' She traces a line that skirts the southern ridge of hills on Maria's model of the landscape. 'That's them, just about there, heading down the brae. It will be Catriona, and someone else with her. A stranger, I think.'

Maria glances out the window. Catriona's land-rover is just pulling up.

'That's not fair, Isa. You heard her engine.'

'Well perhaps I did, and perhaps I didn't. I'm not telling you, dear.'

Catriona bustles in, leading a tall blonde woman festooned with cameras and tape-recorders and shoulder bags bulging with notebooks.

'Well, here we are, Isa. Sorry we're late, but the ferry was delayed. I trust you got the message?'

'Isa, you old charlatan,' mutters Maria.

'Well, Maria herself. This is a surprise. I've a friend of a friend of yours, here. Isa, Maria, meet Gretel Grogan. She's a friend of Stoney Stonebridge, from America. Doing a term at Edinburgh, in the School of Scottish Studies. Stoney's sent her here to collect some authentic Cailleach weaving-songs.'

'And she thinks I'm the one to provide them, does she?'

'Stoney said I really had to come and meet you-all. She said this was a really unspoiled little place and that Dr MacEochan would know just where to take me. It's for a project in ethnomusicology. I'm collecting weaving-songs from all over Europe.'

'And what's the purpose of that?' asks Isa.

'It's to preserve them, so they don't die out.' She puts a tape in her machine. 'Ready?'

'Oh dearie me, do you know something that I don't, Dr MacEochan? I was feeling in fine fettle when I rose up this morning, but if you're in that much of a hurry . . .'

'You look fine to me, Isa.' Catriona lowers her spectacles at her guest.

'Well, I don't know if I'm really in voice for the singing, just now. And I usually just hum to myself as I work. When I'm all alone. I don't think there's anything would interest your scholars and professors.'

'Well, I'd really appreciate it. I've got to do all of Scotland this week, and then it's up to Norway, and over to Finland, and then I want to make it back to France to pick up this Breton lady I heard about before I have to fly home in time for the spring semester. Anyway, I've got to get back on the ferry before it goes out again.'

'But you've only just landed,' says Catriona. 'I thought at least you'd stay for dinner, and spend the night. We can get you a lift on a fishing-boat over to Stornoway tomorrow.'

'I'm sorry, but it really doesn't fit in with my plans. Cailleach just gets this p.m. and then I gotta run.'

'Well, sit yourselves down then,' orders Isa. 'And Maria, pour them out some of that toddy, if we've left any. And I'll get back to my work meantime and see what I can produce for you.'

After pouring out the last cups of toddy, Maria perches on the wide windowsill, with the hills glowing blue-green over her shoulder. Catriona settles herself in the rocking-chair, and Gretel aims her microphone like a gun. Isa begins to weave and, soon, to sing.

Her voice is cracked but powerful, the Gaelic words soft and plaintive, the tune eerily familiar, although Maria cannot place it. She sings until the tape runs out and the machine snaps itself off.

'Well, that was really terrific. Now could you just tell me what the words mean in English?'

'Aah, that I could not,' says Isa. 'For the Gaelic is my mother-tongue you see, and though I could puzzle them out I've never thought of them as having any translation. They mean what they mean. It would take me days to think about them and translate them for you. But you take them back to one of your Gaelic scholars at your university (surely they have Gaelic scholars wherever they collect the ancient tales and songs?), and you ask someone to listen carefully and put them in English for you. They're nothing special really, mind you, just the old sad songs of love and loss. The same in any language.'

Gretel collects up her gear. She beams at Isa, and hands her a five-pound note. 'I really appreciate this. Is that enough for your trouble?'

'Och, I'll no take money for my singing. This is not your Eurovision Song Contest. Give it to your favourite charity, or give it to the doctor here, who can put it to some worthy island cause.'

'If you're going to make the ferry, young woman,' announces Catriona, 'we'd better hurry. She'll be just about ready to turn around.' She puts her hand on Maria's arm, and whispers in her ear. 'And you, my dear, had better come up and join me for dinner. I thought Miss Hit-and-Run here was staying the night, and I've poached a whole salmon-trout. You'd do well to come and help me eat it.'

Catriona starts up the land-rover and they disappear up the brae.

'Well, I'd better go myself, now, Isa,' says Maria. 'Thanks for the toddy, and I hope you like your present.'

'It'll do just fine. And in exchange, I might just weave you a new blanket for your bed. It's going to be a gey cold spring this year, I can promise you, and you get a cutting wind at night up there on the far west side.'

'I liked your singing. I didn't know you could sing.'

'Oh, I've many talents you've yet to discover, dear.'

'I don't know much about Gaelic songs, or old island music, but those tunes you were singing sounded very familiar. I just couldn't place them.'

'They were some of my own old favourites. Ask Catriona about them; she knows them well. It's my own Gaelic translations of Bessie Smith and Billie Holiday. I used to do them all the time as a Hogmanay party piece.'

'And now tell me what you've been up to yourself,' says Maria, as she sits on Catriona's hearthrug and swirls the brandy in her glass.

They have dissected Gretel Grogan along with the salmon-trout, sampled gossip from the souvenir factory and the post office as they worked their way through the Orkney cheese and the Caboc, and speculated on the saleability of Maria's latest sculptures as they sipped their coffee.

'Very dull winter, really. The usual run of fractures and chilblains. A lot of mumps running through the primary school. The children weather it well enough, but it's the queues of worried fathers in my surgery afterwards that wear me out; all fretting about their potency, or whatever. Then, of course, there's been my running battle with the Outer Isles Education Authority over sex education in the secondary boarding school at Stornoway. Need I say that Murdo and his mates are on one side of the line, and I'm on the other? I wouldn't mind so much if the meetings weren't always off the island, and I'm for ever running into the Minister coming back on the *St Rollox*. Can't imagine why he spends the money on the fare; you'd think he'd just walk home, over the water.'

She offers more brandy.

'No, I shouldn't. I'd run my bike into a ditch. What else is new?'

'I've been talking things over with my great-great-great-grandmother.'

'Come again?'

'Your splendid planchette. Far more efficacious than the last one. Would you like to join me in a little session?'

'No thanks.'

'Oh, and I've finally seen her.'

'Seen who?'

'The castle ghost. First time she's appeared in three generations.'

'How do you know? Probably just a little too much Château Latour after your last dinner party.'

'I wouldn't expect such cynicism from you. It's that Stoney friend of yours. I suppose attitudes are contagious. Like *herpes*. Which reminds me . . .'

'I am fine, Catriona. Just fine.'

'Bad company.'

'I haven't seen her for nearly six months.'

'Ah, but she'll be back soon. Easter's early this year.'

'Tell me about your ghost, then. What does she look like?'

'She's mostly shadows.'

'Then how do you know you saw her?'

'I woke up, and all the birds of the tower were glowing faintly in

180

the moonlight. Except there wasn't any moon. She was standing at the foot of my bed. Pale face, almost translucent. For a moment I thought it was you.'

Maria feels a tiny twist of jealousy. 'Then what happened?'

'Nothing. I tried a spell I know – for holding them – but she slipped away. And neither the board nor the pentagram nor the candles nor the words of power will bring her back.'

'You were dreaming, maybe.' Liar.

'She left a trace of her presence . . . an odd sort of iodine smell. It lasted for days.'

'When was that?' I hate you. Why to you now, and not to me?

'Three weeks ago yesterday.'

'Then she won't come back now.'

'And how do you know?'

'The trail is cold now. The door is closed.'

'Forty seconds ago you didn't believe me. Now you're playing the sibyl.'

'I've been studying up on the subject, out there in my western hermitage. It's a fine way to scare yourself to death on long winter nights. The library van keeps me well supplied.'

'And what's the good of that? A bit masochistic, isn't it?'

'This clean island air makes sleeping too easy. And I need my insomnia, for that moment between two a.m. and three, when my best ideas come.'

'Why not try an alarm clock?'

'I'd rather curl up with the Reverend Charles Findlay's *Compendium of Hebridean Apparitions*, published 1886, or *The Report on the Benbecula Poltergeists*, 1925. You'd be amazed what Stuart Macleod can order for you, on an inter-library loan.'

'Mere populist tittle-tattle. If you are seriously interested, I can lend you some far more authoritative works. But you'd have to promise to take care of them. Not read them while you're eating marmalade, or leave them lying around while you're playing with your blowtorch. They're very rare, and some of them are very old.'

'Catriona, I'm surprised you'd trust me with them.'

'Oh, I didn't say I'd trust you. I'd just lay some exquisitely terrible curse on you if you let them come to any harm.'

'Maybe some other time, thanks.'

'Are you certain I can't press you to more brandy?'

'No thanks, Catriona. Anyway, I'd better go. It's very late.'

'You could stay, if you wanted to.'

'I know I could. But I won't.' She squeezes Catriona's hand. 'But thanks for the offer.'

Up the brae, where the road forks, Maria decides against the turning that leads to the far west side. The wind blows out the long red hair from under her helmet; it flaps like a flag. Roaring up the road under a thick black sky, she is speared by a thousand pinpricks of starlight. She passes the Isbister croft – even Ina's asleep; the kitchen light is out – and parks the bike further up the track, near the stones. She walks to the circle; small pebbles, as old as the monoliths themselves, and perhaps more significant, rattle under her boots. She crosses to the far side of the ring, and stops before a thick oblong block of stone; she reaches out her hand and probes until she finds the spiral deeply etched into its surface, where no moss or lichen grows. She presses her face into a smooth hollow – an ancient cup-mark – and whispers into the stone: 'Where is she?' Then listens. A low, low humming that might only be the reverberation of the waves beating up against the cliff on Gosta Ness, a crack in the quietness, a sense of warmth as if the heat of her body were being sucked down into the chilled and thirsty rock. But no other signals. She cannot crack the code.

Stoney, as promised in a postcard, appears briefly at Easter.

'You know, I could stay with you during the summer instead of Ina. The university pays my living expenses for the dig, and I'm sure you could use a bit of rent. Maybe buy yourself a car instead of that clapped-out motorbike.'

'No thanks. Ina counts on your coming. I wouldn't dream of upsetting the delicate balance of the island economy.'

'I thought the whole place was rolling in it these days, thanks to your tacky souvenir factory.'

'It's a modest living for a few people, that's all. Anyway, you know you'll be welcome to stay over any time the spirit moves you.'

'Thanks.'

'I mean it. Now tell me about all the amazing conquests you've made this winter.'

'Don't think I will now.'

'Miffed?'

'No point, if it doesn't make you jealous.'

But the welcome Maria gives her surprises both of them with its warmth.

'JESUS H. CHRIST!'

'Sounds like the big boss is back from America,' they say on the assembly lines.

Much roaring and thumping from the private office. Scotty McCrumb, just off his executive jet from Taiwan to Glasgow, by way of the much slower *St Rollox*, is in conference with his designer.

'He'll be quite surprised by the new line of teatowels,' observes the Loch Ness Monster sewing-squad.

'IS THIS SOME KIND OF A JOKE?'

On the elkhorn keyring and cigarette-lighter assembly line, they wonder what he thinks of the new quotations on the coffee mugs.

'YOU MEAN YOU'VE ALREADY SHIPPED THE GOLD-ANGED THINGS?'

They can hear the moaning all the way to the shortbread-packing department. The shop floor lies in a deathly hush. Not a knitting needle clicks.

'ARE YOU TRYING TO BANKRUPT ME, MARIA MILLENY?'

'It'll be those ashtrays,' say the tartan dolly-dressers. 'Those ashtrays will have done it.'

Surrounded by the new lines for the next season, spread out in all their glory on his Norwegian-pine, Italian-designed executive desk, Scotty McCrumb buries his head in his hand and weeps.

'Ruined. Destroyed. Ravaged. Down the drain.'

Maria watches him with a cool detachment, thinks of Rodin.

'Look at this stuff,' he wails. 'Just look at it. All right, so I asked you to design a teatowel that says "Wha's Like Us?" I don't expect you to answer the question with a hand-lettered breakdown of the Scottish unemployment statistics. And why do these ashtrays have inscriptions about Scottish lung-cancer death-rates and tobacco company profits underneath the thistles? And I know I asked you to expand the Dress-a-Scottish-Dolly Kits beyond Mary Queen of Scots and Bonnie Prince Charlie, but who the hell wants a Scottish Dolly dressed up like John Maclean – whoever he may be – or Jenny Geddes. And who the hell is Jenny Geddes anyway?'

'She threw a stool at the minister in the High Kirk of St Giles when they tried to introduce an English prayer-book into the Scottish service. Sixteen something, I think. We can look it up.'

'Oh that's terrific. Fine and dandy. Just the dab. And what about these dadblasted coffee mugs? I asked for some cute Scotch slogans, didn't I, like "Just a wee doch an doris" and that sort of thing? Well, I didn't ask for a mug commemorating the names and death dates of Highland women burned as witches. And when I asked for a map of Scotland on the shortbread tins, I didn't ask for one that showed the NATO bases and American nuclear missile sites, goddammit!'

'Hang about, Scotty. I haven't finished . . .'

'Haven't finished, Milleny? You bet your sweet ass you've finished. You've finished the factory, you've finished a lot of nice people's jobs, and you've finished my considerable investment in plant and premises, over and above the Highlands and Islands Development Grant. Lady, you are not only finished, you are fucking fired. Pardon my French.'

'Have you looked at the ledgers and the order books yet?'

'Are you kidding, you crazy coyote? Just to give you the pleasure of seeing a strong man cry?'

'Well, before you jump off the Cliffs of Crunig . . .'

'You mean, push *you* off it, honeybunch. Remember, I'm first generation US of A, but I'm second generation Glasgow hardman . . .'

'Just look.' She sweeps aside a pile of hand-knitted, stuffed whales and baby seals all wearing 'SAVE US' badges, and thumps down a thick mat of computer printouts. He studies it, oblivious even to the unaccustomed sound of switched-off machinery and total, breathless silence on the shop floor outside.

'Well, I'll be hornswoggled. I'll be goddamned.'

'The only problem is, demand is outstripping our production capacity with current staffing levels. We'll need about five more full-timers, I think, and about twelve more home-based knitters and sewers if we're going to fulfil the orders on the book. Everyone is doing as much overtime as they can manage, but we're all getting pretty tired. They'd like a home life too, you know. And I'm supposed to be a part-time employee, and I haven't had a day off to work on my sculpture in weeks. Still, nobody would be upset if you offered an across-the-board payrise. I think you'll find it will help your pre-tax profits this year.'

'This is a lot for a good ole boy to take in at one gulp, sugar. Just hold your horses.' He shuffles through the printouts again. 'For a start, what kind of weirdos are buying all this stuff? Never anything like this came up on any of the market research product preference profiles . . .'

184

'Domestic market, mainly. Radical bookshops in Glasgow, some theatres and art galleries. Edinburgh wholefood collectives. Craftshops in Aberdeen. Vegetarian cafés in Ullapool and Anstruther. That sort of thing. Orders from down in England are picking up, too. Word of mouth, mostly; we've never advertised south of the border. And you'll be relieved to know we haven't stopped producing the old stock lines altogether. We know your commitment to exports, and your well-proven markets, and all that.'

'You are one crazy lady, Milleny. Brilliant, but crazy.'

'It wasn't my idea, Scotty. I just put the things down on paper – worked out the graphics and the colours and all. The whole staff came up with these ideas while you were away in America. That's the trouble with running a multinational empire, I suppose, you can't be everywhere at once.'

As Scotty rises, stretches, and opens the office door, the workshops on the other side once again swing into action: industrial sewing-machines start whirring, presses thump, shrink-wrap rattles, and poteen corks are heard popping everywhere from Scotty Dogs to Tartan Tammies. Jubilation reigns.

The Reverend Murdo is not a man of romantic or reflective nature, but he is seized sometimes, as he sits in his manse, for a great nostalgia for the dear dead days when kirk was compulsory and the minister's word was the word of God. He would like, if his prayers as a fully-fledged member of the Elect were ever answered, to petition for a return of public floggings; of the right to close-question and punish adulterers and other naughty persons; of a stool of repentance at the door of the kirk, where sinners would appear barefoot and barehead to be scolded and stared at for as many Sabbaths as it took to drive the Devil out of them; of the right to sentence shrews to the branks and the ducking stool, or condemn doubters to excommunication and banishment; of the privilege of advising parents when and how and with what to beat their children who smile or play in public places on the Lord's Day; of the right to forbid kissing and dancing and all unseemly debauchery among the populace. It seems to him unfair that he was born into a calling that had once enjoyed all these privileges and duties, at a time when it is no longer possible to exercise them. But in his sermons he can do all these things through the power of rhetoric; it only grieves him that so few come to hear them.

Still, he manages to ensure a fair distribution of soul-stiffening guilt by his practice of regular parish-visiting. At Ina Isbister's, he sips his cup of weak tea and shakes his head sadly over the children listening to music in the next room, wondering aloud what her 'poor dead mother, Lord rest her good soul, would have thought of all this'. At the house of the Co-op manageress he nibbles a jaffa-cake and laments the number of automobile accidents, marital break-ups and early deaths that would never have happened if her shop hadn't been licensed to sell spirits for consumption off the premises. At this house he speaks of the unattainable joys of heaven; at that house he warns of the inevitable torments of Hell. In most places the laws of Highland hospitality work on his side: they will not shut the door when once they have opened it to his knock; they will ask him in, and they will offer him food and (suitably decorous) drink. And they will listen politely to his conversation.

He chooses his targets with considerable care; he would no more knock at the door of the castle than at the gates of the Vatican, and a journey to such irredeemable heathens as Isa the Weaver would be a grievous waste of time and petrol. (This galls him; he would like to make capital in his sermons of how well she bears her God-given affliction, but to imply that it was God's punishment would, even he admits, be considered bad taste.)

Once in a while, however, his zeal misfires. During a call to the primary school teacher he makes bold to suggest that she should be vigilant during the children's annual medical examinations: did it occur to her that someone as – eccentric – as Dr MacEochan might fall prey to some uncontrollable temptation when presented with a queue of half-clad twelve-year-olds? Before he can draw breath, on this occasion, he finds his china teacup and saucer firmly removed from his hand, his custard-cream extracted from his grasp only inches from his lips, and his coat tossed out after him as a door slams behind him.

There is talk of a lawsuit; he receives an ominous letter from an Edinburgh firm of Writers to the Signet who have guarded the MacEochan interests since the days of the Forty-five. He has no recourse but to hold his peace, and find another outlet for his righteous wrath. So one dark night he steals out, disguised as a teenage vandal in the unlikely event of witnesses, and overturns all the nuns who stand like brooding crows around the convent ruins. The sculptures are heavy and hard to topple, but he goes home satisfied that he has done good work.

When the archaeological survey team arrives, their first task, at Stoney's command, is to restore the overturned nuns to their original positions around the ruined cloister. The attack on the sculptures has caused much outraged speculation around the island. One of Murdo's elders suggests that it might be high time for the Reverend to produce one of his soul-stiffening sermons on the curse of juvenile delinquency, teenage hooliganism, premarital sex, and their links with the increasing numbers of married women and mothers of children, working outside the home.

Although he complies, the sermon is not one of Murdo's more crackling performances. There is hardly a whiff of brimstone, and no one in the small congregation goes home feeling worse than when he or she came. A mark, according to Murdo's lights, of homiletical failure.

'Well, was it a good winter, up here without me?'

'Yes, if you must know, good enough. I've sold a few pieces thanks to an incredibly pretentious article in an obscure Italian arts review and a passing millionaire yachtsman who fancies himself a patron of young up-and-comings. And I've done a lot more.'

'Where is it?'

'Here and there. Scattered about the island. I did a model of the Cailleach hills for Isa, and . . .'

'Is that the weaver-person down at the south end? The one your friend Catriona introduced to Gretel Grogan . . .'

'You wished her on us, dearie. Don't blame me. Is she a particular friend of yours?'

'Why? You jealous?'

'Don't be funny. Of you and her?'

'She's not so bad.' Stoney bristles. 'But what makes you think there's anything in it?'

'Your sweatshirt, maybe. A parting souvenir?' She taps Stoney lightly on the chest, where a blazoned red-and-yellow slogan states 'Folk You'.

'She was just a passer-by. More to the point – how's Dr Dracula?'

'In fine fettle. At war with the Wee Schismatics over sex education and things.'

'Does she ever ask about me?'

'Not really. Why should she?'

'Aha! Caught you out. So you see her.'

'What do you expect? This is a small island.'

'What does she say about me?'

'Not much.' And I'm not going to tell you what she does say, anyway. 'You're not really part of her landscape any more. Whatever she wanted from you she got, I suppose.'

'Not a damned thing! Am I part of yours?'

'Part of what?'

'Your landscape?'

'Why so insecure this season? Not like our bold, brazen Stoney. Not enough conquests during the winter? No eyes meeting across the seminar table? No hands brushing against yours at the staff club coffee bar?'

'Be nice to me for a change, you swine. I'm feeling fragile.'

'Unlucky in love?'

'Of course not. They're still queueing up for my favours, all the way from the David Hume Tower to the Old Quad. No, a professional disappointment. I almost got on to the big Macchu Picchu project. Missed it by a whisker. Committee said I had to put in another year up in this dreary old hole.'

'You mean you might not have come back?'

'I would have sent you a postcard from Peru. Would you have missed me?'

'Would I?' Maria muses. Stares out the cottage window, watching the tide licking the broad lap of the empty beach. 'Yes, I suppose I might have. Mmmm. Yes. I definitely would.'

'Then why don't you come over here and show me precisely how much?'

In her tower, with reverence and by candlelight, Catriona opens a crumbling, vellum-bound tome on the ancient arts of weather-working. If she has her way, the archaeologists will be in for a wet and muddy season.

If there were still bards and chroniclers, the storms that hit Cailleach that summer would be worth a dozen songs and sagas. The roof is whirled off the kirk, Catriona's castle has half its Victorian lead pipes wrenched off the side of the eastern wall by the winds. Sheep huddle behind the dunes, the beach on the far west side is whipped up into a desert sandstorm, an empty crofthouse on the Cliffs of Crunig is ripped to pieces and its shattered wooden

188

door blown into the sea to make a coracle for some off-course gannets. Three or four times, the ferry is cancelled, and in the calms the Co-op nearly runs out of tinned provisions as everyone battens down.

A band of bad-tempered archaeology students idles away the hours in the Cailleach Inn, which enjoys a season of unprecedented profits; Stoney thinks about sending them away and calling off the dig until the weather improves, but she feels this display of weakness would not go down well with those who make the appointments for Macchu Picchu. So she sets them to drawing site-plans, diagrams, sketches of potsherds and ancient spade-marks. And when the rain is off, she whips them back to the site and brooks no complaints about cold and dampness.

The force of the gales gives new credence to the old tale about the Cailleach herself carrying the stones here from Ireland on the wind; more importantly it dissuades a top-secret committee of far-away generals from siting one of their small but deadly outposts on the far west side. It also, to Catriona's mild annoyance, drives Stoney ever more frequently to Maria Milleny's cottage.

However, the island soon has other things to talk about besides the weather. Scotty McCrumb's subsidy from the Highlands and Islands Development Board expires in a few months, and he is already letting it be known that Granny's Hielan' Hame Industries will probably be closing down. 'Sure it makes a nice little profit,' he tells those who ask him, 'but nice little profits ain't the name of the game. Besides, I'm getting a bigger grant to start up a sombrero factory in South America; I need to reallocate my resources without a cash-flow squeeze. But don't bother your pretty little heads about it, girls. You did OK before I got here, and I'm sure you'll do OK again. Besides, think how nice it will be to have lots of free time around Christmas so you can bake your cakes and knit some nice sweaters for your grandchildren.'

Orders have fallen off at Granny's Hielan' Hame Industries: a seasonal lull, once the tourist trade is in full swing and all possible retail outlets from John O'Groats to the Wee Marriage Hoose Giftie Shoppe at Gretna Green are stocked up for the summer. Maria takes time off from the factory; she's not the only one, for the winds make cycling difficult, and the island's fleet of battered cars are just as easily blown off the roads. She decides to experiment with enamels and fine etching, and makes a series of tiny metal wildflowers, perfectly to scale, growing out of a sculpted rock. The fine detail takes concentration; she is not totally enthralled with Stoney's frequent appearances on the days the weather is too wet for excavations.

'Ina Isbister,' announces Stoney one afternoon, idly fiddling with the buttons on Maria's workshirt, 'wonders why I've been away so many nights.'

'How do you know?'

'She asked me. Just like that.'

'Probably worried about charging you rent when you're never there. Maybe she wants to rent your room to somebody else, another pilgrim solving the Riddle of the Stones, or a repairman from the Hydroelectric Board or whatever . . .'

'Are you serious? Who'd come to Cailleach in this weather? The ferry's hardly ever running. We're bloody marooned.'

'Well, what do you tell her?'

'The truth, of course. That I'm with you.'

'Thanks a lot, Stonebridge! It's all very well for you transients, but I have to live here, remember.'

'What's the matter? Closety, are we?'

'Don't be ridiculous. Nobody has any secrets in this place. I just don't like everyone all over the island minding my business for me. And if I know my Ina, she won't be able to resist telling them all – chuckling over the fact she introduced the pair of us in the first place . . .'

'Don't get your knickers in a twist, pal. I told her you're doing a series of paintings, and I'm your model. I said you work at it half-way through the night, and when you finally stop I'm far too knackered to drive off into the storm. So I just bunk down on your tatty old settee.'

'Did she buy your story?'

'You bet. Said she'd like to commission you herself, to do her portrait. Heirloom for the grandchildren.'

'I'd love to, but I really don't think I'm good enough.'

'Nonsense. Anyway, I told her your prices were likely to be pretty high, now that you're becoming a Real Artist out in the great world.'

'Don't be silly. I'd do Ina for free.'

'When would you have the time?'

'It looks like there's going to be a lot more time about than there used to be. Word is out that Scotty McCrumb's planning to close the factory.'

190

'Well, well, well. And good riddance to him! I know you work there and all, but let's face it, that junk you produce down there is a blot on twentieth-century civilisation, most of it anyway.'

'Fine for you to say, sweetie, but it's going to put a few people out of work.'

'Well yes, granted, but you have to weigh that against . . .'

'Against what? You might not have noticed, on your annual archaeological jaunts, but things are pretty precarious up here. Nobody gets rich off the factory (except maybe Scotty, and I'm not even sure about that), but for some people it makes a lot of difference when the electricity bills come in.'

'Come on, it's only been open for a year or two now, it can't be making that much difference.'

'Go on, disappear up your own academic arsehole. Besides, what's rubbish to you is fodder for archaeologists a thousand years from now. Can't you just see some Dr Stephanie Stonebridge from the year three thousand droning on in her seminar on Materials and Methods in Late Twentieth-Century Thistle Ashtrays? Or producing a scholarly treatise on The Symbolic and Ritual Significance of Scottie Dogs Among the North Atlantic Teatowel People . . .'

'Get off your high horse and tell me what you're going to do when it closes. You can't live off your art just yet.'

'Something will turn up.'

'Why don't you come down to Edinburgh with me?'

Maria shakes her head. 'And be kept by you instead of Catriona? Come on, you're the one who's always lecturing me about . . .'

'I mean it. There are lots of things you could do in Edinburgh, and you'd still have plenty of time for your sculptures and things.'

'It's a kind offer, but you know I can't.'

'It's not a bloody kind offer, it's more than that. I'm asking you to live with me.'

'I thought you said you already lived with . . . "some people".'

'I'll boot them out.'

'Are "they" friends or lovers?'

'Irrelevant question.'

'Not if you're asking me to live with you it isn't.'

'But you won't.' A brief, hopeful gleam. 'Will you . . . ?'

'No. I won't leave Cailleach.'

'Tripe. You're fucking afraid to leave Cailleach. It's nice and safe and cosy here. Nobody challenges you. Makes you think. I think this whole business of needing to be up here to do your painting and sculpting is a load of pretentious elitist claptrap. The mystique of the artist in a lonely outpost. Drivel. You can do it anywhere. And you'd find a lot more stimulation in a city . . .'

'Crap to that, for a start. I was at a standstill before I came here.'

'You probably just needed a change of scene. Anyway, you hardly did a stroke 'til you got out of Catriona's clutches. I think it's time you had a change of scene again.'

'Since when are you my artistic mentor?'

Stoney wanders across the cottage, starts banging teapots and mugs and spoons. She shouts something at Maria, but it is lost in the din.

'What?'

'Never mind.'

She reappears, bangs down the teapot. 'I thought we were good together.'

'What does that mean?'

'It means you're rejecting me.'

'Stoney, I'm sorry. But I'm where I want to be.'

'You could come back in the summers. When the dig's on.'

'I thought next year you were trying for Macchu Picchu.'

'Oh, right. Well then, you could come up here when I'm off in South America.'

'When you can dispense with my services? Terrific. But no thanks.'

'Fuck it.'

'If you look in the press, you'll find a packet of chocolate biscuits.'

'What am I? Your bloody chambermaid?'

Maria fetches them herself.

'Diversionary tactic.'

'Have one.'

'Thanks.'

'I think sooner or later you'll come to another creative standstill. For a start, there's no stimulation here. No one to talk to.'

Maria's face turns as red as her hair. She splutters, nearly chokes on her biscuit. 'You damned urban imperialist!'

'That's a good one. What's it mean?'

'Nobody to talk to? Four hundred perfectly intelligent people living on this island, and you say there's nobody to talk to. Well that says a lot about you, friend. Because I think they're a lot

192

more . . . stimulating or whatever you call it, than your smug little academic wankers at the university staff club. And if you think this place is so boring, why do you spend thousands of pounds of public money every year, dragging yourself and your minions up here to dig holes in the ground? For the greater glory of your *curriculum vitae*? You might as well be up here digging test bores for storing radioactive waste. For all I know, maybe you are, and all this archaeology caper is just a blind. You're not even interested in this place. You're just exploiting us.'

'Cool it, Maria. You're too young for apoplexy. And I think it would amuse the locals to hear you of all people say "us".'

'Stop trying to handle me. You're as bad as Catriona.'

'Please don't choke to death. It's not the corpse that bothers me, it's the headlines in the *Sunday Sentinel*: "Lesbian Red-Head Dies in Island Love Tiff. Horror pictures, page three." And can you imagine Murdo's sermon over your sad little windswept grave? "The wages of unnatural sex and too many graven images . . ." he'll thunder.'

'Did anyone ever tell you your attempt at a Highland accent is diabolical?'

'That's better. You're breathing again.'

For a few minutes, they say nothing, but concentrate on demolishing the rest of the biscuits.

'So why *did* you come to Cailleach, then?'

'Well, I suppose it was, as you say, for professional reasons. At the time, it was the only dig that had an opening, in my field and at the right level. Besides, until now Latin America's been out of the question, Egypt's been done, Southeast Asia's too hot politically and nobody is giving grants for Greece any more.'

'Did you really think I'd go back to Edinburgh with you?'

'Well . . . no. I suppose I didn't. But you weren't very gracious about it. I thought you'd be flattered that I asked.'

'That's what I love you about you, Stoney. Your humility. When do you go?'

'About two weeks from now.'

'Come and see me before you go?'

'Maybe. If I have time.'

The skeleton is almost perfect. Its position is a puzzle; it neither crouches, as in a Neolithic burial, nor reposes supine, hands folded prayerfully, in the Christian manner. Instead it sits upright, leaning against the chamber wall. The dating estimates will have to wait, though, until the specimen is transferred to the laboratory in Edinburgh. For the moment, Stoney and her team are more concerned with the grave goods than with the corpse. Trinkets lie scattered around the body – a cruciform pendant, a bronze snake-ring, an amulet that might be ivory, carved crudely to show three fingers, and a set of interlinked spirals. Fragments of glazed pottery are found nearby – perhaps a jug or dish that once contained food-offerings for the dead.

Stoney is scrupulous about following the correct procedures, advising the correct authorities, arranging for the speedy collection and safe transportation of the find. But professional as she is about doing what is right and proper, she first can't resist a bit of showing off. So she bangs at Maria's door on some ungodly hour, when the late summer sun is just rising, and bundles her, half asleep and cursing, into the expedition van.

'Must show you something absolutely amazing.'

'It had bloody well better be.'

'Don't complain, you've at least had some sleep. I've been up for . . . must be nearly forty-eight hours. Working without a break. Living on tea and biscuits and slugs of whisky. I'm so tired I can hardly see straight.'

'Are you sure you should be driving?'

'Don't worry. I can do this run with my eyes closed . . .' She bangs on the brake. 'Damn! Bloody sheep. Sorry. You all right?'

'Can't you tell me what I'm risking my life for?'

'You'll see soon enough.'

The dig is deserted, except for the sculpted nuns, frozen in attitudes of work or prayer or meditation around the shattered cloister.

'Where's everybody?'

'I've sent them back to barracks for a well-earned rest.'

'Are you sure this isn't some plot of yours to lure me to a remote spot and murder me for my money?'

'Could be. Follow me.'

Stoney leads Maria along a catwalk that crosses the neatly sectioned-off excavation site, and switches on a small generator.

'What's that for?'

'You'll see.' She lifts away a thick covering of tarpaulins and plastic sheeting, and carefully lifts a trapdoor set into the earth. 'I'll go first. There's a ladder. Mind that cable. We've had to rig some lights up.'

They climb down a ladder, Stoney leading.

'What is this place?'

'An earth-house. Souterrain. Possibly Pictish. Maybe a store-house or a hidey-hole or even a home. Housing shortages are nothing new. But it's much, much older than the nunnery. The garden was planted on top of it. The nuns probably never knew it was here. Quite a find.'

'Oh, god!' Maria sees the skeleton.

'She's in wonderful nick, isn't she. And she is a she. That much we could tell straight away.'

Maria has seen skeletons before, stored safely behind the glass in museums, or wheeled out with many sly jokes and puns for a college anatomy lecture. But she's never met one on its own territory, sitting upright and smiling at her. She turns, clambers up the ladder with an agility that would, if she were clearheaded, surprise her, then bounds along the catwalk, gasping greedily at the morning air as if she wants to drink the pale blue out of the sky. Her mind whirls, the garden spins, the cracked walls of the convent hurtle past her. Her mouth is filled with the piercing, briny taste and smell of seaweed; her lips are salty. Behind her, Stoney carefully shuts the trapdoor, covers over the shaft.

'You all right? I didn't think you were squeamish.'

'I'm not,' she retorts through chattering teeth, then turns away and is almost sick before she steadies herself.

'Then why are you trembling? Come into the hut; I'll find you a spare jersey.'

Good question, why am I trembling? thinks Maria, and doesn't like any of the answers that suggest themselves. 'Cold.' In her mind's eye, the skeleton reconstitutes itself, the face is fleshed out into something recognisable, the reddish strands that lay limply along the polished skull grow more luxuriant. An artist's reconstruction.

'A goose walking over your grave?' Stoney grins. 'In my job you have to be tough.'

Maria just stares at her.

'Never mind, the best is yet to come.'

Maria doesn't move.

'I promise, no more horror movies. Step into my office, please.' Maria stirs herself. Stoney unlocks the hut, switches on the light, sits Maria down after clearing a space on a cluttered camp-bed. 'If you tell a soul about this I will kill you, by the way. Now please do close your eyes. I don't want you to see the combination on the lock. Official Secrets Act and all that.' She twiddles dials, curses softly, tries again, and finally opens a large metal strongbox. 'OK. Now look at this.'

The stone casket, lifted out of the box as carefully as if made of cobwebs, is opened to reveal a bundle of protective wrappings – opaque, chemically treated tissue, sterile enough to dress a wound. Stoney, wearing plastic gloves, lifts them clear, exposing a piece of parchment inscribed with a single, sparkling capital letter B. Intertwined ribbons of gold and silver form its outline, while the spaces inside the curves and hollows of the B are filled with triangles of sapphire blue, and emerald hexagons glowing fiercely against the smoothed and creamy calfskin.

Behind the letter, as if reflected in a misted windowpane, Maria sees a whitewashed room, a dying peat-fire and long, sure fingers sharpening a quill with a tiny knife.

Stoney's voice, behind her, comes from a thousand miles away, then jolts her back with a wrench. 'And that's not the half of it. Look at the rest.' Spread out on the work-table are other pages, still covered with their protective skins, together with a bracelet, some highly polished stones, a crucifix, some shards of pottery and – again – the little knife, side by side with a partly blunted quill. Maria fights the urge to pick it up and finish trimming it.

'What will you do with it all?'

'It's all going off to Edinburgh tomorrow, along with the lady down below. The big guns are all back from their hols this week, so we can get everything straight into the labs and get to work. We've just finished photographing everything *in situ*, making notes, drawing diagrams, measuring and measuring again.'

'Do you ever feel like a grave robber?'

'Don't be ridiculous. This is a fantastic discovery.'

'I look forward to seeing your name in the academic equivalent of lights.'

'This is big. This one will even hit the Sunday papers.'

'Congratulations.'

'You know, you're beginning to feel like a wet blanket. Maybe I was wrong to get you over here. I thought you'd be pleased. I think it's time I drove you home.'

'Never mind. I'd rather walk.'

'Don't be ridiculous. It's bloody miles.'

But Maria has already turned away. Soon she finds herself on the far west side, in front of her cottage, with no sense of the time that has passed or the distance she has covered. She starts to go in, then turns towards the beach, and walks down to meet the advancing tide. She stands on the shore until the icy water grips her ankles, then lets out a long, loud banshee howl in a voice that belongs to someone else.

The next night, Maria knows only by checking her watch that the ferry has gone. No sound of the *St Rollox* foghorn, or sight of her lights, reaches the far west side of the island. She stays awake most of the night, frightened to face her own dreams, working on some sketches for a sculpture that has suddenly stopped progressing. She finally falls asleep at her table, slumped over the drawings, and only wakes at the sense of a shadow. Someone is passing the cottage window. She blinks, imagines for a moment that it is Stoney, coming to bring her breakfast, and remembers that Stoney and her band are half-way home; they have sent their prizes away by helicopter, they are themselves kicking their heels on the quay at Stornoway, waiting for the mainland ferry. Maria goes to the door, sees no one, nor any footprints in the sand. The tide is high, but the iodine smell – of sloke and dulse and carrageen and bladderwrack – is overpowering.

'Something's up,' says Catriona, sniffing the wind.

Maria doesn't want to talk about it.

'Very well, I'll find it out myself.'

And she does. It could be bush telegraph (although one hundred and fifty years of sheep have eaten all the island's bushes), it could be her planchette tapping who knows what source of ghostly gossip, or it could be one of her troop of demon servants, with the spiky wings of a gothic gargoyle and a name out of ancient Persia.

'I know what you know,' she twinkles.

'Good,' says Maria, 'now we don't have to talk about it, do we?' And gathers up her library books and buzzes out of the port on her motorbike. Those who notice it attribute her moroseness to the imminent closure of the souvenir factory. Dismissal letters, all signed 'Yours Regretfully' by Scotty McCrumb, have just gone out to the workers.

'Murdo,' says Catriona pleasantly, as they sit in the Cailleach Hall waiting for the Community Council meeting to begin, 'did it ever occur to you that Christianity as we know it might be based on a typographical error?'

The Reverend MacNeish, who has been re-reading with some satisfaction his proposed resolution for closing down the Cailleach Inn, lifts his considerable eyebrows, and looks over his shoulder, where she sits behind him, grinning wickedly.

'With a mere change of a couple of letters in the original text,' she continues brightly 'the Son of God could, in actuality, have been a daughter.'

'TOSH!' replies the Reverend.

'In fact, in some remote communities on the fringe of the known world, before wicked Rome took over the shop, there may have been a female trinity: the Triple Goddess. Mother, Daughter, Holy Spirit. The boy was just a decoy, to distract the Emperor's secret police. A red herring. Hence, perhaps, the derivation of the fish as an early Christian symbol?'

'Absolutely blasphemous balderdash,' sneers Murdo. 'And just what I would expect from a mind as sick as yours, Doctor. I will not even dignify that sort of rubbish with a reply.'

By now the seats around them are filling up. Ina Isbister, Stuart from the Mobile Library, the manageress of the Co-op and several others sit silently, forsaking their usual greetings and gossip for the pleasure of eavesdropping on this contretemps.

'Rubbish you may call it,' declares Catriona, 'and rubbish indeed it may be, but it was once upon a time the practice on this very island. And if you'd ever troubled yourself to sully your holy ears and listen carefully to the local Gaelic oaths and curse-words, you'd still catch traces of it lurking in the common speech.'

'What imbecilic imported theories have you been imbibing along with your strong spirits?' inquires the Minister. 'Sometimes I can scarce credit your stupidity, woman.'

There is a slight gasp from the body of bystanders. To them she may be – after hours – Catriona. But to him she is and always has been Dr MacEochan. This altered attitude bodes no good for the keeping of the public peace.

'There's archaeological evidence. Have you not seen yesterday's *Scotsman*? It's just off the ferry. Or perhaps you only read the *Sunday Sentinel*? Fewer syllables, so you don't have to tire your lips overmuch before your long sermons.'

She unfolds the newspaper, holds up the front page to display a large, blurred reproduction of a tattered but ornately decorated manuscript, adjoined by a smaller, much sharper inset photograph of Dr Stephanie Stonebridge.

'Will you look at that,' sighs Ina. 'The wee soul's only been gone for a few weeks and she looks terrible. I told you Edinburgh was an unhealthy climate.'

'She's found something interesting while grubbing in our convent garden.' Catriona reads out the report of the chance discovery by the Joint Scottish Universities Cailleach Project. ' "While excavating the site of the vegetable garden of the tenth-century Convent of St Bride, Dr Stephanie Stonebridge came upon a souterrain, or earth-house, predating the nunnery itself . . ." '

'What's that when it's at home?' asks the harbourmaster.

'An underground chamber,' Stuart Macleod says brightly, 'you know, like the one on Cailleach Bheag where we keep the mmmmf.' Ina Isbister's hand shoots over his mouth as she gives him a surreptitious kick from behind.

'As I was saying,' Catriona continues loudly, fixing Murdo with a basilisk stare, ' "the chamber was found to contain, as well as some human remains and small artefacts, an iron box of primitive construction, containing within it a stone casket, concealed inside a bundle wrapped in oilskin, the whole enclosed in a large leather sack. Inside these coverings lay some half a dozen vellum quarto folios, apparently a fragment from or copied extract of some more extensive manuscript. After careful transportation," et cetera, et cetera. Anyway, they've tucked it away in the rare books vault at the university so the scholars can have a go at it. They think it's a fragment from a previously legendary heretical gospel, of which no extant copy has ever been found.'

'Get to your point, woman,' says Murdo wearily.

'It is,' says Catriona, glaring over her spectacles, 'an account of some saint, or possibly goddess, who took part in the Nativity. Helped Mary deliver not one but two babies – a twin boy and girl. Working in collusion, the saint or goddess spirited away the female child, and the Virgin presented the boy to the waiting multitude. He, unfortunately, seems to have monopolised all the presents. Further analysis of the text is now in progress, with specialists in attendance from Rome, Berlin, California and Jerusalem.'

The Reverend's robust eyebrows are scuttling up towards his receding hairline. He says nothing, but his face is thundery.

'Quite a turn-up. The Cailleach Codex. Puts us on the map right along with Lindisfarne and the *Book of Kells*,' says Stuart.

'It could be a good thing for us,' muses Ina Isbister. 'Might bring a boost to the tourist trade.'

'It could do,' says Catriona, 'as long as we can accommodate the influx of visitors and control them. We must make sure they confine their drinking to the residents' bar at the Cailleach Inn, where their mainland habits have less chance of corrupting our young people. Don't you agree, Reverend?'

Murdo quietly crumples his draft resolution about shutting the inn. The manageress of the Co-op remembers her responsibilities, moves to the head table, and bangs her gavel.

'Well, we'd better begin the business meeting. First item on the agenda is, of course, to wish everyone a happy Halloween.'

'Thank you for coming,' says Catriona, stepping out of her no-nonsense tweeds and slipping into the opulent court kimono of a Tokugawa princess. 'And thank you for waiting. The meeting went on and on.'

She appears to be speaking to the stuffed skua, or to the taxidermed solan geese, for there is no one else in sight except two cream-lapping cats and her own reflection in the glass.

Scuffed chalkmarks, last vestiges of a pentagram, are faintly visible on the floor, but they have clearly been there for some time, symptoms of Catriona's haphazard housekeeping: there is no smell of incense or brimstone or oil of orris root to suggest any recent conjuring. An inquisitive gull, skimming close in alongside the tower, looks in the window and sees that Catriona is addressing her remarks to Maria Milleny. Half-hidden by the old oak press, Maria sits cross-legged on the floor, in the open doorway of Catriona's so-called cabinet of curiosities. In her lap lies an unwrapped bundle of coarse-woven cloth.

'Well, what do you think?'

Maria looks up at her, shakes her head, says nothing.

'Lovely, isn't it? Much better than Stoney's stuff.'

'Bit of an understatement – lovely!'

'You don't have to talk in that churchy whisper, dear. This is my bedroom, remember? The Unholy of Unholies.'

'Where did you find it?'

'I didn't find it,' replies Catriona, pouring twenty-year-old island malt into two glasses. 'It was given to me. More or less.'

'What's that supposed to mean?'

'That,' smiles Catriona, swirling the amber liquid, 'you will have to figure out for yourself.'

'How long have you had it?'

'Long enough.'

'There's no point in asking you anything. You're worse than Stoney.' Putting her glass well out of the way of the bright, fragile pages, she buries herself again in the *Book of Bride*.

'This one's complete, I think. Stoney's must be only a fragment of it. Perhaps a copy, by someone else. We'd have to look at them side by side to see.'

Some pages display both text and pictures, with birds flying through the paragraphs, and gaily striped serpents busily threading their way along the margins, meeting and tangling to make a dense plaited frame for the words. Other sheets are pure decoration: lozenges, crescents, sunbursts, spirals, or the heads of veiled women who might be saints or goddesses or both at once. Interspersed between the separate chapters of the text are pages filled with trees and flowers. The reader is compelled to penetrate dense forests and gardens, composed of every leaf and petal and bud and fruit ever known to the north. Maria thinks she can almost smell their perfume, and in the silence of the tower on the barren shore she is teased by the sound of wind through far-away branches.

She stays where she is for most of the night, studying the pictures and the ornamentation, touching the vellum as circumspectly as she would a shy new lover.

Catriona goes about other business. It is, after all, All-Hallows Eve. She lights candles, burns incense, throws dice and apple peelings, mumbles over fires, makes incantations, drinks wine that looks like dragon's blood.

For all Maria knows, Catriona could be leading a dance of devils, or interviewing squads of spirits for the post of Chief Familiar; she hardly notices anything, except the flickering of the candles that illuminate the room.

When the morning light floods the tower and slides along the plumage of the motionless birds, Maria puts the book aside. 'Enough,' she says, 'for now.'

She wraps it up carefully, then yields to Catriona's demands that she come downstairs and eat some breakfast.

'Why won't you tell me where you got it?'

'It has always been in my family.'

'Why didn't you ever show it to me before?'

'To be perfectly honest, I'd forgotten I had it.'

'You what?'

'Have you ever considered the accretion of books and papers and documents and boxes full of scrolls, charters, receipts, contracts, old laundry lists, failed blackmail attempts, love-notes, Victorian ladies' calling-cards, proposals of marriage from sorely misguided Regency fortune-hunters, maps of feuds and fiefs, formulas for alchemical experiments, recipes for Lady Grizzel Baillie's Rumty-Tumty Cakes and unpaid tailor's bills this place contains? Do you know that behind my little Cabinet of Curiosities there lies a strongroom that hasn't been cleared out since all the servants went off to die for King and Country in the Great War? That in a lead-lined cupboard alongside my number three wine-cellar there are stacks of deeds with royal seals attached by the last shreds of red tape ribbons, and cases full of architects' plans for rebuildings and renovations that were – thank heaven – rarely carried out. I have always thought I might sort through the stuff, but it's all become reduced to a graveyard of good intentions.

'If I'd been trying to seduce you up here in a more classically-approved gothic–romantic manner, I'd have probably asked you to come up and catalogue the family library and papers. Thank goodness I didn't: you have a fine sense of line and colour and composition, but your spelling – the little I've seen of it – leaves much to be desired. Anyway, there was the Patronise a Struggling Artist gambit . . . and it paid off better in the end, didn't it, for both of us?'

'Catriona, stop hedging. Get back to the manuscript.'

'All in good time. Anyway, as I was saying, the accretion of some four centuries of neglected paperwork by a family of irresponsible magpies is an awesome inheritance – even discounting the baggage brought into the family by the distaff side, or the stuff that was here already and never cleared out from the previous occupants (for the castle, in places, goes back a fair sight longer than my family on the paternal side). Is a person supposed to spend her lifetime sorting it all? I've done my best, but then I've mostly gone through it when I'm looking for something specific . . . the secret papers of an ancestral wizard, say . . .

'Anyway, I came upon it when I was looking for something rather different. Perhaps we'd better make another pot of coffee, first.'

Maria, well-drilled after her months with Catriona, goes to the kitchen, mingles beans from two different mountain regions with the beans from the lower slopes in a carefully prescribed proportion, grinds them together in a wooden coffee-grinder with a handle of highly polished brass, worn silky-smooth by the strong hands of long-gone generations of kitchenmaids. She brews the coffee, warms milk taken from the covered bowl that one of the Isbisters has left, as always, on the kitchen doorstep, then carries everything into the hall on a brass Indian tray – left over from someone's imperial adventurings – and allows Catriona to perform the ultimate mingling of liquids as only she knows how.

Catriona has left the table in the meanwhile, made a swift search along a wall of glazed bookshelves, and comes back with a small octavo volume bound in yellowed calfskin.

'This is part of the story,' she says. 'An early edition of King James's *Demonologie*. Worth a few quid, of course, and if I had any sense I'd sell it for a staggering sum and never have to work again. But I keep it for sentimental value, and I keep it carefully. It was a great bestseller in its day – if the King writes a book, and you have political ambitions, it's best to buy a copy for your library, a copy for your bedside, and another dozen copies to present to guests and friends. I'm sure my respected ancestor bought out an entire print-run for his own purposes, and made sure the word got back to the royal author. Because inside the cover of the book, you'll find a letter from the King himself – there, don't be afraid, hold it carefully, that's right – recommending his magnum opus to my ancestor. On the grounds that it might make all the difference between life and death for him, as strange rumourings had come to the court at Holyrood of the uncanny women who stalked this island: who could whistle up winds, look into a glass and see future events played out before their eyes, listen to the secretmost thoughts and fears of others as easily as if they transformed themselves into fleas and crawled inside their neighbours' ears.

'Now the King had gifted my ancestor the island of Cailleach in the first place, in reward for all manner of intimacies and affections, freely given, yet now it seemed as if he were trying to frighten him away from his brand-new domain. Who knows – maybe Royal Jamie had second thoughts, and the next favourite in the queue wasn't as much fun behind the bed-curtains. But old great-great-great-greatcetera-grandfeyther was not for a return journey to Edinburgh. Once he was in his castle, in his castle he stayed.

'But, fearing that his kingly patron would take offence if his advice was ignored, he began to keep what he called his catalogue of uncanny happenings, presumably to convince His Witch-hating Majesty that he was on guard against Satanic attacks. The notebook, in his own hand, is entitled Cailleach's Dark Closet Opened. In it, he dutifully wrote down everything about the place and the people that seemed eerie and unChristian, and the scope went far beyond the predictable tales of unfriendly neighbours cursing each other's cattle and sheep. There were reports of hauntings, dutifully reported spells and philtres, accounts (always third-hand, and he never names his sources), lists of old pagan beliefs, names of goddesses that were still invoked in times of trouble, heretical remarks passed by the minister of the day – a rather suspicious character, with more than a taint of Papistry and a whiff of something worse besides. But so scrupulous was he in describing the steps of the dances, and words of the songs, that the islanders performed at what he called their 'midnight convocations and naked sabbats' that one might think he was getting rather seduced by it all. He had come to spy and condemn, but it is conceivable that he stayed to worship, for the last half of the notebook is a straightforward list of notes: Implements Necessary for the Rite of Summoning Demons, A Foolproof Receipt for the Purchase of a Reluctant Maiden's Affections.

'He also mentions that he has, in his possession, a secret volume of great antiquity, lettered in the language of the Persian demons (for he could not read it, despite his Latin schooling) and adorned with pictures of a most curious design. I unearthed my ancestor's notebook just before I left Cailleach – found it after a particularly nasty row with my father, when I'd retreated to my Cabinet of Curiosities so I could scream and cry without being heard. There it was, in a metal document box, hidden behind a great heap of Victorian hip-baths and Sheraton commodes. Needless to say, I could hardly make head or tail of it – if you think my writing is indecipherable, my dear, you try sixteenth-century script – but when I left Cailleach to go to university, I took it with me. In my first year at Edinburgh, I lodged with a medievalist (ah, but she's another story, for another time) who helped me learn to read the handwriting.

'The book opened some interesting windows – a counterpoint to all those dreary anatomy textbooks and modern pharmacopaeias. And, of course, when I was homesick, it carried me back to

Cailleach. Then life overtook me, and hospital training, and I put it away and never looked at it again until I came home here.

'At some point, after coming back, I read the note about the so-called secret volume and thought I must someday have a hunt through the castle, see if it was still about. But, at the time, I did nothing about it – I was consulting the notebook for another matter . . .'

'Which must have been pretty important, if it made you forget about a medieval treasure.'

'If you must know, and I suppose, being you, you must, I was looking for a foolproof love charm. At the time, nothing else seemed very important.'

'And who was the lucky object?'

'That's none of your business.'

'Oh come on, Catriona, give me a hint.'

'All right. She's still on the island.'

'Surely not . . . Ina Isbister?'

'And why not – she's a fine woman. But no. Not Ina.'

'I can't think. Isa?'

'She'd never have me. Besides, any love-philtre I tried would bounce back off her and hit me right in the face. She has the best psychic shield on the island . . .'

'I give up.'

'Then I won't tell you.'

'Why not?'

'It was a hopeless case. A completely irrational obsession. Fine if you're sixteen, but I was thirty-five at the time.'

'Catriona, don't you think we know each other well enough to share a few guilty secrets?'

'All right.' She blushes scarlet, looks down at her lap. 'It was Morag.'

'Who?'

'Morag. At the time she was new to the island. The minister's child-bride. Morag MacNeish.'

'Are you having me on? Mrs Murdo? You must have been out of your mind.'

'Perhaps I was, at the time. But don't judge her by the company she keeps. There are hidden depths there.'

'So what happened?'

'Nothing. She never gave a glance in my direction (perhaps I should have taken up going to kirk . . .) and Murdo, despite all my efforts, never developed so much as a pox or an ague. Perhaps my ancestor's formulae need updating. Now wipe that smirk off your face, young woman!'

'So you gave up on the notebooks. But what about the *Book of Bride*?'

'It turned up, of its own accord. Quite recently. Do you remember that fantastic storm in the summer? The one that tore the pipes off the eastern wall? Well, when Ina's husband came along to repair the damage, we had to lift some stones off the inside wall . . . and there it was.'

'You've been keeping the secret well enough.'

'I knew I shouldn't act precipitously. My planchette said so.'

'Your planchette?'

'Of course. Who else should I consult in such a delicate business? I had trouble getting it to spell out anything coherent . . . it was mostly garbled, but the same letters started coming up repeatedly. The message was either BRIDE or BIDE. So I decided to do what I think it told me. Wait and see.'

'And what are you going to do now?'

'Pour us some champagne, I think. Mix it with some fresh-squeezed orange juice and . . .'

'I meant about the Book, Catriona.'

'Ah yes. I am going to wrap it up with the greatest care, take the next ferry to the mainland, proceed directly to Edinburgh, and Tell the World. Dr Stonebridge may have a fragment, but I have the whole.'

'Stoney will be livid.'

'Quite.'

Surrounded by a nimbus of rumour, the *Book of Bride* – in its complete, authoritative version – enters the world. Some whisper that the Wee Schismatics tried to purloin it before it left the island, to burn it ceremoniously as an idolatrous text. But if Murdo and a gang of masked teetotal bandits were waiting at the harbour, they lost their nerve before Catriona turned up to board the ferry. Indeed, other sources say that the Schismatics greeted the discovery of the manuscript with unbridled delight (several independent witnesses confirmed that the corners of Murdo's mouth were seen to twitch and turn up for a brief but perceptible instant): whatever its extravagances in the matter of gilding and graven images, the Book does much to implicate the Papist creed as a distorted form of goddess-worship.

It is murmured, in the discreet antechambers of the better auction rooms and the more important university and national libraries, that the Vatican is after the Book as well. An unknown monsignor has been spotted changing flights at Heathrow, in transit from Rome to Glasgow Abbotsinch, carrying an unusually large but apparently empty suitcase. He is also thought to be carrying a very large cheque, drawn on a Swiss bank innocent of the faintest whiff of freemasonry. Cognoscenti among art historians and antiquarian bookdealers of the better class identify him as Chief Librarian of the Archive of Eradicated Heresies and Spiritual Scandals, last seen in London when the Apocryphal Gospel of Saint Barabbas was auctioned off by the executors of an anonymous estate. Presumably he wants *Bride*, like Barabbas, to be safely locked away from the world's eyes, alongside the Sacred Songs of the Albigensians, the Cathar Manuals of Carnal and Spiritual Love, the Decoded Kabbalah, the Secretmost Siddur of the New Messiah Sabbatai Zvi, the Ex-Cathedra Testimony of the Inquisitors of Toledo, and A Report on the Epidemic of Virgin Births in the Province of Palestine by the Imperial Physician.

Because Bride's Book is an object of rare beauty, even those with no interest in goddess-worship, early Christian heresies or the finer points of Celtic illumination techniques, are salivating. The *Sunday Sentinel* reports that a certain Swiss armaments billionaire would pay anything for it. So would the Royal Family, the Bodleian Library and the Mafia.

Catriona says she's not in it for the money. Few believe her. She wants the treasure to stay in Scotland, in the hands of those who will preserve it, study it and display it to the public with the proper care. The fine old firm of art-auctioneers shakes its collective head over this stipulation. If she opened up the bidding to a wider circle, they venture to suggest, she would realise a price that would keep her in the century's greatest claret vintages for ever. But she quells her agents with a glare that makes their pinstripes ripple.

In the end, Bride's Book goes to an ancient Scottish university with an ultra-modern library, boasting a subterranean Rare Books and Manuscripts department that will withstand earthquakes, nuclear wars and the Second Coming. Catriona, satisfied, goes home to Cailleach. As soon as she steps off the ferry, she hurries home and places a transatlantic telephone call to Scotty McCrumb.

Despite her vastly inflated bank account, swollen with the spoils of the auction sale, she frets and fumes as her call is fielded from one tier of clerks and secretaries and special assistants to another. Finally she reaches the Great Man by a radio-telephone in his golf cart.

'Well I'll be a consumptive coyote! Dr MacEochan of all people. How's the weather over there in bonnie Scotland?'

'Forget the niceties, Scotty. This is business. I want to buy the factory.'

'Which one, Doc? I got hundreds . . .'

'You know which one. The Cailleach one.'

'Granny's Hielan' Hame Industries. But we're closing it down . . .'

'Why not sell it to me, then?'

'I'm afraid you couldn't meet my price, Doc. Unless you've finally taken my advice and turned that quaint little castle of yours into a motel.'

'How's this?' She names a figure well-judged but not extravagant, carefully calculated to offset and exceed any tax loss he is hoping to achieve by shutting down the factory. No fool, she has phoned up an ex-lover who is a very important person in the City, despite her gender, and worked out the perfect price. He accepts.

'Doctor, you surprise me. I didn't think you were a business-lady. What with all your socialised medicine and all . . .'

'Let's not inflate my telephone bill with banter, Scotty. The papers should be forwarded to my lawyers tomorrow.'

'It's a deal. See you at the next Clan Gathering? We're hoping to hold one next summer in Missoula, Montana.'

'It sounds . . . amusing, Scotty, but I think not. Goodbye.'

But Catriona is not finished with her business. Once the appropriate papers for the purchase of the souvenir factory have been drawn up and signed, accompanied by some scathing remarks on the part of Catriona's legal cousin Roddy, she hands over the documents to a small delegation of knitters from the tartan tammy department and packers from the Loch Ness Monster assembly line, in exchange for a crisp five-pound note. Granny's Hielan' Hame Industries has become a workers' cooperative.

Late at night, in her tower, she mulls over other possible projects that might benefit the island – perhaps a research institute to explore the medicinal uses of seaweed? A training college for midwives or speywives? An experimental project to see if grapevines can be produced in the Hebridean climate? The possibilities will occupy her pleasantly as the days draw in. In the meanwhile, she sees no reason to deny herself a few home comforts: her favourite firm of Edinburgh wine merchants is soon observed perambulating Charlotte Square with a smile on its face, oblivious to the bitter wind off the Firth of Forth.

The sculpture of a faceless woman stands outside Maria's cottage; her streaming hair is a tangle of metal seaweed, and she carries a wire basket filled with polished stones.

'What's her name?' asks Catriona, who has arrived, uninvited, with a picnic.

' "The Walker on the Beach". Do you like her?'

'Silly question. Is she for sale?'

'Not for all your gold and silver.'

'I thought not.'

In the house, Catriona unpacks cold chicken, salads and one of Ina Isbister's cheeses, while Maria surreptitiously wipes the smudges off her two glasses.

'We really must get you some proper wine glasses, you know. And a slightly better *batterie de cuisine*.'

'A new tin-opener would do nicely, thanks.'

'Ah yes, alas.'

'You're not looking very cheerful for someone who's pulled off a few spectacular coups.'

'I know.'

'If it's any help, I had a postcard from Stoney. She's seething.'

Catriona brightens, briefly, then relapses into gloom.

'I hope I've done the right thing. Letting the Book leave the island.'

'Why's that? Look at the good it's done . . . saving the factory and all. And at least you know it's in a safe place. It won't be eaten by moths or woodlice or whatever, or destroyed by rot, or . . .'

'Yes, yes, of course, I know all that, don't be silly, girl.'

'Then what's your problem?'

'Something deeper. You wouldn't understand.'

'Don't flatter yourself. I'm a big girl now, I can grasp quite abstract concepts . . .'

'Sarcasm is out of place. I'm simply feeling a bit . . . uneasy.'

'Why? Getting flak from your planchette about selling the manuscript? Abusive phone calls from the Other Side?'

Catriona sniffs. 'Of course not. I consulted Them before I offered it for sale. They voiced no objections.'

'Then what is it?'

'I'm afraid that Bride may have left the island with it.'

'She hasn't. She's here.'

'What makes you so certain?'

'I just know she is. That's all.'

Catriona looks at her over the top of her spectacles.

'And what have you been up to, young woman?'

'My turn to be enigmatic.' She pours out more wine. 'The Book's a wonderful thing. But it's just a document. Her fingerprint on that particular piece of time. She's still here. Promise. If you're feeling sad after selling the Book, it's not the loss of Bride, it's because you've given a piece of yourself away.'

'Maybe that's one and the same thing.'

'Could be. I hope she doesn't strike you down for your arrogance. Anyway, if it's any consolation, I feel depressed every time I sell one of my sculptures. For the same reason.'

'But something feels different.'

'You're the one who's gone off the island. Business trips and auctioneers and press conferences and wheeling and dealing. Come back to us, settle in again. You'll see she's still here. Perhaps you need a little cleansing period – prayer and fasting?'

'Perish the thought!'

'I'll bring her back to you.'

'Who's being arrogant now?'

'Trust me. And watch this space.'

Bravado's all very well, with a tumbler full of Catriona's favourite picnic Rioja in your hands, but how do you deliver the goods? How do you conjure up the spirit of a sometime saint and supposed goddess?

Maria, teased and obsessed by this puzzle, paces up and down the beach in front of her house, and, when the rain or the night comes on, across her floorboards, pondering, and waiting for something to happen.

She uses up, tears up, a dozen sketchpads, and makes little models from her breakfast rolls, then tosses them away into far corners where they gather mildew. She cringes at her own cockiness, and wonders if pre-Celtic goddesses are sufficiently well-read in Greek drama to remember their responsibilities and strike her down for overweening pride. She would love to prove Catriona wrong, and make her happy, which in this unusual instance amounts to the same thing.

She tries the usual island solution, punishing doses of local and imported spirits, and finds they make her sick instead of visionary. She will have to go this one alone, and blunts a few hundred pencils thinking how.

But, in time, the island begins to wake up to a surprise or two.

It has been said of the Cailleach herself, the island's namesake (the sister, rival and one true love of the goddess Bride), that she brought the standing stones to the outer isles in the folds of her skirts, or blew them easily across the western sea in a skycracking gale. When she's friendly and well-disposed, she's the good Old Woman; when she puts on her terrible gown of storms and powers she's the Queen of Stones. All the solemn circles and marching alignments and inexplicably skewed triangular formations belong to her before and after they are registered, protected and controlled by any statutory inspectorates of ancient monuments.

So there are some nervous reactions, in an island where no one has acknowledged her existence out loud for a thousand years, to the new crop of stones that sprout suddenly, half a mile across the field from the ring itself. They are, however, without the province of any Queen of Stones, for they are constructed of an aluminium framework, exuberantly overpainted in bright enamels. So, unless she has decided to rename herself the Queen of Scrap Metals, the Cailleach simply doesn't have a case of complaint that would stand up in any celestial law court.

Bride herself, whose *curriculum vitae* lists the title (among others) Goddess of Smithcraft, naturally takes a more active interest. Particularly because the stones are portraits: of anonymous nuns, of a smiling Ina Isbister, of Catriona with a dangling stethoscope and a high-pointed witch's hat, of the postmistress, and Miss MacEochan from the school, and a blue-eyed Viking maiden with her hair made of coppery plaits, interspersed with island women whose heads are shawled in the heather-coloured Cailleach plaid. They brood all together over a central, slab-like altar, reminiscent of the original ring's putative Stone of Sacrifice. Here, trussed up, lies a black-clad figure in clerical collar, sporting a pair of bushy eyebrows that have been deftly built up from layers of flaking rust.

Still, this is only one of the novelties causing comment in the post office queue.

The Minister decides that he will not dignify the ridiculous caricature with any response or statement, but he loses his patience once and for all when he arrives at his kirk one morning to discover a tall corrugated-iron grotto that has seemingly sprung up overnight on the opposite side of the road.

RIVAL FIRM says the sign beside it, in bold green letters, gothic in style. Within the shed, a heavy-bellied plaster earth-goddess, beaming and good-humoured, folds a double pair of arms across her generous bosom. She stands foursquare on an old copper wash-boiler. Below her, in a gleaming bronze bowl, a fire burns perpetually, constructed from the painted tongues of flame that once adorned a long-departed custom car, relic of the Isbister brothers' long-ago drag races on the west side sands. And next to this sits a little wicker basket, adorned with plastic flowers, bearing a whimsically-lettered sign requesting *Tithes, please. Coins, cheques, all major credit cards cheerfully taken.*

Murdo picks up the basket, shakes it, and finds, to his everlasting disgust, that it already jingles.

Murdo promptly discards his prepared sermon, and instead screams forth an extemporaneous peroration. Although incoherent in patches, it is sufficiently thunderous to keep even the most jaded Sunday morning worshipper awake.

'And the Lord saith that thou shalt bow down to no graven images. Yet here, in Cailleach, we now find ourselves occupied by a veritable invading army of these abominations. First came the television, to fill our young peoples' heads with falsities and turn them away from the kirk. Next came the accumulation of a certain set of so-called artistic sculptures, bits of rusting scrap metal that look like nothing on earth, sprouting up like weeds all over the island. And now, worst of all, we find ourselves harbouring unawares an old serpent in our bosom: a book that crawls out of some pest-hole of the heathen past, rising up like a rotting corpse from a flooded boneyard, bringing with it the putrid stench of Rome, and the persistent noisome pestilence of an even older paganism. Old false saints, the Devil's own work, reeking of papish incense and stinking of the pit.

'And is it not a disgrace that our fair island, which in its day was known far and wide as the flower of Hebridean piety, the quintessential Sabbath-keeper, should now be publicised as the place where the slimy spawn of the old Serpent has been safely cradled? The discovery of the decade, they call it – the *Book of Bride*. A landmark of Celtic art say the museum-keepers. A priceless record of the transition from goddess to saint in early Christianity, say the academics and professors in our ancient universities. Well I say to them, Nay! Nay! Nay! What you have before you is a source of evil, bearing the footprint of Beelzebub. For the Devil is an hoary beast. Satan walked these hills of ours when Abraham himself was but an unplanted seed, when Cain and Abel not even begat by Adam. The reeking spoor of the Old Enemy still scorches our hills and our peatbogs and our cliffs and our sandy shores.

'And those who hope to celebrate this Book, who will flock to see it in all its pagan fripperies and barbarous arrays, all reverentially preserved by dint of special lighting and protective glass in the university museum – let them all be warned! The glass case should be there for your protection – for the danger lies within! Yet no glass, no security system, no electronic alarm devices known to man can protect you from its ancient poison. Only the Lord's Word can provide the antidote – so, I enjoin you, stay away! Spit upon it, as a false idol, a golden calf, a brazen statue of Baal!

'But just as foolish as those who cross the water to worship it are those poor benighted sinners here at home, who rejoice that the filthy lucre earned by the selling of this piece of papistical pornography has purchased them a factory! For the money that bought this factory is filthy, and the products it turns out are themselves but graven images of a baser coin. Beware these seemingly innocent toys and trinkets, beware the hidden messages within them, beware . . .'

'HOLD YOUR WHEESHT, MINISTER!' A woman's voice roars out of the shadows at the back. 'It's all very well for you to say, but what fine words of yours ever put bread into our mouths. You leave our graven images alone!'

And, to a woman, the collective owners of Granny's Hielan' Hame Industries rise and march out of the kirk, the last one banging the door behind her with an angry clang that will – so the elders later avow – be as music to the ears of the cardinals in Rome.

His sermon cut short by a good ninety minutes, Murdo gathers up his dignity and retreats from the pulpit. His loyal wife Morag, waiting with his Sabbath dinner back at the manse, is hardly surprised to discover that he has acquired an instant and acute case of laryngitis. She takes the opportunity to serve herself and the children the tenderest bits of the Sunday roast, blissfully ignoring the Minister's baleful looks at everyone else's well-laden plates.

Rendering under Caesar the responsibilities that he pays his rates for, Murdo – hoarse-voiced and flannel-wrapped – turns to the police in his crusade against the sculptures. But the entire island constabulary, in the person of Archie Henderson, has gone off for a week to Inverness on a Community Relations course, leaving Cailleach temporarily lawless.

Complaining to Catriona, Murdo knows, is bound to be more trouble than it's worth, and likely to backfire. And he will not address the so-called Artist herself. There is, always has been, something that makes him distinctly uneasy about her, ever since he spied her dancing naked with Catriona on the beach, and even more so since she set up her gaggle of scrap-metal nuns at the ruined convent. (These have stayed in place, by popular local demand, in spite of faintly shocked susurrations of disapproval by the Edinburgh bureaucrats who preside over island antiquities.)

So, after a preliminary strategy session with his kirk elders, Murdo brings up the matter at the next Community Council meeting. On the agenda, it follows Strayed Sheep and precedes the Charity Cake Sale. His speech begins with an accusation of blasphemy, heresy, vandalism and pornography, but rapidly develops – with the noisy participation of all present – into an energetic debate on the nature of Art, Politics and Public Property. In the end, the meeting votes sixty-seven to nine in favour of allowing all the sculptures to remain *in situ*. As someone says, en route to the Cailleach Inn for an after-meeting dram, 'you never do know who is actually running things Up There, and a statue or two to a goddess won't do any harm. Always wise to be on the safe side, and I'll have a pint of heavy, Hamish, thanks very much.'

Maria Milleny decides to break a solemn vow. She has sworn, on several occasions, that she will never, never grant another interview to the so-called popular press. But when 'Stone Circle II' and 'Rival Firm' inspire a hot controversy, with angry attacks, vigorous counter-attacks, storms of protest and (failed) injunctions (taken out on behalf of the full Second Schismatic Kirk Assembly after a resolution passed unanimously at an Extraordinary General Meeting, held round a dining table in a manse in Skye), Maria

214

yields to pressure from her co-workers (and now co-owners) at Granny's Hielan' Hame Industries and agrees to see the man from the *Sentinel*.

It is, unfortunately, the same reporter–photographer team she suffered the first time (anything north of Glasgow and west of the Great Glen is their exclusive beat). But this time Maria is better prepared. She agrees to see them in her workshop, where she is putting the finishing touches on a privately commissioned piece called 'Battle of the Titans': two cast-iron stick figures in aluminium dunce-caps, wearing PVC loincloths (or are they nappies?) clubbing each other with enormous space rockets (or, possibly, phalluses). Maria wears her welder's mask and wields her blowtorch throughout the interview. The photographer has few opportunities for any shot that could be captioned 'Cute' or 'Winsome'. The reporter finds that, when his questions become impertinent, she sprays her sparks even closer to his polyester trousers.

In the end, the interview, in spite of Maria's blowtorch, touches only lightly on Maria's sculptures, or on the *Book of Bride* that she claims has inspired them. Nor does it delve too deeply into her response to the storm of protest from the clerical establishment. The reader of the *Sentinel*, as the journalist knows, is interested in none of these. He (which for the purposes of the *Sentinel* embraces 'She') is far more curious about the Red-headed Artist's private life. Does she have a boyfriend? What are her measurements? And who does she bloody think she is to come up here and mess about with other people's dearly held religious beliefs and moral values? So she tells him.

Glad to escape with his skin, the reporter and his photographer retreat, promising the article will appear in early January. They wish her a merry Christmas, and speed away, with a squeal of tyres, up the brae, off the island, and safely home to the haze of the Dundee Press Club.

As long as anyone can remember, it has been the practice on Cailleach to welcome in the New Year with a giant Hogmanay bonfire on the shore. Well-bundled-up against the icy, cutting wind, most of the island's population gathers every year to gossip around the flames, stamping their feet to keep warm, and passing Thermos flasks of coffee well-laced with whisky. The site for the bonfire is always the same: the little strip of beach next to the castle causeway. The preparations are simple: on the last day of the old year, anyone who is passing drops off a load of peat, a basket full of kindling, a sack of coal, a can of paraffin, or whatever fire-feeding materials they have to spare. The slow procession of vans and jeeps and battered cars, coming and going, is visible from the castle kitchen. Here, all afternoon, Catriona and a corps of helpers slice carrots, chop onions, crush garlic, clean leeks, soak dried peas, shred cabbage, peel turnips and parsnips and potatoes. They add them, in a sequence prescribed by common sense, tradition and Catriona, to a collection of soup-pots, preserving pans and cauldrons.

These will be carried, in a careful procession, down to the shore at sunset (which, on this last day of the year comes half-way through the afternoon). Then other hands will bring jugs, pails and jerricans of water, salt mills and pepper-grinders, spices and herbs. A small subsidiary fire will be lit – bonfires, it is well known, being far too aggressive and unpredictable for the gentle nurturing of a serious soup. If necessary, a small lean-to will be constructed to keep the rain off ('We don't want the stock watered down,' says Catriona every year, at exactly six, when the skies open).

Between the helpers tending the bonfire, and the helpers tending the soup, and those who have come to cheer on the workers, and those who have come to carp and say everyone is doing everything the wrong way, the cacophony on the beach drowns out the sounds of winds, waves and screaming gulls.

Everyone has her or his self-appointed role in the proceedings, rarely deviating from year to year unless interrupted by childbirth, death or emigration. But no one is too busy, this year, to notice the burst of unusual activity at the far end of the beach. Someone, unrecognisable at a distance, in bright yellow oilskins, is busy banging and hammering inside a large, high tent of scaffolding and plastic sheeting. This is not part of the annual ritual, and though many people ask about it, no one seems to know. Catriona ignores all questions of any nature, being far too busy worrying that there isn't enough garlic in the soup.

Just after ten o'clock, the Mobile Library van drives on to the castle causeway and parks just outside the door. Stuart, the librarian, emerges in a silver horned helmet and an iridescent purple jumpsuit, leading a small procession of identically dressed Snorri's Marauders – all carrying instruments and sound equipment – into the castle. Rain and sleet being the enemies of

216

electronics, they will set up in the library and entertain the crowd outside through open windows.

'Dear knows they're loud enough even with the windows closed,' says Ina Isbister.

By half-past eleven, the road above the beach is lined with cars, the flames of the bonfire are spitting and leaping, soup-servers are plying their ladles and poteen-drinkers are plying their jugs. The beat of the music blends with the slap of the waves on the shore, and the fire dances.

At a quarter to twelve, Snorri's Marauders take a break, and join the rest of the crowd around the fire.

Five minutes before midnight, someone shouts and points to the far end of the beach, where the mass of scaffolding and plastic has been quietly removed, to reveal Maria Milleny's latest project, imperfectly illuminated by the bonfire: a massive moon-round, smiling female face beams out from an aureole of gold and silver and copper sun-bursts. She is a carnival giantess, of painted metal, with vast piratical hooped earrings dangling from someplace within her crown of metallic curls.

'A privately commissioned piece,' explains Catriona to the now-silent crowd, 'to enliven the view from my library windows. She's called "The Queen of the Fire" '.

From the causeway, the skirl of pipes announces the turning of the year.

By twelve-thirty, the requisite kissings and handshakes and drinkings of health have been completed, and the fire, like the crowd around it, is beginning to die down. Snorri's Marauders have retired to the library van with a few admirers, to share a discreet peace-pipe, and the fiddlers have taken over, with older and wilder tunes. Either the wind has risen and is stirring the clouds, or the new batch of poteen is stronger than usual, and the sky spins.

Suddenly the festivities are shattered by the sound of someone leaning long and hard on a car horn. Then, announced by the angry slam of a door, the Reverend Murdo is upon them.

He stands on the edge of the road, illuminated by the glare of his own headlamps, scowling down at the revellers on the beach.

'Are you first-footing us, Minister?' calls someone on the far side of the fire.

217

Murdo shakes his fist angrily at the sculpture; if he had a set of stone tablets he'd have flung them down by now.

'That,' he proclaims, 'is a graven image to end all graven images. And you – every one of you – whose names I know because I christened you all, or your children, are dancing before it like the tribes of Israel before the golden calf. Have you taken leave of all your moral senses? Have you undone all the Lord's work? Have you forfeited your places among the Lord's Elect?'

'Don't you think you're making heavy weather of this, Minister?' asks Ina, loudly but politely. 'It's the annual Hogmanay do, for goodness' sake. We always have it.'

'And he always drones on about it,' adds Isa the weaver, 'so just take no notice.'

'This bonfire, at an hour and a season when you should all be in your beds is bad enough,' says Murdo, 'but it is an old custom and one best viewed as a harmless nuisance. And, as to the gross amounts of alcoholic poisons you are so happily pouring down your thrapples, I trust the Lord will reward you in the morning, in the usual manner. But I am surprised and saddened that you are conducting your revelries in the presence of that unspeakable object.'

He points at the moonface, which seems to grin at him.

'You all know your Bible. And you know your responsibilities as brethren baptised in the kirk. There is no need for me to remind you. But I must confess that I am sorely, sorely disappointed in you all. It is beyond me how you can tolerate the defacement of this island by the hideous constructions of this former garage mechanic and self-styled sculptress.' He points to Maria, gaudy in her yellow oilskins, who stands by the fire, a rapidly-chilling mug of soup half-way to her lips.

'I realise that an incomer can hardly be blamed for not knowing our ways. But she has shown no respect for them. She has blighted our landscape and, what is worse, perverted the morals and time-tested values of this community, with her obscene, vulgar, ugly images. They reflect half-baked, ill-educated notions of early Celtic history that would not stand up for a moment against the critical scrutiny of any doctor of divinity from our theological seminaries, or any doctor of philosophy from our ancient universities. And what of the mockery she has made of our faith? Have we forgotten those who have suffered and died for it?'

His listeners on the beach shuffle uncomfortably. The effects of the drink are wearing off, and the heat has gone from the fire.

Suddenly a voice booms out of the sky: 'AND WHAT ABOUT THOSE THAT THE FAITH ITSELF HAS FORCED TO SUFFER AND DIE? WHAT ABOUT WITCHES, MURDO, AND HERETICS? WHAT ABOUT THEM?'

The voice is Catriona's, massively amplified, emanating from the castle. Snorri's Marauders, still in the Mobile Library van having amazing insights into space and time, have not yet dismantled their sound system.

'Come out here, where I can see you, woman, if you want a fair fight?'

Something, that might be a thunderclap, crackles overhead. But it might also be Catriona, tripping over the wires of the amps on her way out. Moments later, she stands facing him, a few feet away, the pair of them illuminated by the glow of the headlamps.

'What shall it be then, Minister? A contest of miracles, such as Moses had with the Royal Magicians of Egypt?'

'You know fine who won that one, Dr MacEochan.'

'It depends which side you think you're on, Reverend MacNeish.'

'I'm not going to be tricked into any magic show.'

A voice from the beach cries, 'Come on, Doctor, challenge him to a wrestling match. Two falls out of three. You're tough enough.'

Catriona and Murdo both ignore this. They circle each other like two stags about to enter combat.

Murdo summons up the ringing tones and moral certainties of Old Testament prophets. A white flowing beard sprouts from his chin, his thick scarlet eyebrows are transformed into two snowy ledges over a face like a mountainside.

Catriona wraps herself in the star-stitched cloak of an ancient priestess, her face drains to a dazzling, terrible white, and her eyes are the gleaming green prisms of a cat leaping out of the dark.

He stands, alone and terrible, on the summit of a mountain, brandishing a Bible.

He hears her laughter, far above his head, and sees her passing, riding the rainbow.

With all the strength in his righteous right arm, he throws the Book at her. But misses.

Hands chalk up roman numeral points on a celestial scoreboard. His supporters and hers cheer raucously. Both sides of the field have their fair share of hooligans.

He quotes Scripture. She counters with Pythagoras.

She turns briefly into an owl, a swan, a giant sow.

He makes the sign of the cross, excommunicates her, confiscates her castle.

She turns his wife against him, has her murmuring spells into the Sunday lunch.

He calls out the king's men, the Territorials, the Glasgow police.

She embarrasses him by displaying a trickle of menstrual blood.

He threatens to have her banned from medical practice.

She gives him a plague through witchcraft, then cures it with antibiotics.

He summons God to be his witness, then summons Satan to come and take back his own.

She smiles ruefully when neither of them show up.

He summons down the wrath of the Almighty, fire and brimstone.

They are both drenched in the downpour. Sleet, rain and a force eight gale as per the last Marine forecast of the Old Year. The weather has been terrible for hours, and those islanders not already home in their beds have gone on to first-foot neighbours or attend other parties. It is, after all, Hogmanay.

She offers him a bowl of soup in her castle.

He declines.

'Some bonfire last night, eh, Fiona?'

'Magic.'

'I think I must have passed out. I know the Minister turned up and had a go at Catriona about the sculpture, but I can't remember a blasted thing after that.'

'Neither can I, Fergus. I think there must have been something funny about that last batch of poteen.'

Reverend MacNeish is breakfasting on a Cailleach kipper. Morag stands at the ready with the teapot, should a refill be required. As he eats, he peruses the *Sunday Sentinel*, which has arrived on the Monday night ferry. He reads out choice bits, illustrating human sin and folly. The children, well-drilled, chew their toast in attentive silence.

'Oh my goodness, Murdo, will you look at that!'

'Blast it woman, how many times have I told you not to read over my shoulder. Put that pot down, you're spilling tea on my jacket. Now what's all the fuss about?'

'Down there, on the bottom of the page. Just below the Cheery

Thought for the Week.'

'Is that it? The Letter from the Publisher. Hmmm. "Dear Readers. Time and tide, it has oft been observed, wait for no man, even here in Dundee. And, after a long and happy association with our good friends all over bonnie Scotland and indeed far beyond it, wherever Scots may roam, we must announce with a wee tear in our eye that your favourite Sunday paper today makes its final appearance. For the Old Firm has been sold, lock, stock and printing press to a new publishing consortium. What the nature of their new publication will be, we leave it to our readers – or such as have strong stomachs and stronger curiosity – to discover. Suffice it to say that we, in our forthcoming retirement in the Spanish sunshine, shall transfer our own subscription to one of our former competitors. However, to fulfil the terms of our Agreement of Sale, we must hereby announce to you that our successor will be known as the *Scottish Sunday Deviant and Weekly Dissenter*, incorporated as a non-profit institution fully funded by a grant from the new Catriona MacEochan Educational Trust. So we say to you all, Farewell and remember auld lang syne" . . .'

'That fiend! That . . . cursed . . . woman!'

But Murdo's eye is suddenly caught by something even more alarming, on the opposite page. The photograph of Maria Milleny, just visible under her tipped-up welder's mask, draws the reader's eye to an article entitled 'ISLAND STORM OVER BLAS-PHEMOUS ART'. Murdo reads it, exclaims 'Dear God in Heaven!' spills his tea, and reads it again.

'Morag. Send the children out of the room.'

'But they've not had their porridge yet . . .'

'Immediately.'

Delighted by this break in grim routine, the children vanish.

'What's that? It looks like another article on Maria Milleny. You'd think she'd be fair embarrassed by all the publicity . . .' She reads over his shoulder.

'Although she was brought up in the south of England, Maria has strong family ties with the Isle of Cailleach. "My mother grew up here," says the willowy, red-headed artist, "and she talked about it all the time. She grew up on a croft near the Gosta Ness lighthouse. But she quarrelled with her family, over a marriage they disapproved of on religious grounds, and never went home to the island again. But I think she always missed it." Well, fancy that Murdo, I never knew the girl had local connections . . .'

'Local connections, indeed, you stupid woman. Local connections! That . : . half Roman . . . red-headed . . . sexually perverted . . . whore of Babylon . . . is my *niece*!' He stabs a piece of kipper viciously, and chokes on it.

'A pity about Reverend MacNeish,' says Ina Isbister in the post-office queue. 'It must have been a terrible shock for his young wife.'

'Aye, it was that. Coming so suddenly. Dr MacEochan's post-mortem said it was a kipper bone. But poor Morag herself swears it was that last edition of the *Sunday Sentinel*.'

'Oh, she's a strong, brave lass is Morag. She'll snap back.'

'Aye, that she will. In fact, she was in here herself, not ten minutes ago, seeing about passport applications for herself and the children. She's away to California at the end of the school term with the pair of them. Joining some sort of Buddhist community. I'm sure the sunshine will be good for the wee boy's bronchitis.'

On a mild June evening, Catriona stands on the deck of the *St Rollox* as it eases into Cailleach harbour. At her feet is a crate containing a single case of the most outstanding modern vintage of an honourable and ancient château. It has been conveyed by special courier from the London auction rooms directly to Stornoway airport, and there put into the hands of Catriona herself, who has organised the entire transaction to coincide with the termination of a regional medical conference.

Next to Catriona, leaning over the rail and watching the hills behind Cailleach port loom larger, stands a tall, fair-haired woman in flowing purple and scarlet scarves and luminous silver dungarees. She is listening intently as Catriona indicates points of interest around the bay.

'But you haven't told me,' says Catriona, 'what brings you to Cailleach.'

'I'm doing a pilgrimage around wimmin's sacred places,' she replies in a soft antipodean twang, toying with a double-headed axe that dangles from one ear. 'And I hear that Cailleach has some powerful goddess-connections.'

'Oh, how interesting.'

'Your stone circle emanates some incredible vibrations. Do you ever go there?'

'Oh, I pass by once in a while,' replies Catriona. 'We locals tend to take our landmarks rather for granted, I'm afraid.'

'Well, you really should. I'm going to stay up that way. In a bed-and-breakfast place right near the stones. Do you know it?'

'Oh, it's quite a good one. You'll be very comfortable, I'm sure.'

'Great. I'm planning to go out and watch the sunrise over the circle.'

'Are you staying long?'

'Well next Monday's the solstice, see. And I'm really into sacred fires. Last summer I went over to Brittany and lit one in honour of the Great Goddess at Carnac. But the bloody French police came along and made me put it out. Nasty bastards. I'd really like to do a sacred fire for the Goddess here. Do you think anyone would hassle me?'

'I'm quite sure they wouldn't.'

'Great.'

'There are, of course, a number of other locations around the island that you might find . . . significant. Perhaps you'd allow me to take you on a little tour. I do know the island intimately.'

'Thanks a lot. That would be terrific.'

'Shall we say tomorrow afternoon? Then perhaps you might like to come back for a bite of supper . . .'

The ferry docks. As they step carefully down the sharply angled gangway, Catriona holding her crate of claret and her companion bent nearly double under the weight of a massive rucksack, Catriona sees Maria standing on the quay.

'Well, if it isn't the Mad Sculptress of Cailleach West. Are you here to meet me?'

'Sorry, Catriona. I'm off on the ferry.'

'Well, this *is* a momentous occasion.' She looks at her, piercingly.

'Don't worry, the spell isn't broken. I'm taking a few things down to an exhibition in Glasgow.' She points to an assortment of packing cases and oddly shaped bundles. 'And then I thought I might spend a few weeks travelling. But I promise, Catriona, I'll come home again.'

'This time I'm not worried.' She suddenly remembers the young woman by her side. 'Oh, and let me introduce you to a visitor to our island. My dear, this is Maria Milleny. She's an incomer. Came up for a short visit, just like yourself, and stayed and stayed. The island wove its spell. Now we're all very proud of her. She's on her way to becoming a well-known artist. Maria this is . . . I'm sorry, we've been talking on the ferry for the past half hour, and I don't even know your name.'

'Cinnamon Moonflower. I'm from Adelaide.'

'Here on holiday?'

'Sort of.'

'Miss Moonflower has come to Cailleach in search of the Goddess, Maria. Do you think she'll find her?'

'I think she'll find you first,' says Maria to Cinnamon.

A crew member comes down the gangplank to help Maria with her bundles. Catriona takes Cinnamon lightly by the elbow, and, with her free hand, blows Maria a kiss.

'Well, see you soon then, my dear. I'm going to give Miss Moonflower a run up the road to Ina's. Safe journey.'

Maria pauses, half-way up the gangway, and looks up at the silvery late-evening sky. 'Will it be?'

'This time I can guarantee it. Word of honour.'

As the *St Rollox* moves out across Cailleach Bay, Maria, standing on deck, sees the dark shapes of seabirds poised on the crow-stepped gable of the castle. Suddenly a light flashes on in the tower windows, and the birds swoop off their perches in a single, sychronised wing-beat. Maria hears them calling to each other as the wind rises, and sees them flying above the ferry in an elegant formation, until the light goes altogether from the sky.

Up in her tower, Catriona hears the ferry's foghorn as she rummages in the black oak press, searching for her candles and the chalk to draw a pentagram.

224

TAIL-PIECE
Lizzie Again

When my call from Cailleach comes through, Wee Shuggie Murray is enjoying his ritual 11 a.m. bacon roll in his vast Scandinavian teak-veneered office at CallyTelly.

'It's Lizzie, Shuggie.'

'Well hello, stranger, we thought you'd run off and eloped with the Old Man of Hoy.'

'Sorry I didn't ring back sooner. Only got your message this morning.'

'Are you still not staying at the wee hotel? Well that's fine with me, if you've found someplace cheaper. Just be sure you keep charging the full whack on your expense forms. Don't let the side down.'

'I know I've taken a few days longer than I said I would, but I think I've worked out some really good ideas for the Cailleach documentary.'

'Well, that's just fine, Lizzie love, wonderful. But do you think you could get your sweet self back down here, rapido?'

'But I just said, I've got a script together. I put it in the post yesterday. When are you planning to send up the film unit?'

'Ah. Well. Aye. Yes. Now listen, darling . . .'

'If there's anything you don't like about it we can change it. I don't mind . . .'

'Lizzie, hold on. I'm afraid the plans have changed altogether.'

'What?'

'I said – there's been a change. We need you back at the shop. All hands on deck.'

'But the schedule we agreed says that . . .'

'Forget the schedule. There's been a new development.'

'Shuggie, are you trying to tell me this film is off?'

'No. No. Of course not. Just . . . postponed indefinitely.'

'Why?'

'Fitba', darling.'

'Football? What is football to do with it?'

'Well, it may have escaped your notice, up there in your island fastness for the past few weeks, talking to dear knows what sort of teuchtar crackpots, but Scotland has come through to the finals. We're all going off to Portugal to cover the Cup.'

'What cup?'

'*The* Cup. And despite your woeful ignorance of this important subject, you're coming with us. Firstly because we get a special discount rate from the airline if we fill a certain number of seats. Secondly because we always like to have a few of our own lassies along for the parties. And thirdly because we want you to do a little human interest spot. We're sure you'll love it. It's really female-identified. A special feature on the team's wives. We thought we'd call it something like "Heroes' sweethearts who watch and wait". You know, the nerves, the drama, the last-minute suspense . . . real rolled-up damp handkerchief stuff.'

'Wait a minute, Shuggie. What about the franchise? What about your statutory obligation to provide culturally significant material and . . .'

'Don't worry about it, flower. Football *is* culturally significant. Don't you remember the paper that English professor chappie gave at last year's Edinburgh Television Festival? I know you were there. I sat next to you. You even stayed awake for the whole thing.'

'Well, I'm not going.'

'What?'

'I said, I'm not going.'

'Did I hear you right? You're saying you're passing up a fantastic opportunity for a free trip to Portugal. You're daft. But I'm afraid you don't have a choice, hen. You're on my staff and if I say you're going, then you're going. Finito. Now get back down here. We have a lot of planning to do.'

'I may be on your staff, but in case you've forgotten, my current contract is up at the end of this month. And you can consider me away on sick leave until then. Because believe me, Shuggie Murray, I feel bloody sick!'

I bang down the telephone. Visions of angry bank managers and endless dole queues dance before my eyes. I go back through to the bar, where Maria is waiting for me.

'What's happened?'

'They've cancelled it. That's what's happened.'

'Cancelled the film?'

'Right. Just called the whole blasted thing off. Just like that. Up the spout for the sake of some idiotic football match.'

'What a waste! You've put so much work into it.'

'Damn right I have. And it's a better story than they'll ever get. So I told them where they could put their job.'

'So what are you going to do now?'

'Shoot myself. Throw myself off the Cliffs of Crunig. Walk into the sea off the far west side.'

'No, seriously.'

'Seriously, I don't know. I just don't.'

'Well, why don't you keep working on your Cailleach story? Make it even better. It's far too good for those morons anyway. Why does it have to be a film at all? You'd need all sorts of money and people and things. Why not do it all on your own? Make it into a book. You can stay with me as long as you like. I even have a table you can write on. I'd really like it if you would.'

I know this fantastic offer will not be repeated. So I do.

Also of interest:

Jess Wells
AfterShocks

Tracy 'Trout' Giovanni's life is neat, controlled, ferociously organised. A powerful businesswoman and meticulous houseowner, she has life's every unpredictable possibility covered. Then the earthquake – 8.0 on the Richter scale – hits San Francisco. And Trout's whole world rocks.

Now Trout comes face to face with the chaos she has always, compulsively, tried to avoid, but which has always been waiting beneath the cold, hard layer of her self-imposed order. And as her lover, Patricia, waits in a bar across town, for Trout to find her, and to reimpose that safe security she never knew that she needed, Trout is slowly, inexorably changing...

'This book kept me up all night.' Kate Millett

'Jess Wells makes us face our worst nightmares without flinching. She is a visionary writer.' Irene Zahava

Fiction £6.99
ISBN 0 7043 4383 5